QUITE INCREDIBLY, THE BEAUTIFUL BANDIT WAS GOING TO KISS HIM.

Before he could react, she placed her hand at the back of his neck to hold him still. The kid-gloved fingers dipped past his collar to the skin beneath. As if it were the most natural thing in the world, he found himself reaching for her mouth, forgetting caution, meeting her kiss. Just as her warm lips grazed his, the back of his neck burned. The bandit jumped back to her feet. In her hand, she held his gold St. Christopher medallion swinging from its thick, expensive chain.

"I shall take this instead." She smiled and mounted her horse, holding the chain like a trophy.

"The thieving bitch," MacAfee whispered beside him.

Rey merely watched the highway woman, bemused.

"*Au revoir, monsieur,*" the woman in black called out, blowing him a kiss.

As her men and their horses thundered past, a flawless red rose land

"I'll be da   ring at the
flower. "We   a Rose."

Other novels by Olga Bicos:

WHITE TIGER
BY MY HEART BETRAYED

SANTANA ROSE

OLGA BICOS

A Dell Book

Published by
Dell Publishing
a division of
Bantam Doubleday Dell Publishing Group, Inc.
666 Fifth Avenue
New York, New York 10103

ISBN: 0-440-21152-2

Printed in the United States of America

Published simultaneously in Canada

December 1992

10 9 8 7 6 5 4 3 2 1

RAD

For the two Leilas, my constant sources of inspiration;

For Tina, who always believed;

And for Andy, who taught me the meaning of the words σ'αγαπω παρα πολυ.

The Rose

But ne'er the Rose without the Thorn.

—Robert Herrick,
The Rose, 1647

Chapter 1

New Orleans, 1879

"The Silver Fox." A hint of amusement colored the Cajun's voice—and a good deal of admiration. "You've a reputation for danger, *mais* sure, Rey."

Twilight filtered through the carriage's thick pane, casting Reynard Parks's face half in light, half in darkness. He glanced down at the Cajun seated beside him on the cracked-leather bench seat barely long enough to hold two passengers.

"I'm a lawman, Harlan," Rey answered. "A government agent no different than yourself. The Service pays me to do my job well."

His eyes glittered a pale startling green—the eyes of a crusader, the Cajun thought. The evening's glow frosted Rey's hair a near white, eclipsing its peppering of black. Despite his thirty-five years, scarcely a trace of his original hair color remained other than his pitch-colored brows, making the Cajun wonder if events as well as time could mark a man.

"The men we seek are dangerous," Parks continued, his deep voice mellow, thoughtful. "I myself am only . . . effective."

"Effective. I like that." Harlan Everard—looking hardly old enough to be one of the Pinkerton detectives the United States Secret Service "borrowed" on a regular basis—took out a cigarette case from the handkerchief pocket of his jacket. "I tell you what, we're gonna be real effective, you and me, eh, *mon ami*?" He offered Rey a cigarette. "Smoke?"

"No, thank you."

"Mais oui." A smile lit the Cajun's eyes. "You said you don't smoke at the station."

Rey Parks watched Harlan put the cigarette to his mouth. It had been five long years since Rey had done the same, though he'd never lost the urge to smoke. *A small enough penance,* Rey thought. A lock of brown hair dropped down over one eye as Harlan bent forward and touched a match to the cigarette between his lips. The last rays of the sun filled the brougham's small compartment, catching dust motes in its beam and illuminating Harlan's eyes. They were a unique shade of blue. A color Rey had seen on only one other.

Rey shifted his gaze to focus on the passing landscape. *Not now,* he told his memories. *Not yet.*

Beyond the rippling waves of window glass, the tips of black willow crested the levee of the River Road. Again Rey questioned his judgment concerning his partner—as he had half a dozen times since he'd arrived on the "big J" line from Chicago two days ago to meet Harlan. Young, Rey thought, despite the man's twenty-one years. And a bit too taken with the mystique of detective work.

The carriage wheels hit another rut, almost tossing the two men against the brougham's padded wall before them. "Shoulda taken a steamboat," Harlan mumbled. Catching Rey's eye, he grinned. "But I guess you don't care much for river travel, *non*?"

The smell of stale cigarette smoke and sweat lingered within the cramped compartment, filling Rey's nostrils. Tipping back the brim of his hat, he leaned against the leather cushions. "I'm a poor sailor."

"Vraiment?" The wonder in Harlan's voice gave the single word a wealth of meaning.

"You sound surprised?" Rey asked.

"I jus' thought . . ." Harlan allowed the unfinished

sentence to hang between them. What would the Pinkerton say if Rey confessed that even the gentlest rocking of a ship could make him break out into a cold sweat? But under Rey's watchful gaze, the Pinkerton only grinned. "How long do you think it will take to bring De Dreux down, *mon ami*?" Harlan asked in a quick change of subject.

Rey propped one booted foot on the carriage wall before him. "You speak as if the man's charged, convicted, and sentenced. It's dangerous to take a man's guilt for granted."

Rey's subtle barb stiffened Harlan's smile. A stillness filled the air, disturbed only by the whine of the hired coach's springs and the soft crunch of the crushed shells paving the River Road to De Dreux's plantation. While Harlan mulled over Rey's challenge, Rey glanced out the window on his left at the upcoming bend. A pair of live oaks, their moss-burdened limbs reaching across the road to the levee, formed a hazy gate obscuring the horizon. A teasing prickle stepped up the skin of his neck. He frowned, angling away from Harlan to get a better look at the path ahead.

"*Écoutez,* man. This is my territory," Harlan said, finding his voice at last. "That's why Mr. Pinkerton assigned me to this case when you asked for his help. Let me tell you something 'bout N'awlins." Harlan used the pronunciation of a native, making the city's name one word. "You can track just about any dirty deed from Baton Rouge to Lake Pontchartrain to De Dreux's doorstep, *mais oui*. It's no surprise to me he's involved with counterfeiters and boodle carriers like Sotheby. I *know* Benoit De Dreux. He's guilty."

"Proving it," came the cold response, "is another matter."

A long silence followed. Rey sensed Harlan's determination flare like a bellowed flame. Perhaps there lay his affinity for the Pinkerton, Rey thought. Despite the voice of caution that warned him to keep alert, he'd found a kindred spirit in Harlan. Once, Rey had been that confident. There was a time not so long ago that he'd believed good would conquer the evils of the world—and that he would be a vital part of making it happen. He wished he could get it back, his zeal for justice. What would he give to erase the darker moments of his life when only the promise of revenge could stir him?

Rey faced Harlan, leaving off his concerns for the bend ahead. The man watched him with an intensity that would have quelled a fainter heart.

"Then we'll jus' have to prove he's guilty as the sin that spawned him, won't we, *mon ami*?" Harlan's eyes skimmed over Rey, evaluating. "They told me you're the best."

Rey allowed himself a small smile. "William and Robert Pinkerton seemed to think you'd hold up your end as well."

"With pleasure."

"Pleasure has nothing to do with the days ahead of us. Make no mistake about that, Harlan. Emotions," he said in a voice that conveyed he permitted himself few of those, "cloud an agent's judgment." Unconsciously, he twisted the gold band on his right hand. "De Dreux's just a two-bit crook who's leading us to the bigger game. Yet his name passes your lips with disturbing regularity. Why?"

A smile that could charm a hungry gator at ten paces transformed Harlan's face. "Jus' like to do my job, is all." At that moment, smoking a cigarette and dressed in his checked single-breasted suit and bowler cap, the Pinkerton appeared seventeen and naive; nothing like a twenty-one-year-old agent experienced in detective work—exactly the talent that Robert Pinkerton had said made Harlan so valuable. "He's our ticket to closing down the counterfeiting scheme, *non*? We catch him at his little deal with the men fixing the lottery and 'fore he knows what's what, we got De Dreux *and* Harry Sotheby in the bargain."

"Then you understand, Harlan, that De Dreux is a very small part of our plans?"

The Cajun nodded his head. "Sotheby's the bigger catch, *mais* sure." He tossed his cigarette and ground it out with his boot heel, then tensed when he saw Rey's suddenly distracted expression. "What's the—"

Rey dropped the foot he'd propped in front of him to the floor and held up his hand for silence. He tried to catch the suggestion of sound he'd sensed more than heard. It came again.

The wind?

Or the soft whinny of a horse.

Rey edged aside his black wool jacket and reached for his shoulder holster. He peered out the window as his fingers wrapped around the walnut grip of the Peacemaker. Beside him, Harlan readied his own weapon.

"Com'on, man," Harlan whispered. "What d'you hear? What's out—"

Gunshots exploded like cannon fire. High-pitched shouts erupted on each side of the carriage. Rey cocked his revolver with one hand. With the other, he slammed Harlan down to the floor and crouched down beside him out of bullet range. A loud thump of someone landing atop the brougham sounded above.

More gunfire thundered. Dangerously close.

"Arretez!"

The coach lurched to a stop, dashing both men against the brougham's padded leather wall. Rey inched toward one of the coach windows while motioning Harlan to stay down. He could hear his valet's Gaelic curses streaming from the coachman's seat outside.

"Au dehors, mes amis!"

Both agents ignored the command shouted in French to disembark. Rey watched the bandits surround the brougham, trying to get an accurate count of their number. Their triumphant cries almost drowned out his man's and the driver's protests. The carriage horse reared and shrieked, threatening to overturn the brougham. The carriage lamps extinguished in an explosion of glass.

Rey strained to see the circling riders in the twilight. Alert for any signs of weakness, he immediately focused on one rider nearing the carriage. The culprit appeared particularly young, a boy no more than fourteen years of age. A large hat and a bandanna hid his face, though Rey could make out shanks of dark hair. His gaze shifted to the figure behind the boy and stopped there, arrested by the sight emerging from the parting row of bandits.

Tall and elegantly slim, the rider was dressed in black and masked, as were the others. But this bandit's mask was more elaborate, more like a theatrical domino or a birdlike carnival disguise. Colorful glass beads surrounded the eyes, and feathers crowned the head and curved down the cheeks, creating a costume fit for the most exclusive Mardi Gras ball. In the dim light filtering through the mossy oaks, the flowing ebony hair confirmed what the tight-fitting shirt and pants had already revealed. A woman.

The breeze unfurled her cape, creating a dramatic backdrop for the full curve of her breasts and the sleek line of her finely shaped thighs straddling the horse. An angel in black, Rey thought. The sight of her alone could spark an instant response in the unwary—like a fantasy that was even more alluring for the danger she presented. He scanned the proud carriage, the figure that could never be confused for a man's despite the trousers she wore. After a brief moment of sexual awareness for so magnificent a creature, Rey recognized the image before him for what really mattered—she was a woman, a weakness in the ranks. He smashed the carriage window with the butt of his revolver and aimed.

A piercing fire raced up his arm from his hand. With a curse, he loosed the Colt that had been virtually shot from his grasp and dropped to the carriage floor. Blood welled at a cut where he'd rammed his wrist into the jagged glass of the window.

"Jettez vos armes."

The woman's voice shouted for them to disarm. As he held his bleeding wrist, Rey frowned in a thoughtful expression. A woman led this motley band of highwaymen? He wasn't taken by surprise often. Even the criminal world he'd sentenced himself to for the last five years had become unnervingly routine.

From inside the carriage, he heard the beautiful but deadly lady repeat her command in heavily accented English. He risked a glance out the broken window. The image of the black-garbed figure holding one smoking gun as she aimed the other Smith and Wesson toward the carriage burned into his consciousness as he ducked and turned to Harlan.

"I counted six," Harlan said.

"Seven," Rey corrected. "Possibly more out of sight."

Rey heard MacAfee cursing proficiently in his brogue. He peered outside once again and saw his valet's stocky frame near the carriage, the Scotsman and their driver having dropped down from the paneled boot of the coachman's seat. MacAfee held his arms in the air as he wished the gang of thieves to perdition.

A calm settled over Rey, focusing his energy, shutting out all other thoughts, including the fears that could push him to act rashly to save his friend. *Mac's in trouble. He needs my best.* Rey evaluated his options, saw that any attempt to fight back could cost MacAfee—his valet and comrade-in-arms for a score of years—his life.

"On the count of three?" Harlan asked, looking as if he were ready to execute bravado worthy of the James Gang.

Rey pushed back the barrel of Harlan's revolver. "Do as she says."

"But . . ."

"Dammit man, throw the gun out!"

Harlan's pistol landed beside Rey's on the marshy

ground. The door slammed open. Two bandits blocked the exit, one with twin revolvers trained inside, the other holding a carbine. Unlike the woman, these men were dressed in grubby denim and sweat-stained cotton, their clothes no better than rags. The only other soul to stand out was the small boy Rey had spotted earlier. Wearing a pilot coat hanging to his knees, the child was a good head shorter than the motley crew surrounding him. Scarves and wooly caps disguised all the bandits' identities. The rough-looking character with the carbine pulled both men outside and ordered them to put their hands up. The riders formed a circle around their victims and the bandits waited for instructions from their leader.

The woman in black rode forward. The magnificent silk cape flared over her shoulders and draped across the horse's hind quarters. Again Rey noted her beauty, but in a distant manner, as he might analyze a wanted poster. The mask effectively disguised her face, its red feathers curving down her cheeks to brush her full lips. Black riding gloves encased her hands. Only the exquisite white skin of her jaw showed any delicacy in the picture of strength. Her attire was top quality, more fitting for a masked ball than a roadside holdup with the riffraff currently guarding her back. He looked closer, intrigued, but the waning light and the bejeweled slits of her mask concealed the color of her eyes.

Patting the horse's neck, the mounted highway woman ordered her men to dump the baggage from atop the carriage. Black as his mistress's disguise and with powerful muscled flanks, the Arabian promised power—as did the seven guns trained on Rey and his party as they stoically watched the bandits rifle through their valuables. Everyone was masked; identification would be difficult. The scoundrels had chosen well for their ambush: an isolated bend between landings a few miles outside of New Orleans. But these robbers lacked the blood lust Rey had seen during his last assignment in Chicago. Most likely

Rey and his company would be released unharmed after the rabble picked them clean.

With a grimace for the irony that a trained government agent should find himself a victim of crime on his first day out, Rey watched his fine twilled cotton trousers land in the dirt next to his best linen shirt. A man with a blue muffler hiding his face dug deeper into his portmanteau. Another began emptying their pockets.

"Bloody bastards," the carriage driver mumbled beneath his scraggly mustache as he watched one bandit find and confiscate his coin purse from his coat. The driver lowered his hands a fraction. Two guns swung on him. He jerked his hands back to their original height.

"That's a week's wages," he complained.

"Calme-toi," Harlan whispered from beside the driver as he too watched his wallet disappear into a burlap sack. "There are worse things they can take than your money, man."

Rey looked back at the mounted woman as one of her thugs relieved him of his gold watch and fob. Another robber fingered the fine wool of his jacket, and gestured for Rey to remove it. Apparently taking a fancy to his cravat as well, the culprit attempted to untie the silk with one hand while keeping his gun trained on Rey. He settled for ripping the tie and collar from Rey's neck, taking a few shirt buttons along for his effort.

Handing over the jacket, Rey stood in his yellow silk vest and buff trousers, his shirt open and exposing a gold chain and St. Christopher medal hanging to the middle of his chest. He caught the lady bandit's eye. "You will leave us the dignity of the shirts on our back, will you not, madame?"

The woman holstered one gun and looped a leg around the horn of her saddle, balancing forward on her knee as she held the remaining pistol less menacingly. *"Eh bien, monsieur. Mais,* I am tempted to find out what the shirt conceals."

Incredibly, Rey found himself subjected to a top to bottom inspection—and not for any valuables he might have hidden on his person. A grin appeared below the red-and-black feathered mask, showing even, white teeth. "What I see so far intrigues." She gestured with her gun to his open shirt. "Well, *monsieur*? Perhaps you will oblige?"

For the first time in more years than he could remember, Rey stood nonplussed before a group of criminals. Certainly, his looks had drawn considerable feminine attention in the past. He'd been told he had a young face, that the combination of his unique green eyes and silver hair beguiled. But he'd never expected to exchange flirtatious banter with a bandit at gunpoint. Despite his initial shock, it didn't take long for him to see the advantage in the bandit's regard. He'd not turn down an opportunity to get the leader of this gang of criminals alone and disarmed.

Rey nodded his head to the man now wearing his coat and tie and rifling through his wallet. "May I suggest a more private setting for such an . . . inspection?" Giving her his most charming smile, he added, "Perhaps I could make it worth your effort."

The bandit's throaty laugh, deep and sexy, sounded out of place with her melodic voice and its French accent. Despite their predicament, it was a laugh that invited a feeling of camaraderie. A willingness to laugh at yourself was a rare trait for those in their line of business, regardless of which side of the gun you were on.

"You tempt me, *monsieur.*" She seemed to consider his offer, then shook her head. "*Je regrette,* I am pressed for time and have not enough to take advantage of your inviting offer. Another time, perhaps. Today I must settle for only monetary riches. And lest you think me greedy, I would judge from your fashionable attire that my friends and I need the few *sous* I shall deprive you of much more than *vous* and *vos camarades.*"

"Enforced charity?" Rey asked. "A charming concept, but I gave at church Sunday past."

"Give more, *monsieur. C'est bon pour l'âme.* Good for the soul."

"It's good fer her pockets, the witch means," grumbled MacAfee beside him.

"Undoubtedly her favorite institution," Rey answered.

A sweet smile appeared on her lips. *"Bien sûr.* I can think of no better cause." She nodded her head to the man beside her. *"Lie ses mains."*

Following her instructions, the bandits pushed their victims to their knees and began tying their hands in front of them. Rey kept his eyes on the woman, waiting for her next move.

"Ne t'inquiètes pas, monsieur," she said softly. "We make it simple for *vous.* You untie yourselves, *non*? Once I and *mes amis* escape. *Très simple."*

"We'll do our best." Rey winced as the ropes bit into the cut on his wrist.

"Attendez." The masked woman held up a hand for her men to stop and dismounted. She walked to where Rey knelt on the ground next to Harlan and glanced at the blood crusted on his wrist and staining the cuff of his shirt. Without a word, she untied the bandanna from her neck. Kneeling down in front of Rey, she wrapped the scarf around the bloodied wrist before securing the rope tightly.

"A robber with a heart," Rey said. "Very touching."

Ignoring his sarcasm, she picked up his injured hand. She followed the lines of his palm with the gloved tip of her finger in a fortune-teller's gesture. An uncomfortable warmth spread across Rey's chest as he watched her dark head bent over his bound wrists. Her touch was feather light, and all the more seductive for its restraint. Irrelevantly, he recalled it had been years since a woman had held his hand with tenderness. But when she glanced up, the masked face extinguished such sentimental thoughts, stirring his agent's instincts. He tried again to see the color of her eyes beyond the glass beading decorating the mask.

She held his gaze without flinching and trailed her finger down a path across his palm. At the gold wedding band on his third finger she stopped. She fingered the ring.

"It's not worth much," he said, hoping he'd not lose this last momento.

In the twilight, her eyes appeared almost black within the shadowed slits. "I see by your eyes, *monsieur,*" she said dropping his hand without taking the ring, "that it is very valuable indeed."

Deep within him, something stirred. He didn't have a face that could be easily read. More often than not, no one thought to look beyond his cover—the charming, sophisticated banker who presumably financed more than his fare share of questionable activities. Her comment, her ability to see a pain he hid even from himself, seduced him even more than the tempting curves of her body.

Yet, what truly astounded him as she leaned closer, her head tilting to the side, was the realization that she was going to kiss him.

Before he could react, she placed her hand at the back of his neck to hold him still. The kid gloved fingers dipped past his collar to the skin beneath. He experienced again the sexual response that had ignited when he'd first seen her. It rose up within him, hot and exciting, reminding him that he'd never quite managed to douse it. As if it were the most natural thing in the world, he found himself reaching for her mouth, forgetting caution, meeting her kiss. Just as her warm lips grazed his, the back of his neck burned and the bandit jumped back to her feet.

In her hand, she held his gold St. Christopher medallion swinging from its thick, expensive chain.

"I shall take this instead." She smiled and mounted her horse, holding the chain like a trophy.

"The thieving bitch," MacAfee whispered beside him. "Ye've had that medal since ye were a bairn."

Rey merely watched the highway woman, bemused.

"Au revoir, monsieur," the woman in black called out, blowing him a kiss.

As her men and their horses thundered past, a flawless red rose landed at Rey's feet.

"I'll be damned," the coachman said, staring at the flower. "We've just been fleeced by Santana Rose."

Father Ignacio stared at the beautiful English woman, so young in years to be such a great lady. Her fine silken hair, the topaz hue of a lion's mane, shone gold in the afternoon sun and matched her lovely eyes, the same soft brown as the ginger wine he loved. Tall for a woman, she stood above Father Ignacio, but her friendly smile put them on equal footing. He sighed. She was an angel of mercy, that was a fact, and served St. Bartholomew's Orphan Asylum well. But he worried so about Madame.

"You risk too much by coming here, Madame De Dreux. The roads are not safe." He leaned closer, as if someone might overhear. "Only yesterday two gentlemen were held up at gunpoint just outside Carrollton by the notorious Santana Rose. She and others like her make travel dangerous."

"So I understand from my husband, Father," the lady said, her deep velvet voice clipped by a British accent. "But I could not bear thinking that the children should go without for another week. Nor could Pascal be persuaded to give up her weekly lessons."

"Certainly your efforts and that of the young miss are greatly appreciated. I but worry over your safety."

"Worry about our souls, Father," she said with an odd smile.

But Father Ignacio knew that Madame De Dreux and her stepdaughter, the pretty Pascal, were the last people for whose souls he need concern himself. Their goodness reflected the very epitome of Christian love. Taking the heavy purse of coins reluctantly—fearing he only encouraged this fine woman to continue her dangerous forays from her plantation to the isolated orphanage in Jefferson Parish—he said a heartfelt prayer for her safety. The Good Lord guided in mysterious ways. If He compelled this woman to risk the perilous country roads for Christian good, He would certainly protect her.

"May I see the children, Father?"

"But of course. We have a new foundling I would like you to meet. A young girl who I'm afraid is having a difficult time of it."

Mercedes De Dreux walked regally beside Father Ignacio across the muddied ground to one of several whitewashed buildings. Once inside the mission room where the orphans too young to attend classes played, Father spoke to Sister Anna. The Ursuline nun sought out and ushered forward a blond-haired girl wearing a patched dress. She looked no older than five.

"Poor thing. Just arrived last week. Her mother worked down on Gallatin Street and passed on recently from the French po—" Father Ignacio stared down on the blond head. "Well, that is to say, she's gone now. Resting with our Heavenly Father. A friend delivered the child."

Gallatin Street, the promised land of harlotry, immediately conjured images of what this child's life had been like. Mercy stared down at the small girl whose doll-like size was most likely a result of undernourishment. Mercy knelt down, caring nothing for the yellow Chinese silk that would be stained at the knees, and touched one of the girl's hands gently.

"I'm very sorry about your mother."

The little girl said nothing, but pulled her fingers from the stranger's grasp. Mercy saw the shuttered face, the fear. It gripped her heart. She'd known similar losses in her life.

Unhooking the small bag suspended from her waist, Mercy opened the drawstring and searched inside for a bribe. At the bottom, encased in waxed paper, was a sticky piece of praline candy she kept for just such occasions. She held it out temptingly for the girl. When the urchin reached out for the goody, lightning quick, Mercy caught the girl's hand. She placed the candy in the center of her sweaty palm and wrapped the small fist in both of her larger hands.

These children felt so little warmth in their lives, so little human love and caring. Mercy longed to take the child in her arms and hug her close to her chest. But she saw the girl was uncomfortable with her touch so she released her. Instead, Mercy sat down cross-legged on the dusty floor and reached back in her bag for a second bit of candy and broke off a piece. Behind them, Father Ignacio stepped away to let her do her magic, as she'd done on so many other occasions with the new orphans.

The child watched her slyly, as if trying to discover Mercy's game. From the look in her blue eyes, Mercy would guess she had spent a fair amount of time living on her own in the streets. It was a look Mercy knew well. A look she saw most mornings in the mirror.

"Well, my dearling," Mercy said, nibbling on the edge of her praline. "What's your name?"

"Harriet," the girl said in a childlike lisp.

"Harriet." Mercy looked suitably impressed. "That's an awfully pretty name. Unusual too. How ever did you come by it?"

"Ma mère," she said around the wad of sticky praline. "But she called me Harry."

Mercy lifted a fine, arched brow. "That sounds like a boy."

"Don't it just," the girl giggled, as if she'd been granted a great compliment.

Mercy shook her head, tugging one of the child's curls. "You're much too pretty for that, dear Harriet."

Intrigued by the woman's familiarity, obviously starved for attention, Harriet inched closer to Mercy. Again she hunted in her bag until she found some string. She began forming an elaborate cat's cradle and smiled when she watched the girl's eyes light up. "Do you know this game?" Mercy asked with an air of innocence.

Within minutes, Harriet and she were talking and laughing as they exchanged the piece of string in ever more complicated patterns. For Mercy, watching the web and listening to the child brought back memories that were both cherished and painful—recollections of a time when, though her life had been a daily struggle, she'd been truly loved. *Oh Laura, Beth. What's become of you, my dearest friends?*

Seeing by the sun's position in the noon sky that it was well past time to leave, Mercy surveyed the mission room. A dark-haired girl with skin the color of creamed coffee sat in the corner watching them. Mercy urged the child to join in their game and soon enough the little ones were engrossed in the cat's cradle. Mercy stepped away quietly, giving Harriet and her new friend one lingering glance before searching for Father Ignacio. She found him waiting outside.

"You work miracles, madame," he said, nodding his head to where the girls played and laughed just beyond the opened door.

"I wish I could do more." She handed him a few coins. "Please have the sisters buy something special for Harriet when the peddler comes by. A dress, a soft toy, whatever they think would make her happiest."

"Of course. Will you be leaving us now?"

"I'm afraid I must." She reached over and gave Father's hand a squeeze. "But Pascal and I will return next week."

"Have a care for your safety, madame," Father Ignacio called out as he watched Madame De Dreux cross the courtyard to the classroom. Again he wondered how a woman with such a gentle manner around children could be denied one of her own. Yet, in the ten years since she'd joined Monsieur De Dreux at L'Isle des Rêves as his bride, their marriage had been blessed with none. And though anyone could see that Madame cared deeply for her stepdaughter, the high-strung Pascal seemed distant, and at times outwardly hostile to her stepmother. Father Ignacio shook his head as he watched Mercedes De Dreux's retreating figure. Truly, God's ways were mysterious.

Mercy stepped onto the planked-wood porch of one of five whitewashed buildings that made up the asylum compound. The familiar ache came as she looked inside the classroom filled with girls and boys of various ages, all listening attentively to their lesson. Seeing the children she would never have, remembering her own past—at times reliving it through the eyes of streetwise girls like Harriet —tore through her carefully constructed walls. For a moment, she remained outside the door, a spectator.

She turned her gaze to the deceptively perfect profile of her stepdaughter at the head of the class. The noon sun colored Pascal's hair a rich burgundy red as her head nodded in beat to the children chanting the alphabet. Her smile showed a monument of encouragement for the chorus of reedy voices stumbling through their letters. In her lavender walking gown, its wrists and neck trimmed demurely with Belgian lace, Pascal looked so young, so innocent.

So different from the girl blackmailing Mercy.

Her eyes never leaving Pascal, Mercy's hand fell to her stomach. Her fingers clenched into a fist and pressed the stays of her corset into her waist as she recalled the life that had briefly flared there. A year ago, when Benoit had told Mercy his daughter was returning to live with them at L'Isle des Rêves, no longer welcome at the many boarding schools he'd shipped her to over the years, Mercy had hoped for another chance at motherhood . . . but her stepdaughter had never given Mercy the opportunity to show her love. No, blackmail was definitely not endearing.

How ironic that the poor girl didn't know half of what she'd involved herself in.

As if sensing her stepmother's presence, Pascal turned toward the door. She smiled, a vibrant, angelic smile, that like her moments of teaching confused Mercy into believing she might find love and companionship there. How could the lovely creature who watched her now with a look that almost begged for acceptance be the same girl who'd approached Mercy a year ago with her threats? How could the girl who insisted on accompanying Mercy on these trips to teach a classroom of orphans be the same hellion who just shy of seventeen—only eight years Mercy's junior —had been tossed out of every school she'd attended? No institution would accept Pascal now, no matter how much Benoit offered as a bribe. The response was always the same whenever the girl's father made inquiries: He could not pay enough to smooth over his mannerless child's many transgressions.

Mercy's gaze lifted from the girl's smile to her dark mysterious eyes, eyes that melted the years and, as they often did, evoked the image of the man who had given to Mercy in worldly goods, but had stripped her of love—even its possibility. Benoit had smiled just as charmingly while initiating and destroying Mercy's only chance at happiness. Benoit De Dreux, the man who had fathered Pascal on another woman. The man Mercy despised. And had married.

Mercy blinked, slowly bringing the classroom back into focus. She caught her stepdaughter's expectant expression.

"We're late, Pascal. Please hurry." Mercy turned and left.

Inside the classroom, Pascal's features twisted into familiar pain. She glanced up, making certain her stepmother could not see her, and brushed away her tear. She dismissed the class and packed her books and papers into her travel bag.

Once outside the mission-style classroom, her sixteen-year-old stepdaughter brushed past Mercy, granting her only a sneer. Mercy sighed and followed, crossing the grassy quad crowded with frolicking children to the De Dreux landau. She expected no more from Pascal.

The entire journey back to L'Isle des Rêves, Pascal remained silent, though her frequent glances at Mercy made it clear she chafed to speak. Mercy reminded herself to be patient. Pascal had never had a woman's influence, or a parent's love judging from the way Benoit ignored the girl. Her mother had lived only long enough to name her infant daughter. But when the carriage reached the cedar groves on the outskirts of Benoit's vast sugar plantation, Mercy could stand the venomous stares no longer. She dug her fingers into the seat's red moroccan leather, ready for Pascal's worst.

"You've obviously something to say, Pascal," she said. "I'm listening."

The girl's lips pressed together.

Mercy glanced toward the plantation house. "We're almost home."

Pascal's gaze slipped from the white mansion back to Mercy, as if judging how much time she had left before reaching the plantation house. Both knew any candid discussion could occur only outside L'Isle des Rêves' walls.

"I'm trying to understand," Pascal said at last, "*why* you did it."

Mercy stared at her stepdaughter, rocking gently with the motion of the carriage as it turned down the drive. "I'm afraid I don't understand. What have I done to offend you this time?"

"Why take such risks? You acted downright foolishly. The danger—" Pascal's eyes widened. "Is that it? Is it the danger you're after?"

"You are giving me entirely too much credit for perception, Pascal, if you think I have the slightest notion of what you are talking about." But even as she protested, Mercy's hand crept to the neckline of her dress.

"Of course you do! Why do you pretend not to!"

Before Mercy could stop her, Pascal reached across the

carriage. She knocked Mercy's hand aside and grabbed the chain around Mercy's neck. With a tug, she slid the gold out from beneath the silk bodice until she held the stolen St. Christopher medal in her hands.

"Why keep such a valuable medal when Santana Rose can sell it for badly needed money? Why wear it around your neck like some badge to your foolishness? Anyone could find it!"

Mercy's fingers covered Pascal's hand around the medallion. "That choice is mine alone to make."

Pascal opened her mouth to protest, but then her lovely eyes narrowed. "Oh, I see the way of it now. Is it a momento? A cherished reminder of your romantic tryst? How sweet. How romantic. How *selfish*!" She tugged harder on the chain, until Mercy feared the clasp she'd fixed just that morning would give way again. "Did you enjoy yourself when you kissed him?" Pascal hissed.

Mercedes yanked the chain from Pascal's grasp. With an angry glare, the girl fell back into her seat.

"Monsieur Murard would have given Santana Rose a pretty penny for that chain," Pascal said. "It's a danger to keep it."

Mercy undid the clasp and tucked the St. Christopher into her purse. "Do you think the risks I take too great, Pascal? Whenever you wish to quit, you know that would make me exceedingly happy. It was never my choice to have you ride with Santana's men. It's getting to be a bit of a wear to watch after you on our runs."

Pascal's expression crumbled, as if Mercy's words had sorely wounded. Mercy instantly regretted her attack, knowing what she'd said was not true. Quite the contrary. Pascal had required minimal training before becoming a vital part of Santana's group. The only burden was to keep secret the true nature of their thefts from her stepdaughter, which Mercy and her men did diligently. But with all her heart Mercy wanted to keep her stepdaughter home where she would be safe.

"You simply refuse . . ." Pascal sputtered. "You don't want to believe . . . you need . . ." Pascal looked away, blinking back what looked suspiciously to be tears. The pained expression in the girl's eyes moved Mercy to the point that she reached out to console her.

Pascal slapped Mercy's hand away. "You'll not get rid of me easily. No matter what you say to me, I'm still part of Santana's gang. Just you remember that. The minute you oust me, I run to my father and tell all . . . *maman*." The last word Pascal saved as her greatest insult.

Mercy shook her head. "What is it that you really want from me, Pascal?"

"Stop taking needless risks! You put yourself—*all* of us —in danger."

"Then stay safe, Pascal. Remain home and leave Santana and her men alone."

In the silence that followed, Pascal's gaze turned sharp, making her eyes appear hard and glassy like obsidian—a replica of her father's. "If I don't come along," she said in a voice filled with venom, "who will make sure that the goods don't end up lining Santana's pockets?"

The girl's insinuation struck Mercy strangely as a betrayal. She'd not expected such a low blow, even from Pascal.

"Someday," Mercy said softly, "someone is going to teach you how to curb that poisonous tongue of yours."

"Possibly not before your love of danger gets us both killed."

Mercy tightened her grip on her bag, feeling the medallion through the silk. "When will you learn, Pascal? That is the one choice neither you nor your father shall ever succeed in taking from me."

Chapter 2

Rey lifted the Baccarat tumbler to his lips and sipped his absinthe and water. "My thanks again, De Dreux, for having us as your guests."

"But of course, *monsieur*," answered the soft, almost sibilant voice from across the parlor. "Whatever are neighbors for? Until repairs to the plantation house at Bizy are finished, you and *Monsieur* Everard are most welcome to stay here."

Rey nodded at the dark-haired gentleman whose sharp features and olive skin bespoke Creole ancestry. De Dreux held his compact body flush against a Belter armchair, its pierced rosewood design towering over his head like a rococo throne. Gray tinged the temples of his thick black hair. A perfectly manicured mustache accented lips that were a bit too full, a shade too delicate, to belong on a man. Though he was dressed in a style befitting Harlan's age, Rey suspected the planter neared the half-century mark.

Here in his plantation kingdom, De Dreux had surrounded himself with riches Rey knew the man could ill afford. The floor to ceiling windows of the double parlor bowed under the weight of their gilded cornices and damask curtains. The Midas theme echoed across the room, repeated in the gold-patterned wallpaper and the gilt-edged mirror over the fireplace. Behind De Dreux, Harlan examined a white marble mantle that bloomed in an overabundance of carved flowers and fruit. Yet the planter's dark, almond-shaped eyes seemed to negate the richness of the room, evoking the image of a river rat—cunning, hungry despite the opulence.

Rey had learned as much as possible about De Dreux before coming to New Orleans. De Dreux was a man willing to do anything to achieve his ends. A man who had, it was rumored, killed his own brother in a duel. Seated beneath the coved ceiling of his parlor, he exhibited the one trait that allowed Rey to use him as a pawn in his game to beat Sotheby: greed. No matter how much the Creole gentleman possessed, he schemed for more. His very gluttony threatened to make a pauper of him.

"*Eh, bien.* We shall make a fine start of it with your planting cane, *m'sieur,*" Harlan said, pacing the lavishly furnished room in a manner Rey found annoying in the extreme. From time to time, Harlan would pick up a statuette, a Ming vase, scuff a toe of his boot to the plush Wilton carpet, taking inventory of each costly item. "It's a good thing for us you could spare the seed cane, *mais oui.*"

"You are paying a fine price," replied De Dreux. "I am always a man with his eye out for a healthy profit."

A man in desperate need of one, Rey thought. If his banking connections were correct, De Dreux's kingdom teetered on the brink of ruin. He needed Sotheby's lottery scheme to save him from losing everything. But without the money Rey offered, De Dreux would be cut out of Sotheby's dirty dealings like a poker player without the blunt to ante up. Rey had been only too willing to oblige.

"Profit is what we all seek," Rey said out loud. "I shall make certain to learn what I can from you, sir."

De Dreux folded his hands on his lap in a manner that portrayed instant attention. "I believe, *monsieur,* it is you who can teach me a thing or two. I have made several offers on the tract of land you purchased. I wished to add the *batture* to my plantation." One corner of his full lips twisted upward. "Never was I able to acquire the property."

Rey allowed himself a slow lazy smile. The land, like many plantations after the war, had been government owned and still was. "It was not an easy negotiation, I must admit. But Everard here promises he'll make the land pay back within a season."

De Dreux cocked an eyebrow. "You have experience with sugar, *monsieur*?"

Harlan looked up from the Japanese ivory carving in his hands. "Cuba."

"Ah. The best." De Dreux passed a hand through his graying temples before resuming his languid strokes of the rosewood arm. "But with the trouble the Spanish are having there now, not as profitable as before. There are only two things the Louisiana sugar planter need fear: Cuban independence or annexation by the United States."

"Neither is too likely," Rey said.

"A gamble, nonetheless."

Rey took up his glass and raised it in a toast. "To a good gamble, then."

"You certainly *do* enjoy games of chance. It was your past investments that led me to approach you with my business proposition."

"I could hardly pass up such a lucrative offer. According to your figures, I stand to more than triple my investment." Rey allowed just a hint of hesitation in his voice. "That is, if the man you work with really has as much influence as he claims. The reports in the *Democrat* this past week suggest the lottery bill might be repealed. It's difficult to believe there will be a drawing at all come June, much less that the outcome can be . . . guided."

"I assure you, *monsieur,* things will progress just as planned. You will lose nothing. There is really no gamble at all for the Silver Fox." De Dreux cocked his head. "An intriguing name. Is it your cunning with money that makes people call you that?"

"I think the name is a reference to this head of hair you see," Rey said, touching a lock. "Nothing more significant than that."

"If not cunning," De Dreux added, "then certainly an instinct for the profitable. That was why I was so surprised when you wrote that you were purchasing the Bizy plantation. Given the current slump in the sugar market, I hardly believed my inquiries to you would result in such dramatic measures."

Rey held back a smile. He was certain his move had shocked De Dreux, who wanted Rey's money for his lottery scheme—not his presence. Five years it had taken him to hook into one of Sotheby's deals. Thanks to De Dreux, soon, very soon, Rey hoped to put both the Creole planter and Harrison Sotheby behind bars.

"You are asking for a substantial investment." Rey shrugged. "I feel better when I can keep an eye on my money. I want to be involved first hand."

De Dreux's circling fingers stopped. "Leonard Marcus seems to keep you in high regard."

Rey nodded at the mention of the petty counterfeiter turned government informant. Marcus had been paid well to serve as Rey's entrée into De Dreux and Sotheby's circle. "The money I made for Mr. Marcus recommends me. When can I meet this gentleman you're working with?" Rey continued, acting as if the meeting with Sotheby were a foregone conclusion. "I'm eager to find out firsthand how my funds are being spent."

De Dreux shifted in his chair. "I'm sure something can be arranged. I shall look into it. In the meantime, let me give you my condolences on yesterday's misadventure. It truly is a shame you should experience such a violent introduction to our city." The smile on his face belied his sympathetic tone. "Not a happy prelude to our future enterprise."

"*Que diable,*" Harlan said. "We would have arrived here yesterday if not for *les bandits.*"

Rey placed his glass on the marble-topped table in front of him, losing interest in the half-filled tumbler. "I can't say the bandits made off too well. A few personal items. I make it a habit to travel with as little cash as possible."

"A wise course with villains such as this Santana Rose—"

"—Villains? Why Benoit," a mellow voice with an intriguing British accent and an edge of laughter called from the entryway behind Rey. "I believe Santana Rose sounds much too dashing to be lumped with the other rabble of our fine city."

Rey turned toward the double doors leading to the music room. The woman who stood at the entrance of the parlor, her hand poised above the white molding, could have stepped out of the Gainsborough landscape hanging from a gold cord on the wall behind her. The walking gown of coral pongee flowed down a figure superb despite the exaggerated curves created by crinolines and the gown's elaborate draping. Her creamy complexion, the wisps of golden hair escaping the cascade of curls and brushing her cheeks, made her seem almost ethereal.

For the second time in less than twenty-four hours, Rey experienced an overpowering sexual response to a beautiful woman. Interestingly enough, the woman could have been the bandit's opposite. Where the highway robber had been dark, this lady was golden light. While the masked woman aroused with fierce power, the lady's air of refinement seduced by its very gracefulness. Yet, despite the differences between the two, Rey's reaction to both had been the same: instant, powerful—not to be ignored.

"Mercedes, my dear." De Dreux stood. "Our visitors have arrived at long last. Monsieur Reynard Parks and Monsieur Harlan Everard, may I present my wife, Madame De Dreux."

Wife. It took ten years of detective training to hide Rey's reaction to the title. He told himself it was her age, certainly half that of De Dreux's, that had caught him off guard. But then the fragrance of lavender reached him and the sweet warmth of desire crept unerringly through his muscles. If he weren't careful, this woman could prove a greater foe than the bandit who'd robbed him at gunpoint.

Rising to his feet, Rey bowed his head in her direction. "A pleasure, madame."

"Your name is *Renard*?" Eyes a soft brown smiled at him from across the room. "Like the fox?"

Though her British accent ravaged her French, the smile she delivered more than made up for the flaw. The curve of her lips made her look teasing, as if she and Rey already shared a secret. The gesture coaxed a responding grin from Rey despite his determination not to be charmed.

"Spelled differently," he said watching her walk across the room. "*R-E-Y*. As in the Spanish word for king. I was named after my mother's side of the family." He took up the hand she extended toward him and touched his lips to the smooth skin in a formal kiss. He had played many roles during his years as government agent—some he was not proud of—including that of seducer. He found it unnerving that the mere sight of De Dreux's wife could tempt him to consider a strategy that in the past had weighed so heavily on his conscience.

Rey released her hand and took a step back, distancing himself from temptation. But his smile remained easily just the same. "My name was always a sore subject for my poor father. Luckily, I have a younger brother whom Father named as he pleased."

She tilted her head. A light of intelligence sparked from her too-lovely eyes. "I believe fox suits you better, sir. A silver fox."

De Dreux's head jerked toward his wife. Rey let none of his surprise show on his face. He wondered if the fair lady made it a habit of eavesdropping and how much of his discussion with her husband she had overheard. It would be quite a coincidence for her to come up with the name on her own, though not entirely impossible.

"Imagine." Madame De Dreux swept past Rey and offered her hand to Harlan. "To be initiated into our dear city by such an infamous figure. They say"—she looked over her shoulder at Rey and her husband—"Santana Rose is quite beautiful." She stepped to the low courting couch and rested the long elegant fingers of one hand on the meridienne's single arm. Built to accommodate wide skirts and still provide a comforting support for the lady's escort, the back of the meridienne scooped down to disappear halfway down its length. "That would be rather fanciful, I suppose, considering her employment. She probably has the face of a hag with the muscles of a stevedore. Was it terrible?" she asked, startling Rey by her quick change from humor to sympathy.

"As I was telling your husband," he said. "We did not lose much."

"That's wonderful news. I'll make it a point to see that your stay at L'Isle des Rêves is so pleasant as to erase its unfortunate beginning." She lowered herself gracefully onto the meridienne. Her skirt spilled over the edge of the couch making Rey think of cream poured over berries. She gestured for each man to be seated.

"Mr. Parks"—again the teasing humor in her voice—"I do not mean to make light of your misfortune, of course, but I am terribly curious. *Is* she as beautiful as rumored?" A dimple appeared to the left of her soft mouth. "Or is it the bulging muscles after all?"

Rey had trouble keeping back a grin. He could see the lady enjoyed being just a bit outrageous. "That would be difficult for me to judge, madame. Under the circumstances."

She raised a brow, looking as if Rey's response disappointed her. "My curiosity shall not be appeased, then. She has become quite a figure of speculation on the coast," she said, referring to the plantations along the Mississippi shore. "Tossing a Santana Red rose at your victim's feet is rather flamboyant. It captures one's imagination. And you, Mr. Harlan? Do you venture an opinion?"

Harlan shrugged and leaned against the scrolled rosewood arm of the low sofa. "She was masked. I guarantee, I was looking at her guns more than her figure."

"Mercedes," De Dreux interrupted, impatience making his French accent more pronounced. "Is everything prepared for our guests?"

"Why of course, Benoit." Her tone and the sweep of her eyes downward held just enough of the submissive wife to shield the spark Rey saw—a subtle light in her gaze that made him believe she enjoyed her husband's irritation.

She glanced up in time to see Rey staring at her. Instantly the look dimmed.

"You must be extremely tired from your travels," she said, standing. "Excuse my bad manners for being absent at your arrival. When you didn't appear yesterday, Benoit's daughter and I went to the opera. I thought it best to stay at our *pied à terre* in town rather than journey back so late. I'm afraid Pascal insisted on doing some shopping before I could get her out of the city. I will have Nathan show you to your quarters now." She walked to the tapestry bell pull. "It's a lovely walk to the *garçonnière*. I'll have a bath prepared for you both and you'll have plenty of time to rest." A tall, white-haired negro appeared immediately, as if he'd been waiting just outside for this summons. "Dinner is served at eight," she said.

Rey stepped to the door. "I shall look forward to your company, madame."

As he followed the servant and Harlan to their quarters, Rey caught Harlan's stare. A boyish grin spread across his face as he nodded his head back toward the double parlor. "A real beauty, *mais* sure." Harlan kissed the tips of his fingers in appreciation.

"Yes," Rey said distractedly, shaking off the woman's disturbing attraction as he thought of her husband and the meeting with Sotheby Rey must coax from De Dreux. But even as the group traveled down the thick runner of the corridor, the scent of lavender lingered in the air.

Pascal tossed herself on the mahogany sleigh bed, ignoring the small daybed at its base despite the fact that the servants would now have to roll out the lumps in the moss-and-horsehair mattress before nightfall. The duvet swished up around her body, buoyed by its feather stuffing. Dressed only in her cotton chemise, drawers, and corset, she relished the touch of satin against her bared skin as a remedy to the afternoon's moist heat. She let out a dramatic sigh and stared up at her companion, a tiny Chinese girl whose exotic eyes and prominent cheekbones amplified her amused expression. Pascal pointed an accusing finger despite her own smile. "Now don't you dare laugh, Ling Shi. He *is* the most beautiful man I have ever seen!"

The Chinese girl, only a year older than her sixteen-year-old charge, pressed her lips together as if trying to subdue her smile. "And you have seen so many to make a proper comparison."

Pascal twisted her lips into a look of annoyance. "I've led a life that would make a monk proud, as well you know since you were sequestered right along with me. Educated by Madame de Flambeau at her exclusive *Académie des Jeunes Filles,*" she mimicked in a thick French accent. "Subdued at Mrs. Beasley's Institute of Etiquette. Beasley and her Beasties!" She made a face. "But"—her eyes darkened—"even if I'd never seen a man before in my *entire* life . . ." She threw her arms up, trying to hug the very air. "I would recognize such masculine *perfection*!"

Ling Shi bent down to pick up the gown and petticoats that habitually littered the parquet floor and English hook rugs. She couldn't help a small laugh. She shook her head, sending her dark braid swaying against the shining blue silk of the gown she wore, a dress no less fine than the one her mistress had carelessly discarded on the ground. "Pascal, you are incorrigible."

Getting the reaction she'd hoped for, Pascal swung around to face Ling Shi. Pascal's dark red hair, a color so deep it appeared almost black, flicked across her bare arms. "Oh, I definitely made a mistake teaching you how to read English. Now you're constantly spouting five-syllable words. As if you didn't know enough ways to discourage me."

Ling Shi added another petticoat to the tower in her arms, ignoring her companion, but Pascal saw the tilt of her lips just the same.

"He has these blue, *blue* eyes," Pascal continued, encouraged by her friend's response. "Like indigo blossoms on the hillside. And his hair is the color of café au lait." She licked her lips in a way she thought outrageously seductive and mature. "*Mmm,* just the way I like it." She climbed down from the mattress. Taking the clothes from Ling Shi's hands and dropping them on the bed, she pulled the Chinese servant girl into a waltz stance. "If we should dance"—she swung Ling Shi about the room in a lilting rhythm, swaying right then left—"his steps would be expert and light, the embrace of his arms strong and guiding. . . ."

"Pascal! You're supposed to be resting." Ling Shi pulled away and began folding the clothes on the bed.

"Ah yes, the arduous task of staying awake through the day may be too much for my frail self." She stumbled to the bed, as if already weak, then pounced onto the mattress, sending the gown and petticoats fluttering into the air. The neatly folded items landed in a tangled heap on the duvet. With a toss of her head, Pascal swung her waist-length hair out of her face and grabbed Ling Shi's wrists before the Chinese girl's hands reached the clothes. "Ling Shi. I am in love."

Ling Shi's gentle eyes darkened and the corners of her mouth turned down. For a moment, it appeared as if Pascal—someone who loved the servant girl like a sister—had purposely hurt her.

"What's the matter?" Pascal whispered. Her heart pounded in her chest. Ling Shi was the only person on this Earth who cared about her. Even if her father paid the girl to be her companion, over the years Pascal had forgotten that their relationship was based on anything other than mutual caring.

Taking Pascal's hands in hers, Ling Shi gave them a comforting squeeze. "It is nothing." She shooed Pascal aside and grabbed the gown, all business once more, making Pascal want to sigh from relief. "It's just that, you don't even know this man."

"How well did Apollo know Daphne? Could he help loving her on first sight?"

"As I recall, his feelings were not returned . . ."

"I am in *love,* Ling Shi." She clasped her hands dramatically to her chest and swooned on the bed in a performance worthy of the St. Charles Theater. "Struck through the heart by Cupid's golden arrow as surely as Apollo."

Pascal stared up at the canopy of mosquito netting as Ling Shi watched on disapprovingly. She could feel her heart pound beneath her hands as she recalled Harlan Everard's handsome features. Love—true love—pulsed within her, something to replace the ugliness that had grown inside her with each passing year.

When Pascal had been allowed to come home to L'Isle des Rêves, she'd thought to change her life. She would no longer be a nuisance as Beasley's Beasties had called her, or the misfit shunned by her classmates because she hadn't the slightest notion of proper social behavior. For once, she would be a cherished member of her family. Reality had been a jarring blow. To her father, Pascal was about as important as the Spode creamware. Her stepmother watched her with a look that showed Pascal would never find love there. No matter how she tried to impress Mercedes with feats of daring as one of Santana's gang, things remained bad between them.

The frustration of it all goaded Pascal into nastiness that surprised even her—and certainly astounded Ling Shi. Pascal had kept her friend carefully ignorant of Mercy's dual identity or Pascal's participation in Santana's gang. Though her companion never judged Pascal harshly, Ling Shi often lectured Pascal on her rudeness toward Mercedes. Pascal frowned, thinking of the afternoon's ride back from the orphanage. She hadn't meant to say those vile things. She'd only wanted Mercedes to understand she shouldn't take needless risks. Her forays as Santana Rose were dangerous enough! If only Pascal could make her see. . . .

Pascal sighed, shifting her thoughts back to Harlan Everard, the man who had proven she was capable of something honorable after all. At last, she had found goodness inside herself. Love. She would not let Ling Shi dampen the wonderful feelings warming her now.

Propping herself up on her elbows, Pascal said, "Ling Shi, I need your help. Tonight at dinner I must look *stunning*." Rising to her knees, she declared from her bed-stage, "I shall bring him to his knees with my lovely countenance as surely as the nymph Daphne."

"You are a beautiful girl, Pascal—"

"Girl." She stuck her tongue out. "Tonight, I want to be a *woman*."

"Do not be in such a hurry to grow up, dear friend," Ling Shi warned.

"You don't understand!" She jumped off the bed and ran to the armoire. Throwing open both doors, she tossed gown after gown to the floor, searching deep inside. She called back in a voice muffled by the oak, "There must be something in here I can wear that isn't designed for a twelve-year-old child!"

Ling Shi watched, this time leaving the clothes to their

fate on the floor. "I do not believe your father would approve."

"Forget Father," Pascal said almost to herself. "He wouldn't notice if I walked in to dinner with a hogshead of sugar balanced on my head. Ah!" She pulled out a beautiful turquoise gown and swung around to face Ling Shi, holding the gown in front of her. "We can fix this one." Flashing her best smile, she added, "I mean, *you* can fix it. A trained chicken could sew a straighter stitch than mine."

"Perhaps if you'd not been so busy reading medical texts to discover how to make knock-out drops for Beasley's Beasties you might have paid closer attention to your sewing lessons."

Undeterred by Ling Shi's censure, Pascal ran back to the bed and shoved the other gown and petticoats aside. Spreading the turquoise dress for Ling Shi to see, she said, "Your touch is magic. If you can take down the bodice . . ." She stopped, her hands still above the silk. Almost as an afterthought, she glanced down to her budding breasts beneath her chemise.

"*Arghhh!*" Pascal flopped back onto the bed, crushing the lovely gown beneath her. "If you fix the bodice, he'll have a lovely view of what a flat-chested ninny-hammer I am. Hopeless. Doomed."

After a dreadful moment of silence during which Pascal contemplated the years of spinsterhood looming ahead, she felt Ling Shi's cool fingers grasp hers and pull her off the dress. Pascal huddled into her friend's embrace, placing her head on Ling Shi's shoulder as the Chinese girl stroked the curls from her face.

"It is important to you, Pascal?"

Pascal nodded, giving Ling Shi a watery smile. "More important than the knock-out drops."

Ling Shi shook her head. After giving Pascal a squeeze, she nudged her gently aside and turned back to the gown. With an encouraging smile, she motioned her over. Pascal hovered above the smaller Ling Shi, watching the girl's hands straighten the rumpled silk on the bed.

"Perhaps the cut of the gown is a bit youthful," Ling Shi agreed. "Look here. I could lower the corsage a bit without ruining the line of the dress. And with a corset"—she spared Pascal's small breasts a glance—"we might be able to improve on nature."

Pascal's mouth dropped open. "You can make me"—she stared down to where her chest pressed against her chemise—"bigger?"

Ling Shi shook her head, laughing. "Only time can do that. But perhaps some cotton padding will help."

Pascal hugged her friend. "You're wonderful, Ling Shi. Absolutely wonderful!"

Rey sat beneath the dining room's punkah fan. The heavy moist air of the day had coalesced into a light drizzle that pattered against the window panes. The evening was not near warm enough to require the silk embroidered fan hanging from the high ceiling and the punkah had been tied stationary by its cord. Bronze and crystal wall sconces with amethyst drops illuminated the feast that spanned the length of the table in a culinary parade. Rey turned his glass of burgundy in his hand, half-listening to Pascal De Dreux regale Harlan with stories of bullfrogs in the bayou. The girl was certainly knowledgeable about the different species and their habits, though Rey could see from Harlan's expression that his partner didn't find frogs particularly interesting.

Distracted himself, Rey watched the candlelight from the ormolu candlesticks reflect off the cut-crystal edges of his glass. Periodically, he would express a diplomatic "certainly" or "interesting" to encourage Constable Gessler's soliloquy on the benefits of convict labor. Given the choice, Rey would rather hear about bullfrogs. Unfortunately, Gessler was seated beside him. Rey scanned the military formation of Sevres china, each dish hand-painted with a different pastoral scene, until his gaze reached the evening's greatest diversion: the lovely vision in lilac at the table's end.

Mercedes De Dreux returned his gaze directly—as she had done many times while the guests sampled their way through the odyssey of French cuisine. As Harlan had said, she was indeed a beauty. The perfect curves of her body, the sweet oval face and eyes the color of burnt sugar, could dazzle any man—even one determined not to be. Rey's gaze dropped to her breasts, caressed by the silk pansies decorating the low décolletage of her gown. As he watched, Mercedes straightened her shoulders until the material rose to a more concealing angle across her pale skin. He glanced up, saw by her expression that she'd caught the direction of his stare. A slight flush colored her cheeks as she lifted her glass marginally in a silent salute and granted him her dimpled smile.

Rey felt something delicious and irresistible unfurl inside him. Nothing she could have done would have been more provocative. The teasing innocence of her flush as she strove for a more demure pose combined with the inviting smile left him just a bit off balance. Oddly enough, he found he enjoyed his giddy brush with desire. In the past five years, he'd thought himself beyond the feelings this woman inspired.

"The fifteen convicts I brought you today," the florid-faced constable said, raising his voice to an attention-grabbing level, "can reditch all of L'Isle des Rêves for twenty cents a day in food and the cost of guard hire. Can't do better than that now, can you? And not a chance they'll be off steamboating elsewhere like them Eye-talians you hired last year." Rey watched the man accept an enormous helping of potato croquettes despite the bulging buttons of his waistcoat ready to give way like a crevasse on the levee during flood season.

"*Ah, bon.* Sounds almost as good as slave labor," Harlan said.

At his words, the De Dreux girl stared down at the turtle soup the servant replaced with the next course, obviously chagrined at losing her audience. Rey was none too pleased himself with the comment, but he thought Harlan's engaging smile successfully camouflaged his baiting tone.

"Ain't nothing as good as slaves, sir." The constable's red-veined jowls shook with emphasis. "But convict labor comes right close. Only problem is making sure there's enough to go around. Been a real demand since the war."

"Tell you what. I'm sure you could . . ." Harlan seemed to search for the right word ". . . round up a few, *non*?"

Gessler shot Rey a sly look. "I might be able to help you out at Bizy if you're looking for some—"

"*Mais, non,* man," Harlan cut him off. "We're not interested in your goods."

A stunned silence fell over the room. Rey gave Harlan a hard look before saying, "Not at this moment, in any case."

From her end of the table, Mercy watched the exchange between Gessler and Everard with interest. She suspected she and Everard shared a few views, particularly concerning the scheming opportunist, Gessler. The letter Santana's men had found hidden in Everard's wallet during the holdup confirmed it as surely as the look he gave the slow-witted constable.

Mercy hid her smile behind her wine goblet as she thought of the note written by Robert Pinkerton. The missive had been an unbelievable boon. Addressed to Pinkerton detective Harlan Everard, it stated simply when Secret Service agent Reynard Parks, the Silver Fox, would be arriving for their mission at L'Isle des Rêves. They were to pose as two financiers interested in an illegal lottery scheme. Obviously, the two were here to investigate Benoit. From Everard's actions tonight, Mercy suspected that Gessler might well land in jail beside her husband.

Staring at the constable, Everard did nothing to hide his hatred for the man, watching him with an expression one might reserve for a slug before giving it the heel of his boot. Parks was much more circumspect. As she took a sip of the burgundy, Mercy wondered if Rey knew about the missing letter and if he might stop his mission because of its theft. Though under different circumstances Mercy would try to encourage Parks to go forward with his plans against Benoit, Mercy alone knew that the lottery scheme was one crime her husband could never be convicted of.

"You'll have to excuse Mr. Everard if he seems a bit hesitant to accept your help, Constable," Reynard Parks added when Gessler began to grumble over Everard's rudeness. "He did a superb job of making sure all the workers we needed were contracted before the sale of the property became final." He winked at the constable. "I've found Harlan is a bit proprietary about the workings of Bizy."

Mercy examined Reynard Parks through lowered lashes, unable, despite the peril he represented, to get her fill of the enigmatic Secret Service agent.

Or could Pascal be right—the danger itself draws you.

Mercy rejected the possibility immediately. Of the men Benoit had entertained in their home, many of them handsome, the only effect his cronies had ever spawned was complete and utter disgust. But here was a man commissioned by the government, who'd dedicated his life to justice and righting wrongs. What could be more seductive to a woman seeking a modicum of fairness in the world?

She admitted she found him painfully attractive. He was a good head taller than she—few men were. The cut of his frock coat and matching black trousers displayed a firm and admirable body with wide shoulders and long, muscular legs. The cleft in his chin accentuated the sensual mouth she had barely grazed as Santana Rose; the salt-and-pepper blunt-cut hair feathered across his forehead, making him look young. On him the silver with its sprin-

kling of jet left no appearance of age. It was merely another unique feature permitted only Rey. Like his eyes.
His dark brows and lashes emphasized the pale green hue,
turning it almost iridescent.

She'd never met a man who had such an effect on her.
At twenty-four, after ten years of this facade Benoit called
a marriage, could she really be experiencing her first girl-
ish crush?

She looked away, suddenly annoyed with herself. Why
question her feelings? Why not relish the excitement
coursing through her? Parks frightened her, yes, because
she was unsure how high a price those seductive eyes
might cost her. But could she turn her back on the pos-
sibilities they offered?

"I find it interesting, *monsieur,* that you were able to
contract sufficient labor for Bizy. *I've* had a damnable time
finding workers for L'Isle des Rêves."

Her husband's raised voice nudged Mercy from her
thoughts. Immediately, she saw Benoit was watching her,
assessing her interested stare at Parks. She lifted her glass
to take a sip and gave Benoit a devil-may-care smile.

Benoit's lips thinned with his slight frown as he continued, "I'm curious to know how you managed to outfit Bizy
so quickly, *monsieur.*"

Rey sat back against his chair, drinking his wine as he
witnessed the drama played between De Dreux and his
wife. Clearly, the lady enjoyed baiting her husband. "Bizy's
workers are immigrants mostly," he answered De Dreux.
"Arranged, as I mentioned, with the sale of the property."

De Dreux looked as if he didn't quite believe Rey,
whom he had good reason to doubt. A lack of a viable
work force was a problem that had plagued planters since
the war. But then, Rey didn't plan to be around long
enough for a harvest when his lie would be discovered.

"You'll have to let me know how it works out," De
Dreux said. "I've tried Swedes, Italians, Virginia blacks
. . . other than Chinese labor, convicts have produced the

best results. The others I can't seem to keep on board for the wages. Especially around cutting season."

"Convict labor," the constable repeated with emphasis. "Only thing that works. Mark my words, sir. You'll be coming around the penitentiary mighty quick."

"It's a shame you can't capture Santana Rose and her group and put them to work," Mercedes said, a mischievous glint in her light brown eyes.

"It's just a matter of time now, ma'am, before we catch that thief." The constable's beadlike gaze expanded to almost normal proportions. "She's gone too far. Imagine a holdup on the River Road in broad daylight! I've set extra men all along the road. We're sure to catch her soon enough."

"So you've said for the past year."

At De Dreux's words, the constable's face turned the color of his burgundy. "It's true she's slippery. It's as if she knows what my people are up to before I can trap her—"

"That woman's a menace." Benoit lifted his fork and focused on the quails in wine a servant had just placed before him, communicating he'd lost patience with Constable Gessler's many promises. "If something isn't done about her soon, I'll take the matter into my own hands."

"If you have plans to catch Santana, I would like to help, if I may."

"You sir?" Constable Gessler stared at Rey, his heavy jowls lifting in surprise.

"Why not?" Rey asked. "She's certainly captured my attention, robbing my coach on my first day here."

"You men and your talk," interrupted Mercedes. "Is the lady really such a menace? Why she's never even shot a man. Half the men on Gallatin Street can boast more harm than she. I've heard it said she has a code against killing. Could it be possible that Santana Rose is something other than corrupt? She strikes me as a bit heroic."

Across the table, De Dreux's daughter choked on her wine, sputtering and coughing.

"Pascal, are you all right?" Mercedes asked solicitously.

"Yes." She coughed again, grabbing her napkin.

"Pascal," her father said, "you may be excused."

The girl's eyes flared open and her mouth dropped as if she couldn't quite believe her father's command. "But . . ."

"Now." De Dreux looked to the door.

"Benoit," Mercedes intervened. "I'm sure Pascal will be fine in a moment. Let the child finish her meal at least—"

"The least the child could have learned at all those expensive schools I sent her to was how *not* to inhale her food. I've spent a fortune trying to teach her some semblance of manners. To no avail, apparently. The *child* can finish her dinner in the kitchen until she learns how to conduct herself properly."

Rey watched Pascal blush with each condemning word and glance anxiously at Harlan. Her father's criticism would not sit well on a girl trying newfound wings of femininity. A jolt of pity rushed through Rey. Pascal De Dreux had spent the evening lavishing attention on the oblivious Harlan. Too much attention from the expression on De Dreux's face.

"I won't ask again, Pascal."

When daughter turned to father, the angry tilt of her dark, almond-shaped eyes immediately marked the resemblance between the two. She dropped her napkin onto her plate, her gaze never leaving De Dreux. The dark wine sauce immediately soaked through the pale linen, certain to leave an indelible stain. Her eyes narrowed and she pushed back her chair. It fell to the ground with a loud crash. Without a word, she bolted from the room.

Rey watched the extraordinary exchange. What he'd seen was a lack of control that he would not have associated with the man he'd studied in preparation for this operation. Even his annoyance with his wife's flirtation had not affected De Dreux so visibly. Yet, despite the emotional scene, the planter's face was now a frigid mask as he turned to his wife, acting as if nothing untoward had happened.

"I find it rather interesting, Mercedes, that you should see anything the least heroic about a common footpad." He spoke as if his daughter had never quit the room, had never been there at all. "Especially one that is stealing me blind."

"Santana Rose does seem to have taken a special liking to you and your associates." There was just an edge to her voice as she glanced anxiously at the door. In that moment, Rey suspected Mercedes De Dreux did not like her husband. But then she turned her devastating smile on Rey. "I was recalling the legend of Robin Hood," she said. "He was certainly considered quite heroic."

"But," Rey answered, "he gave the money away. Hardly an accurate comparison."

Her smile brightened as if he'd made her very point. "And who's to say Santana Rose doesn't do the same? She's not your average thief. She is a woman, sir. Would it be so peculiar that one of my gender would rob for motives different than a man? Certainly, if it were I fleecing my husband"—her gaze slipped back to De Dreux with an expression of sudden innocence—"I would give the money away as well. Perhaps Santana Rose is robbing for a good cause?"

"You, dear wife," said De Dreux from the head of the table, "do a better job of disposing of my money than any bandit."

Her husband's baiting remark only deepened her smile.

"Speaking of spending your money, Benoit, I am planning a special dinner to introduce our guests to society." She looked to Rey. "Is there a Mrs. Parks lurking about somewhere?"

"Mercedes!"

Her eyes shone despite her husband's scolding tone. "I merely want to know whether I should invite all the proud mamas and their brood."

Rey leaned back against his chair. He turned the stem of his glass, suspecting he knew exactly why she asked about his marriage status. "I am a widower."

The lines of her face softened from mischief to the sweetest sympathy. Her expression showed a compassion that said she would set things right if she could. The change from seductress to consoler was quick and complete. The latter struck him as the first genuine emotion he'd seen from the lady.

As his fingers played with the stem of his glass, Rey thought there was something familiar, as well as compelling, about her regard. It nudged at the back of his mind, like a word on the tip of the tongue, until he recalled Santana Rose, her hand dropping from his wedding band, leaving him that lone treasure. How strange that after so many years of calculated dispassion, two such different women should breach his control. And yet Mercedes's expression moved him just as deeply as the exchange he'd experienced with the highway woman at twilight. Hers was a look uncomfortably seductive because of the understanding it offered. The regard of a woman who knew of pain, and was strong enough to help share its burden.

"I'm sorry to hear of your misfortune," she said, her voice slipping over him like a soothing balm. Rey drank the burgundy, concentrating on the taste of his wine. He wanted to break the dreamlike quality of her words. God, to actually experience the comfort she promised by her tender voice and expression.

"It's been five years. Time heals all wounds, as they say." He tried to sound glib, to show her he no longer felt pain—was no longer vulnerable to what she offered. But her look of empathy remained, as if she'd not been taken in by his dismissing statement. She couldn't possibly know, of course. She couldn't guess that time had not made a dent in his anguish over Sophie's death. Or diminished his guilt over the role he'd played in it.

"Then you and Mr. Everard shall not mind if I indulge in a little socializing?" she asked, her tone subdued.

"Mais, non," said Harlan. "I'd not mind at all, I guarantee."

"I am sure, madame"—Rey captured her eyes in a look designed to erase her expression of sympathy and change it to quite another emotion—"I will thoroughly enjoy any entertainment you might devise."

For a moment, she stared at him nonplussed, as if his blatant invitation surprised her. He'd meant to incite her flirtation, finding it an easier menace to cope with than her compassion. But instead of a coquettish smile, her full lips remained slightly parted in an achingly seductive look of innocence, as if she were trying to discern if he'd intended the double entendre. Her soft eyes stayed fixed on him, unblinking, until she pushed back her chair and stood. "If you'll excuse me gentlemen. I believe I'll just look in on my stepdaughter."

"Mercedes, leave the girl—"

"You men will soon retire to your port and cigars, Benoit. I'll join you within the hour."

Her husband didn't bother to argue as the men watched her quit the room in a rustle of satin. Nor, Rey suspected, as he tried to brush off the effects of his last exchange with Mercedes, would it have done De Dreux any good if he had.

Chapter 3

Mercy rounded the newel post and walked past velvet curtains puddled in a display of wealth on the hall floor. A flash of lightning ignited the hallway as she stepped silently onto the oriental runner. Benoit would be livid that she'd left him and their guests so abruptly. She didn't care. He'd had no right to humiliate Pascal. Why not give him a taste of his own medicine?

Mercy's steps slowed as she neared a solitary door on her right. Her hand reached out and her fingers grazed the enamel door handle in a feather-light touch as she passed the nursery—a silent but familiar tribute to happier times. By the yellow glow of the hall lamps, accented by intermittent bursts of lightning, she sought Pascal's room at the end of the hall.

Standing before a cedar door whose faux grain had been painted to resemble bird's-eye maple, she lifted her hand to knock, then lowered it before her knuckles touched the wood. *I will thoroughly enjoy any entertainment you might devise.* Those final provocative words, said almost like a warning, had given her a taste of what she'd courted all evening. Her skin prickled as she remembered another's hands, Benoit clawing, grasping, his thick lips devouring hers as he pushed, pressed, hurt her. Mercy sucked in her breath and closed her eyes, shoving back the ugly memories. *That was ten long years ago. He hasn't touched you since the baby. Forget, Mercy. Forget.*

She rested her forehead against the cool door, calming her breath. Rey had stirred something in her that promised better than pain, more than fear. He was the first man to awaken that tingling deep in the pit of her stomach that she suspected could be passion. He was a good man. A decent man. A man who put criminals like her husband behind bars. She didn't want to run away from the honest look of desire she'd seen in his eyes. If she did, if she allowed Benoit to control her through memories, he would win. And she would lose the chance to experience the full force of the joy that bubbled teasingly inside her, like a kettle on the verge of its whistle, every time those enigmatic eyes looked at her with longing.

Mercy smoothed her palms on the silk of her dress and knocked. No, she wouldn't allow Benoit the satisfaction of ruining her life further. Nor would she let him torment his daughter.

When she heard no response to her knock, Mercy reached for the painted ceramic knob, worried Pascal might be too upset to respond. The door swung open. Her stepdaughter lay huddled on the daybed, her knees tucked up around her stomach like a wounded animal. Ling Shi sat beside her, her fingers combing through Pascal's long red hair. The tapping of rain against the windowpane combined with Pascal's soft weeping filled the room with its somber tone. Pascal looked up from Ling Shi's shoulder; surprise registered on her face until it hardened into anger.

"What do you want?" Pascal brushed back her tears.

"I came to see if you were all right."

Ling Shi stood to give Mercy and her stepdaughter some privacy, but Pascal grabbed her hand. "Don't leave." A strange desperation edged her voice. Immediately, Ling Shi sat back down beside Pascal, patting her hand in a motherly fashion. The vulnerability in Pascal's eyes ebbed when she faced Mercy. "Take a good look, *maman*. The *child* has been properly chastised for her bad manners."

"Pascal, don't," Ling Shi whispered.

Mercy ignored her stepdaughter's jeering remark. "Annette made your favorite dessert, bread pudding. Would you like some brought to your room?"

"I'm not hungry."

"All right. I suppose, under the circumstances, that's understandable. Pascal . . ." She paused, trying to think of the right way to console her stepdaughter, to let her know she found her father's outburst unfair and intolerable. "Pascal, I'm sorry about what happened—"

Harsh laughter cut Mercy off. "Sorry? You're *sorry*? Not as sorry as I am." She lifted her eyes to the ceiling as if fighting back tears. "You spend the entire evening making a fool of yourself over Parks and I'm the one punished! There's justice for you."

Pascal's words cut deep into Mercy's conscience. She hadn't thought Benoit's rage could be connected to her flirtation. "Don't blame your father's actions on me."

"Oh, no, *maman*! How could I blame anyone but myself? I'm the one with the bad manners to choke on my wine while you tell everyone in the room how heroic Santana Rose is! I am the ill-bred child who worries while you bait the constable into hunting Santana down."

Mercy remained silent, condemned by the truth more than Pascal's anger. Tonight she'd courted disaster. At times, Santana appeared to take over her life even here at L'Isle des Rêves, an entity Mercy could not always control. But she'd never wanted her war against Benoit to hurt Pascal. She needed her risks to be hers alone.

Glancing at Ling Shi, she realized this was not the time to speak candidly, to beg Pascal to stay home and enjoy the privileges of childhood while she still had the chance. Nothing had been the same since the night Pascal had followed Mercy and discovered the truth of Santana Rose —knowledge that Pascal had used to blackmail Mercy into allowing her to ride with the gang.

"I see you're in fine form as ever," Mercy said, deciding

to leave before she made matters worse. Thus far, Pascal had kept her word and had not divulged Santana's identity to anyone, even Ling Shi. Mercy couldn't afford to give herself away. "I'm sorry I disturbed you, Pascal. As I said, I was merely concerned."

"Well you needn't be!" Pascal shouted as her stepmother shut the door behind her. "You don't ever have to worry," she choked out, then huddled closer to her friend's shoulder. "I worry enough for the both of us," she whispered to herself.

Rey accepted the brandy MacAfee, his valet, handed to him. He turned to watch Harlan as the man leaned against one of the *garçonnière*'s hexagonal walls, nursing his drink. When Harlan raised his glass in a toast, Rey asked, "What the hell were you trying to accomplish tonight with Gessler?"

The grin on the Pinkerton's face faded. Harlan stared at the mahogany bed, one of two in the small room, examining the mosquito netting as if it were Renoir's latest. He shrugged his shoulders. "The man's about as sharp as a coon's ass. He'd wouldn't know sarcasm if it kissed his eyeteeth, him."

"So you were trying to prove your superior intelligence against a coon's ass?"

Harlan said nothing.

Rey placed his drink on the washstand and stepped toward him. As Harlan looked up, Rey knocked the glass out of his hand and grabbed his wrist. "I don't work with fools, Everard."

Harlan's blue eyes burned like the center of a flame. He glanced over Rey's shoulder at MacAfee. Though his servant grumbled as he picked up the glass, Rey knew Mac would do nothing to interfere.

Harlan made no effort to pull his wrist from Rey's grasp. Rather, he looked up with the same charming smile he'd used so effectively at dinner—only this time, there was an edge to his mouth Rey had not seen before.

"Do you know what 'convict labor' good ol' Gessler peddles?" Harlan asked. "Men riding the rails, vagrants, sometimes they don't even do anything wrong, them, jus' end up in jail 'cause Gessler *needs* workers. Poor white trash, that's who. Some, Cajuns, jus' like me, *mais oui*. The ones who don't have two cents to rub together end up cutting De Dreux's cane. Ten dollars or sixty days the law says. Only, it's never jus' that, *tu comprends*? They're sold, man! Some never leave these plantations alive."

"We're not here," Rey said the words carefully, though he'd loosened his grip on Harlan's wrist, "to find evidence against peonage."

Harlan tore his hand away, giving Rey his back. In the silence, Rey could hear the irregular cadence of the shutters banging and rain striking the panes. Thunder rolled in the distance.

"If we get the bastard for the lottery scheme," Harlan said, still facing the wall, "I'll be satisfied, I guarantee."

"Will you?" Rey asked, thinking of the passion he'd seen in Harlan's expression.

Harlan turned around. His eyes darkened under the light of the oil lamps. "*Mais,* sure, man. I came here for the lottery operation. Nothing more."

Rey nodded as if he believed Harlan, which he wasn't sure he did. When the Pinkerton relaxed, Rey said, "I've been working years to build my cover for this case. It wasn't on Leonard Marcus's word alone that I came to De Dreux's attention. My involvement with the Havana lottery and with counterfeiters in Chicago gave me the exposure I needed to earn De Dreux's confidence." Rey spoke in a low sure voice. "If we can bring De Dreux down, it will mean twenty-five years imprisonment and confiscation of any money he's stolen. But that's only the small stuff. De Dreux is nothing—a gnat, a bothersome insect. I'm after the man who put this deal together. De Dreux's my ticket into a circle of criminals so powerful, a crime so pervasive, De Dreux looks like a kid filching a stick of penny candy in comparison." Rey watched Harlan closely, trying to decide if he trusted him. "You're a professional, Harlan. If you're going to work with me, you'd better start acting like one."

"*Oui.* I understand."

"No more goading the constable. No stalking about evaluating De Dreux's belongings as if they are already part of the national treasury." As Harlan opened his mouth to defend himself, Rey continued, "Can you do it? If you can't, it's MacAfee and me. Alone."

"Give me another chance," Harlan said. "You can count on me."

The charming smile vanished. Only an earnest young man stood before Rey, one who wanted to prove something. And that, of course, was the problem. What exactly did Harlan Everard want to prove and to whom? He should push Harlan for those answers, interrogate him until Rey knew for certain Harlan spoke the truth rather than rely on the verbal hand slap he'd just delivered . . . but the resemblance Rey saw between Harlan and another nudged at him. Rey gave a mental sigh. Robert Pinkerton knew what he was about when he assigned Harlan to this operation, he rationalized. Harlan was young, capable of brashness. But he was also smart. Having been shown his errors, the Pinkerton would settle down and do his job. Rey would just have to keep a close eye on him.

He glanced back at Harlan who waited for his decision. Against his better judgment, Rey nodded.

Harlan dropped his chin to his chest. With a flash of teeth, he said, "I can help. You'll see. You need me, *mon ami.*" He let out his breath, making a sound between a laugh and a sigh of relief. Straightening his shoulders, he looked to the door, then back at Mac and Rey. "*Eh bien,* I think I'll take a walk."

"In the rain? Are ye daft, lad?" MacAfee looked doubtfully out the window where wind-swept branches snapped against the glass.

"Why not, *mon vieux*? I could . . . use the fresh air. *À bientôt*." With a salute made cocky from relief, he turned and left.

Hearing the door shut behind Harlan, Rey walked back to the washstand and picked up his drink. He rested one hip against the marble top, watching MacAfee check the mosquito netting and turn down the beds. He waited, knowing his man would not keep his silence long.

"If ye be wanting my opinion . . ." MacAfee said, not disappointing Rey.

"I'm sure you're dying to voice it."

MacAfee crossed arms thick with muscles. His close-cropped red beard shot with gray grazed his chest as he cocked his head in a stance Rey recognized from prior lectures. His piercing black eyes glanced up beneath his bushy brows. "Maybe the laddie will save us all the trouble and catch his death out there."

Rey smiled staring at his brandy glass before he finished off the drink. "Maybe."

"He's got other plans he's not speaking of."

"It's a possibility."

"Aye. And despite it, ye keep the lad on." MacAfee's lips tightened beneath his mustache. "Sure as I know why."

"Oh?" Rey leaned against the washstand. His grin challenged his servant-partner, but inside the walls of his chest, his heart pounded like the thunder outside.

"A fine strong lad with brown hair and blue eyes." In his lilting brogue, MacAfee invoked the image he described. "Smart, too, even if he doesna always act as wisely as he should. A boy some man would be proud to call 'son.' " He raised his thick auburn brows. "Makes ye think, does it not?"

Rey remained still, hating the pain, the weakness that coursed through him with Mac's words.

"There! Ye see?" MacAfee pointed at Rey with the righteousness of a traveling preacher discovering sin. "There's an expression I've seen one too many times since the Pinkerton crossed our path."

His face once more set in the hard lines of a man who couldn't afford the luxury of emotion, Rey asked, "Are you suggesting my lack of judgment has put the mission in danger?"

"I ain't suggesting nothing. I'm saying it plain! I've seen ye dispose of lesser fools than that young buck out there soaking his brains in the rain. Yer an exactin' man, Rey. These past years ye've expected perfection from yerself and those who work with ye. You think the world's all black and white with no gray. Now, I'm not saying it's yer best quality, but damned if it hasna served ye well a time or two. Dinna let what's eating ye up inside muck up yer good instincts. They've kept us both in one piece since the war."

Rey walked to the nightstand and refilled his tumbler. A burst of lightning filled the room. "Perhaps you would like to contact Chief Brooks and let him know about this sudden incapacity of mine?"

MacAfee's eyebrows shot up, disappearing beneath the graying red curls on his forehead. "That ye'd even suggest such a thing makes me think yer addled worse than I thought."

Rey raised his glass to his lips. "Then why not leave me to my insensibilities?"

MacAfee jabbed his finger in the air like a rapier. "Blast yer black soul to ol' Nick himself. Have I not dedicated myself to you and yers since Fran's passing, God rest her soul?"

"Hung on with the tenacity of a leech."

"Och! I couldna even say how often I've watched yer backside, laddie."

"The number seems drilled in my brain through your persistent tutoring."

"I've kept ye alive—"

"—More times than you can count," Rey finished the familiar phrase.

"Why don't ye just go back to yer boy?" MacAfee shouted, losing what little composure he had. "It's been almost a year. It's not right for a father and son to be apart—"

"Enough!"

Both men glared at each other, each waiting for the final condemnation.

"Enough is it?" MacAfee asked, his barrel chest heaving from the emotion blazing color in his face.

"Damn you, Mac," Rey whispered. "What do you think?"

Instead of finishing his attack, MacAfee softened his gaze. His broad shoulders slumped forward. "Aye," he said. "Perhaps it is at that."

Shaking his head, Mac lumbered toward the bed, occasionally glancing back at Rey. Stopping to reexamine the stain where Harlan's tumbler had fallen on the rug, he bent down and brushed the carpet with his calloused fingertips. "Bit of yolk and honey mixed with salt ought to fix things here," he said, a valiant attempt to break the angry silence. "I was heading back to the house to fetch some blacking for yer boots in any case." He scratched at the stain a bit longer, then sighed, his great shoulders heaving. He squinted up at Rey. "So why dinna ye just tell me to bugger off?"

"I just might some day, Mac. I just might."

He nodded, gazing off into the distance before a grin lit his face and he rose to his feet. "Say now, laddie. I've a fine idea. Why don't we go into town, ye and I?" His eyebrows bobbed up and down in a suggestive fashion. "Find some nice lassies to chase away what ails ye?"

"Mac. The incurable romantic."

"Maybe so, but seems to me it's been a wee bit too long

since ye've occupied a woman, if ye ken my meaning. Does something to a man when—"

"I don't pay you to mother me, Mac."

Mac waved him off. "Ye don't pay me at all. I work for Chief Brooks."

"I deposit your wages every month in an account held in your name." Rey shrugged. "Whether you use the money or not is entirely up to you."

Mac shook his bearded face with a knowing smile. "The minute I touch it, I'd be working fer ye in earnest. It's only my cover, that I'm yer man. Oh, sure enough, ye need someone to take care of ye, and I might feel sorry enough to take on the task—"

"For the past ten years."

"—but there'll be no kowtowin' fer me, Rey. Ye keep yer money, and I'll speak my mind. As fer the other matter." His mustache drooped in a look of sympathy. "I only long to see ye happy, lad. It's not been the same fer ye since Sophie died. Ye should find a nice lassie to marry. Give Christopher a brother or two—"

"I said enough."

Mac's mouth snapped shut. "Aye. That ye did."

"You and Nan." Rey shook his head. "Picking away at me as if I were some unfeeling bastard who needs prodding to show he has some soul left."

MacAfee walked past Rey to the door. He lifted his hand to clasp Rey's shoulder, but let it fall without touching him. "Problem is, ye feel too much." When Rey said nothing, he finished, "Think about what I said. Ye know where to find me if ye change yer mind."

A click of the lock and Rey was alone.

He stared down at the drink in his hand, then tossed back the liquor. He grabbed up the crystal bottle again . . . but didn't pour. No amount of alcohol would wash away the loneliness.

He set down the decanter on its silver tray and glanced at the escritoire across the room. Almost against his will, he walked there. He began sifting through his correspondence, then placed his glass on the table and searched in earnest until he found Nan's letter.

Of all his many siblings—five sisters happily married back home in Boston and one younger brother in charge of the family banking firm since Rey's resignation—Nan always knew where to find him. Even if he was as far away as Havana, she would have an address where messages could reach him. She held charge of his most precious gift.

He picked up her recent letter. The curled edges and smudged ink showed he'd read it several times, as he did all her letters. Lightning flashed, drowning out the muted light from the oil lamp. Seconds later, the *garçonnière* shook with thunder. He read the familiar words:

I really believe you are in error, Rennie, and I must tell you what I think. Have you forgotten your son will soon be seven years old? You cannot simply disappear for almost a year and think it won't affect the child. He misses your fishing trips and practicing his letters at your desk while you work beside him. Will you be absent for his birthday? I cannot honestly predict how it will affect Christopher if you are. He is each day more aware of your rejection. I know what you say, but it is rejection nonetheless for him. Surely you must see that? It is not enough that Michael and I love him or that you visit him in the station between trains. He needs the love of his father, to be at your side as he was for the first six years of his life. Won't you reconsider and stop this endless wandering? You have money enough. Are these investments more important than your own child? I simply refuse to believe it of you! At the very least, allow Chris to come to you.

Another burst of light flared through the room. Nan's words radiated through him with the force of the thunder that followed. A year. It was the longest he'd left Chris with Nan. Rey imagined his carefree boy—his ready smile, the spark of mischief in his blue eyes. Were those eyes sad now? With a curse for Sotheby and the circumstances that kept him from Christopher's side, Rey vowed he'd make it up to his son. Once he had Sotheby behind bars, he'd never leave his child alone again.

He glanced toward the window, watching the oak branches thrash against the glass with the banging shutters. Nan, of course, did not know the danger he risked or she would never suggest that Chris come with him on his ventures. His family thought his frequent trips concerned banking business only. After Sophie's death, he'd learned to keep secrets, to lead a double life for the safety of his loved ones.

Rey closed his eyes, remembering his young wife, the tender, sometimes tentative, brush of her fingers against his skin before she would break into giggles and whisper, "Have your way with me, Mr. Parks, or I shall be forced to take aggressive measures." Sophie had always understood him. After they'd married, when the service approached him about their operation to catch Sotheby, she'd only smiled and returned to her tatting, saying, "I knew you couldn't stay away."

There'd been no one since Sophie. No one to love, no one to share tender emotions. Other than perfunctory visits to prostitutes, couplings about as intimate and satisfying as brushing one's teeth, his romantic life had been limited to one disastrous liaison with Leticia Farnsworth, Sotheby's old mistress: the result of a quest for information against Sotheby. It had turned into a sorry affair that Rey had confessed to Mac like a penitent seeking absolution he couldn't find within himself.

Rey glanced down at the letter. Perhaps Mac was right. He was driving himself just a little mad.

Rey folded the fine parchment in his hand, hoping to put away the power it held over him. Dammit, he needed to feel something other than pain and desolation. He wanted more than the numbness of resolve—the healing power of a righteous cause.

In the darkness of his mind appeared a set of eyes, warm with sympathy, soft with longing. The flirtatious smile and lovely form that complemented Mercedes De Dreux's hauntingly innocent gaze triggered within him a desire that blotted out the memories. Rey dropped the letter on the desk. He walked to the window, opened it and the shutters. Rain spattered on his face, pelted the hardwood floor. Lightning and thunder burst into the room.

He *could* feel again. He could blanket out this loneliness that threatened to incapacitate him. Even if for only a moment.

But at what cost?

Harlan leaned against the stuccoed brick walls of the great plantation house. The vines and trees shielded him from the rain that was thankfully letting up. He held the lapels of his jacket tightly against the wind as he smoked his cheroot, wishing he'd thought to bring his overcoat. Then again, he was glad he hadn't taken the time. He'd needed to escape the Silver Fox's too-knowing gaze, needed to leave the small, overly warm room before he confessed too much.

He'd told the story of the convict labor, hoping that Rey would take it as sufficient reason for him goading the constable. He'd been caught off guard when Rey threw in his face his fascination with De Dreux's wealth.

He didn't know he'd been so obvious.

Yet, he admitted, it made him madder than a hooked gator to see those riches, knowing the blood that had paid for De Dreux's money. Lucky for him the Silver Fox had let him stay on, despite his slip. He would not make the same mistake again. *Mais, non,* man. He wouldn't get another chance. That's why he hadn't mentioned the missing letter.

Tonnerre! What would the famed Silver Fox say if he knew Harlan had lost a confidential letter from Robert Pinkerton? Thankfully, that particular note hadn't mentioned Sotheby and the counterfeiting, but it sure as hell told plenty about their identities as government agents trying to hoodwink De Dreux. If Rey ever found out, he wouldn't just get rid of Harlan, *mais non*—he'd cancel the whole mission. The fact that someone else might know what they were about added risk. But Harlan didn't think there was any chance of the letter reaching De Dreux. The note had been hidden in the lining of his wallet when those thieves picked him clean. *Les bandits* were interested in money, not some folded piece of vellum that they probably couldn't read even if they found it. *Ah non,* they'd toss the letter with his wallet as soon as they took the bills inside.

At least, that's what he hoped.

Something more substantial than a raindrop hit Harlan atop the head. With a smothered oath, he glanced at the broken twig near his feet, then looked up in time to see slim trousered legs seek purchase on the branches of the tree above him.

Dousing his cheroot, Harlan ducked behind the thick trunk of the tree. The figure above scrambled out the window ledge, oblivious to his presence. A foot slipped, and Harlan heard a voice that could belong to none other than Pascal De Dreux curse fluently. He waited, wondering what *l'enfant* was up to. Soon, she dropped down the last few feet to the ground, landing smoothly on two legs, then took off running toward the stables.

Harlan smiled. At first, he'd felt sorry for *la petite* when De Dreux told her to leave the table like she was some *vermine* nobody wanted around, but then he remembered who she was—the devil's own spawn. She was up to something all right, sneaking out of her room after hours. Harlan followed at a slow lope. She was his enemy's daughter. Perhaps she could be of some use.

* * *

Mercy watched the sparkling glitter of the salon's chandelier as she held the decanter of port. Benoit had surrounded himself with such exquisite things. Why couldn't some of that beauty reach inside him, the way candlelight brightened the salon's Waterford chandelier? She poured a glass of the sweet wine and handed the drink to Benoit, a wry smile on her lips for her fanciful thoughts. Benoit was evil. Nothing, not even the seven wonders of the world, could bring out goodness from the man.

"That was an interesting exchange between you and Pascal at dinner," she said, sipping her drink.

Benoit's harassed eyes flitted over her. "Don't change the subject, Mercedes. I brought you here to discuss *your* behavior. Your . . . performance for our guests. In the future, I must ask for more subtlety on your part."

"She did do her best to look older than her sixteen years," Mercy continued, ignoring Benoit. Pascal had accused her of goading her father into punishing her. Mercy had quite a different theory of the evening's events. "You know, Benoit, for the first time since I've known your daughter, she looked like a woman grown."

He shook his head, disbelieving. "Your tactics are obvious. And so unlike you. You've never run from a fight before."

"Did her appearance bother you, Benoit?" Her eyes skimmed over the tight fitting jacket hiding the corset she knew he wore beneath and rested on the mustache whose gray Benoit's valet touched with blacking each morning. "Did it make you feel . . . old?"

He looked for a moment as if she'd scored a direct hit. His delicate lips twisted into a sneer, ruining the perfect line of his mustache.

"*Touché,* my dear. I see you're not running at all."

"I never have, Benoit." She toasted him with her drink. "Nor will I ever."

"Then answer my questions, Mercedes! What possessed you to act like a whore displaying her wares?"

As he prowled the length of the salon, she set down her glass and leaned against the meridienne's arm, trying for a casual pose. "Worried Benoit? Concerned I may be unfaithful to you?"

Benoit stopped. His dark eyes narrowed like a threatened animal's. "That's not a possibility, Mercedes, as you well know I would kill you."

"Ah, yes." Mercy stepped away from the sofa. The long satin train of her lavender gown whispered against the Wilton carpet. "*Le nom de la famille.* No scandal permitted. Pride and honor above all." She laughed. "All so ridiculous don't you think, Benoit? Given the circumstances?"

In an instant, Benoit was beside her, digging his fingers into the tender skin of her arm. "What I think, my dear, is that you'd better watch your step. There was too much sparkle in your voice, a bit too much color to those lovely cheeks this evening. You think to torment me by your outrageous behavior with Parks, to make me look the fool, but I fear you might fall into a trap of your own making."

As he spoke, she could feel her face grow warm, further condemning her. She smiled as if it didn't matter.

"He's a handsome man, Mercedes." His voice dropped to a whisper. "And certainly taken with you. I do hope, for your sake, that you will resist the temptation. Don't break the rules of this game and force my hand."

Mercy's smile faded. Emotions she'd suppressed for years bubbled to the surface. "Haven't I always played the faithful wife?" she whispered. "Have I yet to go back on our arrangement?"

His eyes searched hers, as if curious of the vulnerability she'd allowed to creep into her voice.

"An arrangement that suits you, as well," he said.

"Benoit." She grabbed both of his arms. "Let's be done with this charade!" Compelled by ideals of lost love brought on by the evening, she allowed herself the luxury of trying to persuade her husband. There were men like Rey Parks outside this prison Benoit had titled L'Isle des Rêves, his island of dreams. Good people with whom she could lead a normal, perhaps even happy, life. Looking for a quicker escape than her plans had promised, she pleaded, "Tell me where Beth and Laura are. Leave them and me to our own fates. You have reason enough under the laws of the church to abandon me. I can never give you children!"

"Pascal is my heir."

"But a son, Benoit!" she said, targeting this one last vulnerability. "Think of it. One to carry on your name. Isn't that reason enough to divorce me?"

"Be quiet." He turned away from her, but she could see by his expression that she'd tempted him.

"Even your own noble Creole family has known divorce—"

Benoit turned on his heels to face her. *"Tais-toi!"*

Mercy stared into the black depth of his eyes and knew she had lost. The urgent longing for a child she'd seen had been replaced by a burning desire to possess. He would never leave her—never allow one of his beautiful possessions to leave him. This man had done every despicable deed there was in order to achieve his ends and she, unfortunately, remained part of his plans.

"They'll never accept you," she said lightly, letting the hate and anger she felt fill her, giving her the strength to goad him. "No matter how much money, no matter how much political power—no matter what illusion you've created over who your wife is. You'll have to kill every single one of them, like you did Henri."

"Henri was a fool. He forced that duel on me. It was either pull the trigger or die."

"Is that how you justify killing your own brother?"

"Half brother," he corrected. His lips twisted into a cunning smile. "Why should I give a damn about Henri? He never cared about me."

"That's right. None of them care about Benoit the Bastard, do they? Your family will never accept a *cachumas*—"

His hand swung out faster than she could react. The force of the blow against her cheek sent her to the floor.

When she recovered from the blinding pain, she stared up at Benoit. He stood panting above her. Slowly, she smiled.

"If I didn't know better," he said, watching her with dark excitement in his eyes. "I'd actually believe you enjoyed my hitting you just now."

She wiped the corner of her mouth and stared at the blood on her fingertips. "I did. It reminded me of why I despise you so, dear husband."

The light in his eyes extinguished. His thick lips pressed together. "Perhaps you've changed your mind about other things, as well, Mercedes. There's nothing I would like more than to continue our bed games."

Mercy steeled herself, knowing that with Benoit she could never show fear. "You'd have to kill me first."

"Damn you, Mercedes!"

"You have," she answered.

He looked as if he might hit her again. Mercy braced herself, but he crouched down beside her instead. "Despise me if you must, but remember. You are my creation. I made you from nothing. As God created man from clay." With the crook of his finger, he tilted her chin up, forcing her to look into his hate-filled eyes. "You, my dear, are nothing but mud I have formed into the illusion of wealth and breeding. And because of that, you are mine."

He thrust her away and stood, smiling cruelly down at her. "That which I possess will always *be* mine."

In the silent room, the gilded clock over the mantle chimed the late hour as Benoit turned to leave. Mercedes watched the door shut behind her keeper, before she answered, "We shall see, Benoit."

Ling Shi cracked opened the door connecting her room to Pascal's. In the past, it had been a relief to see her friend's empty bed. Though she worried about Pascal's evening excursions, these occasional absences made Ling Shi's life less complicated. But tonight, Pascal had been so deeply upset. Ling Shi sighed and walked to the door, intending to take advantage of Pascal's absence just the same. She'd check on her later, when she returned.

From her own doorway, she peeked into the empty hall, watching for servants who might still be up. Clutching the beautiful silk kimono she wore, she stepped into the corridor. Quickly, she traveled to the far wing in darkness.

She took small careful steps, as she'd been schooled to walk in her homeland. Pascal had taught her to take wide strides. "Like you own the ground, not like you think it's going to open up and swallow you," she'd said. Her friend had taught Ling Shi many other things as well. Her perfect English, spoken with the accent of the American governess Pascal's father had hired to rid his daughter of her Creole lilt. But on these clandestine trips, Ling Shi couldn't help but retreat to mincing paces.

Turning the corridor, she pushed her fears for Pascal aside, consoling herself that her charge could take care of herself. When they'd been at Beasley's and the other schools Pascal and Ling Shi had attended together, Pascal had dragged Ling Shi along often enough to make Ling Shi believe these escapades were harmless. More likely than not, the only thing she need fear was Pascal slipping and falling out of the tree she used to climb from her window down to the ground two stories below, and certainly Ling Shi would have heard by now if something like that had occurred.

When Pascal had first begun to disappear at night almost a year ago, refusing to tell Ling Shi of her activities,

Ling Shi had been sorely wounded, disturbed that in this one thing her friend would not confide in her. She'd even worried that Pascal might be visiting a boy. But she'd soon learned her friend was a complete innocent. Discussions such as tonight's, in which Pascal expounded on the romance of love, proved it. Ling Shi knew that kind of love was every bit a myth as Apollo and Daphne.

Even before she reached her destination, Ling Shi felt a familiar dread creep into her heart. She almost gave into her desire to flee down the darkened hallway to the safety of her room. But she forced herself to stay where she was. It did no good to delay the inevitable. If she didn't visit him tonight, perhaps she'd be free for an evening or two. But eventually, he would summon her. And above all, she did not want Pascal to know about this secret life. Better to choose her own time for these visits.

She knocked on the heavy cedar. When she heard the low voice call *"Entrez,"* she swallowed her fears and entered.

Standing by the door, Monsieur De Dreux watched her with his dark hungry eyes. He smiled and gestured for her to enter.

"Ling Shi. Your timing is exquisite."

She shut the door behind her and, her gaze trained on the carpet at her feet, she allowed the expensive silk kimono to fall to the floor.

Chapter 4

I . . . am . . . not . . . a . . . child. The horse's hooves dug into the soaked earth. Mud whipped up, splashing Pascal's thighs, stinging her face. *I . . . am . . . not . . . a . . . child.* Tears blurred her vision, but she dared not release her hold on the reins to dash them back. Though the rain had ceased for the moment, the storm had turned the road to Bayou Metairie into a deadly quagmire.

Pascal guided her horse around a broken limb blocking the road. The animal lost its footing. Horse and rider slipped sideways down the raised path. Her mount struggled, almost dumping them both into the swamp. With a muffled oath, Pascal brought the horse under control. To her left, lightning flamed a patch of the night sky. The roll of thunder swelled in the distance. She looked over her shoulder, back at the cane fields of L'Isle des Rêves, then kicked her horse into a canter, hoping to reach Lena's house before the rain that threatened flooded the swamp road.

In her head, the horrifying scene at dinner replayed itself. *The child has no manners. Can't conduct herself properly.* Harlan's pity-filled stare had devastated her. Again, Pascal witnessed her infantile response to father's words— the napkin thrown at her plate, her chair dashed to the floor—while dinner guests watched on like judge and jury. "Let the child finish her meal," Mercedes had said. How dare she! How dare she call Pascal a child when it was Pascal who guarded her back with a loaded revolver? *Child. Child!*

A low sob escaped her clenched teeth and she dug her heels into the flanks of her mount, Phoebus, holding on for dear life. How could Harlan ever see her as a woman after tonight?

I am not a child!

The wind sliced through the thin coat she'd not bothered to button. Another jagged arrow of blue split the night sky, followed by a clap of thunder. *I'll show them! I'll show them all!* If a dress couldn't bring out womanly curves enticing enough to catch Harlan's interest, there was another way to get what she wanted.

Pascal followed the narrow cart road toward Bayou Metairie. The moss dripped from bald cypress and swayed in a macabre dance to the wind's howls, accompanied by the crash of palmetto fronds. She slowed Phoebus to a trot; she was cold and wet. But though the storm tempered her pace, it could not lessen the pain of humiliation raging inside her or quell her determination to brave the wild night. Amid the tangle of cypress and drenched Spanish moss, Pascal dismounted and hunted the roadside. By the light of the moon, she found her marker: an alligator skull covered with voodoo markings nailed to a cypress bordering the footpath. She clutched her coat as she passed the skull, her boots sinking ankle-deep into the mud. "Come on, Phoebus." She pulled her reluctant mount forward. "Don't quit on me now." The horse whinnied, fighting the bridle, then trotted forward down the narrow trail.

Pascal battled the overgrown shrubs and low-hanging trees, urging Phoebus to hurry as the thunder grew louder. Every child in Jefferson Parish knew the location of Lena Larouse's cottage as well as the terrifying stories of her magic. As a little girl, Pascal had been warned to stay clear of the black priestess who drank the blood of black cats and feasted on white babies for power. And even though the voodoo priestess had made many attempts to befriend Pascal when she'd first returned to New Orleans the year before, Pascal had heeded Ling Shi's warnings against involving herself in the dark world of black magic. While acknowledging the woman's salutations in town or on the outskirts of L'Isle des Rêves, Pascal had never shown any interest in the potions and gris-gris magic Lena had offered. Until now.

As she and her horse broke into a clearing, lightning flared; Phoebus shrieked and reared. Pascal gripped the reins and whispered soothing words, calming her mount. Another flash of lightning showed the gable-ended shack in a halo of light. Tall cypress trees encircled the *briquette-entre-poteux* cottage like bearded old men guarding an ancient prize. Pascal tied the rein around a tree stump and walked up the footpath to the batten porch. The weather boarding had peeled back in places, exposing the soft bricks beneath. The house rose half a story above soggy ground, its generous gallery sinking drunkenly on one side under the weight of the gabled roof. When her foot stepped onto the first rotting board, a wail pierced the night air, blending with the wind's cries. The sound shivered up her spine until it ended in a sharp tingle at the top of her head.

Pascal closed her eyes, reaching deep inside herself for the courage to climb up to Lena Larouse's door. With each step, she thought of the voodoo queen's powerful magic and what it could give her. Her birth had killed her mother. Her own father hated her; her stepmother watched her with guarded distrust. Surely, nothing short of what the voodoo priestess offered would buy Pascal the love she craved.

Standing at the front door, Pascal again heard an eerie wail. It seemed to curl around her, as tangible as smoke, as cold as the north wind. Gooseflesh skidded up her arms and neck. She thought of Harlan's handsome face, concentrated on the firm lips she'd wanted to touch—and re-

membered his distracted expression. During dinner, he'd
gazed right through her, as if she mattered not at all. Pascal raised her hand and knocked on the door.

The tap of her knuckles sent the door creaking open.
For a moment, she wondered why the door hadn't
slammed open with the same force that sent the shutters
banging against the whitewashed walls. Magic? But then
the image exposed by the muted candlelight and fire glow
from the hearth silenced her thoughts.

A cavern of curios lay within the shanty's four walls. A
long wooden table abutted the wall to her right, adorned
with skulls—human skulls. Pascal's pulse doubled as she
glanced down the row of offering candles burning before
the hollow-eyed, grinning faces. Dried toads and lizards
festooned the wall above. On her left, the glass eyes of a
dried black cat, forever frozen with its back arched in a
hissing stance, warned her to turn back. Swallowing the
knot of fear in her throat, Pascal took a cautious step
forward.

Dressed in blue calico, Lena Larouse rocked next to the
fire, her back to Pascal. Seated across from her on a
straight-back chair, a much younger woman fingered a set
of beads. Lena's burnt orange hair, tresses that had earned
her the name "Larouse," meaning "the red one," were
wrapped in a tignon with seven points directed toward the
heavens. The priestess hummed as she rocked. In her lap,
a snake coiled and uncoiled, writhing to the sway of the
voodoo priestess's chair.

The woman toying with the beads stood and snapped a
few herbs from the bunches hanging to dry over the
hearth. She crushed the spices between her fingers, dropping them into a black kettle suspended from a crane adjusted high to keep the contents from boiling. Lena picked
up the snake and the same queer keening Pascal had
heard outside filled the room. The serpent wound around
Lena's arm, attuned to her cries, and brought its head
close to her face. The slick tongue slipped past scaly lips to

feather across Lena's cheek. She cooed and stroked the beast.

"You gonna stand der all night, Pas-cal De Dreux? Or you gonna come in?"

Pascal started. Lena had never turned to see who stood behind her, yet somehow she'd known it was Pascal.

"She hides at da door, Zombi," Lena whispered to the snake. "Do you think we scare Pas-cal De Dreux?"

Pascal crossed the plank wood floor, not wanting to offend the priestess before she could make her request. She stumbled over a mesh cage she'd not seen in the faint candlelight. Her eyes fixed on the large rat scurrying inside, she nearly collided with a pile of bones and snakeskins before she sidestepped the grisly obstacle. A sweet, musky smell filled the air.

"Simone, make da girl comfortable."

The younger woman shooed a mangy black cat off a wooden chair before dragging it to the fire. Though of mixed blood like her queen, Simone's skin was darker than Lena's. With a smile that was too predatory to be inviting, she motioned for Pascal to be seated. Pascal watched the cat lick its paws in the corner, then glanced up to the stuffed cat hanging on the wall. She shivered.

"Why chil', you soaked clear t'rough. You come sit down," Lena encouraged her. "Simone, somet'ing hot for Pas-cal De Dreux to drink."

The way the voodoo priestess called her by her full name, almost emphasizing the name De Dreux, increased Pascal's apprehension. Cupping her hands around the warm ceramic cup she was given, Pascal sat down beside Lena, thankful the cup held a dark herbal tea and not some queer voodoo concoction. She sipped while Lena waited patiently, stroking the snake she called "Zombi."

"What d'you want child? What brings Pas-cal De Dreux to my home in dis storm?"

"I've come to buy a potion."

"Ah! And what can I git Pas-cal De Dreux?"

"I would like . . . a love potion."

Lena threw her head back and laughed; her pale brown eyes glittered almost yellow with firelight. Beside her, Simone chuckled. Pascal glanced down at the tea, wondering if she should have come at all.

As if sensing the effect of her laughter, Lena settled back to examine Pascal. "My little Pas-cal De Dreux's all grown up, Simone. Come, look. Don't she look like a full-grown woman to you? An' now she got a woman's appetites."

Pascal blushed as Simone stared at her with her dark eyes.

"A love potion." Lena rose from her chair. "I got lots." She wrapped the snake around her like an elegant shawl. Pascal could have sworn the creature watched her over Lena's shoulder as the priestess walked to her shelves. Its tongue flicked in and out.

Lena searched the shelves, shifting the bottles. The chiming of glass striking glass filled the air, a magical, lighthearted sound that seemed strangely out of place in Lena's dark quarters. "A potion to make a man jealous. A potion to make him lust for you until he burns wit desire so strong he don't want nobody bu' t'you. An' . . ." She turned, displaying a small blue bottle like a priceless gem for Pascal to see. ". . . a potion to make a man love you truly."

Pascal's heart doubled its beat.

"Is dat what you wan', Pas-cal De Dreux?" Lena smiled, showing sharp yellowed teeth. "You wan' True Love?"

Pascal licked her lips and nodded her head. "That's the one."

"Den, it's yours."

Lena held the bottle outstretched toward Pascal. The girl rose and walked across the wood floor toward the voodoo priestess and her prize. As she reached to touch the blue glass, the snake swung around. Its tongue flicked out and touched her fingers like cool fire. Pascal snatched her hand back. Lena's smile deepened.

"H-how much?"

Lena held the bottle out closer to Pascal. When she still hesitated, Lena picked up her hand and placed the potion in Pascal's grasp. "It's a gift."

"I can pay . . ."

But Lena had already turned her back to her, giving Pascal the sense that their business was done. "Pour da contents in strong liquor," she said in a singsong voice. With the instruction, Pascal realized the enormity of the step she was taking. "An' den make sure," Lena turned from her chair to look directly at Pascal, "dat young man see you first! Understand?"

"I understand."

"Make sure he drinks it all up," she said, stroking the snake.

"All right." Pascal turned to leave, then faced the older lady once more. "Are you sure about the money . . . ?"

Lena held her hand up. "I only ask dat you come visit ag'in."

Outside the shack, Pascal took a deep breath. For the first time since she'd arrived on Lena Larouse's doorstep, she could breathe freely. She glanced at the bottle. Cryptic markings, odd crosses and snakelike swirls, covered its label—voodoo markings. Her heart pounded and she held the bottle against her chest. "It may not be cupid's arrow," she shouted into the night, "but it will make you mine, Harlan Everard!"

Praying the potion would work, she ducked her head against the drizzle that had just started and ran to her horse. For a moment, she thought she heard something. She glanced behind her, but in the moon's glow she saw nothing. Shaking her head, she mounted Phoebus and concentrated on the path ahead. In her hands, she held True Love. At last, it would be hers.

Inside the shack, Lena Larouse stroked her snake. Beside her, Simone watched her carefully.

"I thought you despised Benoit De Dreux—"

"An' anybody close to 'im," came the rabid response.

"Then why help the girl?"

"I got plans for dat girl, Simone. Pas-cal De Dreux gonna come in real handy."

The quadroon gasped. "You have seen something?"

The priestess nodded. "I ain't waitin' for Saint John's day like I tol' you. Dat girl come to me, an' I'm gonna use the gift she give me." Her yellow eyes slanted up to Simone beside her. "For years, I plan to git even wit dat man. De Dreux kill our sistah, Simone. Now we gonna git one of his." She held the snake back up to her face for an affectionate kiss. "Dat girl gonna come back, Simone. And next time my magic will cost her plenty. I gonna feed that devil's child to Papa La Bas."

Mercy stared at the red satin mask with its black trim, stroking the feathers at the crown. The eyes drew upward, the cat-eye effect amplified by gold and silver glass beads she'd sewn in a serpentine pattern around the eye slits. She'd decorated the simple domino with feathers from the kingfisher, egret, and pheasant. By her own hand, the quills had been dyed blood red, a few black like her costume, and stitched carefully in place to cover the satin in a design inspired by the colorful birds of the swamps. In making the mask, she'd stripped some of the feathers of their vane at the base, leaving only the bare quill with a spray of color at the tip that danced like a fine mist above the headdress as she rode. The feathers slipped through her fingers, granting her the sensation of freedom that had first drawn her to use bird feathers.

Santana's mask. The guise that had granted Mercedes De Dreux the power to fight when she'd been powerless. The romantic illusion that helped one of Benoit's victims assure the world that there would be no more.

She thought of the years she had trained, the men from Barataria she'd convinced to aid her cause. It hadn't been difficult to persuade the fishermen, oyster and moss gatherers, in whose veins ran the blood of the Laffite brothers and other pirates, to join Santana's quest. But the careful planning, the rigorous instruction she'd put them and herself through had taken time. Ten years after Benoit had imprisoned her at L'Isle des Rêves, Mercy could at last mete out justice.

She glanced into the dressing table's mirror. Reflected there she saw a woman of twenty-four, whose unlined face, rich dress, and carefully designed hair showed no signs of hardship. The wounds Benoit had inflicted were etched on her soul, hidden away like the secret drawer she opened at the base of the marble-top duchesse. Into the hidden compartment, she slid Santana's half-mask, carefully slipping it into the satin bag. Her cape, clothes, wig, and guns remained at the *pied-à-terre,* the modest town house she'd chosen knowing Benoit would disdain its lowly comforts and grant her privacy. Her black horse, Little John, was stabled at a secret location outside of town. Soon, very soon, she would be free to find Laura and Beth.

Mercy crossed the Brussels carpet to her *chaise longue.* The room was still in winter dress, and the midnight-blue Victorian drapes attached to the ceiling fell over the bed in a cascade of silk taffeta and mosquito netting. Pushing aside her reading stand, she reclined on the lounge, making herself as comfortable as the wide skirts of her evening gown permitted. In her own room, she was assured privacy. No one would enter without warning. She'd earned that much after the miscarriage.

She reached for the reading stand and unhooked the beaded bag hanging there. From inside, she drew a thick gold chain. She tapped the St. Christopher suspended from one hand with her forefinger and watched the medal swing back and forth.

Mercy twined the gold links between her knuckles. Tonight, she had fearlessly baited Benoit. It was as if, with his financial ruin only months away, she no longer feared him or his power over her loved ones. Mercy felt omnipotent, almost completely free.

You are my creation. I made you from nothing. As God created man from clay.

She closed her fist around the medal. It wasn't true. She'd broken the shackles of his control over her. As soon as she made certain he no longer had the resources to harm Laura and Beth, her escape would be complete.

But soft, seductive doubts still called inside her heart. Who but a creature of Benoit's making could plan, to the last devious detail, to destroy him in such a dastardly manner? Do you think that giving the money away absolves you of his taint? Benoit *had* educated her, polished her speech and appearance, trying to create the woman his first wife had never been. It was a process that had taken two haunting years of isolation. At times, Mercy had been starved and beaten into learning. But in the end, wasn't it his efforts that turned the twelve-year-old London street urchin into Mercedes—the elegant, sophisticated wife of Benoit De Dreux?

But never of my choosing. She'd wanted none of it.

Mercy closed her eyes. The edges of Rey's medallion cut into the skin of her palm as she squeezed the precious gold tighter. She could still see Laura, remember the way she looked that last time they'd been together over a decade ago in that cold London alley. Beth, a fellow soldier in their battle to survive on the streets, had sat across from them knotting the hem of her gown in her hands, watching Mercy with a look that begged her to make everything all right. Mercy had held Laura in her arms, rocking the friend she loved like a sister as Laura made her terrible confession. . . .

"Oh, Laura, why?" a twelve-year-old Mercy whispered against her friend's straw-colored curls. "We'd 'ave made it on what we could filch here an' there."

Across the London alley, Beth sniffed. With the back of her hand she swiped her soot-smudged nose and pushed back an oily swag of brown hair. She balled the muddied hem of her dress, worrying the cloth between her fingers.

Though she was the same age as Laura, Beth's large innocent eyes made her appear younger. Mercy and Laura always treated her like the baby, the one who needed to be held to sleep . . . and woken from the nightmares that always followed. Though Mercy was in fact two years younger than either girl, in the five years they'd been together at London's Home for Abandoned Children, she'd always been their leader. She'd taken each orphan under her care, mothering them as fading memories of love reminded her she'd been mothered. The three had been inseparable. They were all the family Mercy had. It was up to her to solve Laura's terrible problem now.

"What do we really 'ave, Mercy?" Laura wailed. "We live on the bleedin' streets. We beg . . . we steal." She waved her hand at the brick buildings lining the alley. The fetid odor of rotting garbage poisoned the air. Among the trash piled in the doorways, telltale sounds of rattling paper and tins gave away the beastly occupants. "We make our 'ome with rats! I thought anything would be better than the workhouse, but we ain't 'ad anything decent since . . ." Laura looked away, but her accusation lingered in the air.

Beth shot Laura an angry glare. "Stop your grousing. It's not 'er fault—" Beth said.

"Mercy, I'm sorry," Laura said. "I didn't mean—"

"It's all right," Mercy answered. "I know it was my idea to run away. I jus' figured they'd put the three of us to 'horing, like they did Shelly and Jim . . ."

"And I just go and do it anyways," Laura finished. She sniffed back a sob, then said, "He tol' me he'd give me two guineas."

Mercy's eyes widened. Two guineas was more money than she'd ever seen. But even before the fabulous amount registered she realized how Laura's story would end. Laura would never hold back money from her and Beth. "He didn't pay you, did 'e?"

Laura shook her head. "After the bastard rolled off me, 'e just gave me a cuff and tells me to go 'ome. I never tol' you, 'cause I knew you'd be mad. But now . . ." She wiped her eyes clear. "I'm in trouble, Mercy. Ain't I?"

"Shhh." Mercy tightened her arms around Laura. "Don't you worry none. We've been in a bigger fix than this."

Beth crept over on her hands and knees and huddled closer to her friends. "What we gonna do, Mercy? With Laura aproned-up . . ."

"Hush now, Beth." Both girls looked to Mercy for direction. She tried to smile reassuringly. "We got ourselves out from under the workhouse. This ain't gonna be no 'arder than that."

"But a baby . . . ?" Laura said. Her blue eyes clouded.

"Not much different than us, I wager," Mercy said, looking at the two dirty orphans who, for the last four months, had carved a life for themselves on the streets of London with Mercy. "I expect we'll take care of it jus' the same when it comes."

"We don't got enough money for the three of us as it is!"

"I'll take care of the money, Laura. I promise," Mercy swore.

"You ain't gonna . . ." Laura stared at her, unblinking. Beth knotted the hem of her gown tighter in her hands.

"I couldn't Laura." Mercy shook her head. She brushed a curl from Laura's dirty face. "Though I understand why you did."

"Two guineas."

" 'Tis a bloody fortune," Beth offered, as if trying to justify Laura's actions.

"I know." Mercy put her arms around Beth and Laura

both. "You did it for us, Laura. We're family. And I'll not let you down. You'll see."

With the desperation of both Laura's and Beth's hungry faces imbedded in her mind, Mercy went to seek her prey. The heavy evening fog swirled around the rich coat and breeches of her victim, giving her tempting glimpses of the elegant gentleman who stood on the street corner. Mercy wrapped the scrap of cloth the girls used as a shawl tighter around her arms and crept forward, ever watchful lest she lose her mark in the fog. He seemed to be waiting for someone, a coach perhaps—would flip open his watch every so often. The gold chain glittered under the gas lamp and Mercy wet her lips inching toward him. Her hand itched to slip inside that coat pocket. The gold watch and fob would be worth a good deal more than two guineas.

If only she'd not been so squeamish about stealing before now. Beth and Laura had both suggested it, but Mercy had talked the two out of filching anything other than food. Maybe if she hadn't, Laura wouldn't be in trouble. Mercy's guilt only hardened her resolve and, keeping in the shadows, she advanced. She had never before stolen from the gentry—fruit from a vendor, maybe a sausage, but never something so bold as picking a pocket. She wasn't even sure she could do the thing right. But she had to try.

She crept nearer, stepping away from the cold brick wall where she hid. She could almost hear his breath. Or was it her own thundering in her chest, giving her away? She moved closer. The smell of the alcohol sweetened the air. Another step. She reached her hand forward. . . .

Two powerful arms grabbed her from behind, pulling her back into a dark alley where just seconds ago she had planned her assault. Mercy gasped for breath, trying to rip away the hand covering her mouth, suffocating her.

" 'Ere, ye bloke. 'Elp me with her."

"What's the matter, Billy Boy. Is that wee bit of a girl too much for ye?"

Raucous laughter followed a loud curse as Mercy clawed at her attacker, trying to kick the man behind her.

"She's a 'andful, she is."

"Stop yer grousing. If ye cain't take care of her, I will."

The agonizing blow to her head radiated down her spine, stealing her breath, crumpling her knees, until the world went dark and she felt no more.

When Mercy awoke from the pain of a blinding headache, she looked up into a pair of exotic eyes. In the lamplight, they appeared dark and completely unknown. Her abductor? She looked around the hull that reeked of stale beer and mold. She could feel the ship sway beneath her.

With the rush of memories, she remembered her plans to filch the watch fob, and her agonizing capture. Blinking her eyes, she tried to focus on the man hovering over her, tried to make her lips form the plea for help. He looked young and elegantly dressed. Handsome. A stab of hope ripped through her. Certainly this was not the bloke who had struck her senseless in the alley. She managed to prop herself on her elbows, ready to seek the man's aid, but hard hands grabbed her arms and pinned her to the damp floorboards.

"Well, Mr. De Dreux. What do ye think? Madame's in France? Or is it to Sweden with this one?"

A cold fear raged through Mercy as she realized the man kneeling beside her was not her rescuer but the devil himself. She'd heard of young girls being carted off to work in bawdy houses. The hungry eyes that watched her confirmed her fate. Their black depths threatened to devour her, reaching down to ignite a fear she didn't even know she possessed. She closed her eyes and turned away. His hand darted out and steadied her chin. He passed his fingers down her cheek in a chilling caress. "No, not France," he said in a whisper.

"Sweden then?"

He shook his head. "Have you ever seen anything so beautiful, Bill?"

"She's a bleedin' gem aw right."

"An angel. I have special plans for *la belle.*"

"Please, sir! I cain't go nowheres. I cain't leave me friends!" Mercy fought to get free. "They need me. Laura and Beth need me." As if from a distance, Mercy saw herself flailing, fighting, heard her voice echo in the chamber. "They need me. They need me! Laura! Beeeth . . ."

Mercy opened her eyes and stared at the gold St. Christopher in her hand. Two brackets of red marred the soft flesh of her palm. A familiar dread of not knowing what had happened to her friends weighed her soul. Her attempts to locate the two girls, the detectives she'd hired, the desperate inquiries she'd made, had all proved fruitless.

Benoit claimed he knew where they lived and would hurt Laura and Beth if Mercy didn't do his bidding. But Mercy wondered if he were just as ignorant as she of their whereabouts. The time she'd rebelled almost ten years ago —after her miscarriage, when she'd been unable, even for Laura and Beth, to succumb to the horrible man she'd married—Benoit had backed down. As soon as he saw no threat would bring his wife back to his bedchamber and the beatings he always administered there between the cool satin sheets, the rules to their game changed. As long as she stayed by his side, played the elegant planter's wife for the benefit of his political cronies and the family who'd rejected him, he swore not to harm Beth and Laura.

It seemed so unlike him, that concession. But she reasoned her supposed barrenness might have been cause enough to keep Benoit from her. After her miscarriage, she'd convinced the doctor to tell her husband she could never bear him children. Appalled by the fruits of Benoit's perfidy—a fourteen-year-old wife, only a babe herself, beaten into a miscarriage—the gentle-minded doctor had readily agreed. Certainly, the idea that there could be no children might keep Mercy free of Benoit's advances. Yet, her instincts told her that if he had the power to do so,

Benoit would have her under his complete control, in and out of the bedchamber. It was a theory she dare not test. Until she found Laura and Beth herself, she wouldn't risk their lives to prove her suspicions.

Mercy thought back to the tomb in the family plot behind the plantation house. For five short months she'd carried her daughter, dreaming of happiness—until that too had been ripped away. During those two days of agonizing labor, when her body expelled the pocket-size bit of bloodied flesh, Santana Rose had been born. A woman who, by destroying Benoit's financial empire, would take away his power to reach London, to create more victims like her daughter.

Never again would the guilt of stealing still her hand, as it had so many years ago. She'd spent the past half decade honing her skills until she became a sophisticated instrument of crime. And there was only one requirement for her victims: Each must have some connection to Benoit and his illicit deeds. That's why she'd held up Reynard Parks, whom Benoit had led her to believe was his newest cohort. The letter she'd found in Harlan's wallet had told a different story.

Mercy rose from her chaise with the same elegance that Benoit had paid to drill into her. She had only one regret —Pascal's involvement. She'd never meant to include the girl in her father's destruction. Nor did she have the heart to inform her stepdaughter of Benoit's perfidy. When Pascal blackmailed Mercy into letting her ride with the gang, Mercy had told her only that they stole from the rich and gave to the poor, nothing more diabolical than that. Why tell Pascal her father was a fiend, a white slaver who deserved Santana's constant vigilance? Why tempt the darker side her stepdaughter displayed at random by weighing the girl down with the sins of her father? For the same reason, Mercy hadn't shared the Pinkerton's letter with Pascal. Her stepdaughter need never know that her father was a man whose crimes had gained the attention of the United States government.

Mercy unhooked the clasp of the Saint Christopher medal and put it around her neck. The medallion rested between her breasts, a symbol of justice. She remembered her stepdaughter's concern over Mercy keeping the medal. Pascal was wrong. Nothing could happen to Mercy by carrying the medallion with her. No one could stop what Santana had set into motion. Nor could she leave her husband's undoing in the hands of agents investigating him for the wrong crime. Benoit's destruction must be quick and complete. More than she and her friends depended on that now. Only Santana could assure her of it.

She searched for paper in her escritoire as she thought of the upcoming dinner she must plan for Rey and Mr. Everard. It was too early for a Mardi Gras ball. In any event, many were reluctant to celebrate due to the number of people who'd died from the fever. Rumor had it there would be no public celebration by Momus this year and only Rex would parade the streets of the city. But the dinner must be extravagant. Benoit was already in debt to most of the tradesmen in town. Her efforts as well as his own vanity had seen to that. It would take some delicate negotiations to convince the merchants to allow her to purchase goods on their overburdened accounts.

Putting pen to paper, she thought perhaps Santana might even make an appearance that evening. It took a lot of money to right her husband's many wrongs. But even as she wrote the note and summoned her driver, her most trusted servant, to deliver it to Catalan Kate's, Mercy remembered Pascal's warning.

Your love of danger will get us killed.

Harlan threw off his wet jacket, brushing back his soaked hair with his hand. He settled in the room's single chair, heedless of his wet trousers. Across the *garçonnière*'s six-sided room, Rey leaned against one wall, smoking a cigar, watching Harlan with his startling green eyes.

Merde, there was something gripping about those eyes. Almost like, if he stared long enough at you, you'd tell the man anything he might want to know. They were eyes the color of *feu follet,* the phosphorous luminescence that comes to life when a man's paddle strikes the still marsh waters at night. But as Harlan looked closer, it wasn't Rey's eye color that struck him as odd. The cigar. That first day, at the station, Rey had turned down the cigarette Harlan had offered. Later, in the carriage before the holdup, he'd done the same.

Harlan shrugged. One cigar late in the evening hardly made the man a liar. Stretching out his legs, he crossed them at the ankle, once more concentrating on the evening's events. This time, he could meet the Silver Fox's stare without reservation, *mais oui.* He'd not fallen short of his objectives this night—had in fact surpassed them. Rey would surely see Harlan's worth once he recounted the night's endeavors. His smile firmly in place, Harlan laced his fingers behind his head and leaned back. The smoke that billowed and plumed around the tall figure in the shadows did nothing to lessen the intensity of his regard.

"Why am I grinnin' like a coon with a catfish in both paws?" Harlan asked, unable to wait out Rey's silence.

"The thought crossed my mind," Rey answered mildly.

Harlan jumped to his feet and began to pace, too excited to remain seated. "I jus' came from a most incredible trip, *mon ami.*"

"I'd wondered what had happened to you. It's past midnight."

"I went exploring," he said, slipping his muddied boots off with the boot jack. "Led through the bayous by a guide of some experience, I'd wager."

"Your touring seems a bit ill-timed."

"*Ah, non!* My guide made the trip worth my while, *mais*

sure." When Rey said nothing, Harlan added, "It was Pascal De Dreux. I followed the girl clear out to Bayou Metairie."

Rey lifted one brow, unable to hide his surprise. Harlan laughed aloud, not checking his elation at being one up on the experienced agent.

"And?" Rey asked.

"You'll never guess, I guarantee. Not in a million tries."

"Then tell me."

"I saw *l'enfant* climb out of her window and skinny down an oak to the ground." Harlan sat back down, leaning forward with his elbows on his knees. "She was dressed like a stable boy an' definitely up to no good, so I followed her. *Merde*"—Harlan shook his head, impressed despite his hate for De Dreux by the girl's horsemanship—"she rode like a dream. Almost lost her twice when she left the main road. I thought for sure we'd get caught in the storm an' end up in the middle of the gum swamp. I couldn't imagine what made De Dreux's kid take a turn around the swamp at that hour." He paused dramatically, looking to see if Rey was impressed by his good judgment in following the De Dreux girl. "She went to see a conjo woman for a voodoo potion. A love potion." He grinned. "Meant for me. The girl, she wants to cast a spell on me!"

For the longest time Rey said nothing, and Harlan wondered if he needed to spell out the significance of the girl's infatuation. But then the silver head nodded and Rey answered, "It could be useful."

"*La petite* thinks herself in love with me." The words came out in a rush. "I overheard the old crone who gave her the potion say she had to mix it with strong liquor." He chuckled. "I'll have to watch what I drink 'round here."

"If you can cultivate a relationship with the girl perhaps she might be of some use against De Dreux." Rey snubbed out his cigar, exhaling a last stream of smoke. "Are you prepared to do that?"

Rey delivered the request as if he asked a great sacrifice. Harlan almost laughed. What could be simpler than to encourage the girl? "*Mais,* yeah, man."

"You sound sure of yourself. You've done this sort of thing before? You have experience in seducing young girls who have their hearts in their eyes for you?"

Harlan hesitated. "No."

"Then don't commit yourself so lightly." Rey walked over to Harlan. "She's young. A beauty. If you hurt her, you'll be responsible for that pain. It may be more difficult than you think."

The image of Pascal fluttered into his consciousness. Harlan recalled her clumsy conversation at dinner and the look of elation he'd seen when she'd cradled the bottle to her chest and shouted his name. Something unfamiliar knocked at his conscience, a hesitation he'd not have thought possible under the circumstances. Harlan snuffed it out quickly with thoughts of De Dreux. Whatever he had to do to bring the man down, he would gladly accomplish and the consequences be damned.

Chapter 5

"The garfish has the head of an alligator and the body of a fish," Pascal continued the dissertation she'd begun when the party of five had left her father and L'Isle des Rêves for New Orleans. Swaying with the motion of the open carriage, she smiled at Harlan seated across the landau from her. "It can grow over six feet long."

"I've seen 'em, *mam'selle,*" responded Harlan as he glanced at Rey beside him. "Floating like logs in the duckweed."

Catching Mercy's eyes on him, the Cajun winked at her, letting her know he had the situation well in hand. His silent assurance had quite the opposite effect. Obviously, the gentleman was well aware of her stepdaughter's regard. He'd have to be blind, deaf, and dumb not to be. Since the first night Harlan arrived in their midst a week ago, Pascal had done little but shower attention on the man.

"That's right. You did say you grew up around here," Pascal said. "Gosh, I have never actually *seen* one." Disappointment at having failed to impress their guest threaded her voice. Pascal glanced down at Ling Shi on her right. At her companion's shy smile, Pascal seemed to rally. "Did you know their eggs are poisonous?" Her eyes brightened when Harlan shook his head. "And green . . . big as an egg yolk. Why, the garfish can . . ."

Mercy tucked a curl beneath her straw cap and its cockade of feathers, shutting out the conversation that gnawed at her conscience like the action of an unoiled rifle. Pascal's outrageous behavior could surely be a mocking echo of Mercy's own struggle to engage Rey Parks's interests over the past week. An ugly voice inside hinted that Pascal wished to show, through example, just how ridiculous her stepmother appeared in her infatuation. But a gentler side counseled that a naïve girl, barely out of the schoolroom, wouldn't know her expansive gestures and dramatic tone did not place her in a good light.

Mercy cast a brief glance at Rey seated directly in front of her. The cut of his stylish Cambridge jacket and matching plain cloth trousers showed off his lean muscles and emphasized his elegant height, renewing a curious warmth inside Mercy. Since that first night at dinner, there'd been no more suggestive overtures. Mr. Parks was all a polite guest could be as they'd discussed politics in the salon, dined together under muted candlelight, or listened to Pascal play Mozart on the piano while the guests sipped a glass of sherry. His benign congeniality over the past week only increased his appeal, providing a safe haven from which she could admire him. The few occasions she'd caught him watching her, she'd seen a hint of something familiar in the pale green depths of his eyes—the same needy stare of the orphans at St. Bartholomew's. Its allure tingled deep within her, as intoxicating as the dreams that each night returned her to the roadside holdup where they'd shared their brief kiss.

". . . And that's how they've survived so long. Now, the blue crab . . ."

Mercy's gaze flitted back to her stepdaughter beside her. If Mercy could fall just a little in love with the looks of a man and the ideals he represented, how much more susceptible would a sixteen-year-old girl be to Harlan's youthful charm?

She rubbed the satin cloth of her bag, feeling the edges of the St. Christopher medal inside as she watched her stepdaughter. Apparently, no one at the many institutions Benoit had paid so handsomely had succeeded in teaching Pascal demure feminine behavior, or its benefits. Mercy's subtle attempts to focus the conversation elsewhere had been met by sharp glances and hostile retorts. But it wasn't just Pascal's humiliation that concerned Mercy. Detective Harlan Everard, here to investigate Pascal's father, could very well have ulterior motives for his admiration of the girl.

". . . And sheds the hard shell twenty times. Maybe even more before it reaches its full size."

"Twenty, you say, *mam'selle*?"

Mercy crushed the purse in her hand upon hearing Harlan's superior tone. Though she'd warned Pascal the two men were government agents—that she should have a care what she did and said around them—Mercy still hadn't mentioned their investigation of Benoit. She had spent many a sleepless night evaluating her decision to keep the letter and her suspicions from Pascal, had questioned her wisdom a dozen times as she'd watched Harlan play up to her stepdaughter. Yet, Mercy wanted Pascal ignorant of her father's crimes. If Mercy could feel tainted by her association with Benoit, how much more susceptible would Pascal be, his own flesh and blood? The girl already seemed driven by some demon. No, Pascal must never discover her father's true character.

". . . And when hooking the alligators, they bring them up into the pirogue, and, I'm told, use a huge stick to knock them out."

"Incroyable."

Mercy's knuckles turned white around the handbag. Unbelievable, he'd said? What was truly unlikely, Mercy thought, was that a Cajun like Mr. Everard wasn't familiar with every detail involved in hooking an alligator. How could she warn Pascal against the charming Everard without telling her of her father's treachery? How could Mercy make her stepdaughter understand her behavior must be tempered without inciting all-out rebellion from the girl? How could she—

Out the corner of her eyes, Mercy saw Pascal stand and, with a wide swing of her arms threatening her equilibrium, demonstrate the amount of pressure exerted by an alligator's jaws.

Dear God, Mercy thought, watching Pascal's hands clap shut to mimic the animal's mouth. How could she get the girl to shut up!

"Do you hunt, Mr. Parks?" Mercy asked, her voice loud, loud enough to draw the group's attention from Pascal and her alligator jaws.

He took a moment to respond, his expression that of a man who never spoke without deliberation. "Often, madame."

"Pheasant, perhaps?"

"I prefer more challenging game, something I might have to outwit, rather than merely hunt down." As he spoke, he took Pascal's gloved hand and guided her back to her seat with a smile so charming that it brought a flush to the girl's cheeks. "But never something as exciting as alligators, I'm afraid."

Still gripping the medallion beneath the purse's cloth, Mercy held back a sigh of relief for Rey's perceptive interference. "The prey's intellect is therefore important?" she continued as they entered the outskirts of the city. She prayed that between herself and Rey they might control Pascal's quest to be center-stage.

"Just so."

"And are you often successful?"

His thoughtful silence made her question appear something other than simple conversation. He seemed to seek out hidden meanings with his steady gaze, bringing to mind his profession: an agent trained to hunt down criminals. Criminals, like Benoit—and Santana.

"My time is limited these days." He leaned against the red moroccan leather. His body appeared relaxed but struck Mercy as strangely alert. "When I hunt, I do so in earnest. And I'm almost always successful, madame."

A knot formed in her throat as his innocuous responses took on a different meaning all together. "What a pity. For your prey, I mean."

"I hunt too," Pascal chimed in, apparently begrudging Mercy even a moment's attention. "I'm an excellent shot," she said proudly. "*Maman* is only passing fare."

"Pascal," Ling Shi whispered behind her gloved hand.

"You must take me hunting some time, *mam'selle*," Harlan said. "Maybe you could teach me a trick or two, eh?"

"I would be honored," the girl whispered, as if the governor himself had asked for her to strap on her guns in the country's defense.

A movement caught Mercy's attention from the corner of her eye. Her gaze fixed on Pascal, she did not see Rey lean toward her until it was too late. She watched him reach for her hand—the hand grasping the thin satin bag and absently fingering the chain and medal inside. He closed his fingers over hers. The motion squeezed the medallion against the soft satin, revealing the round outline of its shape against the cloth.

"You've been clutching your purse as if you think someone might steal it," he said with a smile.

"No, of course not." She eased her fingers beneath his, trying to manipulate the medallion further into the folds of satin beyond his touch. *You're being silly. He can't possibly know.* "Then again"—she forced a laugh—"one never knows with Santana Rose still unaccounted for."

"I think we're safe enough." He glanced to the crowded streets of the Garden District.

She slipped her gloved hand from his, and set the purse back at her waist, out of his reach. Mercy met Pascal's gaze. The dark eyes watched her anxiously, the full lips pressed in a look of concern. Mercy wondered if she'd guessed the St. Christopher was inside.

With a smile to all, Mercy adjusted her hat and took up her parasol. "I feel quite safe with you and Mr. Everard." To the carriage driver, she said, "To Jackson Square. Quickly."

Pascal strolled with their party down the banquette of the Pontalba Apartments beside Harlan, holding her closed parasol at her side. Cast iron railings with the *AP* of Almonester and Pontalba woven into their arabesque design adorned the balconies overhead as the group of five browsed the ground floor shops on Rue St. Ann where they'd left the landau. Constructed to revitalize commerce in the Vieux Carré almost three decades ago by the Baroness of Pontalba, the red-brick buildings that fronted Jackson Square had fallen into disrepair since the war. Still, their lovely galleries attracted passers-by to peruse the glass-front stores at street level housing a variety of hardware, dry goods, and clothing shops. From second-floor balconies, apartment dwellers could view couples strolling amongst the greenery of the public grounds and children playing in the shadow of the enormous bronze statue of Andrew Jackson astride his rearing horse. Horse-drawn cabriolets and coaches rumbled down the paved street as the St. Louis Cathedral chimed the late morning hour.

In front of Pascal, her stepmother's skirts swayed with her elegant glide beside Mr. Parks. Pascal, Ling Shi, and Harlan followed at the rear on the wide banquette. Occasionally, Mercy stopped her conversation with Parks to glance over her shoulder. Pascal would smile, letting her stepmother know that nothing was amiss. But, in her mind, she plotted furiously.

She could almost feel a tantalizing warmth from Harlan, who walked close beside her. The sight of him in his elegant striped pants and brown suit jacket caused her heart to take a nervous jump. Pascal concentrated on her boots stepping across Mercedes's dark silhouette on the flagstones. She was *almost* alone with the man she loved. But how could she ditch Mercedes? In her stepmother's shadow, she could do nothing.

Mercedes caught Pascal's eye. At that moment, a gentleman stepped out from the store where a life-size winged devil advertised Mephisto cigars. Staring down at his feet, he didn't seem to see Mercedes. Before Pascal could give a warning, the man slammed into her stepmother, knocking her to the ground.

Pascal's heart drove to her throat. She hurried to her stepmother's side. Mr. Parks and Harlan barred her way as they joined forces with the offender to give aid.

"Pardon, madame!" the gentleman apologized. "I did not see you."

Pascal swallowed her gasp. She remained frozen in place. That voice. Her gaze darted past Mercedes, fixed on the man kneeling beside her. And his face.

Jean Claude. Santana's number-one man.

"That's all right." Mercedes accepted Jean Claude's gloved hand. There wasn't a hint of recognition in her eyes as she smiled up at the tall, dark-haired man. "I'm afraid I wasn't watching where I was going as well." She laughed, brushing her skirt.

A chill of fear touched Pascal's heart and she took a step back, away from the group. It was the same with each holdup. Unlike Mercedes, the love of danger could never motivate Pascal into feats of daring. Only a pathetic desire to make sure nothing happened to Mercedes drove her— and, she admitted, a need to impress Santana, perhaps into someday showing more than begrudging respect for Pascal's riding and shooting talents. It hurt, more than Pascal cared to admit, when Mercedes branded her a nuisance last week coming home from St. Bartholomew's. Apparently, Pascal had yet to prove herself.

With a mouth made dry from fear, Pascal watched Jean Claude fuss over Mercedes, dusting her skirts and apologizing, until he slipped a piece of paper into her hand. Her stepmother expertly palmed the white square and hid it in the folds of her skirt as Jean Claude tipped his top hat and walked away, his cane tapping on the flagstones. The note could mean only one thing. Another raid. Pascal tried to marshal the courage she would need to follow Santana.

"If you'll excuse me, gentlemen." Mercedes took a deep breath and smoothed the emerald foulard of her gown. She glanced at the shop's door. "I think I'll just step inside a moment. A drink of water wouldn't be amiss right now."

"Allow me."

Rey stepped in front of Mercedes, blocking her way. He knew his smile remained friendly, that his face showed none of the emotions twisting inside him. Nothing would alert Mercedes that he'd seen the handsome Frenchman give her the white slip of paper.

Mercedes held him back with a gloved hand. "Please, I'll be just a moment," she said, not quite meeting his eyes as she swept past him.

The door slapped shut behind her. Rey wanted to follow. She was of course going inside to read the note. But the thought that she couldn't wait two minutes to read the gentleman's missive incited an anger that stunned Rey by its very potency. Instead of pursuing her, he waited, pretending to watch the strolling couples, afraid that, for once, the skilled agent would give himself away.

Meaningless anger, he told himself. Even if his suspicions were correct, he had no investment in the lady's virtue. He wasn't the wronged husband who'd caught his wife planning a tryst.

He released a long slow breath, relying on his training to regain control. Accustomed to analyzing mistakes, dissecting errors until he knew they would not be repeated, Rey faced the emotions brewing inside him. Did it matter so much that the week he'd spent admiring her, studying her, he might be wrong about her character? Was that the genesis of this numbness that felt incredibly like betrayal?

Or did something more dangerous than professional pride—more intimate—provoke him? Seeing her take the folded scrap of paper, he'd felt curiously robbed of the innocence he'd attributed to her. He'd believed in her sweetness, the naïveté that for the past week tempted him to forget plots and plans and seek only the comfort he saw offered in her eyes.

"Rey?"

Harlan stood before him, a puzzled look on his face. Rey immediately glanced at the two waiting girls. He gave each a reassuring grin as he reached for the door. "I'll see what's keeping her."

Pascal jumped to attention. Slipping past Harlan, she grabbed Mr. Parks's hand on the door. "She said she'd be right back." She had to make sure he didn't catch Mercedes reading the note.

"It was a bad fall," Parks answered. "I'll just step in and make sure she's all right." He nodded to Harlan, passing the baton of responsibility for Pascal and Ling Shi to him. Pascal felt Harlan's hand on her arm, holding her back.

A cold knot formed in her stomach as she watched Parks step inside the shop. Santana would have been able to stop him. Her actions would have been interesting enough to keep a man occupied. Pascal turned away, thinking furiously of what to do, sure that her lax vigil would cost her stepmother dearly.

Almost as she formed the condemning thought, Reynard Parks reappeared. Pascal watched Harlan raise his brows and Mr. Parks give an almost imperceptible shake of his head. The silent communication between the two men was followed by Mercedes's exit.

"Here she is now." Mr. Parks gave his hand to Mercedes as she stepped down from the doorway. "Feeling better?" he inquired.

"Much," she answered. "Inside the patron gave me a splendid idea on how we might spend the afternoon. I should have thought of it myself. It's simply required for anyone visiting the city to see Marie Laveau for a palm reading. We're not far. Just up the street a few blocks.

Afterward we can visit Congo Square. If we're lucky, we might witness some secret voodoo rite."

Pascal frowned. A palm reading? Obviously, the note hadn't been urgent or Mercedes would have made some excuse to return home.

Rey glanced at Harlan. "It seems we can't refuse. . . ."

"Oh, I insist," Mercy added.

"I'd rather not," Pascal said, her hands almost shaking as she formed her hasty plan.

Her stepmother watched her with an intensity Pascal couldn't miss. But with the mention of the palm reading, Pascal saw an opportunity she dare not let pass.

"Why don't you and Mr. Parks go ahead, *maman*?" She looped her hand around Ling Shi's elbow and wrinkled her nose, digging up every last bit of acting talent Ling Shi was always attributing to her. "I am not partial to black magic. I would rather visit the market."

"But it's past ten," Mercedes said. "You won't find anything there at this hour—"

"Harlan can escort the young ladies." Mr. Parks stepped to her side and took up her arm, already steering her down the street. "We'll meet here at Jackson Square before noon," he said to Harlan. The younger man nodded as Rey continued to guide Mercedes forward with a hand at the small of her back. "Perhaps Miss Laveau can foretell some good fortune for the days ahead. I understand New Orleans has quite a few establishments where a gentleman can try his luck."

Mercedes dug in her heels, turning to look back at Pascal. "I'm not sure. . . ."

"Oh please, *maman*," Pascal urged. "Ling Shi and I will be fine with Monsieur Everard." She gave Mercedes her back, leading Ling Shi down the banquette. "The market is just up ahead, Mr. Everard."

When she didn't hear a final protest, Pascal almost gave a whoop of relief. By the time they reached Decatur Street, her mouth ached from her wide smile. She left her parasol closed at her side, enjoying the feel of the sun warm on her cheeks. A mule-drawn vegetable wagon rumbled past as a woman balancing a wide basket on her head called out, "Bla-a-ack berries," on the street opposite. Soon, Pascal could see the barnlike "Red Store," in front of the French market place. As Mercedes had predicted, not much remained in the way of merchandise when the group arrived at the pavilion. As early as three o'clock in the morning buyers and sellers crowded the open-air market. English mixed with Spanish, French, and German normally lent an eerie sense of foreignness to the place. Even the Choctaw Indians would come to sell herbs and roots here. At this late hour, few vendors remained. Only the smell of fish still lingered in the air.

Making a quick excuse to Harlan, Pascal pulled Ling Shi to an apple vendor's cart, one of the few enterprises still remaining. Pretending to be interested in the fruit, Pascal whispered, "I want you to leave me and Mr. Everard. I'll make up some excuse. We'll meet you later, back at Jackson Square—but don't hurry!"

"Pascal," Ling Shi whispered anxiously, "I couldn't!"

Not often the recipient of Ling Shi's censure, Pascal paused. She allowed herself one look at Harlan, at his handsome features, his broad shoulders. She swung back to Ling Shi. "*Please!* What harm could it do?"

Ling Shi bit her lip. "You still believe yourself in love with Mr. Everard?"

"Hopelessly."

Ling Shi seemed to watch Harlan as if she were trying to decide if she could trust him with her charge. Then, slipping her parasol over her head, she stepped off the banquette and said, "I'll be at the apothecary."

Pascal watched Ling Shi disappear down the street, not wanting to return to Harlan until it was too late to call back her friend. Examining the wrinkled fruit in her hand as if it were Diana's golden apple, she nearly jumped out of her skin when she heard the raspy voice call her name and felt Lena's hand clutch her arm.

The voodoo priestess's eyes appeared even more yellow in the daylight. She smiled, showing small jagged teeth. She nodded her head toward Harlan. "Is dat your man, Pas-cal De Dreux?"

When Pascal didn't answer, Lena chuckled. She leaned closer, lowering her voice intimately, "You give him da potion yet?"

"Miss Pascal?" Harlan's voice behind her sent a surge of relief so great Pascal actually felt her knees wobble. She gave Lena an apologetic smile and took a step back, then turned and almost ran to Harlan's side.

"Ling Shi had to go to the apothecary," she said as nonchalantly as possible. "I thought we might walk back to Jackson Square and wait for her and my stepmother there."

Harlan peered over her shoulder, a slight frown on his face. When Pascal followed his gaze, she saw Lena weaving through the crowd down to the levee. Pascal bit her lip, thinking perhaps Harlan might not agree to her plan, but then his mouth curved into his familiar smile. "Sounds fine, *mam'selle.*"

Pascal let out a breath. She walked close beside him—and realized she had absolutely no idea what to do now that they were alone. At the same time, she felt a desperate need to do *something*. She thought of her stepmother and her polished manner. Mercedes could certainly get a man's attention, if only with a smile. Pascal had seen her do just that with Mr. Parks. Pascal opened her parasol and twirled it on her shoulder, thinking of how to imitate Mercedes. She needed some excuse for Harlan to touch her. She searched madly for a possible prospect. Not her reticule, she thought. Too obvious.

Harlan watched the girl beside him. She'd pulled her hair back, sleek against her temples, and tucked it into an elaborate French roll. It looked like she had quite a bit of it hidden there and he wondered just how far the girl's hair would reach down her back. The sunlight made it look real pretty, like burgundy wine. *Beaux, très beaux.*

He frowned as he thought of the conjo woman. He'd recognized her right away, though he'd only seen her through a crack in the door that night he'd followed *la petite* out to the cabin. Where he came from, folks weren't social with the voodoos, *mais non.* He thought of warning the girl, then reasoned it was probably none of his business what she did.

He glanced back down to the bit of womanhood walking beside him. How different she looked from the trousered kid he'd seen crawling down the oak. The dress made her figure look fine—like a woman's. But despite the dress, she showed her age. Very young. Especially when she glanced at him with that desperate, nervous smile. . . .

If you hurt her, you'll be responsible for that pain.

Harlan looked away. Well, yeah, her father didn't worry none about causing people pain. If Harlan had to talk smoothly and get *la petite*'s heart to flutter a bit for information he needed against De Dreux, that was his job. His mission.

Harlan sighed, watching her look of intense concentration. *L'enfant* was probably thinking up some important fact about bullfrogs she thought he'd be dying to know. He racked his brain for a way to get her to talk about De Dreux before he spent the afternoon listening to her lecture on the habitat of the whooping crane.

Giving his most charming smile, he took up her hand and placed it on the crook of his arm. The bones of her wrist through the gloves felt small, delicate. She sure was a little thing. "You know, *mam'selle,* I am truly interested in sugar planting. I bet your *père* taught you plenty 'bout sugar."

Pascal stared straight ahead. It was all she could do to keep her mouth from dropping open. She'd been so busy thinking of some way to get Harlan to touch her, she'd nearly fallen from shock when he'd just taken her hand, as if it were the most natural thing in the world! Once she thought she had her composure, she looked up. "My father doesn't really talk to me about sugar."

Harlan frowned. She probably knew more than she thought. "Then tell me about your life in N'awlins. I'd be interested in knowing 'bout the famous *Famille De Dreux,*" he specified, not willing to give *la petite* any choice on the topic of conversation.

The overhead bell rang as Ling Shi opened the door and stepped inside the apothecary. The dark rosewood counters and beautifully carved cabinets gave her a familiar warmth. She passed the glass container of orange water, taking a gratified sniff and skirted past the ceramic jar filled with leeches. Browsing the glass display cases containing beetles, snake bones, gold and silver covered pills and other curatives, she waited for Doc Chiang to step out from the back.

"Ling Shi!" she heard him call out happily. Looking up, she watched the Chinese man in his late thirties cross the stone floor to her side. His dark-haired queue swung past his waist in stunning contrast to his western suit. The ends of his long mustache turned down, bracketing his mouth and chin.

"I was not expecting you today. Sit, sit," he urged her over to a wooden stool at the counter. "I will get my assistant to start on your powders immediately, then we can have a nice visit while you wait, yes?"

"I would like that very much."

Ling Shi watched Doc Chiang hurry to the back room. Nicknamed "Doc" because he was able to cure even patients the Western doctors had given up on, he had no true medical credentials, though he was one of the first Chinese to be educated in the United States as well as China. Like the apothecary itself, his therapies were a curious mixture of old-world Eastern arts and Western medical science. In Doc Chiang's shop, a Chinese herbal teapot and scales could be found alongside a variety of inhalers and fleams used for bloodletting. The shop and therapies were a reflection of the man himself—tolerant of all cultures, seeking the good in all things. Aside from Pascal, he was the only friend Ling Shi had in the world. To Ling Shi, he personified kindness itself.

Pushing back the nightmare memories of the night she'd first met Doc Chiang, Ling Shi thought of the medicine she purchased here monthly. Since taking his powders, she'd not had the problem recur.

Doc Chiang returned balancing a porcelain Chinese tea set on a tray. He placed it on the counter before Ling Shi and rubbed his palms together. His impressive mustache only emphasized his beaming smile.

"You have time to join me for tea, I hope?"

"It would be my pleasure," Ling Shi said, her heart lifting as her host arranged the delicate teacups with their distinctive blue-and-white willow design. She inhaled the jasmine scent as he poured. "That smells wonderful."

"For you, Ling Shi, I wish it were from the Dragon well itself."

"This is my favorite," she said raising the handleless cup to her lips.

She pointed to the lacquer plate filled with almond and walnut cakes. "Mrs. Meyer's?" she asked.

Doc Chiang stopped mid-bite, lowering the walnut tea cake back to its dish. He nodded at the mention of the German widow running the restaurant up the street.

"When are you going to marry the dear lady?" Ling Shi teased.

Doc Chiang shook his head, then took a bite of the cake. His expression showed he'd just tasted a bit of heaven. "Delightful. I still marvel where she learned to cook Chinese."

"She wants to show you what a good wife she would make."

He caught her eye. "Perhaps, Ling Shi, I wait for another."

Ling Shi looked away, wishing she'd not seen the sudden light that came to Chiang's eyes or felt the seductive warmth it kindled inside her. Mrs. Meyer could make Chiang happy. Mixed marriages, such as the one she'd suggested with the German widow, were not uncommon. Immigration laws requiring Chinese women to prove their "good character and correct habits" had caused a shortage of Chinese wives and a severe hardship for men like Chiang. Thanks to Monsieur De Dreux's smuggling, Ling Shi had not faced the stringent government standards. Her papers had all been forged courtesy of De Dreux's men. She was in fact one of the few women Celestials in New Orleans. But she could never consider marriage, no matter how handsome she found Chiang or how thankful she was for his friendship. It was not his age that made her discount his desire for her. He was at least ten years younger than Monsieur De Dreux, after all. She merely refused to put the horrible taint of what she experienced at L'Isle des Rêves on this one place of happiness.

She felt his hand on hers and looked up. Chiang pointed to the counter. "For you."

A beautifully carved jade bird lay caged in gold before her.

She touched the delicate jewelry. Inside the cage, the tiny bird no larger than her thumb swung on its golden perch. It was truly a work of art in the detail of the feathers and face. To her embarrassment, Ling Shi felt a tear slip down her cheek.

"Ling Shi?" Doc Chiang lifted her face, watching her with a worried frown. "Why have I made you cry? Please tell me what I have done?"

"It is nothing," she said, brushing the tear away with her gloved hand. "It is just that . . . the bird . . . it reminds me . . ." *It reminds me of myself,* she thought sadly. But instead, she said, "It is so lovely. It moves me. That is all."

He looked unsure. "My gifts are meant to bring you happiness, not tears."

"They do. Very much. You have seen so many sad tears from me. These are tears of joy." Ling Shi put the bird in her purse, not bothering to argue about the present. Doc Chiang had made it clear he would not allow her to refuse his favors. In truth, his small gifts of jewelry made her feel very special and she allowed herself that much.

Ling Shi finished her cake and sipped the jasmine tea. Across the counter, Doc Chiang smiled happily, taking true delight in her pleasure. He tried to place yet another tea cake on her plate but she stopped him.

He sighed in mock disappointment and patted her hand. "Please, stay as long as you wish. I'll see if your powders are ready."

When he returned with the paper package, Ling Shi paid and slipped the powders into her purse. He knew of course why she needed the "medicine." She would have bled to death in the shack at Smoky Row if Doc Chiang, a Celestial like herself, had not been summoned to help her. During the ordeal, he'd coaxed the story from her of why she'd risked her life to be rid of Benoit's child.

"Ling Shi, why do you not leave this terrible man?" he asked, as if reading her mind. "I could help you. Let me take care of you."

She shook her head. "I have another obligation." Though Pascal had everything in terms of worldly goods, Ling Shi knew she was the girl's sanity. She would not leave her to her devil father.

Doc Chiang frowned. "I could do better for you than this man."

Ling Shi looked up, surprised. "You misunderstand. It is not you I reject."

He shook his head. "Perhaps some day you will explain this to me in a manner I *can* understand. For now"—he escorted her to the door—"take the medicine."

Chapter 6

"There it is."

The dilapidated fence enclosing the house on Rue St. Ann was almost as tall as the house itself. Only the tops of a few trees could be seen over the board fence. Once beyond the gate, Mercy released Rey's arm and lifted the veil she'd worn to conceal her face. Though it was rumored that even politicians sought the advice of the great Laveau, sometimes paying thousands for aid in political machinations, meetings at the house on Rue St. Ann usually took place in the dead of night, when all was quiet and identities obscured.

"It doesn't look like much." Rey nodded to the small cabin.

"Looks can be deceiving."

Mercy rapped her knuckles on the door, thinking that the pounding of her heart could be no less audible. During the short walk to Marie's, she'd sensed an almost coiled anticipation in Rey, as if the Silver Fox were preparing to pounce. One moment he'd grant her his quiet smile, the next, he'd watch her with a keenness that nearly made her turn back and forget Kate's note. Mercy told herself she was overreacting. The message, delivered so precipitately by Jean Claude, had caused her fears and not Rey's company. And yet, the careful way he examined her, as if his agent eyes missed nothing, made her wary.

Mercy knocked again, the wait only fueling her nebulous worries. She'd sent a note ahead and hoped they would be granted an audience—and that Marie Laveau would be amenable to her plans. If they were turned away, she doubted she'd find another way to distract the Silver Fox while she kept her meeting with Kate.

The door screeched open. A small child poked her tawny head through the opened doorway and glared at them.

"We seek the advice of Marie Laveau," Mercy said, handing the child twenty dollars, the cost for two readings. The girl gave the bills a thorough inspection before gesturing for them to enter.

The floorboards creaked. Crumbled red brick, used by Creole housewives to scrub their floors, rasped beneath the soles of Mercy's shoes. Many claimed the soft brick could keep a home safe from evil spells as well as clean. In Marie's house, Mercy suspected the brick powder was used for magic. Everyone knew the voodoo priestess had enemies.

In the room's corner, a withered old crone rocked quietly. She watched them through sunken eyes. A madras handkerchief encompassed her skull like a headdress. From beneath the tignon, swags of white hair tumbled to her hunched shoulders.

Rey touched his hand to Mercy's arm and jogged his head to the white cloth-covered altar with statues of the Virgin Mary and Saint Peter. He raised a dark brow.

"Marie Laveau is a devout Catholic," Mercy whispered back.

From the back room entered a regal-looking woman with skin the color of honey. Her vivid black eyes seemed to reach deep in Mercy's soul, seeking secrets before she even spoke a word. Like the old woman in the rocker, she'd covered her head with a scarlet and blue tignon. Heavy gold bracelets jangled at her wrist as she brushed away a length of long black hair.

"You want I tell your future?" she said in broken English.

"Yes." Mercy glanced up at Rey. Though she knew Marie Laveau preferred to speak Creole French, Mercy would not give herself away by addressing her in any language other than English. "Yes, we do."

"Come." She gestured them into the next room.

Rey stepped forward. Mercy stopped him with a hand on his arm.

"I would like to go first," she said. "Alone." She had to convince him to allow her this private audience with Marie for her plan to work.

His inscrutable gaze seemed to test the truth of her words, but his smile gave her the most pause. Before that moment, she had never seen Rey appear mocking.

He stepped back and bowed his head, extending his hand forward. "By all means . . . madame."

She followed Marie and a jolt of relief blazed through her. She'd managed the first of her hurdles well enough. She glanced at the watch pinned to her gown. She must hurry.

Walking inside the clapboard room, she heard the door click behind Marie. The altar that commanded this chamber was distinctly unlike the holy table found in the front. Carved statues of a bear, a tiger, and a wolf rested on a black cloth like guardians to Marie's black magic. As she stepped around a small table bracketed by two cane chairs, Mercy saw a large box beneath the altar. Brightly painted voodoo signs covered the crate. Slithering and brushing noises came from within. A soft tapping followed. Mercy frowned.

"Do not fear." Marie pulled out a chair. "It is only my snake. You wish I show him to you?"

Mercy shook her head and sat down. "No. That's fine."

With a smile that said the voodoo priestess knew she'd just earned some healthy respect, Marie picked up Mercy's ungloved hand. Mercy unfurled her fingers to reveal not the guiding lines to her future but a ten dollar note.

Marie glanced up. "I have money already . . . you paid enough."

"Not for this service." Placing the bill in Marie's hand, Mercy leaned forward. "This must be a long reading. Very long. I want you to keep the man outside waiting. When he will wait no longer, tell him I left because I was deeply upset with your predictions. Make up some excuse why you didn't call him right away. Say you were afraid he might be angry and take back the money. Say anything but the truth. When he asks where I am, tell him I went for the carriage and will return for him shortly."

One quick nod and the bill vanished.

Mercy looked to the back of the room where a door hung precariously on its hinges. "Does that way lead outside?"

"*Oui.*"

"Remember." Mercy stood. "Make him wait!"

The priestess grabbed her wrist. "You paid for a reading, madame. I will be quick." Marie's dark eyes and lilting voice held Mercy's attention as securely as the woman's grip. Behind her, Mercy could hear the snake slithering and tapping against the sides of its box. "The man. He is bright, with white hair, like an angel, *non*? But you. You are darkness. Darkness that seeks the light." She turned Mercy's hand palm up and looked down. "You will be lovers."

Mercy jerked her hand away. "I don't have time for this."

"Very well, madame, but I give you this warning for your money—he is like flame to the moth. A very dangerous man."

The echo of Pascal's warning joined the priestess's laughter as Mercy pulled the veil over her face and plunged outside. Careful not to be seen, she ran to the street corner where a carriage waited. She blanked her mind of all thoughts but the minutes ahead, trying to forget the palm reading. Marie Laveau was known for her mischief. She'd probably guessed Mercy was married and wanted to cause trouble. There was nothing mysterious or supernatural about her prediction. After a sharp knock, the carriage door swung open. Mercy climbed inside.

"You took long enough, Santana," said the same gentleman who had passed her the note at the Pontalba Apartments.

She flipped back her veil. "Then let's not waste any time now, Jean Claude."

He pounded his cane to the roof of the cabriolet. Her back hit the leather as the coach sped off.

Eight blocks later, the carriage slowed to a stop only long enough for Mercedes to dismount on Royal Street. The cabriolet continued down the street at a fast clip to Jackson Square where Jean Claude would instruct her carriage driver where to pick up his mistress. Her veil once more in place, Mercy rounded the corner of the three-story concert-saloon called "Catalan Kate's." The sour smell of refuse and discarded beer filled her nostrils as she hovered at the side door off the narrow street.

"*Dios!* Get away!" Kate bellowed in her unmistakable Spanish accent. A cat dragging a fish between its clamped jaws sped down the steps before Kate appeared waving a fist. "*Estúpido animal.* Steal my good fish!" With a look of disgust, she lifted the train of her scarlet gown out of a puddle of ale. Cinched tight at her waist and cut low across the shoulders, the dress displayed an incredible hourglass figure that challenged belief. Over her shoulder, she yelled, "I see that cat in the kitchen one time more, Anaise, and I swear it is *sopa* by morning."

"Kate," Mercy said from the shadows.

"*Dios,*" the lady held a palm to her abundant bosom. "You scare the life out of me, *chica.*"

"Sorry," Mercy said. "But I'm in a rush." She took Kate's hand. "How is she?"

Kate gave Mercy a wide smile. She brushed back a lock of hair a questionable shade of red. "Carolina is fine. She have *una niña*—a baby girl." She shook her head, bemused. "That baby, she take all night and all morning. Carolina swear she dying. She scream for you. We worry plenty. When Jean Claude say your carriage in town, I send him after you because I think you make Carolina calm. Two minutes after Jean Claude leave"—Kate snapped her finger—"that baby slip out like a greased pig."

Mercy laughed, happy to hear mother and daughter were fine. "Can I see her?"

Kate nodded. "Come. Carolina in her room."

Upstairs, in a chamber overheated by boiling water and a roaring fire, Mercy held the newborn baby girl in her arms. She blinked back the tears filling her eyes, cooing down at the perfect pink angel wrapped in swaddling.

"I named her after you," Carolina said in a weak voice from the bed. "I named her Rose."

Mercy turned to the blond woman, touched by Carolina's gesture. Carolina appeared no older than Pascal—though there was a knowledge in her gaze that Mercy would never see in Benoit's sheltered daughter. Mauve circles darkened the skin beneath Carolina's gray eyes and her night rail was sweat-soaked under her breasts and arms. She looked tired, but very satisfied.

"I'm honored, Carolina." Mercy gazed down at the baby girl. "Rose," she whispered reverently. "It's the symbol of love," she added, remembering the day a flower vendor had said the same as she'd handed Mercy her first Santana Red rose. Mercy had determined then to use the flower as her calling card. It was a tribute to the love she held for the child she'd lost. "It's a lovely name," she said, handing the baby back into her mother's arms reluctantly. She'd already risked too much time by her visit. "A lovely name for a beautiful girl."

Carolina grabbed Mercy's hand before she could leave.

"I just wanted to show my thanks for . . . for everything."

"You're *very* welcome," Mercy whispered, squeezing Carolina's fingers warmly.

Mercy turned to find Kate waiting at the door. Fine lines, admitting more years than her figure, appeared around the Spaniard's kohl-darkened eyes as she grinned. "Come, *chica.* Your carriage is waiting outside."

The two women traveled downstairs to the kitchen. At the back entrance, Kate took Mercy aside. She glanced over her shoulder, as if nervous that someone might be listening, then stepped close to whisper, "I hear news in the taproom this morning." Her dark blue eyes widened. "I think maybe I shouldn't tell you, but Jean Claude say he will if I don't. They bring a new shipment. *Hoy.*"

"Tonight?"

Kate nodded. "Can you do it, *linda*?"

Mercy thought back to Carolina and little Rose. She met Kate's anxious gaze. "Just keep the door unlocked."

Kate nodded. *"Dios te ayude."*

To the stream of Spanish curses once more directed at poor Anaise and her cat, Mercy left Catalan Kate's. As Kate had said, Mercy's carriage waited at the corner—the landau's cover was up, just as she'd instructed Jean Claude. Without even a lift of his brow, the well-trained driver made for Rue St. Ann.

When they reached Marie's house, Rey waited outside. He was leaning against the fence, his tall body held rigid, his expression tense. The sight of him sent a corresponding tautness through Mercy. Immediately, she regretted taking the time to see Carolina and the baby. She watched his long strides as he approached the coach: precise, fluid —the image of a panther stalking his prey.

"I'm sorry to have kept you waiting," she said once he'd settled inside and the carriage lurched forward. "I do hope it hasn't been too long?"

"Not at all." His hands rested on the crease of his trousers at the knees. "Did your meeting go well?"

The words sent her mind reeling. Across the carriage, the planes of Rey's face were set in an unreadable expression as he waited for her response. He could have said anything. Asked about the weather, made a comment on traffic, his voice had been that calm, almost disinterested.

"My meeting?" she asked.

"Yes. With the fellow who passed you the note." Nothing in his expression changed. He watched her with an unnerving nonchalance. He shook his head. A hint of disappointment crept into the line of his mouth. "Such clumsy hands."

In a gesture so quick, so unexpected, that Mercy could do nothing to stop him, he hooked his finger under the drawstring of her purse at her wrist. He stared at the tiny swath of satin. "I'd wager the note's still inside. Should I search it out for you? Refresh your memory?"

Mercy snatched her hand back, holding her purse tightly. Kate's note she'd thrown away at the shop. But the St. Christopher medal remained inside.

"Ah." He leaned against the squabs. "It seems you remember after all."

The red moroccan leather accented the silver color of his hair. An angel, Marie had called him. At the moment, the pale green color of his eyes seemed to glow, contributing to quite a different image.

"Was he worth it?" he asked, his voice barely above the sound of the carriage wheels.

Her heart skidded to her throat. Worth it? Jean Claude? Dear Lord, he thought she'd kept some romantic assignation. She almost laughed. She'd thought he'd discovered the true intent behind her meeting, that the agent in him would somehow ferret out her connection to Santana Rose. He didn't know the truth, didn't even suspect.

"In my opinion," he continued, "the fellow lacks finesse. And passion."

He leaned across the carriage until his knees pressed against hers. With the back of his hand, he stroked her cheek. It was the first time he'd touched her. Always, as Santana or Mercedes, she had sought his touch. Only in her imagination had he reached out and caressed her with the sweet desire communicated by the simple brush of his fingers.

"Were I your lover, Mercedes, I would never have left your side without some sign that we'd been together."

His thumb grazed her bottom lip. The warmth inside her fired white hot.

"Perhaps a slight redness here," he whispered almost as an afterthought as he followed the curve of her neck. His fingers stopped at the base of her throat, and circled, slowly circled. "Or a trace of a kiss here."

"I didn't meet any man, Rey." The words sounded harsh, without breath. She could hardly hear them for the pounding of her heart. "Please, believe me."

He nodded, then sat back. The silence that followed gave her hope she might persuade him, but a voice inside her counseled caution.

"How I would like to believe that, Mercedes." She marveled at how one word—her own name—could hold such accusation. "Over the past week, I started to believe only I could bring that charming blush that colored your cheeks when your gentleman friend slipped you his note. I thought it was my touch that could make your fingers tremble as they did when you took that slip of paper. Each night in the *garçonnière,* I wrestled with my conscience, telling myself that you are married . . . Yes. I would most definitely like to believe you."

He studied her, waiting as if for some response. Mercy agonized for the right answer—none came.

"May I see the note?" he asked.

A hundred protests rose to her lips, even more excuses

followed, but she voiced none. She knew he'd never believe her, not without seeing the letter. "I threw it away," she said, sincere regret coloring her words.

A small, cynical smile turned one corner of his mouth, accenting the dimple at his chin. She sensed he'd expected her response all along. "Before I left Marie's," he said, his voice once again cool, "she gave me some rather interesting news about my future. I wonder if she said the same to you?"

You will be lovers. Mercy dropped her gaze to her gloved hands, feeling a hot blush color her face. She could hear the prediction as clearly as if she were at that moment sitting before the great Laveau. Had the voodoo priestess actually repeated her prophecy to Rey?

"Just so," he answered.

Her head jerked up. Dear Lord, that he could read her so easily.

He reached across the carriage with his hand. In one lingering stroke, he caressed her cheek. He pulled his hand away, haltingly, communicating regret.

His touch struck her oddly as more intimate than a kiss.

"Think about it, Mercedes."

The carriage slowed until it came to a halt. The sounds of children playing and vendors calling their wares crept past the carriage walls. Jackson Square already.

Rey glanced outside. "We're here."

At any moment, Pascal, Ling Shi, and Everard would open the door and come in. Mercy had perhaps seconds to make some excuse for her absence rather than what he'd just assumed. She opened her mouth to explain—Rey pressed two fingers across her lips.

"Don't say anything now," he said. "Just think about it. But understand this. I'll be your only lover." He dropped his hand. "I think it's enough that I have to share you with Benoit, don't you?"

* * *

John MacAfee gulped down the good Scotch whiskey. Its mellow barley flavor did nothing to wash away the bad taste left by the sight of the lovely lassie sidling up to the overfed glutton, Gessler. Rey had asked him to follow the constable while he and Harlan spent the day with the ladies of L'Isle des Rêves. Much good it had done so far, Mac thought as he finished off the drink and signaled the barkeep for another. It was almost evening and he'd learned not a thing by dogging Gessler's steps. Thank the good Lord, this stop was proving a bit more interesting than the rest.

Mac glanced down to the lace reining in the creamy flesh of the lassie's bosom as she bent down to whisper something in the constable's hairy ear. Burgeoning with charms she was. Mac shook his head and took another belt of the liquor. It wasna his place to tell the lassie who could scratch her itch, but damned if she weren't cockeyed to think much of the mound of flesh taking in an eyeful of her now.

MacAfee rested his elbow on the polished oak bar, his back to the seventy odd bottles lined up like good soldiers beneath an etched glass mirror announcing WELCOME. He put a boot up to the brass footrest. Scanning the interior of Catalan Kate's, he admitted Gessler at least had good taste. Unlike the other concert-saloons he'd tramped through in the Vieux Carré, Catalan Kate's showed some class. Not a tinny piano or a shrill fiddle, but a four-piece band played while couples danced on the hardwood floor. The girls slinging beer and serving food at the small tables were a cut above the "beer-jerkers" who tended tables at the other bars, their dresses showing only a dainty bit of ankle and a tempting glimpse of bosom. There was even a real curtained stage for the evening's entertainment. And, he thought, taking another swig, the Scotch was fine.

"Señor!"

Mac glanced up to see the lovely redhead give Gessler's hand a teasing slap. He frowned. Truly a waste.

"You would tempt a saint, Kathleen." Gessler made another go for the lassie's backside, but she sashayed out of reach.

"Your Kathleen has something much more tempting for you, *señor,* coming from her kitchen."

MacAfee watched the constable's eyes light up. He gave a disgusted shake of his head. Imagine being distracted by food when an entire feast lay before your eyes.

"Is it my favorite?" Gessler asked.

"But you know it is. La Sadie make it special for you." She gave his bulbous nose a tweak and poured him another glass of claret. "I hear that robber lady, Santana Rose, strike again." She turned her back to the room and dropped her voice. Mac strained to listen but couldn't make out her words.

Tapping the glass with his fingers, he thought quickly. Though it werena the business Rey was particularly interested in, Mac drifted down the bar, taking his glass with him. When he thought neither the lassie nor Gessler was watching, he stepped up to the bar right next to their table.

". . . got my sights on her. It's just a matter of time."

Mac heard the scrape of a chair pulled out behind him as the womanly confection in red sat down. "This, your Kathleen knows . . . feel safe just knowing *el señor* is such a good . . ."

Losing the conversation, Mac casually turned and scanned the room, inching closer.

". . . tell me what you have planned for this robber woman."

Out of the corner of his eye, Mac saw the lass edge forward, displaying her admirable wares for Gessler. From where he stood, Mac judged the good constable had more to salivate over than his lamb cutlets. The lassie's bosom practically heaved beneath his nose.

"I really shouldn't . . ."

She tapped his hand. "*Señor!* You know you can trust

your Kathleen!" Her beringed hand gave Gessler's pudgy fingers a tempting stroke. "You have plan, no? You get this . . . this . . . she-devil, *sí*? I fear for my life each day now. Make me feel safe. Tell me, Tomasito. Tell Kathleen she need not fear this woman."

"Well, I do have a rather brilliant plan."

"But of course, *señor*!" she said, filling his glass once more.

MacAfee almost groaned in disgust as he witnessed how easily the constable succumbed to the lassie.

"I've set a trap for that witch. Tonight."

She raised a thin arched brow. "*Hoy?* But *señor*, how do you know this devil-woman will rob tonight?"

"I got a client see, a real upstanding citizen that has particular trouble with Santana Rose. Oh, he's her target all right. It never fails that when we bring gir—this particular cargo, she heists the loot. I'm betting she'll do the same thing tonight. These henchmen, they've no smarts." He tapped a fat finger to his temple. "They just do whatever works over and over until it doesn't work anymore. The gi—er—cargo will come up through Barataria. At the Little Temple, me and my men will be waiting."

"And the *señor* will catch her!"

He belched. "I plan to."

Mac watched the constable reach across the table for the lassie, but she was on her feet and out of the way before he even touched her. Mac had to tip his hat to her; she knew how to work a mark.

"I will bring you the rum cake you like so much. I will make sure La Sadie adds some sweet cream, *sí*?"

"You take good care of me, Kathleen."

She smiled, stroking his double chin. "You are Catalan Kate's best and most important customer, *señor*. A big, important man."

Big in any event, MacAfee added to himself.

"It is not often we have a government man here." With a wink, she turned and left.

MacAfee bid his time at the bar. A line of high-stepping girls performed the *clodoche* on the stage, kicking up their red frilly skirts and yelling with the music. When the constable finished his meal and left, Mac didn't follow. He knew the man's haunts now. Knew how to find out what he was about. Damned if that cute little Spanish redhead wouldn't do the work for him. All he had to do was buy a drink and let that pretty lassie ply the answers from that loose-lipped lump of lard.

Mac glanced back at the lassie. Despite her heavy Spanish accent and bright red curls, she reminded him of his Fran. All curves and softness, the lass was. The bar had a good business upstairs by the look of the gents and ladies making for the stairwell. But as he watched the toothsome lassie strutting across the room, Mac felt no desire for the slim girls serving drinks that looked young enough to be his bairns. Interesting woman, the redhead, he thought. He could tell by the way she talked with the customers and kept the girls on their toes that she had a hand in running the place. Did a fine job of it too. Mac finished his drink and signaled the barkeeper for a final one.

Over the rim of the shot glass, he kept his attention on the lass. Though he wasna young, he'd not had too many problems catching a lassie's eye in the past. Ready to put his most charming self to the test, he motioned her over.

Even the sway of her skirt called his peter to attention. *Hold on boy,* he thought. *We've not got her yet.*

"Can I buy ye a drink, lass?"

She gave him a sharp look with the prettiest set of blue eyes he'd ever seen. "I only pour the drinks here, *señor.*"

He glanced down at her fine breasts. "Can ye not find a bit a time to make a stranger feel welcomed? I work out at a plantation up the river, but it's my day off and I plan to make the most of it." He leaned over, letting her know with the stroke of his hand at her skirt what it was he was after.

"Remove that hand, Scotsman, or lose it."

Her eyes looked like a pair of blades ready to do just as she'd threatened. Mac flushed. "Now that ain't at all friendly." He gave her his best smile and reached for his purse. "I could make it worth yer while."

She pushed his wallet back into the pocket of his jacket. With a carmine-painted nail, she pointed to the logo etched in swirling letters on his shot glass. "Do you read, *señor*?"

He nodded. "Catalan Kate's. Saw it on the marquee coming in."

She pointed to herself. "I am La Kate. If you want a *señorita*, I have plenty." She jogged her head toward the stairs, then pointed a finger to her chest. "But Kate"—she wagged the long-nailed finger in front of his nose—"is not for sale. *Comprende*?"

Mac's eyes sparkled. "Not for sale, ye say?"

"*Sí.*"

"Looks like I'm going to have to woo you, like a real gentleman then."

Her eyes widened, as if she'd not expected his response. She shook her head, looking at him as if he were a bit teched.

"Because you new in town, I will help you. Marcela there"—she pointed out a dark-haired girl with an inviting smile—"will take *very* good care of you, *señor*. You like what you see?"

MacAfee slapped down the money for his drinks on the bar. He tilted Kate's head up with a finger under her chin. "I like what I see just fine." He dropped his voice an octave. "I may be new in town, but I know what I want. I'll be back, Katie."

Chapter 7

Rey yanked off the dustcover. A cloud of fine gray powder billowed around the three men, sending Mac into a fit of coughing. Tossing the sheet to the floor, Rey dropped to the S-shaped tête-à-tête and swung one leg over the armrest. "Home, sweet home." Excitement thrummed in his veins, pulsing into the sweetness of anticipation. It felt good. Right. He should have acted long ago. "I say we stay here tonight."

"Are ye daft?" Mac scanned Bizy's salon, taking in the peeling wall paper, the spiderwebs glittering like tinsel from the mantel. "They just fixed the roof. But half the rooms are ready."

"It looks ready enough for me. What do you think Harlan?"

Harlan shucked off the sheet covering the settee and sat down with a grin. "*Mais*, yeah, man. *C'est bon.*"

Mac threw up his arms and glowered beneath his brows. "Ye said we'd not be moving till next week! There's nae but a servant, maybe two, and they've surely gone and found their beds elsewhere fer the night."

"We'll stay just the same."

"What the devil happened on that carriage ride this morning that sent your skull rattling?" Mac jerked his head to Harlan. "Or did the lad here put ye up to this?"

"Take it easy, *mon vieux.*" Harlan lit a cigarette and

squinted through the smoke at the room's bare walls. "I'm as surprised as you."

"Faith! The place isna habitable."

"We've had worse, Mac."

"Oh, aye. But only during the war, I'd wager!"

Rey loosened his cravat and pulled it free of his collar. He smiled, almost drunk with the plans he'd made. The bubbling exhilaration inside him was new—and intoxicating. It struck him surprisingly like happiness. "I rather like the place. It's not bad for temporary quarters."

Mac grabbed a sheet off the floor and wadded it into a ball. "We dinna have supplies. No linens. No food," he grumbled, gathering the dustcovers off the furniture in capitulation.

"De Dreux—our wonderful host—has agreed to send over whatever we need."

"*Eh bien,* and be glad to see our backsides." Harlan expelled a stream of smoke with a laugh.

"I wouldn't mind some distance myself," Rey said under his breath.

"Would ye now?" Mac's dark eyes narrowed above the piled linens in his arms. "An' I'm wondering why that might be?"

"It's obvious, Mac." He folded his arms behind his back and stared up at the plaster medallion of vines center-ceiling. "We need to get out from under De Dreux's nose. Make our own camp, so to speak."

Mac watched him skeptically. A begrudging smile quirked Rey's lips as he met his valet's gaze. He rarely managed to fool Mac. But there was enough truth in what he'd said to convince even Rey that the move *was* necessary. This wasn't just for Mercedes.

"Aye. It makes sense. Enough to make me wonder why we didna leave afore?"

"Ah." Rey dropped both his feet to the ground. "Before today, De Dreux hadn't made his move. Now, I know when he's going to see Sotheby. Tonight, or so De Dreux told me over a glass of port this afternoon. He's going to discuss the possibility of Sotheby meeting with us."

Harlan popped forward on the settee, his muscles tensed. "I'll go with you, of course."

"You'll go with me, of course *not*," Rey answered.

"He's making me cool my heels as well, laddie," Mac said with regret as evident as that on Harlan's face.

"This isn't a two-man job, just a simple surveillance," Rey said. "My chances are better of going unnoticed if I'm alone, you both know that. Harlan, you just make sure you keep your meeting with that reporter from the *Democrat*. He says he has proof that Sotheby's been using the mail to distribute counterfeit bills through the lottery outside the state. If we can't trap Sotheby through De Dreux, I want a backup plan."

"*Bien*, all right." But Rey could see by the man's expression that Harlan didn't care for the job assigned to him.

"Do ye really think," Mac asked, "that they can rig the lottery like De Dreux's promising? With two war heros and a couple of orphan boys picking the winning tickets, I'm thinkin' it's a mite unlikely."

"In this town, nothing is impossible—if you have the money. De Dreux has certainly taken enough of mine to grease a few palms." Rey reached inside his jacket pocket for the cigarettes he'd bought that afternoon. A green square fell to the faded carpet as he pulled out a package of Choctaws. Setting the carton on the arm of the tête-à-tête, he picked the folded bill off the floor.

"What's that?" asked Harlan.

Rey unfurled the note carefully, revealing a five dollar bill. "Queer money, boodle." He sat back against the cushion of his seat, staring at the center engraving of the pioneer and his dog and Sully's portrait of Andrew Jackson in the left corner. "It's counterfeit."

"Is that one of Sotheby's?" Harlan asked, coming closer to examine the bill.

Rey held up the greenback for Harlan to see. "One of

his earlier attempts. Quite good actually. Not dull or sunken." He pointed to the carefully etched bands. "No broken lines from cheap plates. It would take a lens to find any imperfections in the lathe work. The shading is light, like in the real bills, with only a few dark spots to give it away." His fingers rubbed the paper. "Nice. Difficult to tell it's no good even if you've studied Heath's book on counterfeit detection. Aside from being the worst sort of back-street scum, Harry Sotheby is really very talented. A genius. And that, my friends"—Rey studied MacAfee and Harlan; both listened carefully—"is why we have to make sure he and his gang are completely shut down. Sotheby could destroy the nation's currency, ruin our credit structure. And he's just greedy enough to do it. Right now, there's enough boodle coming out of this state to make itself felt at the national treasury."

"Rigging the lottery *and* counterfeiting." Harlan shook his head. "*Mon Dieu.* The man's a regular crime gang, him." He pointed to the bill in Rey's hand. "Did that come from N'awlins?"

Rey shook his head, folding the bill back into a small square. "No." He placed the bill back in his pocket, and picked up the package of Choctaws. With a flame of a phosphorous match, he lit a cigarette. "I've had that particular note for quite some time."

Harlan nodded, watching Rey with an odd expression.

"Anything wrong?" Rey asked as he dragged deeply on the cigarette.

"Ah, no." Harlan shook his head, snubbing out his own cigarette. "I was jus' under the impression you didn't smoke, is all."

Rey's hand shaking out the match slowed to a stop. He glanced up at MacAfee, who also watched him, then looked down at the lighted cigarette. "I haven't smoked for a number of years."

"Leave the man be," MacAfee said. "He's nae need to justify his actions to you, laddie."

"*Mon vieux,* I meant no offense."

"None taken." Rey turned the package of Choctaws between his fingers, examining them thoughtfully. He'd purchased the cigarettes in town after he'd made his proposal to Mercy. After so many years of controlling his impulses, he was tired of denying himself what he wanted. "I stopped smoking five years ago, but I decided to take it up again. Did you find out anything in town this afternoon, Mac?" he asked, changing the subject.

"That I did. But not what ye expected."

Rey caught the note of interest in Mac's voice. "I'm listening."

"I followed Gessler, just like ye told me." Mac dropped the sheets on the chair in front of him, then waved off the cloud of dust that lifted around the pile. "The best place to find the constable is bellying up to a bar name of 'Catalan Kate's.' Well, I watched Gessler guzzling an' overindulgin', as appears to be his want, playing the big important man fer a lassie who cozens up to him." Mac paused and looked to each man. "While I'm sittin' there, drinkin' my Scotch, the lassie starts to ask him about Santana Rose. How does he plan to catch the thief, she asks? What are his plans? Oh, he seems a wee bit reluctant to discuss government business at first, but the lassie presses him, ye ken? Next thing I hear, every blessed detail of his plan to catch the bandit races past his fat lips." Mac's brows rose in dismay. "The man's got a mouth as big as the Mississippi, he has."

"That certainly explains why he's having trouble taking the woman into custody," Rey said.

"Aye. I'm thinking the same. She has spies a'plenty and hears what's afoot before Gessler even sets out to catch her. Seems he's planning a trap for her tonight."

"Tonight?"

"At a place called the 'Little Temple.' Could be," Mac added, "we might be of some assistance to the constable?"

A slow sure smile spread across Rey's lips. "Perhaps."

He took another puff and leaned comfortably into the chair, his legs stretched forward and crossed at the ankle. The thought of catching the woman highway robber was very appealing, indeed. "But not tonight, I'm afraid."

"Why waste our time with a highway robber?" Harlan objected. "I thought we were here to catch De Dreux and Sotheby?"

"Crime, my friend, is wrong—in any form." Rey pictured his St. Christopher medal sliding into the bandit's gloved hands. "I wouldn't mind seeing justice done in this case."

"I'm guessing Gessler's comin' up empty-handed tonight. But with a little direction from us . . ."

"Next time, he might have better luck," Rey finished for his valet. "Why not?" He watched the smoke from his cigarette curl around him. "Mac, you keep an eye out at Catalan Kate's. Obviously, the place is connected to Santana Rose."

"That I'll do," Mac said with broad smile.

Rey cocked his head back to Mac, catching the unexpected note of enthusiasm. "That must be some fine Scotch they serve."

"The best," Mac said.

"In the meantime," Harlan asked impatiently, "what about De Dreux?"

Rey stood and walked to the wood mantel cunningly painted to appear like marble. He tapped a finger against a dusty cobweb. "I've already given word that we plan to move here to Bizy. Tonight, I'll follow De Dreux and see if Mr. Sotheby is amenable to our meeting." He glanced at the clock on the mantel. "You'd best be off, Harlan, if you want to meet that reporter." When Harlan turned toward the salon door, Rey called out, "And Harlan, one more thing. The girl, De Dreux's daughter." In his mind's eye, he saw Mercedes, her anxious expression during the carriage ride, her attempts to protect her stepdaughter from Harlan and her gratitude when Rey had intervened. "Let's leave her out of this, shall we? She's just a child. She can't possibly be of any help."

"But . . ."

"She's out, Harlan."

Though his hands remained fisted at his sides, Harlan smiled nonetheless. "*Bien. Bonne chance* tonight, eh?" He turned on one heel and quit the room.

Rey flicked the ashes of the Choctaw toward the hearth. Good luck, Harlan had said. Rey smiled, feeling very fortunate indeed. Since that afternoon, when he'd met the anger stirred by the white slip of paper passed to Mercedes—tasted its bitterness, dissected its cause until it lost its power over him—a sort of peace had settled inside. He'd made his offer. And he knew to a certainty it was merely a matter of time before Mercedes accepted him. Everything seemed different now. The old excitement was back. He lifted the cigarette to his lips and grinned. And all because he'd propositioned a woman.

"So, ye finally made yer decision, have ye?"

Rey glanced over his shoulder at Mac. "Decision to move against De Dreux?" He turned slowly to face his valet. "It was always my intention to do so. You knew that. I was waiting for a chance."

"T'aint that De Dreux I'm speakin' of."

The muscles of Rey's chest constricted, but his smile remained carefully in place. He inhaled deeply from the Choctaw.

"Oh, she's a fine bit of goods, and it's clear she's sweet on ye. I'm not blaming ye fer succumbing. Ye've held out longer than most against what's she's offering. But she's married, fer God's sake. Ye'll not find a life with her! She'll not give ye bairns—"

"Just so, Mac." Rey tossed the cigarette into the hearth. "Don't you understand? That's exactly what I need. You're always condemning me for Christopher. Why would you even think to wish me more children?"

"You're a fine father to the boy! It's just that ye've

mucked up yer mind with Sotheby and revenge. Ye'd never have left him with yer sister fer so long otherwise."

"No children, Mac." Rey shook his head, sensing his contentment slipping. "I had my chance at marriage and family."

"It wasna yer fault, Rey. Why must ye torture yerself so? Ye werena even the agent in charge. Ye warned Sophie to stay away from the bank that day. How were you to know she'd disobey and come looking fer ye?"

Rey didn't answer immediately, just stared at the hearth. "Sometimes," he whispered almost to himself, "I think I lured her there with my cryptic message to stay away. She knew the colonel had contacted me. She might have thought I was in some kind of danger—"

"An' she could have come to tell ye Chris was teething or to get money fer a new bonnet! It wasna yer fault they took Sophie. She was one woman in a bank full of people. They could have taken anyone."

Rey swung away, not listening. He grabbed the dusty mantel place, digging his fingers into the wood. It hadn't been just anyone Sotheby's men had taken. Sophie had been their hostage to secure the release of the men seized that day at the bank. And it had been Rey's decision that put them there—his choice to allow Colonel Whitley to set up the sting operation at the family bank. No matter how much Mac tried to soothe him, Rey couldn't forget those choices. His anguish over Sophie's death kept him entrenched in the past. Yet, every night for the last week, when he returned to the darkened *garçonnière,* alone, with only visions of Mercedes to keep him company, he burned to be released from his lonely, five-year vigil.

Mac wouldn't understand the battle raging inside him. How could anyone understand? But even as he formed the thought, Rey remembered Fran, Mac's wife, and how his friend had grieved her passing. Perhaps Mac wasn't haunted by the tragedy of his wife's death, as Rey was, but certainly he'd lived through the loneliness.

"Don't you miss it, Mac?" He rested his head against his arm braced on the mantel. "Don't you . . . *miss* the tender touches, the sweet smiles." He turned, scanning Mac's face for traces of awareness. "You had Fran for ten years to my three with Sophie. Don't you want what you had? It's not enough to bed a woman, then slap money on her table and leave the second I fasten my pants." He shook his head. "Sometimes, I watch their disinterested faces and it . . . sickens me. I tell myself I should have serviced myself"—he laughed—"and don't think I haven't done that enough. Do you know how many years it's been since I've fallen asleep holding a woman in my arms?"

Mac's sad eyes remained steady on Rey. "I've paid a lass or two to hold me through the night, Rey. They'll do that, ye see, if ye pay them enough coin."

Rey shook his head. "It's not enough. Not anymore."

"Aye." Mac sighed. "Not when an angel like De Dreux's wife stares at ye with eyes that would eat ye up if they could. But Rey, yer young, handsome as sin. There are plenty of lassies—"

"Virgins with tender hearts and marriage on their minds —that just can't be for me now." Again, he saw the white note slipping from the Frenchman's fingers to Mercy. "But a married woman, one bored and cosseted, whose husband turns a blind eye to her occasional indiscretions. One used to clandestine meetings—and their partings. What could be a better match?"

"So ye've convinced yerself, have ye?" Mac's bearded chin jutted out. "It's against the kirk's laws."

"Oh, for the love of God. Against the church? I've *killed* men. I'm sure God's more concerned about that blot on my soul."

"In the war, in the line of duty. It's different, as well ye know." He crossed his arms over his chest and spread his legs wide. "I didna want to say it, Rey, but ye force my hand. Have ye already forgotten Leticia?"

Leticia. Sotheby's old mistress. Rey pressed his lips together as he saw Leticia's tear-filled eyes as she'd begged him not to desert her, swearing she'd leave her husband for Rey. No, he hadn't forgotten, could never forget the woman he'd used so poorly. "That, was different."

"Why?" Mac examined him from beneath his brows. "Because yer heart was not involved? Because ye were groomin' her more fer information against Sotheby than to give ye pleasure? I say it's worse, worse fer both of ye if ye fall in love."

"Bugger off, Mac."

He nodded, picking up the linen to leave the room. "Aye, I thought ye'd say as much."

In south Jefferson Parish, the reeds grew thicker than the blades of grass. Jammed together like coiled wire, the tall golden rods chocked out the sun, creating a dark underground world of tunnels that patrols could never guard. If a body were willing—risked the floating marshes that could suck up the unwary and suffocate them like quicksand, or the alligators that would snap a leg in one chomp of their jaws—there was money to be made in the swamps. People said the spirit of pirates and smugglers still haunted the Barataria swamps. It was here that Santana Rose and her band felt most at home.

Boots soaked, Mercy crouched by Jean Claude and Pascal behind a curtain of cane. The pungent smell of damp earth and leaves permeated the air. Spanish moss dangled to a hundred feet above their heads, swaying with the breeze as the duckweed-clogged water drifted past. The group of three waited at the bayou's edge with a half a dozen men hidden in the cane behind them. All listened for the telltale splash, the fading whisper. A message had arrived by pirogue, the slim, fast-moving dugouts a man could pole over dew if necessary: De Dreux's shipment was making its way up the bayou toward the Little Temple.

Santana would make sure it never got there.

The ruffled swoosh of birds taking flight followed the

plop of alligators sliding into the water, alerting the group. Their quarry neared. Soon, moonlight glimmered off the deck of a skiff. The boat passed in and out of the cover of reeds and mossy curtains, weaving like a snake. One man poled the boat; two others stood guard. Mercy raised her hand, a signal to be ready. The skiff edged closer, almost on them. She glanced at Pascal. The girl whispered to the men around her, then pulled her bandanna over her face.

Mercy lowered her hand.

Two men jumped on the boat, knocking the guards to the deck. Before the third man could cry out, Mercy landed at a low crouch beside him. He swung his pole. She rolled to the side as the paddle hissed past her ear.

Mercy lunged. Ripping the pole from his hands, she jammed the end into his chest. His hands flailed, swinging wildly as the man sought his balance. With her boot heel, Mercy helped him over the edge. A spray of water and gurgling shouts followed as wave after wave slapped against the sides, rocking the skip.

A gunshot fired behind her.

The blast echoed down the bayou. Deafening. Branding their presence in the still night air. Santana cursed, holding the pole tight with two hands. Out of the corner of her eye, she saw a man grab his revolver. Thwack! The gun spiraled end over end into the water. Another swing of her pole and the man fell unconscious.

"Au plus vite!" she whispered to her men to hurry. The job was not going well. Gessler knew their location, alerted by the gunfire. With the back of her Smith and Wesson, she knocked out the man wrestling Jean Claude to the deck. Her men pulled the last of Benoit's smugglers out of the water. Off in the distance, she heard shouts.

"Merde," Mercy cursed, turning her attention to the cargo in the middle of the skiff.

A dozen women huddled together. A sick sense of kinship drove through Mercy, causing a familiar weakness. She experienced the same emotions each time she confronted this scene: girls, some no older than children, imported by her husband as fodder for the flesh marts of New Orleans. A few cried quietly, some sat shaking, their arms held tight around their stomachs. Still others lay lax on the floor of the boat, undoubtedly drugged.

"The gun," she heard Pascal say behind her. "They'll be here soon." The shouts of men's voices in the distance grew louder.

"Prenez les filles à les pirogues!" Mercy commanded her men to take the girls quickly to the boats that waited at the mouth of a cane tunnel. She and Pascal herded a pair onto their boats while Jean Claude and two others tied up Benoit's men. When the last girl boarded a waiting pirogue, Mercy turned to Pascal. "You go with the men. I'll join you later. *Viens avec moi,*" she called to Jean Claude.

"You can't take him," Pascal argued. "He'll make the best time in those tunnels."

"I don't have much choice," Mercy said harshly. "You know the escape route well enough. Now get on the boat. I'll distract Gessler's men."

Mercy turned back to Jean Claude. Behind her, Pascal headed not for the pirogue, but scrambled down to the bank in the opposite direction.

"What the hell do you think you're doing?" Mercy cried.

Pascal glanced back, then continued onto the stumplike knees of a cypress growing out of the water. Holding onto a gum tree, she jumped onto a felled cypress. She glided down its length, her hands held out for balance.

"Zut alors!" Mercy cursed, not believing her ill-luck.

"Go with her, Santana," Jean Claude said. "I'll take the women. I'll leave a man with a boat down the tunnel for you."

With a quick nod, Mercy hurried after her stepdaughter. As soon as she caught up with the girl, Mercy grabbed her shoulders and swung her around.

"What do you think you're doing out here? Get back to the boats."

Pascal pulled her bandanna down off her face. "I'm helping you." She tugged on Mercy's elbow. "Come on. We can decoy them up at the bend."

Mercy held firm. "*We* aren't doing anything. You get back to the tunnel where it's safe."

"And leave you to Gessler by yourself? Hardly." Pascal pushed off. She skipped to another cypress. Before Mercy reached her, she jumped to a small islet.

Mercy followed, her heart in her throat. She caught Pascal's arm. "No more playing around. Go back—"

A bullet whizzed over her head. Both women dropped to the muddy swamp floor.

"Too late to turn back now," Pascal said, pulling up her bandanna with a shaking hand. She snatched her gun from its holster.

Mercy pushed Pascal to a low crouch as another shot blasted. Leading the way, she brushed aside the creepers and moss, making for the opposite shore. Once there, she fired across the bayou. Pascal did the same. Both moved down the swamp, away from the mouth of the tunnel where Jean Claude led the boats to safety. Within minutes, they heard answering gunfire.

"They've taken the bait." Mercy said. "All right, let's go."

The two women wove past black willow and maple, deeper into the swamp. Mercy led, following the bayou's edge, careful not to lose sight of their direction. Their boots ankle-deep in swamp water, Pascal and Mercy kept up the parley of bullets, always drawing Gessler's men away from Santana's escape route.

When the sounds of pursuit grew scarce, Mercy stopped. She held her gloved finger across her lips and motioned Pascal to stay put. Cautiously, she circled back. Finding no sign of the men that stalked them, she returned for Pascal.

"I think we've lost them," Mercy whispered. "Let's—"

"Look out!"

Pascal knocked Mercy to the ground, rolled to her knees, and fired. One of Gessler's men stepped out from behind a swag of moss. He dropped his pistol and clutched his arm.

Mercy jumped to her feet. She grabbed Pascal's hand and ran. Pascal stumbled, cried out, but Mercy dragged her, never stopping. *Run,* a voice inside her called. *Run. Run!*

Dark trees whipped past them. Branches clawed, tore at Mercy's cape. Santana's mask felt suffocating, hot. Still she ran, hauling Pascal deeper into darkness. Shouts erupted from both sides. Dear God! Surrounded!

Mercy pushed to a stop. Her breath gasped in her chest. She scanned their surroundings, spotted a dense copse of palmettos overgrown with vines. She thrust Pascal into the cover of the short palms and dove in after her. Holding her hand over Pascal's mouth, she hugged the girl to her chest and covered them both with her black cape. Pascal huddled close with a soft whimper.

Seconds later, Gessler's men tramped past their hiding place, smoking torches held high. Too intent on pursuit, they failed to spot their prey.

Mercy collapsed against Pascal. She released the breath she'd held. The girl's arms tightened around Mercy. She burrowed closer, clinging to Mercy, squeezing the little air that remained from her lungs. Mercy cradled Pascal's head against her shoulder. She rocked the girl in her arms and kissed her temple. The gesture came naturally, as if they'd never exchanged a harsh word. "It's all right," she crooned in Pascal's ear. "It's all right."

Only a chorus of frogs and crickets sounded through the swamp when Mercy gently unwrapped Pascal's arms from her. Gessler's men long since gone, the two women doubled back to the pirogue. Santana's man waited just inside the mouth of the escape tunnel taken by Jean Claude and the others. Both women boarded and Eric pushed off the riverbank with his pole. The waterway would eventually hook up to the river and relative safety; all they need do now was rest.

Mercy kept her weight balanced, as she'd been taught, careful not to tip the pirogue. Occasional moonlight filtered past the tall reeds and shone on Pascal seated in front of her. A thin scratch twisted up the girl's face, past her cheek. Mud caked the other half. She looked younger than ever. Mercy recalled how she'd trembled in her arms as they'd waited in the palmettos.

"You saved my life," Mercy said softly.

Pascal's face slanted up. She watched Mercy, her eyes wide and glassy. "I did, didn't I?" A tremulous smile tipped the edges of her mouth, hung there but seconds, before the girl dropped her head in her hands and began to cry.

Rey stepped off the running board of the moving carriage and blended into the shadows. Beneath a street lamp four doorways up Gallatin Street, the landau stopped and De Dreux dismounted. The planter wrapped his cloak around himself against the night's chill, instructed his driver, and stepped up the stairs to the saloon.

Fifty feet away, two men watched Rey. Their faces gnarled by scars and weather, their clothes were no better than a stevedore's. The eyes of one glittered under the lamplight as the other shot Rey a gap-tooth smile. Trouble. Rey moved up the street, pulling the brim of his hat low over his distinctive hair. Gallatin was no place to remain idle.

He crossed the roadway and settled against the building opposite the saloon's facade. Though dressed all in black and with his hair tucked up in his bowler, he still wouldn't risk following De Dreux inside. Within minutes, a light flickered through the shutters on the second story of the bawdy house. The timing was right. De Dreux would have climbed to the second floor just about then.

Rey jogged across the brick-lined street, dodging a carriage, and slipped around the *porte cochère* to the back. A few servants hustled back and forth from the main building to the kitchens across the courtyard. Shouts and off-key singing accompanied the tinny piano playing inside. Where he stood beside the cistern, Rey felt certain no one could see him. Shedding his greatcoat and jacket, he glanced up to the railing of the second-story balcony.

He crouched down and fished inside his jacket pocket until he found a coil of sturdy cordage. A three-prong steel hook gleamed from one end. When the courtyard emptied, he stepped back, released a length of braided rope from the coil. With a flick of his wrist, he twirled the hook in a tight circle at his side, then released it. The rope caught against the railing, the weight of the hook twisting around the wrought iron until Rey anchored the steel with a sharp pull. He tested the rope, found it secure, then jammed his bowler hat on tightly. Climbing hand over hand, he reached the gallery, then swung over the cast-iron rail.

The shutters of the floor-to-ceiling windows were shut against the cold, but the warped and weathered planks prevented a tight seal. Leaning against the peeling paint, Rey could see inside through the crack where the two shutters met. The gaslight's yellow glow showed a faded carpet, a table, two chairs, and the back of one man seated in the chair closest to the window. Two voices spoke in quiet tones, one distinctly Creole by its accent—De Dreux —the other not nearly as educated. Rey moved to the next window and carefully pulled the edge of one shutter, widening the gap between the two. Inside, he saw De Dreux talking to the seated gentleman. The man turned toward the window, into the light.

Sotheby.

A tremor of hatred pulsed through Rey. As if waiting

for the proper trigger, his loathing erupted with a force that overwhelmed him. Five years slipped away. He stood in the Boston jail house again, hovering over a man half his size, the one they'd caught escaping from the boat after the explosion. He listened to the thug's whining refusal to name his accomplice—until Rey calmly cocked his pistol and jammed it against the man's temple, as if such violence were common for him. "It's Sotheby that put us to it," the henchman said quickly enough. "Harry Sotheby's the man you want! He done think up the plan to hold the lady hostage."

He'd wanted to pull the trigger. To rid the earth of the vermin responsible for Sophie's death. He'd stood there, tasting the salt of his sweat in his mouth, his fingers pressed against the trigger, until MacAfee pried the gun from his hand. The man had paled as he'd whispered one final time, "It's all Sotheby's doing. He didn't want no witnesses. We didn't mean the lady harm."

Sotheby.

Rey studied Harrison Sotheby by the light of the gasoliers. He'd never met the man, only knew him from pictures—yet he would never fail to recognize him. He'd committed the mud-brown curls, hawkish nose, and thin lips to memory. As Rey stared through the opening, a cold, almost chilling, calm bathed him. His breathing deepened. He felt strangely composed and very focused.

"I'll not hand over another penny, *monsieur,*" he heard De Dreux say, "unless I have assurances that the drawing will go on as planned."

"And what's to say it ain't going to, Benny boy." Sotheby answered, talking around a cigar stuffed between his lips.

"The vote in the legislature yesterday! You assured me the act would not pass. According to Louisiana law, that drawing will never take place and I will lose every dime I have sunk into this venture! More than I can afford to lose, damn you!"

"Don't get yourself all fired up, Ben. Come June, the Louisiana Lottery will be just as buzzing as ever, don't you doubt it for one moment."

"And how will you accomplish it, *monsieur,* given yesterday's vote?"

"Now good ol' Governor Nicholls ain't signed it into law yet, has he?"

A long pause followed before Rey heard Benoit De Dreux respond, "Do you have reason to believe he will not?"

Rey watched the lamplight from the gas jets burn in Sotheby's eyes as he clamped down on the Havana. "Let's just say, it ain't happening soon. And even if the governor did sign the bill, it will just go to court. Get my drift?"

"The Lottery Company hasn't lost a case yet," De Dreux answered with a relieved smile.

"Now you get it, Benny. Don't you worry none. By June, everything will be taken care of. The drawing will go ahead as planned. And you"—Sotheby poked De Dreux in the shoulder with the hand holding his cigar—"will be one rich Creole sonuvabitch." Sotheby burst into loud guffaws and stuck the cigar back between his teeth.

"You'd better be right, *monsieur.*"

Rey watched De Dreux drop a leather pouch on the table beside Sotheby. The other quickly picked it up and flipped through the money inside.

"By the way, *monsieur,* I've taken on a partner in this venture, a financier from Chicago—"

Sotheby glanced up, his face set in a snarl.

"Leonard Marcus vouched for him," De Dreux quickly assured him. "Reynard Parks is his name, but many know him as the Silver Fox. Perhaps you've heard of Parks? He's quite a reputation for . . . exotic investments, such as the one you offered me. He's recently arrived in New Orleans."

Sotheby returned to counting, his lips moving around the cigar as he silently added up the bills.

"He wants to meet with you," De Dreux continued. "In fact, he won't commit any more funds until he has, I'm afraid."

"Any time, Benny boy, any time. You just send a note to my man, and he'll make sure to set things up." Sotheby folded the bills together and tapped the ends against the tabletop, stacking them into a neat pile. "Good thing you got that partner too, Benny, 'cause we're gonna be needing some extra blunt now that the bill has passed."

A vicious smile slashed across Rey's lips. Of course Sotheby would bleed De Dreux for more money now that he knew about a partner.

"But you said there wouldn't be any problems!"

Sotheby shook his head, the cigar lolling from one side of his mouth to the other. "It's not a problem, just added security, Benny." He stood and tapped De Dreux's cheek with his open hand. "We wouldn't want anything to go wrong now, would we? Listen, anything you want downstairs, it's on the house." He glanced up at the carriage clock on the mantel. "I got to be going, but you just make yourself right at home. And Benny, you got any more shipments coming in soon?"

De Dreux smiled. "*Oui,* tonight." De Dreux's eyes turned sly. "But I'm afraid that due to recent losses, my prices will go up with this shipment."

Again, the loud guffaw. "We'll see what you got, Ben." Sotheby granted De Dreux a quick nod and slipped out into the hall.

With the click of the door, Rey loped to the railing. Whatever Sotheby was up to, Rey planned to witness it firsthand. Unhooking the rope, he checked to make sure no one was watching, then threw the cord and hook down. He scissored his legs over the railing, then jumped to the ground, landing in a roll. Grabbing his rope and coat, he was just in time to see Sotheby dodge past the door and flag down a cab. Once Sotheby was inside, Rey jumped onto the back of the carriage, using his coat to cover his face from the light.

On Royal, Rey sensed the cab slowing. He bounded off and hid in the darkness as he watched Sotheby pay the cabbie and step inside a brightly lit concert saloon. The sound of a brass quartet mixed with clapping and female cries of delight streamed onto the street as the door swung open and closed. Rey glanced up to the marquee. A knowing smile curved his mouth.

Catalan Kate's.

Chapter 8

Mercy sank back into Kate's favorite chair, an exotic piece with roaring lions for legs and two camels connected at the top rail for a back. Her stockinged feet rested on a footstool near the fireplace. It seemed as if the chill of the swamp had penetrated her heart and she would never be warm again—not after tonight's near catastrophe. She cupped a snifter of brandy between her hands, hoping the liquor could give her some measure of comfort. Santana's black and red mask with its crown of feathers dangled from one of the camel's heads. Its glass beads shimmered under the light of the wrought-iron chandelier.

Across Kate's sitting room, Pascal sat perched on the edge of a divan, mesmerized by the coals burning in the grate. Kate paced before the fireplace, her arms crossed beneath her voluminous breasts, the red train of her Andalusian-style gown dragging across the Persian rug. Just as Kate glared at Mercy, she in turn watched Pascal, still haunted by the image of Gessler's men hunting the girl in the swamps.

Pascal rose and walked to a low table inlaid with ivory that was characteristic of the haremlike furniture decorating Kate's parlor. She studied the brandy decanter resting on the Moorish table before reaching for it. As Pascal's fingers wrapped around the bottle's neck, she glanced at her stepmother. Mercy said nothing, only watched the girl whose trousers and jacket were stained with mud from the swamp.

"Since when does *la chiquita* drink brandy?" Kate asked, turning her scowl on Pascal.

Pascal lingered over the bottle. The Meissen clock on the mantilla-covered hearth chimed half-past midnight. She glanced at the timepiece, ignoring Kate's question. "Just about now, father thinks we're leaving the theater."

In one quick motion, Pascal unstoppered the decanter and tipped it over a glass. "I wonder if I liked *Othello*. I do hope Mr. Richards attained the right touch of pathos in the closing scene." As she picked up the snifter, her fingers shook. She steadied the glass between both hands and, catching Mercy's stare, added, "*You're* not going to tell me I'm not old enough to drink, are you?"

"No," Mercy said. What she did plan to tell Pascal would be much more difficult for the girl to accept. "It was a rough night. The brandy will steady your nerves."

"*Dios mío!*" Kate threw up her hands. "This is what I fear always to happen. We stop now, eh *chicas*? No more Santana Rose. No more shooting. No more!" Her hand slashed through the air with a jangle of bracelets. "We stop. *Paremos.*"

Silently, Mercy wished she could follow Kate's advice. In the year and a half since Santana began her raids on Benoit, she'd never come so close to disaster. She'd always believed the information Kate fed her and what Mercy herself gleaned from Benoit and Gessler would keep her safe. Now, even that security had proven false.

Mercy sipped the brandy, thinking that her quest must continue, no matter how great the danger. But after tonight's close call she would never again risk her stepdaughter. The girl might hate her, might shun her attempts to mother her, but she was the closest Mercy had to a child of her own. In that wet copse of palmettos where she'd quieted Pascal's whimpers, Mercy had realized she must start taking responsibility for the girl.

She turned her gaze toward her stepdaughter. Pascal lingered over the table, examining Mercy with eyes that urged her to second Kate's counsel. So, Pascal wished Santana to stop as well. Mercy's hopes raised a notch. Perhaps the evening wouldn't be as difficult as she'd thought.

"I can't change course now, Kate," Mercy said softly.

Pascal's fingers curled tight around her glass, bleaching the skin beneath her nails white. Without another word, she tossed the brandy back and gulped. The strong liquor sent her into a fit of coughing.

She wants to stop, Mercy thought. *This time, I'll make her stop.*

When Pascal regained her composure, she made a show of sipping the brandy—without mishap—before returning to the divan. "I suppose for you the more dangerous the better," she said. "Where would be the thrill, otherwise?"

"I admit Gessler had more men than either Jean Claude or I anticipated. We made a mistake. We missed his scouts." *I don't have any choice. I must continue. But you, Pascal, still have choices.* "Perhaps Gessler's even getting cagier—"

"*El gordo* is getting cagier?" Kate lifted a perfectly penciled brow. "Or La Santana Rose is getting too confident? Tonight, after *el gordo* tell me about trap, I say to you, 'stay home, Santana. It is too dangerous with *la policía* waiting at the Little Temple.' But did you listen to Kate? You should have called off tonight."

"That was never an option."

"Not an option, eh? *Dios*!" Kate's blue eyes narrowed. "When you first come to me, Santana, and ask that I help, I think . . . this, a good woman, *muy buena*. She wants to help girls. She don't want no money . . . she gives *me* money to take care of things." Kate shook her head. "I think, I wish I have someone like Santana to help me when I forced to work with my mother in the cribs. A good woman, and very brave. But I never think you *loca*! Now, I

not so sure. Something drives you, Santana, something
that scares Kate."

Mercy set her brandy snifter on the table beside her.
"This isn't a game I can stop and start as the whim suits
me. There's too much at stake to quit now."

Kate waved her hand and her bracelets cascaded down
her arm. "*De verdad,* I do not care! I like you, Santana.
And I no want to see you hurt. I say, listen to me and *la
niña.*" Kate tossed her head toward Pascal. "You stop
now. Before it is too late."

"It's *too* dangerous to keep going," Pascal added.

Mercy rose to her feet. She picked up her mask from
the camel-head chair and studied it. "So I should stop
now." She looked at the two women. "Leave the girls so
they can be sold to bordellos or worse, be pandered to the
highest bidder or the cribs on Smoky Row?" She tossed
the mask on the table. "I can't. I can't do it, Kate. It *eats*
me up inside to see these girls and think that someone is
living off the money they bring. How can you close your
eyes to it, Kate? You've lived their nightmares."

Kate shrugged her shoulders. "I do what I can to help.
But I no risk my life! Santana, no one can stop *prostitu-
ción.* Not the church. Not the law. If you want, we think of
some other way to help. But I say it's time Santana Rose
disappear."

"Not quite yet."

In a trail of rose scent, Kate marched across the room.
A stream of Spanish curses floated over her shoulder. At
the doorway, she glanced back at Mercy and her blue eyes
softened. "I'll see to the new girls, eh?"

"Do we have enough money to get them back to their
homes?"

"*Sí.* Thanks to you *niña,* the only girls staying at Catalan
Kate's are the ones who choose to."

As Kate disappeared into the hall, Mercy turned and
prowled the room, restless. In her head, she quelled Kate's
predictions of disaster, not allowing doubt to upset the

plans she'd crafted. She was too close to fulfilling her goals to falter now.

"Haven't you risked enough?" Pascal asked in a quiet voice behind her.

Mercy stopped and turned to Pascal. "I'll be ready for Gessler next time. He can't stop me."

"And what about the man who nearly put a bullet in your back? Do you think he might have stopped you?" Pascal stared at Mercy as if she'd grown a second head. "Why, Mercedes? You have everything. Mistress of L'Isle des Rêves, beautiful clothes, money when you need it. Everyone of the *beau monde* admires you."

Mercy smiled sadly. How different her world was from what Pascal had just described. "You wouldn't understand." Nor could Mercy tell her stepdaughter of the gilded cage she lived in or what kind of monster had spawned the girl.

"I know my father and you don't"—she seemed to search for the right word—"care for each other. Is that what drives you to seek danger? For goodness sake, have an affair with Parks if you need excitement," she shouted. "But what you do now, it's plain madness!"

"Yes, Pascal, it *is* madness." Mercy hurried to the girl's side and knelt before the divan. "I'm driven by demons you wouldn't dream of—and simply insane to have ever allowed you to share in that madness. But no longer. From now on"—Mercy dropped her voice to a soothing tone—"Santana rides alone. And you stay home, where it's safe."

Pascal's glass slipped from her fingers. It rolled across the carpet, leaving a trail of brandy. "W-what?" A fear Mercy could not comprehend showed in her eyes. Pascal laughed hesitantly. "Are you joking?"

"It's done Pascal. Tonight was your last ride."

"But you can't do this. Not now. Not tonight. I saved you! If not for me, you'd have a bullet in your back or be in leg irons right now."

"I am truly grateful for what you did. But I can't risk your life as well as mine. Not anymore."

"No," she whispered, her eyes growing haunted. "It's something else. I did something wrong. What did I do wrong?"

"You did nothing wrong. *I* was wrong, wrong from the beginning to let you come along. You said it yourself, we were almost captured . . . or killed. Never have we come so close. Even Gessler's dull wits could bring me down."

"Then you stop too!"

She shook her head. "I can't."

"I thought . . ." Pascal seemed to shrink into the divan. "After what I did tonight, I believed . . ." A suspicious shine came to her eyes, as if tears glimmered in their depths. But then she threw her shoulders back, shrugging off her weakness. "I won't let you get rid of me. I'll tell my father. I'll tell him the whole thing. About Santana. About how you flirt with Parks. I can ruin you. I can still ruin you, just like I swore to do that first night!"

Mercy rose to her feet. "No, Pascal. You won't convince me this time."

"I . . . I—I will! I'll tell him."

Mercy said nothing.

Pascal jumped to her feet. "I'll do it!" she shouted. "I'll . . ." For a moment, Mercy thought Pascal would run from the room, but instead she dropped back to the divan, her head sinking to her chest. "You don't believe me."

Mercy shook her head. "A year ago, I thought you might. But tonight, you saved my life. No, I don't think you'll say anything to Benoit."

"I saved you." She choked back a breath. "I . . . *saved* you. How can you not want me?"

Mercy frowned. "Of course, I want you. I care for you, Pascal, and I don't want to see you hurt."

"It's not that! Stop pretending that you're doing this for my own good." Her dark eyes narrowed and she watched Mercy with the expression of a gambler trying one last role of the dice. "All right. I won't tell my father. I never would have. Not even that first time. I just said that because I wanted you to let me come with you, to prove myself." She stood and grabbed Mercy's hands. "Don't send me away," Pascal whispered. "Everyone sends me away."

Mercy glanced into Pascal's eyes and what she saw left her stunned. There was a desperate need in her gaze—and not just for acceptance. For the first time, Pascal allowed Mercy to peer beyond her defenses to the hunger driving the girl to be part of Santana's gang. All of Pascal's cries to stop taking chances echoed in Mercy's head, a grim accompaniment to tonight's intrepid rescue. With startling clarity, Mercy realized that it had never been the daring of riding with armed men that Pascal had sought. The girl who'd blackmailed her, who'd made Mercy's life hell for the past year—who had shunned every attempt at friendship—wanted Mercy's love.

"Please," Pascal repeated, squeezing Mercy's hands. "I want to stay with you. I want to help you."

Mercy shook her head, disbelieving of how blind she'd been. Pascal's mangled efforts to get Harlan's attention, all her misdeeds at school, acquired a completely different significance than Mercy had given them in the past. She thought of the countless times she'd been repelled by what she'd termed Pascal's dark side. Why wouldn't a girl whose mother died at birth, whose father ignored her scandalously, strive for love in such a contrary manner? The only attention she'd ever received *had* been through bad behavior. Such a girl might see blackmail as her only means to gain acceptance. Wouldn't scheming and force be the sole manner she would know to attain Mercy's admiration?

Oh, Pascal, how could I have been so wrong? All Mercy had ever wanted was someone to love. Why hadn't she realized that Pascal's temper and ill-treatment of her were a cry for help?

Because she's Benoit's child, a dark voice insinuated. *You see him in her eyes; she even looks like him. She's a part of him, evil like he is, and you want nothing to do with her.*

"No!" Mercy shouted her thoughts out loud, startling Pascal and herself by her vehemence. She wouldn't hold that horrible man against Pascal. She would never do that!

Pascal released a sob and stepped away. Quickly, Mercy realized what she'd just said and how it must sound. "Pascal, listen to me," she said, grabbing the girl by her shoulders. "I've been so wrong. We can be friends now . . . but not by risking your life. Never that."

"You can't fool me." Pascal pushed Mercy away, stumbling back. "You don't want me. Nobody wants me!"

"Pascal! That's not true—"

"Y-you'll be sorry. You'll see. You need me. You'll get caught or something awful will happen to you without me there to watch your back." She wiped the tears from her cheeks. "You think you don't need anyone and you're . . . so . . . wrong."

"Stop it Pascal. Please listen to me!"

Mercy reached out but Pascal slapped her hands away. She raced to the door. "To the devil with you, *maman*!" she shouted.

The slamming door rattled the pictures hanging by cords on the wall. Mercy reeled back, dropping to the divan. "What have I done?" she whispered.

The door creaked open. Mercy's heart propelled to her throat; hope dawned that Pascal had returned—but only Kate peeked inside.

"*El hombre* you wait for, he is here. Do you want to see him, *niña*? Or do I tell him to come back another time?" Kate's tone let Mercy know it was the latter response she hoped for.

Mercy pushed the heels of her palms against her eyes, taking a deep breath, then clasped her hands in front her. It was difficult enough to evade Benoit once a week for supposed visits to the theater and expeditions to the orphanage. If she delayed this meeting, she would not be able to come back until the following week, perhaps even later. "No, Kate. I'll see him." With a slew of promises to speak to Pascal at the first available moment, she put on her soft leather boots and picked up her mask, clearing her mind for the meeting ahead. "I don't have any choice."

Kate stared at her, disapproval etched on every line of her face. "You sleep with *perros,*" she said in a hiss just loud enough for Mercy to hear, "and you wake up with *pulgas,* Santana."

"I can take a few fleabites, Kate, but thanks for the warning."

As the door closed, Mercy tied the feathered mask over her face. She walked to the mirror hanging over the mantel and stared at the image reflected in the glass. Santana Rose, the fearless highway woman, had dedicated her life to stopping Benoit and helping his victims—and, by her single-minded determination to reach that goal, had sorely wounded a sixteen-year-old girl. How could she ever reach through that wall of hostility surrounding Pascal or ease the fears that caused the girl to refuse love because she expected rejection? Mercy knew she had to try, but right now, Santana's business again tied her hands.

Adjusting her wig, Mercy turned back toward the door and called for Kate to enter. She prepared to greet the man who sponsored her attempts to destroy Benoit, the only man in New Orleans who could divest Benoit of his ill-gotten fortune. The door opened and Kate signaled their guest inside.

With a jaunty step and a slick smile Mercy had come to despise, Harrison Sotheby stepped into the room.

There was actually little substance to him. He was just an inch short of average height and very thin. His outdated clothes didn't flatter; the excess of material seemed to hang on him. Unlike her husband, who flaunted wealth he did not have, Sotheby played the beggar. Between his thin lips, he chewed his ever-present cigar. It was difficult to believe this man had half the city in his power—even harder to conceive that she had joined forces with him. *All for a good cause,* she reminded herself.

"*Monsieur* Sotheby," she said in Santana's French accent when they were alone. "May I pour you a brandy?"

"I'll take a nip if you're offering."

Mercy passed him the glass. As always, his cadaverous finger lingered on her hand, making her wish she'd put on her gloves as well as her mask. When he'd taken a healthy swallow, he said, "I had an interesting meeting with Benny tonight. Did you know he's taken on a partner?"

"I make it my business to know everything about Benoit De Dreux."

"Yeah." His gray eyes gleamed in the gaslight. "I guess you do." He strolled about the room, examining it as if he'd not been there countless times. "I'm still trying to figure that one out. I love a mystery." His eyes scanned an oil painting of a Spanish gentleman and his horse. "You think up this deal to bankrupt Benny, come to me for help, but you let me keep the blunt so there's no money in it for you." His lower lip jutted out as he puzzled over his words. "You do good work for me in return, delivering my bribe money so I don't lose interest and stop bleeding Benny." He turned his gaze on her, watching her as carefully as the painting. "I wonder why?"

"I should think it is *évident, monsieur.* I seek revenge. Whatever it may cost me."

"Vengeance is mine, sayeth the Lord." He chuckled. "But why, Santana? What did poor ol' Benny do to you?"

"Let us say only that my family suffered a great loss because of *le salaud.*"

"Makes sense, I guess." He shrugged. "Me, I don't worry about that kinda shit. A waste of time."

"Perhaps that is because you are not French, *monsieur.* The French believe in honor."

"Oh, I like that, Santana. All that hot passion a' sizzling." He puffed on the cigar, his eyes skimming down her body, touching every inch. He wetted his lips with the brandy. "Benny doesn't stand a chance. And did he ever take the bait." Sotheby whooped with laughter.

Mercy turned her back on the man's lascivious gaze, suppressing a shudder of disgust. "Like many Creoles, Benoit De Dreux loves to gamble. A simple weakness to take advantage of, *non*?" She picked up the brandy decanter, ready to refill Sotheby's glass. "If you truly could rig the lottery, the prize *c'est incroyable,* a fortune. Of course, De Dreux would want a chance at that kind of wealth."

"Come June fifteenth, he ain't gonna have a plug nickel to his name."

"J'espère, monsieur. It is that day I live for."

As she poured, he grabbed her hand. The snifter still cupped in his palm, he stroked her fingers with the back of his knuckles. "Let me tell you about the day I live for, Santana."

The door slammed open. Mercy stepped back, yanking her hand from Sotheby's as Jean Claude and two of Santana's men burst into the room. They dragged behind them an unconscious man, sliding his dead weight across the peacock blues of the carpet as Kate followed at his feet.

"We got *problemas,* Santana. Your men caught this *gringo* trying to break in."

Mercy barely kept her grip on her glass and the decanter. At her feet, facedown on the Persian rug, his distinctive hair tucked inside a bowler hat, lay Reynard Parks. Out cold.

She dropped to his side and set aside the brandy bottle and snifter to examine his injuries. She carefully placed herself between Rey and Sotheby. Rey was a government agent. If Sotheby even suspected his connection with the law, he'd think nothing of slitting his throat. *"Mon Dieu,* Kate," she said. "What have you done?"

"Jean Claude said—"

"Prenez l'homme à la chambre à coucher," Mercy in-

structed her men while dealing Kate a look that warned
her to keep quiet. As her men carried Rey into the bedroom, Mercy stepped in front of Rey, blocking Sotheby's
view. "*Excusez-moi, monsieur,* this will take but a moment."

"What the hell's going on, Santana?" Sotheby growled.

"*Vraiment, monsieur,* just a moment," Mercy answered,
ushering Kate into the bedroom with her. With a reassuring smile as she closed the door, she added, "I will explain
everything when I return."

As the door clicked shut, Kate whispered, "What *rayos*
are going on, Santana?"

"Be careful with him!" Mercy said, ignoring Kate as her
men dumped Rey on the bed.

"*El gringo* is a spy! Jean Claude caught him picking the
lock with these." Kate thrust her hand in front of Mercy.
In the center of her palm rested a leather case with its flap
closure thrown back. Several metal picks of differing sizes
nestled within the wallet-size container. Mercy merely
skirted around the outstretched evidence.

Kate dogged her steps to the bedside. "Jean Claude said
he came off Sotheby's cab before trying to break in." Kate
ticked off the facts on her finger tips. "Jean Claude recognized him. He says *el gringo* works with your husband! You
hold up his coach just a week ago."

"All true, Kate, but it's not what you think." Mercy
brushed back the silver strands of hair matted with blood
just above Rey's ear. He'd been following Sotheby?
Though the Pinkerton's letter hadn't mentioned Sotheby's
name, she could well imagine Rey would be interested in
such a notorious criminal.

A low moan slipped past Rey's lips. Mercy backed away.
Her gaze sought out Jean Claude, who leaned negligently
against the bedpost.

"Listen to me," she told her number-one man. "You
must take him away from here, before he regains consciousness and realizes where he is." Riffling through

Rey's coat pocket, she found his wallet and threw it on the nightstand. "Hopefully, he'll just think he was robbed. Take him outside through the next room. I don't want Sotheby to see him again." As the men hurried to do her bidding, she added, "And be gentle, this time! Stand guard over him until he comes to his senses. I don't want him hurt any more than he has been." With another groan from Rey, the men hauled him out the door.

"What are you doing, *chica*?" Kate asked with a worried expression.

"I can't talk now, Kate. Please, just trust me."

Mercy stepped back into the salon and closed the door. She leaned against the oak, her arms crossed behind her. "*Pardon, monsieur* for this interruption," she said to Sotheby, who still prowled the salon's length. "The man is merely a spurned lover." She shrugged her shoulders in a Gallic gesture of nonchalance. "They caught him listening outside the door. He thinks I meet a man here and is jealous. His jealousy makes him do this *stupide* thing. Nothing more."

Sotheby smiled showing tobacco-stained teeth. "Can't say I blame him. But I don't want trouble, Santana."

"Do not give this man a second thought, *monsieur*. He is my problem alone."

Mercy picked up her brandy glass where she'd left it on the carpet and replaced the decanter on the table. She pressed her hands against the glass to keep them from shaking and gave Sotheby her most winsome smile. *Dear Lord,* she thought, *what else could go wrong tonight?*

As if in answer, Sotheby swaggered toward her. He tossed his cigar in the hearth and took her glass from her hands, placing it along with his on the mantel. "You know, I feel for the gent. Losing you must have been hard to take." He brushed his fingers along her exposed cheek beneath the mask. "You're a tempting piece of goods, Santana."

He turned her in his arms and pushed his full mouth

against hers. Santana struggled not to gag and forced herself to endure the man's embrace and sickening kiss. She wanted his mind off Rey. But when his hand pinched her breast, she could endure the humiliation of his touch no longer. With a great heave, she shoved him from her. Sotheby stumbled back against the table and overturned the brandy decanter. As he gained his feet, the look in his eyes said he wasn't finished with her.

Mercy reached for the knife she kept hidden in her boot and unsheathed the blade. "I hope, we can keep our relationship on a . . . professional level, *monsieur.*"

He laughed, eyeing the knife. "Whatever you say, Santana. I never argue with a toad-sticker." He reached in his coat and pulled out a small burlap bag. He tossed the sack of money at her. She caught it in one hand. "Senator Bickel will be waiting for you in his carriage at the rendezvous point near the River Road. There'll be another payment next week. We'll see each other then."

When she gave him a quick nod, Sotheby grinned. He took a step toward her. Mercy could feel sweat gathering between her breasts, stinging under her arms as he moved, hunting her. She held the knife tighter. Sotheby's smile never faltered. When he stood within an inch of the blade, he leaned forward until the steel tip touched his waistcoat. He cupped her chin in his hand, ignoring the knife. His breath reeked of brandy and stale cigar smoke.

"It's a real shame we can't deal with each other a bit nicer. Sure you won't reconsider?"

She forced an answering grin, but kept the knife steady. "Under the circumstances . . ." She nodded toward the bedroom door.

"Not such old news, then? Too bad." He stepped back and adjusted his coat before walking for the hall door. "Well, if you ever get tired of the gent, you just let me know." Reaching for the door, he snapped his fingers and spun back to her. "I almost forgot to tell you. When I met with Benny tonight"—Sotheby shook his head, chuckling as if the uncomfortable scene between them hadn't happened—"stupid idiot really thinks I'm rigging the lottery."

"I myself would not put it beyond your powers, *monsieur*."

"Oh, I'm not saying I couldn't do it. But why would I? I'm making a bloody fortune as it is." He took out a cigar from his coat pocket and bit off the end. "Listen, Benny asked me to meet this partner of his. A Reynard Parks. We're setting something up for next week. I don't think he'll be any problem, but I thought you might be interested. I'll let you know what happens." He chomped down on his cigar and winked. "Might even be a little extra money in it. See you later, Santana."

Mercy stood speechless and watched the door shut behind Sotheby, her knife still in her hand. She shut her eyes under the burden of yet another cartridge dropping into the chamber of tonight's calamities. He was going to meet with Rey—her spurned lover.

Kate charged through the door like a bull seeing red. "Start talking, *niña*! Since when does Santana Rose have a lover? What is this man to you that you protect him?"

Mercy ripped off her mask and flung it to the farthest corner of the room. She almost threw the knife, handle over blade, at the camel-headed chair, envisioning its carved handle sticking from the striped fabric. She sheathed the weapon against the temptation. Anger churned inside her, a frustration that sought control over a situation that had just spiraled out of her grasp.

She whirled around. "All right, dearest Kate. I shall explain everything." She extended her hands outward, a performer addressing her audience. "I present to you Santana Rose the crusader! Santana, who steals from the wicked and delivers their booty to the hands of the needy. The advocate of the poor." She flung back her cape dramatically. Its folds brushed against her hips. "A woman who brings justice where there is none!" The frenzied energy inside her threatened to explode with the force of her doubts. The faces of those she'd failed danced before her vision: Laura, Beth, Pascal, Rey. "A woman who brings nothing but peril to the people she loves! Protect him? Kate, I pray to God I haven't exposed him to great danger."

Kate frowned, shaking her head. "*Chica*. What are you talking about?"

Mercy paced the room. She tried to recall each detail since her men dragged Rey past the threshold. "I think I convinced Sotheby." She spoke low and to herself. "He was certainly jealous, I saw it in his eyes when he kissed me." She pivoted and retraced her steps. "The hat covered most of Rey's hair. Only the temples showed. Many men have graying temples. I'm not even sure Sotheby saw his face."

Kate grabbed Mercy's arm, hauling her to a stop. "Who *is* he, Santana?"

Mercy stared at Kate. "A spy. An agent." She backed away from her friend's touch. "Perhaps even a man I could love."

"*Dios mío!*"

There was terror in Kate's voice. It radiated through Mercy and added to her own uncertainties until she forced herself to forget those considerations. Whether she had truly fallen in love with the Silver Fox or was merely bewitched by her fantasies about him was not the issue to face this night. The precautions she'd taken might not be enough to save him from Sotheby.

"I must protect him, Kate." She had to make sure Rey wouldn't be recognized. "I've got to stop that meeting."

Chapter 9

"God be with us! What happened to ye?"

MacAfee wrapped an arm around Rey, anchoring him to the Scotsman's side as they stumbled up the stairs. Passing the open salon, he guided Rey into his room, careful to match his steps to the injured man's. As Mac kicked open the door and half-carried Rey to his bed, a tide of Gaelic curses sputtered under his breath.

With a low groan, Rey settled back against the counterpane. He thought he'd never survive the carriage ride to Bizy. With each rut in the road, his head had erupted with an explosion of pain—once almost sliding into the beckoning darkness of unconsciousness. As Mac hovered over him anxiously, helping him off with his coat, Rey touched the lump behind his ear and winced.

"Here, now. Leave that be. I'll get something to clean ye up a bit."

While Mac emptied the pitcher into the washbasin, Rey knocked off his hat and surveyed the room. Through the door, he could see across the central reception area to a small section of the salon. Though it was not quite morning, both parlor and bedchamber had been swept clean, the furniture rearranged, the cobwebs gone. Despite the overwhelming pain in his head, he was impressed. Bizy looked almost habitable.

"You've been busy."

"I had little to do but wait fer ye and the laddie to show

up." Mac hustled back to Rey and pressed a wet cloth against his head.

Rey sucked a breath and grabbed the cloth from his valet. "Christalmighty, Mac. I've had enough torture for one day, thank you."

"Och, I knew in me gut I shouldna leave ye to the task alone! Ye look like ye've been given a good hiding. Did Sotheby find ye out?"

"No. I'd be a dead man if he had." Rey touched the rag to his head, gritting his teeth against the sting. "I was jumped from behind and my wallet stolen."

"Bloody hell! Ye got jack-rolled?"

Rey nodded, then stopped the motion when a blade of pain sliced down his neck from his head. "I woke up a good distance from where I last remember standing, my head pounding like someone had taken a sledgehammer to it." He parted his hair back and dabbed at the dried blood behind his ear.

Seeing his contortions, Mac swiped the cloth from Rey and bent over him to do the job. "It's a bonnie miracle yer still alive, maun. Let's hope the lad faired better."

The moan of the rear entrance opening was followed by a loud bang as the door slammed shut. The sound of footsteps echoed up the stairs.

"Speak of the devil," Mac said.

By the noise Harlan was making as he bounded up the stairs, Rey guessed the Pinkerton was taking them two at a time. A surge of relief spread through him. After his own close call, he'd be glad to see the younger man safely home.

Harlan swept into the bedroom, an energetic force that seemed to reach every corner of the chamber. But when he saw Rey, he stopped in his tracks. "*Mon Dieu!* What happened to you?"

"I had a little trouble at a place called"—Rey slanted a glance at Mac—"Catalan Kate's."

Mac's eyebrows shot up. His hand holding the cloth stilled. "Kate's ye say?"

"Yes, Mac. Kate's. After I overheard Sotheby tell De Dreux that he had another meeting set for tonight, I decided to follow him and see what I could find out. He went straight to Catalan Kate's. I was knocked out before I had a chance to find out what he was up to."

Harlan tossed off his hat and dropped into the overstuffed armchair, whistling softly through his teeth. "*Eh bien*. That's the place where Gessler spilled his guts—where Santana has her spies."

MacAfee frowned. "Perhaps he was looking for a bit of sport? He wouldna want to be telling De Dreux he'd a 'meeting' with a soiled dove."

"Com'on, *mon vieux*," Harlan argued. "It's too big a coincidence."

"I have to agree with Harlan. Kate's seems to be a hub for more than one criminal. Mac, I think it's important you keep acquainted with that concert-saloon."

"Aye." MacAfee nodded, his eyes unfocused as he walked back to the washbasin, deep in thought.

"What did you hear 'bout De Dreux?" Harlan asked.

"Nothing I didn't know before," Rey said. "De Dreux has developed some healthy skepticism about Sotheby's lottery scheme since yesterday's vote in the legislature. Sotheby tried to convince him the governor wouldn't sign the bill outlawing the Louisiana Lottery. He even suggested the legislation would get thrown out in court. I think De Dreux is in so deep, he can't afford *not* to believe Sotheby. When De Dreux mentioned setting up a meeting next week with his new partner, Sotheby didn't waste any time asking for more money."

Harlan snorted in disgust. "The man's greedier than a gator out of hibernating."

"So it would seem. What about the reporter? How did your meeting go?"

Harlan smiled. "Sweet as a praline. Sotheby's man goes

regularly to the post office to pick up several parcels, *tu comprends*? The reporter says it's all lottery stuff. He told me the man's due back to the post next month. I plan to be there. Maybe Sotheby's boy might misplace a package or two, hein?"

"Good work," Rey said. "If I'm right, Sotheby's using the Louisiana Lottery to pass his counterfeit bills. This could be a big break in the case. We'll shut down Sotheby's operation one way or another."

"And De Dreux?"

"Don't ye worry about him, laddie," Mac said, ringing the cloth over the basin. "If all bowls roll right, we'll get De Dreux as well."

Though Harlan's pleased expression niggled at Rey, he staunched his doubts about the Pinkerton. Tonight, Harlan had proven his worth. Though he'd complained about his assignment, he'd done his job and met the reporter while Rey followed De Dreux. Harlan's plan to snatch one of Sotheby's packages from the post office was a good one. Even Mac seemed to be warming up to the Pinkerton.

Taking the moist cloth Mac offered, Rey scanned the newly straightened room. His gaze stopped at the foot of the bed where a pile of mail waited. A familiar tension gripped him as he stood, steadying himself with a hand on the counterpane. Catching Mac's eye, he handed the rag back to his valet.

Nan's stationery peeked out from the stack of mail.

"It came with our things from L'Isle des Rêves after ye left," Mac said, knowing exactly what held Rey's attention. As Rey picked up the letter, Mac dropped the cloth to the bedside table with a sigh and turned to Harlan. "Come on, laddie. We'd best be findin' our own beds."

Harlan rose, his eyes holding Rey's for a moment. Then both the Pinkerton and Mac walked to the door. Rey's heart pounded with more force than his head as he fingered the letter, staring at the seal.

"Ye'll be all right, Rey?"

His eyes followed the sound of Mac's voice. His valet stood half-in, half-out of the chamber, holding the door against his chest, his brown eyes set in a look of concern.

"I'll be fine, Mac. You get some rest. We're due back at L'Isle des Rêves by noon."

Rey waited until he was alone before unfolding the paper. Though he looked forward to these messages, filled with news of his family and Christopher, Nan's letters always brought on a disturbing melancholy. This time was no different. With her usual wit, Nan described the antics of his family. His niece had beaten her two brothers in a foot race, taunting the boys unmercifully for days. Aunt Clair had taken up phrenology—despite Mother's advice that a person could learn nothing about themselves by studying the lumps on their heads. Christopher had lost another tooth, and for the first time he'd questioned the tooth fairy's existence, until Nan assured him that only little boys who *really* believed received a silver dollar under their pillow.

The last paragraph contained Nan's usual tirade about his neglect of his son, tempered by her concern for Rey and the loneliness he must feel. She knew her brother loved Christopher dearly. At the bottom of the page, scrawled in large print, Chris had penned his own message.

Nana says you are not to miss my birthday and I should tell you that myself. But I think it is all right if you are too busy this year, though you do give me the best presents and I will miss you very much. Could we celebrate when you come back? Uncle Michael showed me how to play billiards, but Greg and Tim shoot much better than I. Hurry home Daddy. I love you.

Rey folded the paper along its creases and sat down on the bed. The throb at his head no longer concerned him.

So, he had Christopher's permission to miss his birthday.

He tried to recapture the anger that had consumed him when he'd first seen Sotheby that evening—but all he could think about was Christopher, a child who'd lost his mother, and who, for the past year, had seen his father only for short visits in the station before Rey mounted the next train out of town.

I think it is all right if you are too busy this year.

How simply Chris had offered forgiveness for his father's neglect.

Rey lay Nan's letter carefully on the bed beside him and buried his face in his hands.

Harlan looked across the sea of sugarcane at the workers battling the weeds that threatened the young plants. As half a dozen guards watched on, convicts dressed in thin cotton pants and shirts bent over the neat rows of cane with long hoes. Each guard carried a bat, a six-foot-long leather strap weighted with lead on one end, and used it without hesitation. Right now, the work was light. Come cutting season, these poor bastards and others would arrive early each day, beaten, half-starved and ill-clothed, forced to work until after sundown or feel the whip of the bat.

A bitter taste filled Harlan's mouth as he studied the workers. This was a group of Gessler's finest—prisoners, all of them. Just like his brother Jules had been.

How well Harlan remembered the day they'd come to tell his *mère* that they'd found Jules. The family had been so happy, his mother, his two sisters, and younger brother. The whole village had turned up to see Jules back. But Harlan's joy had been cut short when he laid eyes on what was left of his oldest brother. Jules, the hulking youth who'd towered over Harlan's five feet eleven inches, outweighing him by a good two stone, had been transformed into a thin and frail waif who gasped for each breath as if it might be his last. The *traiteuse,* the healer his mother had sent for, said Jules had been beaten to within an inch of his life, that the bottoms of his feet were so cut and infected, he wouldn't be able to walk for months. As it turned out, he hadn't lived long enough to see his feet healed.

Harlan shut his eyes against the image of his brother, the purple bruises on his ribs, the bleeding sores on his face and hands. Within a few weeks of finding him, they'd lost Jules to a fever. But not before he'd told Harlan his stories. He'd been sentenced and tried by a local magistrate for riding the rails without paying, even though Jules swore over and over he'd been given a ride in the engine cab for free. He'd been forced to live in a shack with twenty other men, eating putrid sowbelly. Each morning before the sun rose, the guards would wake him and make him and the other prisoners run the ten miles to work at L'Isle des Rêves, De Dreux's plantation. And the beatings —always with the bat, the leather stinging, the lead weights cutting, as the other prisoners held Jules down. Harlan still woke up in the middle of the night, soaked with sweat, thinking he could hear his brother screaming in his sleep, "Not the bat. *Mon Dieu,* I can't take anymore."

Harlan pivoted away from Gessler's convicts. He focused on the shacks where De Dreux housed his regular work force and their families year round, dropping his fisted hands to his side and deepening his breathing. It had taken him six years, but he was finally going to make that bastard pay for Jules's death. Six years of training and waiting. Revenge against De Dreux had been his whole reason for joining the Pinkertons.

"Mr. Everard!"

The shout carried over the whistling breeze. Harlan turned and watched Pascal De Dreux running toward him. She held her skirt bunched in her hands, above her ankles, so she wouldn't trip. Even at this distance, her face looked shining with happiness. Her long burgundy hair trailed behind her as she ran.

His enemy's daughter. The sole heir to De Dreux's fortune.

Last night, Rey had warned him not to involve the girl, but in this one instance Harlan thought the Silver Fox was wrong. The Pinkerton Detective Agency had taught him to use every advantage in order that justice be done. Oh, he wouldn't purposely hurt *la petite,* but if she had information he could use against De Dreux, nothing would prevent Harlan from getting it.

Pascal pitched to a stop before him. She was out of breath and couldn't talk. Her face shone with excitement as she put her hand on his coat sleeve. "Do you want me to show you around?" she asked when she got her wind back.

Today, her lovely dark eyes looked red, not the clear gaze she'd had yesterday while they'd walked through the French Market together. He frowned. Had she been crying? Or had she stayed out all night, riding half-cocked through the swamps to the conjo woman's again?

As if catching the disapproval in his thoughts, Pascal stepped back, dropping her hand from his sleeve. "I thought . . . I mean . . . Yesterday, in town, you seemed interested in the plantation. I thought maybe you'd like to see a little of it."

Harlan forced himself to smile. "I'd like that well, *mam'selle.*"

Her face lit up like a taper and she took his hand in hers. With a tug, she led him forward, skipping backward in front of him, watching him with a delighted expression. "I'll show you the sugar mill. The foreman said we just got a new vacuum pan. But we still use the open-kettle for part of the sugar making. The vacuum pan only adds to the quality and the quantity of the sugar, you see."

Without so much as taking a breath, the girl launched into a narrative about modern technological advances in sugar-making. When she diverted into the genealogy of Ribbon cane, the variety of cane used on most plantations in Louisiana, Harlan stopped mid-stride.

"I thought you told me yesterday you didn't know much 'bout the plantation?"

She looked down at the toes of her shoes. A pink flush crept up her face, making her look quite pretty. "Well, I've done a little reading since then."

"Sounds like you've read a whole library."

She laughed. "Not a *whole* library."

Her shy giggles made him grin, a genuine smile this time. "Is that how you got those dark circles under your eyes, *petite*?" Harlan drew a faint line below her lower lashes then tapped her nose with the tip of his finger. "You stay up all night reading 'bout sugar-making for me?"

Her flush deepened. She rocked back on her heels, looking a little less sure of herself. "Well you just reminded me that I should be more familiar with the family business." She bit her lip, then blurted out, "Will you be attending the dinner dance here next week?"

Harlan's grin widened. "*Mais,* yeah. It's in my honor, isn't it? Mine and Rey's."

She clasped her hands in front of her, and let out a breath as if his answer had taken a great load off her mind. "I just wanted to make sure." She turned on the balls of her feet, her eyes taking in the cane fields around them. Her happy expression lifted Harlan's own spirits and he was surprised to discover he found Pascal De Dreux very attractive. She slanted him a look from beneath her lashes and her expression turned coy. "You know, Mr. Everard," she said wetting her lips. She didn't meet his eyes as she spoke. "Some day this will all belong to me. It's my legacy. And when I marry, it will all go to my husband."

Harlan's smile vanished. She was trying to lure him with the possibility of riches. He pictured his brother. Beaten. Bruised. Above Pascal's dark head, he could see the row of convicts hunched over the cane.

With more force than he'd meant to use, he grabbed her hand and pulled her to his side. "*Allons,* Pascal. Let's go back."

She almost stumbled before she managed to match her steps to his. He steered her back to the house, disgusted with himself. She was just a child. Why vent his anger on *la petite*? She wasn't responsible for the acts of her father and probably too naïve to know how the man made his money.

"It's getting late," he said, trying to explain his previous harshness. "I've a meeting with your father back at the house."

"All right," she said, skipping to keep up with him, but her voice sounded subdued.

The Mask

Men take more pains to mask than mend.

———

—Benjamin Franklin,
Poor Richard's Almanack, 1757

Chapter 10

Mercy looked around at the crush of guests at L'Isle des Rêves. The small dinner party she'd planned to introduce Reynard Parks and Harlan Everard had blossomed into a soiree attended by New Orleans's high society. She had, as always, spared no expense. The ballroom shimmered with candles. Flowers arranged in Chinese vases lined the walls, filling the room with the sweet fragrance of hot house roses. Champagne and delicacies exquisite enough to tempt the most jaded palate awaited guests in the banquet room across the hall. The crush of guests and the incessant buzz of their chatter pronounced the gala a success. How odd that watching the dancing couples swirl past on the parquet floor, Mercy experienced not an ounce of satisfaction for her social coup.

She twisted the double strand of pearls around her finger. In the past, she'd taken enormous pleasure in spending Benoit's money. Such expenditures brought her closer to her ultimate goal: her husband's bankruptcy and complete incapacitation. But over the last week—since the night she'd almost lost Pascal in the swamps and exposed Rey to Sotheby—she'd been torn in too many directions to allow herself even one minute of jubilation.

All her attempts to reach through Pascal's hostility had failed. The girl wouldn't even speak to her, claiming she had nothing to say to Mercy unless she allowed Pascal back into Santana's gang. Strangely, the pain of Pascal's rejection lingered like a miscarriage, another lost attempt at even a thread of happiness. To her concerns about her stepdaughter Mercy added fears about Rey's meeting with Sotheby. Had Sotheby seen Rey? Should she take the risk and intervene, or was the danger to Rey only imaginary? So far, she'd heard nothing to confirm that a meeting with Sotheby had been set. She was afraid she'd become conspicuous in her attempts to garner information from Benoit and Gessler.

Releasing the pearls, Mercy smoothed her hands down the coral faille of her gown. She fingered the red poppies that caught up the square train of ivory Sicilienne and turned down an offer to dance with a polite smile, pleading fatigue. She'd spent the last week questioning herself and her decisions. Laura and Beth. Certainly it was farfetched to believe that she would ever find her friends after so many years of fruitless effort. Yet, Benoit's threats that he knew their whereabouts made it impossible for Mercy to give up now. Pascal. Mercy still couldn't forgive herself for not realizing her stepdaughter's true motives for blackmailing her. Time and again, she wondered if perhaps she hadn't allowed some of her hatred for Benoit to prejudice her against his daughter. And Rey. Her romantic notions about the secret agent were at worst dangerous, and at best silly and certainly ill-timed. Yet, even as she dismissed her attraction, repeating her decision to tell him that a relationship between them was impossible, she found herself searching the ballroom for his tall figure.

Rey leaned against the doorjamb behind Mercedes, watching her as she scanned the dancing couples. An almost empty glass of champagne dangled from between two of his fingers. Was it really only a week ago that he'd told Mac all the reasons why an affair with the charming Madame De Dreux would cure what ailed him? How simple he'd made it sound. How easily he'd convinced himself. She had a lover. De Dreux thought nothing of his wife's promiscuity or he'd have put a stop to it rather than allow her the considerable freedom Rey had witnessed over the past two weeks. Or perhaps she was merely discreet enough that De Dreux had no notion of her assignations. Whatever the case, both arguments assured him that, with a little caution, he was safe in courting De Dreux's wife. The lady desired him; she'd made that abundantly clear. An affair had never sounded so simple, so appealing.

Opportunity, desire, lack of risk—oh, he'd made it sound easy all right. But after Christopher's letter, when he'd sat, clearheaded, and mulled over the personal cost of his decision to put Sotheby behind bars, Rey had seen through his flimsy arguments to their core truth. He wanted Mercedes De Dreux, in a way he'd never wanted a woman, even Sophie. His need was mindless, and confusing—a physical hunger that did not abate no matter how he tried to control it. His desire for her frightened him because he'd never before fallen into self-deception. No agent did and stayed alive. If he dared to get involved with De Dreux's wife, he had to keep his eyes open to the dangers, not discount them.

He'd decided then to stay away from the lady. And until tonight, he'd managed to do just that. But now, like a man watching a stranger, Rey saw himself push off the doorjamb and place his glass on a passing servant's tray. She was an addiction he'd played with, then sought to leave off when he'd sensed the danger—only to find caution had come too late. Ignoring the voice that commanded him to stop before he did something he regretted, he walked toward Mercedes. Her hair looked the same color as the champagne under the candlelight. It tumbled down her back, pinned with ivory combs in multiple layers of curls. The advice and decisions of the past week scrambled from his head at the thought of how those champagne curls would feel dripping through his fingers.

The touch on her arm caught Mercedes by surprise. She turned, prepared to dismiss yet another expectant dance partner until she saw Rey. Her blithe excuse faded from her lips. A week. They hadn't been alone together since the carriage ride. One simple week that had lasted a lifetime. She'd avoided him, true, afraid that once she saw him her well-intentioned plans would be forgotten. During their carriage ride, he'd let her know he wanted her, had asked her to leave her supposed lover. It was on the tip of her tongue to answer him, "No, I can't do this." But she wanted to. She wanted to very much.

He took her hand. Without protest, she followed him to the dance floor and walked into his embrace as the lilting beat of a Viennese waltz swelled around them. She'd never been so close to him and her skin tingled where he touched her hand and waist. She could smell the soft pine scent of the cologne he favored.

"I believe we have some unfinished business."

Nothing had prepared Mercy for his seductive whisper. Desire flowed sweetly through her as he brought his mouth close, close enough for his breath to caress her neck. She nodded, unable to speak.

"Come to Bizy, Mercedes."

His softly spoken words were more than an invitation. They were a call, a demand that affected her physically, almost stinging in its intensity. *Come to me, come to me.* Mercy shut her eyes, silencing the message of his gaze as well as the echo of his voice. So many things had changed since that carriage ride when she'd courted the look of desire in Rey's eyes—her relationship with Pascal, the danger to Rey. It was as if she teetered on the edge—of triumph, or disaster, she didn't know which anymore.

His hand under her chin urged her to look at him. She opened her eyes, saw he expected an answer. She tried to keep the regret from her voice. "I can't." She couldn't allow herself the luxury of loving him.

His expression stayed exactly the same, almost calming in its power to keep her gaze. "Can't? Or don't want to?"

"Is the difference so important, Rey? Both amount to the same thing. My answer is still no."

"There's a world of difference between the two. Say you don't want to, and I'll leave you now and never bother you again. But tell me you can't, and Mercedes"—he squeezed her hand and tucked her nearer as he turned—"I'll make sure to change your mind."

The parquet floor shifted. The vaulted ceiling twisted by more degrees than Rey's fluid turns allowed. *I'll change your mind. I'll change your mind. Come to me.* It seemed so tempting. For once, another besides Mercy would make the decision. Someone else could shoulder the burden of the choice and its consequences. All her life—for Beth and Laura, as Santana Rose—Mercy alone had been the one responsible. How enticing to be convinced, to make Rey accountable for changing her mind after she'd done the right thing and said no.

She could feel the tension of his shoulders beneath the cloth of his frock coat where her hand rested. The fox ready to spring. There was a slight smile on his lips. Only his eyes showed her answer mattered.

"Say it, Mercedes," he coaxed. "I can *see* your answer. I can almost smell its scent. Say it, love. Just say it."

She dropped her chin to his chest, leaned against him as they danced. She thought of the honeyed weakness only Rey could bring her, a softness at the core of her, a passion strong enough to conquer her memories of Benoit's abuses. *I deserve this. I deserve this one chance.* She'd read about love. She'd seen it in the eyes of other women. Even Kate had spoken of it, long-ago and lost but still a cherished memory that brought a smile to her lips. Mercy's life had been filled with hardship and pain. She wanted to smile like Kate when she thought of Rey—not spend her life wondering if she'd given up too much for the path she'd chosen.

She brought her face up. He watched, waited.

"Change my mind, Rey. I want you to change my mind."

Before she could protest, he led her toward the balcony doors. They were so close, only a step away, she wondered whether their position hadn't been calculated throughout their dance as he steered her to the exit. To an observant bystander, they would appear to be nothing more than hostess and guest, going outside for a breath of fresh air. Rey took her arm and placed it on his, wending their way through the crush of guests on the gallery that wrapped around the house. He slowed when they turned the corner and reached a pair of French doors. The sound of voices drifted toward them, but no one remained in sight.

He opened the doors and pulled back the curtain. With his hand around her waist, he plunged them into the darkness of an empty guest room.

"Oh, no, Rey. Please, not here—"

His mouth covered hers in a sweeping kiss, flooding her with confused emotions. Passion, fear, excitement, all three rippled through her, taking the strength from her arms as she pushed against his chest. She arched back, but rather than granting Mercy the space she'd intended, the movement only pressed her hips against his. He coaxed her lips to open with light brushes of his tongue. *No. I can't. It's too much,* she argued with the building sensations. But the tangy sweetness of champagne and desire nudged at her until she parted her lips, tentatively at first, then without hesitation. Mercy felt like water rushing past a break in the levee. The release was so powerful, she knew there was no turning back. He savored her, giving her a taste of him. She wrapped her arms around Rey, digging her fingers into his hair. She forgot caution and focused only on the touch of his mouth. She heard herself whimper as she pressed her breasts against his hard strength. She couldn't seem to get close enough. Marie Laveau's words flitted through her consciousness. *Darkness seeks the light.*

The music from the gallery came as a low whisper on the wind, as faint and tempting as the smell of magnolias in spring. Rey picked her up and carried her to the bed. Her mouth covered his in frantic kisses, never stopping as he lowered her onto the counterpane. The mattress dipped as his body followed. The planes of his chest and his thighs fitted against her and a tempting hardness settled where her thighs met, nudging her, prompting her to press closer. The curtains fluttered. The light of the moon reached but a few feet beyond the French doors. She couldn't see. It made his touch all the stronger a sensation.

His mouth trailed down to the tip of her chin and his palm cupped her breast. As his thumb stroked its curve and his lips cherished her neck, Mercy gasped. Rey captured her breath with his mouth.

"I won't stay away, Mercedes."

Her hands traveled up his shoulders. Her fingers crushed the material of his coat to the muscle. Squeezing. Clutching. "I don't want you to."

He brushed his lips against hers, once, twice, again, his touch an enticement. As he pushed himself up and balanced on his hands, his breath teased her neck. "Come to Bizy."

"Yes." She reached for him, hungry still for his taste. "Yes, I'll come."

His kiss became a promise, slow, lingering, an assurance of what awaited her. Gradually, he pushed away, hovering inches above her. He caressed her cheek with the back of his fingers. "I'll be waiting."

She heard the bed ropes creak beneath her as he moved off the bed. In a flash of light, he pulled the curtains back and stepped beyond them. The moonlight crowned his head from behind, shading his face as he stood at the threshold. "And Mercedes—" As she watched, a most extraordinary smile curved his lips, gripping her heart. It was the kind of smile she imagined a man might give his first love. "Make it soon."

The curtain dropped and she heard his footsteps fade down the gallery.

* * *

With the stealth of a Cajun hunter, Harlan followed Pascal. He made sure to keep just far enough behind *la petite;* it wouldn't do to be spotted. He smiled as she raced past her father's study, the long train of her ball gown trailing behind her. How sweetly she'd asked if he cared to drink something stronger than the champagne he'd been served. Just a short nod of his head and she'd fled faster than a fish off a hook.

A woman with a purpose, for sure.

And he suspected he knew what she had in mind, *mais oui.*

Now, he just had to catch her at it.

She entered the upstairs library where he'd visited her father just the day before to arrange a meeting with Sotheby. The girl was so busy going about her business, she didn't even bother to look behind her to see if anyone followed. Harlan just walked in and watched her run to the walnut shelves. She pushed back a set of heavy leather tomes. Behind the books, she brought out a familiar blue bottle—the same bottle she'd gotten from the conjo woman. Harlan waited in the shadows as she dashed to the decanter of brandy with her prize.

Pascal couldn't believe it. All week she'd worried about this moment and now everything was progressing as smoothly as the silk of her emerald Worth gown. She'd hidden the love potion here in the library earlier, then volunteered to bring Harlan a brandy. He was much too manly to be satisfied with the champagne or the syllabub served at the soiree. All she had to do now was lace the drink with the love potion.

Pascal finished pouring the brandy and raised the blue bottle. Seeing the cryptic voodoo markings, she suffered a moment of misgiving. Uncorking the bottle, she took a cautious sniff and wrinkled her nose. Absolutely vile! She wondered if she dared give Harlan the love potion after all.

As it had for the last week, the scene with Mercedes returned with painful clarity. Immediately a sharp sting came to Pascal's eyes. Her days as one of Santana's gang were over. She no longer held the leverage that had allowed her for the first time to belong—even if it were only to a gang of criminals. Her throat choked up as she thought of that last time in the swamps, when she'd disarmed Gessler's man. She'd finally seen the admiration she'd worked so hard to earn in her stepmother's eyes. She'd always thought Mercedes's esteem would be reward enough for any danger, that once she had it, her stepmother's love would naturally follow.

That's why her rejection had hurt so much.

Pascal stared hard at the voodoo bottle. Lena had said a strong liquor. She put the cork stopper down, ready to empty the bottle into the glass of brandy.

Hard fingers dug into her arm at her elbow, preventing her from dumping the love potion into the brandy glass. Pascal gasped, hoping against hope it was Mercedes, even her father, who held her arm.

"I asked for brandy . . . not poison," came the low voice behind her.

For the count of one breath, Pascal wanted the floorboards to open up and swallow her. Lord in heaven, of all the people to find her . . . Harlan! She pivoted slowly, thinking desperately of an explanation for what she was doing.

"It's not poison," she said breathlessly.

"Non?" Harlan picked up the hand holding what he already knew was a love potion, but frowned when he saw the voodoo markings. On the other hand, who the hell knew what was really inside?

Pascal sent a silent thanks that Lena did not label the bottle's contents in simple script. How horrible if Harlan should find out just how low she would stoop to get a man's love.

"What is it then?" he asked, his blue eyes boring into

hers. He'd make the girl think twice before she tried a
trick like this again.

"Nothing that could harm you, I swear it!"

"Really?" He took her hand and guided it to the glass.
He forced her to dump the liquid into the brandy. Releasing her, he took a step back. His normally friendly countenance hardened into uncompromising lines. "Then you
drink it, *chère.*"

Pascal's heart rushed to her throat. That's all she
needed! She was already madly in love with Harlan. What
would happen if she, and not Harlan, swallowed the potion?

She looked up into the challenge of his blue eyes, knowing she would find no sympathy if she refused. She would
rather die than tell him what the bottle truly contained
and why she couldn't drink it. Yet, the hardness in his face
told her she would not leave the room without some sort
of explanation. She had to prove she wouldn't hurt him.

Slowly, she raised the glass to her mouth.

Harlan slapped the glass out of her hands just as the rim
touched her lips. The snifter fell with a thud to the carpet
and rolled away. He'd thought to give her a taste of her
own medicine, make her confess what she was up to. But
the stupid girl really meant to drink the concoction rather
than admit what she'd done. *La petite* thought it was only a
love potion, but Harlan didn't trust the witch's brew. He'd
seen that old conjo woman with her strange yellow eyes.
No telling what was in the bottle.

La petite stood like she'd taken root. Her eyes looked
big, larger than he'd ever seen them. They were a dark
brown color and suited her olive skin and burgundy hair.
Meaning only to reassure her, he raised his hand to the
red locks held back in a net of gold. Problem was, *la petite*
was real pretty. He frowned as he saw his tanned fingers
brush her cheek, then caress the soft skin. He reminded
himself that she'd almost poisoned him, unintentionally
true, but the harm would have been the same if he'd drunk

the mixture. Still, it was hard to stay mad at her for trying to buy his love. He dropped his hand to her chin, cupping the delicate curve in his palm. Her breath came faster past her full red lips.

She'd wanted loving so bad, had been willing to buy it through black magic. Refusing to think of the consequences, Harlan bent down to her tempting mouth. What's the harm in giving her one kiss?

Pascal felt the firm lips brush against hers tentatively at first, just a featherlike touch, then press more firmly. Slowly, his arms wound around her waist and pulled her against him. No one had ever kissed her before. No man had even hugged her.

Tentatively, she dared to touch his face. She stroked his hair with her fingertips, seeing that it was indeed as soft as she'd always thought. She leaned into him, arching up to receive his kiss. *Thank you,* she sent the silent message. *Thank you for this.*

Harlan pulled back from the girl's embrace. Something had knocked at his heart when she'd finally kissed him back. She was just a kid, and yet, her kiss had been strangely adultlike, as if she'd waited a lifetime to give it.

He glanced down at her, confused. She looked calm, almost at peace, while his heart hammered like a clock wound too tight. She looked older too, not like the girl who had just tried something as silly as putting a love potion in a man's drink. As he studied her, she smiled, and he realized for the first time that she'd shed a tear. He touched the drop sliding down her chin, almost needing to make sure it was real.

Pascal took his hand and brought it to her lips. She kissed his palm then looked at him as if he'd granted her the world.

"Thank you," she whispered.

An unfamiliar heaviness settled in Harlan's heart as

Pascal laced their fingers together and pulled him to the door.

"Come on," she said over her shoulder. "Let's go dance."

Chapter 11

MacAfee nestled his face between the two generous globes of womanly warmth and inhaled the scent of roses. The rhythmic strokes of ten soft fingers rippled up and down his bare back and he sighed appreciatively.

"Qué hombre," he heard Kate whisper. Mac grinned. He didn't understand the words exactly but he kenned their meaning well enough. A good week it had taken for the Spanish lassie to warm up to him, but once she had, she'd stoked a fire in Mac like none he'd ever experienced before.

Her hands traveled up his arms, caressing his biceps before giving the muscles of his shoulders a squeeze. She cupped his face in her palms and tilted his head off the nest of her bosom, making him look into her eyes. They shone as blue as the deepest waters of Loch Maree.

"Juanito." A catlike smile curled her lips. "You very stubborn *hombre*. I am one lucky *mujer* you no give up so easy. I pray for a good crop at Bizy so you stay a long time here."

He leaned forward while he curved his large hands around her bottom and kissed her full on the mouth. "Ye needn't worry about my leaving, lass. I never give up when the prize is worth the effort," he whispered between kisses. "And you, lassie, are a priceless treasure."

She dodged his kiss and slapped him playfully. "Why do you call me this 'lassie'? I am a woman of forty—" She stopped, then grinned wickedly as her hands crept between their bodies. "A woman of much experience, *no*?"

Mac sucked in his breath as her "experienced" hands wrapped around his dearest member. "I be a few good years ahead of ye, lassie. To me, yer as young as a lamb and as fresh as spring rain."

Her hands stilled and he heard her intake of breath before her eyes narrowed on his. "*Dios.* I think I better watch my heart with you, Juanito."

He wrapped his hand over hers and tightened her grip around his already engorged self. "Best watch out for more than that, lass."

"*Qué hombre,*" she repeated with a moan.

After activity furious enough to send the bed ropes squealing, the two of them collapsed against each other. Mac relaxed on the moss-filled mattress of the tester bed, examining the pineapple bedposts at his feet. Kate had told him the pineapples were a sign of hospitality in New Orleans. Well, he'd surely been welcomed.

Kate's breathing tickled his chest. Mac leveled his head up to look at her—but instead of Kate's peaceful features his eyes met a disturbing statue on the bedside table. The wood carving looked religious, like something he'd see in a kirk. A black woman with a crown atop her head sat on a gold throne like the mother Mary. In one hand she held a gold ball; on her lap sat a laddie, black as coal, crowned and dressed in gold as well. A candle glowed before the two. Mac reached over Kate and turned the statue to face the wall.

Kate's brilliant red curls popped off his chest. "What are you doing? That is *la Virgen de Montserrat,* the patron saint of my people!"

"Makes me nervous to see those eyes watching us when we . . ." Seeing her beautiful eyes smolder with anger, he took advantage of her upraised position and passed his thumb over a nipple the size of a twenty-dollar gold piece. He continued his circles until her black pupils grew. See-

ing the lass subdued, he ventured a question. "If yer so
Catholic, me dearest Katie," he asked softly, "how is that
you . . ."

"Was a *prostituta*?" She shrugged and flipped onto her
back next to him. "*La tradición*. A tradition in my family."
She chuckled deep in her throat, but Mac couldn't find the
humor in her words. She buried one hand beneath her
head, giving Mac a distracting view of her upraised
breasts, but he forced himself to think on her words and
not on her fine figure as she said, "My mother, she was a
Spanish noblewoman. Her family throw her out because
she had the bad luck to be a beauty. She was seduced by
her uncle. The uncle . . . nothing happen to him. My
mother? She not so lucky. What else could she do? Her
family tell her she is whore . . . so she become whore."

Mac could see faint shadows in her eyes, making him
want to soothe the hurt inside her. He reached out and
brushed back the curls from her face. "Tell me, lass."

She turned onto her side and propped her chin on her
hand, watching him as if she were deciding whether to say
more. She shook her head. "*No*. I tell you only that I am a
smarter whore than my mother. She died in the cribs. La
Kate no work like that anymore." Her eyes trailed across
his body. The sheets lay bunched at the foot of the bed,
leaving Mac bare to his toes. Her expression showed she
liked what she saw. "The men I sleep with *I* choose. Not
for money. *Comprendes*?"

He rolled on top of her, placing his two calloused hands
on either side of her face. "If that's yer way of tellin' me
lassie that I pass muster, then I accept the compliment."
He kissed her, his lips caressing her eyes, her cheeks, her
chin. But when she bucked her hips up to meet his, he
stopped and smiled down at her. "I have a compliment of
me own to give, lass. Yer one hell of a woman, Katie. And
I'll not leave ye alone. There won't be anymore men,
money or not."

He knew immediately by the sharp look in her eyes that

he'd said the wrong thing, but he wasn't sorry he'd spoken. The sooner she knew his feelings, the faster she'd get used to the future he'd hatched over the week he'd courted her.

"Bah! You too serious, *hombre*. You take the fun out of a tumble."

Kate grabbed the dressing gown at the bottom of the bed and wrapped it around herself. She stepped into high-heeled slippers and walked to the mantel where she took out a long ivory filter and popped in a cigarette. Behind her, the glow of the coals burning in the grate showed the dark curves beneath her wrap. Mac sighed. "A hell of a woman," he said under his breath.

Remembering that he was to do more than bed the luscious Spaniard, Mac sat up, propped against a legion of pillows. He'd had his pleasure sure enough, now it was time for some business. Tonight, Rey and Harlan attended a dinner party given in their honor at L'Isle des Rêves. But come morning, Rey would expect to hear something of more substance than bedroom antics.

Mac sighed. How to help the lass straighten her life and still see justice done? He knew his Katie—as he'd come to think of her—had a heart of gold. He'd watched how she took care of her girls, and he'd seen her feed more than one hungry man who didn't have the coin to pay. That and her charming figure had drawn him to her bedchamber. Sure as hell he hated to believe she fraternized with criminal types. But facts were facts and he wasn't the kind of man to close his eyes to them. Now it was up to him to see the extent of the damage.

Steeling himself for the business ahead, Mac patted the mattress beside him and grinned. Kate lifted a fine penciled brow and walked toward him with slow swinging hips that set his blood to simmer again.

"*Más,* Juanito? So soon?"

"I just want ye close."

She sat down, running her painted nails through the curls on his chest. The lass had a way about her, and that was a fact. A stream of smoke slipped past her reddened lips as she put her cigarette and filter on the bedside table and inched closer to him.

"Your words turn even an old whore's head."

"Don't call yerself that, lass," he said. When he saw her thin brows meet in a frown, he took up her hand and kissed each of her knuckles to take the sting out of his words.

"Do not get silly ideas about me, Juanito."

"Are ye telling me it's foolish to give ye my respect?"

Immediately she withdrew her hand. Her eyes glowed as hot as the coals in the grate and she picked up her cigarette holder and inhaled. "You misunderstand me, *hombre*. I am a powerful woman. La Kate demands respect. But in matters of the heart . . ." She shrugged. "You do not put water in your Scotch, *no*?" When he shook his head, she finished, "It is the same with me. I do not like romantic notions to . . . water down my enjoyment."

Mac watched her smoking the cigarette on the edge of the bed, realizing that she believed what she said. But he'd seen more than enjoyment in her eyes when they'd made love the past two nights.

"A powerful woman, ye say." He massaged the knuckles of her hand, getting to that other business. "What do ye have power over, lass?" He cocked a brow. "Except me hanging Johnny that is?"

She laughed. Again her clever fingers reached out to stroke him. He responded immediately. "You do not do too much of this 'hanging' when I am around."

"Now lass." With the utmost of regret, Mac coaxed her hands away. "I asked ye a question."

She took another slow puff of the cigarette. Watching her lips wrap around the ivory holder did nothing to aid his condition. He could see from her glance and wicked smile that Katie knew her effect on him.

"*Dinero*. Money, Juanito. You're a working man. You understand. When a woman has her own business," she said through a puff of smoke, "she has money, security. That is power."

He nodded, trying to focus on her words and not the lips that formed them. "I see Constable Gessler is a regular. Is he part of that power?"

A wariness crept into her dark blue eyes. She watched him, forgetting the cigarette until the ashes threatened to spill onto the counterpane.

"Lassie." He pointed to the inch-long ash.

She tapped the cigarette over the edge of the bed. "*Sí,* he comes here many times."

"Do ye give him yer favors, lass?" he asked quietly, thinking to make her believe him jealous. She might tell him her true intentions with Gessler to ease his anger. But after posing the question, he realized that he wasn't completely free of that green-eyed monster. Even if he knew the lass couldn't care for Gessler, how far would she go to get the man to talk?

She laughed, a soft fluid sound that reminded him of crisp mornings on the moors. "*El gordo?*" She glided back to his side, perching herself on the edge of the bed. She pulled the cigarette from its holder and snuffed it out, carefully laying the ivory stick on the night table and turning the Virgin around to face forward again. "Gessler could close my business in *un minuto.* It is better that I keep the constable as happy as possible—"

"How happy?" he asked, surprising himself with the edge to his voice.

She shook her head smiling. Her hand curved around his bearded chin. "You jealous, *mi amor?*"

"Might be that I am."

"Let us just say . . . not that happy, eh?"

He kissed her as he pulled her down to him and peeled back her wrapper. "It warms my heart to hear it, lass." Time enough for business later.

* * *

Mercy glanced down the hall. The light of the sconces flickered off the walls, creating deep waving shadows. The last guest had finally left for home. Not even a servant disturbed the quiet as Mercy wrapped her fingers around the enamel doorknob before her. A sprig of violets had been carefully painted onto the flat knob. A matching keyhole cover hung beneath. She'd chosen that detail herself. Everything about this room had been the product of careful deliberation. She'd been young then. And she'd believed the happiness denied her in the first fourteen years of life had finally come.

Her fingers gripping the cold glaze, she turned the knob and pushed the door open. She didn't visit the nursery often, but tonight she thought it was the only place where she'd find the courage she needed to make her decisions.

Mercy stepped inside—and immediately experienced the pain of memories. The Jenny Lind cradle that had been all the rage the year she'd bought it sat in the corner. She'd thought the baby would have a beautiful view of the magnolia trees outside through the window there. The carefully chosen toys still lined the shelves, untouched, unloved. The miniature furniture she'd begged Benoit to purchase—actually merchant's displays for L'Isle des Rêves's own furniture—waited under the shuttered window. Mercy placed the lamp she carried on the mahogany dresser and picked up a small china cup, part of a set she'd searched out from Pascal's old toys in the attic. She'd so hoped the baby would be a girl. In that one thing, she'd not been disappointed.

She turned the frail cup in her hands, seeing it had been dusted clean. The room remained spotless at all times. Not as some shrine to her lost child, but because she hated to think of all the things she'd chosen with such love moldering in a dark corner of the house.

The creak of the door swinging open drew her attention and Mercy spun around. Her fingers around the cup tightened. The fragile handle snapped in her hands.

At the threshold, the light of the hall lamps outlined Benoit's dark figure.

"I will not allow you to make a cuckolded fool out of me, Mercedes."

He slurred his words. In his hand, he clutched an empty whiskey tumbler. Mercy dropped the broken china cup to the table. "Benoit, it's almost two in the morning—"

In a flash of light, Benoit threw his glass at the fireplace, barely missing Mercy. The fine crystal shattered against the brick.

"I could kill you, you know," he said with deadly softness. He stumbled toward her, kicking aside the table and its china set. The precious pieces scattered on the carpeted floor. Mercy remained still, refusing to retreat as she'd done ten years before in this very room. Benoit's dark eyes shifted as he neared. His breath came in heavy pants. He reeked of whiskey.

He lifted his hands, wrapped his fingers around her neck. "I *want* to kill you," he said in a low voice, slowly squeezing his hands.

The pressure increased. Tighter and tighter. Benoit gnashed his teeth, burying his fingers, blocking her air. Inside Mercy, the woman she'd created to fight this man rose within her, combating her panic. Santana didn't fear Benoit; she only despised him.

"You wish to kill me, Benoit?" she gasped, a smile coming to her lips. "Then do it."

Sweat beaded on Benoit's forehead. The fingers on her throat began to tremble. Using her last breath, Mercy whispered, "Coward."

With a gurgled shout, he pushed her away. She crashed against the mahogany press, her cheek striking the door.

"Damn you, Mercedes! I *want* to kill you!"

"And what is stopping you?" she asked, her hand rubbing her neck where the skin still burned. She looked at the hearth where the light caught the shards of broken glass. "Am I not as easily replaced as your fine crystal?"

"I saw you on the dance floor! I saw the way he touched you! Are you lovers? Has that man bed you?"

She gave him a pitying look. "It's amazing to me that you should still care, Benoit."

"Answer me!"

"No." She stepped around him, brushing close in a manner that let him know she didn't fear him. She leaned her back against the post of the nanny's bed, both her hands resting behind her. "No, Benoit, he has not."

His dark eyes narrowed. "Why do I believe you?"

"Probably," she answered, "because you know I wouldn't give a damn if you knew that he had."

With a growl deep in his throat, he rushed at her. Mercy swerved to the side, but he caught her around the waist and threw her up against the bedpost, falling on her. He crushed his mouth against hers in a sickening kiss. His hand squeezed her breast, bruising her, hurting her. "After all these years, do you finally want a man, Mercedes?"

She pushed him away, barely able to stay standing, fighting him. He clawed at her dress, his slobbery mouth biting, humiliating, bringing back the ugly memories.

"I am your husband!"

"Husband? You are my nightmare, Benoit. You kidnapped me, forced me, you use my friends to keep me at your side . . . that is no marriage in the eyes of God!"

"To you, I *am* God. Everything you are, you owe to me. And if you crave someone between your legs it shall be me—"

Mercy punched him in the stomach, then kicked his feet out from under him. He staggered back, falling to the floor, so utterly shocked by her practiced move that his mouth hung open. Mercy raced to the door. In the last ten years, she'd learned how to protect herself. Never again would she be his victim. But she wouldn't confront him in the nursery. *No, not in the baby's room.*

She rounded the newel post and scrambled down the steps. She could hear Benoit shouting her name in a drunken slur. The sounds of chase stopped in an abrupt shout of surprise, followed by Benoit crashing down the stairs. She didn't look back but bolted along the corridor. Again she heard his curses as he regained his breath and continued his pursuit. Mercy hurled the library door open. Before he could reach her, she grabbed the heavy iron poker. Benoit careened into the library. She faced him, holding the poker, ready to swing it if necessary.

"Ten years ago"—her words came out between pants—"I made it perfectly clear that I would rather kill you than submit to you again, Benoit. I may not have pulled the trigger when I held you off with that gun, but my absolute *loathing* for you has not changed!"

He diminished with each word, looking for an instant like a defeated old man. How she hated him. How she hated herself. But then his features sharpened, and he took a step toward her.

"If this is another ploy to get a divorce, you are sadly deceiving yourself," he said almost lovingly.

"I know how valuable I am to you, Benoit. The only way you could get a wife was to steal her and train her to your liking! How will you ever find another to take my place? Clarissa, the one woman who would actually marry you, wasn't good enough to please your precious family. Oh, no! Only bloodlines as blue as the ones you created for me could do that!"

"Shut up, Mercedes!"

"But Henri wasn't fooled, was he, Benoit? Isn't that why you killed your own brother? Because he told you to your face that no matter how much money you have, no matter how beautiful and cultured and white your wife, your family would never accept a *cachumas*—the son of your father's quadroon mistress."

"Damn you, that's enough."

"Oh, your father may have educated you, he may have given you a taste for all the fine things you enjoy, but he could never make you part of his family. Even in his eyes, you were never as good as Henri, his legitimate son—"

"I was better than him!" he shouted over Mercy's voice. "Twenty times better! I made the money to keep this house from moldering into ruin! I made my father's last days worth living when Henri didn't have a *sou* to give him."

"And despite it all, he still loved him best."

"Dear God, that you would dare . . . you who are nothing! Nothing! A whore I took off the street and made into an illusion of gentility." He jumped at her, catching the poker in his hands as Mercy swung. They struggled over the weapon until Benoit pushed her up against the mantel, ramming her back against the wood shelf. "You don't seem to understand the power I have over you. You're too stupid to even fear me anymore! I could lock you up or send you away. I could destroy you."

Mercy laughed. "Destroy the elegant lady you created? The only thing the society you cherish so much respects about you?" She shook her head, looking at him with contempt. "Do you think they would even come to your island of dreams if I didn't ply them with exquisite foods and entertainment. I tempt them here with the best money can buy! You want me to fear you, Benoit? Well, I acknowledge your power over me because of Laura and Beth. But I will never show you the respect of fear. Never again."

Grabbing the poker with both hands, she pulled it from his grasp and threw it to the carpet. She tried to walk around him, but he stepped in front of her, blocking her path.

"Ten years I've had you by my side. Ten years I've thwarted all your attempts to leave me. You won't leave me now, Mercedes. Not even for the handsome Parks. You mentioned your friends. Remember that their welfare depends on your pleasing me."

Mercy's heart belted against her chest as she met Benoit's dark gaze. "I sometimes wonder if you really know where they are."

His eyes shifted from hers, then darted back. "You can't be sure of that, can you?"

"I wish to God I could be," she whispered.

He smiled, finally winning the victory he'd sought.

Mercy shouldered past him, disgusted with him, disgusted with herself. "If your little show is over, Benoit, I bid you *adieu*"—she walked to the door and stopped, pivoting back to him—"on second thought. Go to hell."

Ling Shi looked up at the sound of the door to her room opening. Her heart sank as she saw Monsieur De Dreux. He marched to her side, his face twisted into the mask of a demon. He slapped her book aside and grabbed her arm, practically dragging her up to him. She could smell the alcohol on his breath.

"Whore!" He threw her back on the bed, climbing up on the mattress as he shrugged off his coat.

"Please, *monsieur.*" She cowered before him, crawling away from him.

He pulled her back by the collar of her nightgown, almost choking her. "Ungrateful bitch! I've given you everything! Money, education." He jerked her against him, using the tremendous strength of his fingers to dig into her arms. "I made a lady out of a tramp!"

"Oh, please, *monsieur*!" She wept, seeing the strange unfocused look in his eyes. "I am not her! Please, I beg you."

He pushed her on the bed. Ling Shi crept up the mound of pillows, trying desperately to get away from him.

"Do you think you can reject me, as they did? You should idolize me! You should kiss my feet. Call me a coward will you? I'll show you a coward." He struck her across the face, flinging her back against the headboard. "Kiss my feet, bitch."

Ling Shi fell forward and obeyed him. "You are not a coward, *monsieur*. You are brave and strong."

He ripped off her nightgown, shredding it down the front. "Yes, brave and strong." He kissed her feverishly, whispering against her mouth, "God, I love you, Mercedes. I love you. Why didn't you keep the baby?" His hand squeezed her breast painfully. "It was nothing, what I did to you that night. Nothing. A real woman would have kept the child." He kissed her again, and again, sucking against her mouth. "Not my fault."

He buried his face in her breasts. Ling Shi cradled his head while she sobbed.

"Tell me I mean more to you than any man. Tell me you love me, Mercedes."

"I love you, Benoit," Ling Shi said between sobs. "I love you."

Rey unfolded today's letter with one hand as he inhaled deeply from his cigarette. He dropped the vellum on the desktop and straddled the back of his chair. Picking up his glass off the table, he smoothed the creases from the paper, then drank the bourbon as he reread his favorite line.

Rennie, pardon me for taking the liberty to say this to you, dearest brother, but you are a ninnyhammer as well as a fool!

He laughed aloud, the alcohol making him relax. He pictured Nan at her worst. With her eyes smoldering, she'd stamp her foot in a manner she'd found effective since she'd turned five. Rey took another drag of the Choctaw and continued reading.

And so help me, if I don't get a satisfactory answer from you soon, I'll pack up Christopher and we'll come find you.

It wasn't the first time she'd threatened to follow Rey. And, as always, the response he'd given Mac to post told her in no uncertain terms that she and Christopher were to stay put.

Rey drained the whiskey glass, the moment's euphoria passing as quickly as the sharp sting of the liquor in his mouth. He stood and walked to the window, thinking of Christopher's birthday next month. He'd already written to Nan about his present—a "safety" bicycle made especially for his son. Last year, Christopher could talk about nothing else after seeing a man riding an "ordinary," a bicycle with an enormous front wheel. Rey had determined then to buy one, but had chosen the safety model because its two, equal-size wheels made it more stable. How Chris's eyes would light up when he saw the shiny red bicycle made just for him. Of course, Rey wouldn't be there to see him ride it. Not that day.

Rey leaned his head against the cool glass pane. He should be with Chris. He belonged home with his son. But Sotheby was still out there, free—free to kill again. Part of Rey knew he couldn't return to a normal life until he stopped Sophie's murderer. The other half warned that Sotheby's capture might cost him too high a price. And nothing he could do would ever bring back Sophie or ease Rey's guilty conscience over her death.

He studied the burning tip of his cigarette. Questions, questions, so many questions—and no good answers. It had been a long time since he'd allowed himself to doubt his plans for Sotheby. Yet, since that first day he'd boarded the coach for L'Isle des Rêves, the fine threads of his resolve had begun to unravel. With the aid of the bourbon, he could feel the strands slip their moorings. The pattern he'd set for his life fractured as each fiber snapped and separated under the weight of five years of loneliness. Tonight, his conscience had proven no match for the surcease offered by Mercedes De Dreux.

He could almost smell her lavender scent, feel the softness of her skin beneath his fingers instead of the cold window glass. Mercedes. The name didn't really suit her. It was too formal and pious-sounding. He closed his eyes and remembered her mouth when she'd stopped fighting and returned his kisses. It excited him just to think about her lips seeking his, as hungry for his touch as he'd been for hers. He couldn't regret their brief retreat into that darkened bedchamber, even when he acknowledged the great risk he'd taken. Those few moments of pleasure had blanked out the world, bringing him a taste of peace. No, regrets were far from his mind. With the bourbon in his veins and the shadows of his past calling from each dark corner, he could only think of her promise. *I'll come.*

It took a moment before the tapping registered, the knocker striking the door at the rear entrance. He snuffed out the cigarette and left his room, racing past the back loggia, halting halfway down the staircase to watch the servant open the back door. He heard Mercedes's voice. His blood rushed to his head at the sound, more intoxicating than the bourbon. *I'll come.*

The servant stepped aside, permitting Rey his first view of Mercedes. Her pelisse covered her from neck to ankle. The plumed bonnet shadowed her face. Just as he'd wished her, just as he'd imagined her for the past two hours, she'd come to Bizy. To him.

"Send madame up, Sissy," he called down.

In the salon, he leaned against the mantel, watching the arched doorway for her entrance. His pulse beat twice as fast as the ticking clock and he couldn't stop the grin that turned his lips. He felt like a schoolboy, hot, eager. He wanted to pace, but forced himself to stay with his arms crossed and his shoulder propped against the wood. The oil lamps gave the room a hazy yellow glow. The bourbon heated his blood. She'd come. At least for tonight, he wouldn't be alone with his demons.

With the grace of a queen, she walked into the room. She glanced around the salon, not meeting his eyes while she took off her coat. She was dressed in the same coral gown with the ivory train she'd worn at L'Isle des Rêves. The off-the-shoulder sleeves and low neckline displayed her breast to advantage. Pulling off her gloves, concentrating as she eased off one finger at a time, she sat down on the tête-à-tête.

"You said to come soon." She slid the kid leather across her palm, then crushed it between her hands before looking up. "I hope I haven't been premature?"

He walked to her chair and dropped to his knees before her. She looked almost hesitant sitting there on the edge of her seat. He set aside her gloves and took up both her hands. "I'm glad, Mercedes." He kissed the white tips of her knuckles. "I'm very glad you came."

Releasing her hands, he tugged the bonnet strings and pulled off her hat. By the light of the fire, her hair burned golden, her eyes shone like amber chips. The corners of her lips trembled and Rey reached out to smooth them.

She gasped at the brush of his fingers, as if the touch pained her. He frowned and stared at her mouth, then down at his hand. He rubbed his fingers together. A powdery residue rolled off the tips.

"Mercedes?"

She turned away and stared at the fire.

He set the bonnet down. Very gently, he tilted her face back to him, shifting it so he could see her better in the light. The cheek he examined looked just as soft as he remembered but now he saw the slight discoloration—not shadows from the fire playing across the curves of her face, but a bruise clumsily covered with too much powder. He touched the slight swelling. She winced and drew back.

"Who did this to you, Mercedes?"

Leaving the chair, she walked to the fire. He followed, taking her by the shoulders and turning her back to him. His heart pounded, not with desire now, but with an anger that threatened to snap his control and send him back to

L'Isle des Rêves to find the culprit who had hurt her. "Tell me what happened?"

She lifted her chin. The defiant gesture brought the highway woman strangely to mind. Rey blanked out the image of Santana Rose and focused on the woman in front of him.

"A slight miscalculation on my part," she said. "I walked into my armoire in the dark."

"You're a terrible liar. Was it your husband? Did Benoit strike you because of me?"

"This has nothing to do with us."

"The hell it doesn't."

She twisted out of his grasp and took a step back. "If you're going to interrogate me, I'll take my leave now." Just as quickly as she'd found it, her defiant stance crumbled. Her eyes wide, her fists balled at her sides, she whispered, "Please, Rey. Don't make me sorry I came."

He walked slowly toward her like a man approaching a skittish mare, his hand outstretched. "Did he see us, Mercedes? Did he guess that I kissed you?" He touched her arm, pulled her gently back to him. "I have to know." He kept his voice low, reassuring. "I couldn't stand it if I caused you pain."

Unexpectedly, she flew into his embrace, hugging him with the ferocity Christopher used after a bad fall. He could feel her head shaking against his shoulder as she whispered, "No, it wasn't your fault," over and over. And then, more urgently, "Let's not talk about it, Rey. Please, I want to stay." He closed his eyes, holding her, smelling the lavender perfume, hating the instant desire that filled him and swayed him to leave off his questions. Her hasty denials only reinforced his suspicions. She didn't trust him enough to tell the truth.

"Someone hurt you, Mercedes."

Instead of answering his question, she kissed him, digging her fingers in his hair. He'd seen the bruises on her mouth. He knew these desperate kisses must hurt, but she wouldn't allow him to pull away, only crushed her mouth against him harder when he tried.

"I don't want to leave, Rey," she said. "I don't want to go back tonight. Let me stay with you. Help me to forget."

Like a fire that had been carefully banked but suddenly fed with a bellows, his passion overcame his caution. They were both hurting. Why not give each other solace? He coaxed her lips open and slipped his tongue into the sweetness of her mouth. He tugged the off-the-shoulder sleeves until he exposed her corset cover and kissed the warm silk of her breasts above the material. Picking her up in his arms, he carried her to the bedroom across the reception hall.

Mercedes buried her face in his neck. He smelled of tobacco and bourbon. She'd never been so frightened in her life, yet she wanted to be with this man, wanted to experience the wonders his kisses promised. Benoit had given only pain. His attack tonight had pushed Mercy to find whatever happiness she could.

Rey lowered her to the bed. For the first time, she realized she'd kept her eyes tightly shut. She opened them now, smiling at him, then allowed her gaze to drift around the chamber. The room seemed to fit Rey. Dark, rugged, unfinished—but what furniture he had was in perfect order and spotlessly clean. He waited above her as if wanting the next move to be hers. She almost laughed at the notion. She didn't have a clue what to do.

Rey sucked in a breath at her inviting smile. She lay across his bed, waiting, looking more beautiful than any woman he'd ever known. How often had he imagined her there? How many times had he dreamed of loving her in the dark walnut bed? But when her expression turned uncertain and a glimmer of apprehension returned to her eyes, Rey frowned. Her anxious gaze reminded him of the bruises. He'd thought she was a young woman bored with her aging husband. What if there were more to the story than that? What if tonight were not the first time she'd known abuse?

He sat down on the bed beside her and stroked back the hair from her face, then reached around and took out her ivory combs. He twined his fingers through the long curls, unfurling them past her waist. The shoulders of her gown slipped lower as she inched up the pillows, exposing more of her breasts. But his gaze only flitted there for a moment. It was the expression in her eyes that held him.

I'm doing something wrong, Mercy thought watching his frown. Certainly her inexperience showed. Would he turn her away? Or like Benoit had so many years ago, lose patience and attack? She reached for his waistcoat, haltingly at first, then with more confidence. When she unfastened the coat, he shrugged it off. Again, she hesitated over his shirt. At the back of her mind, phantom devils jeered her. *He'll hurt you, just like Benoit.* Mercy bit her lip and reached for his shirt buttons.

Rey stilled her hand. He could see she was breathing hard. "Second thoughts?" he asked.

Mercy tried to push back the memories—Benoit slapping her, punching her chest as he rammed into her, as if the violence stirred him more than the sex act. Ten years and still his abuse haunted her. She knew he wasn't normal. Kate had assured her few men enjoyed that kind of coupling, that love and passion were to be enjoyed and should never involve pain. Rey made her want to find out if Kate was right. Mercy looked into his eyes, seeking reassurance. They weren't dark and turbulent like Benoit's, but cool green, as serene as the waters of a bayou pond. She knew she wanted this man. Would she allow Benoit's cruelty to destroy that?

She edged Rey's hands away. No, Benoit had ruined too much already. Briskly, she continued to unbutton his shirt.

Rey caught her wrists. With an almost loving smile, he said, "That's the way Nanny used to undress me. With that same determined look." He raised his dark brows. "She always made me feel as if we were in a bit of a rush."

Mercy laughed, but the nervous giggles somehow choked in her throat, threatening tears. She dropped her chin to her chest. *Please, Rey, help me.*

He cupped her face in his palms and tilted her face up. "Tell me what happened tonight. It might help to talk about it."

"No," she said firmly.

"Mercedes." He kissed her ever-so-softly on the corner of her mouth. "Trust me, Mercedes." Another touch followed, like a whispered breath on the tip of her chin. "Trust me."

She longed to confide in Rey. She dreamed of telling him about Benoit, how she hated him, what he'd done in the past that made her feelings for Rey so difficult to express. Recklessly, she answered, "Yes, I'll tell you." And as soon as she said the first word, relief flowed through her. She needed to confide in him, to receive his reassurance that their lovemaking would be different. But at the same time, her easy capitulation made her wary. This man was an agent, trained to coax even the most dangerous confession.

"Sometimes, when Benoit drinks," she said, giving only half the truth, "he can get violent."

Rey cursed under his breath, then cut off the words as soon as he saw their effect on her. The last thing she needed was to hear his brutal thoughts about her husband.

"Does he know where you are right now? Will he retaliate for this?"

"No. We . . . we don't share a room. We haven't for a number of years. He stays in the wing on the opposite side of the house from mine. I'm sure by now he's passed out in his bed from too much drink."

He could hear the truth in her voice, see it in her eyes. She lay before him, open and unguarded. Her vulnerability called to something buried deep within him, something that told him this woman needed tenderness more than passion. She didn't sleep with her husband. No wonder she sought lovers.

"And no one has ever tried to protect you from him?" he asked, thinking of the young Frenchman in town.

"There is no one else, Rey." Instantly, Mercy saw the change in him, the slight tensing, a panther feigning sleep. But she wanted him to know he was the only one, needed for him to make their time together special, and she knew instinctively how the knowledge that she had no lovers would affect him. "The man who gave me the note, what I told you in the carriage is true. He isn't my lover. I have a friend, a woman friend, of whom society doesn't approve," she said, giving him the story she'd concocted to explain her absence from Marie Laveau's. "Benoit would make my life . . . very difficult if he knew of our association. She needed me that day. I didn't know you very well." Unbelievably, she heard her voice crack. Tears threatened. "I couldn't risk telling you anything—"

"Shhh. Don't," he soothed. Wrapping her in his arms, he lay down on the mound of pillows next to her.

"I don't have lovers, Rey."

She nestled against his shirt. With each ragged breath against his chest he tightened his grip and called himself ten times a fool for the things he'd thought and said of her.

"And if I unbutton your shirt like your nanny," she said, her voice rising with choked laughter, "it's because I haven't the foggiest how to do it otherwise."

A halcyon delight bathed him. Her hesitation, the anxiety in her eyes, were no act. She'd sought only him to soothe the pain of her marriage to Benoit, a man Rey knew was capable of perfidy. He kissed the fine curls at her temple. She deserved better than De Dreux. With his lips, he brushed the curve of her ear, then gently bit the lobe before whispering, "Then let me show you."

His lips teased the edge of her mouth until she turned

her head and kissed him. Bringing her hands to his chest, he eased her lips apart and explored the tender skin within. He skimmed her teeth then sucked on her tongue, relishing her whimpers as he lowered her hands to the shirt buttons. *She deserves better.*

He kissed the tip of her nose, then her chin. "I am the oldest in a large family, five sisters, one brother. There was always a slew of nannies running about. The one you reminded me of, she was always in a hurry." She reached for his mouth, but he pulled back and set her fingers to unfasten another button, then the next. "I told her that slow and steady would be much nicer for both of us. Why rush?" Leaving her hands to his shirt, he circled her nipples through the silk of her dress, watching her through half-closed eyes. "But Nanny was always so eager."

Her hands on his shirt stilled. "You make it sound as if . . ."

"As if what?"

"As if . . . how old were you when you had this nanny?"

He smiled. "I don't recall saying she was my nanny."

"Rey—"

"The buttons, Mercedes," he said, nuzzling the skin of her neck, making it tingle. "Slow and steady."

There was nothing slow about the way she removed his shirt. He made her feverish, and she dispatched the last button and pressed her heated cheek against the muscles of his chest as quickly as she was able. His palms burned on the skin of her shoulders and she arched up to meet his skillful mouth. His kiss made her blood sing with a frenzy that snuffed out the last of her fears. The tension of her gown and corset eased. The room's air chilled her skin as Rey guided her arms from the silk sleeves and the bodice dropped to her hips.

One hand reached beneath her skirts, drawing the layers of petticoats up her ankle to her knee. The cold swirled under the gown, following the path his hand exposed as he continued his kisses. She could feel the heat of his calloused palm, stroking then squeezing her calf. He teased the back of her knee as he unrolled her stocking, then worked up the inside of her thigh. His touch made her lightheaded, but when his fingers reached beneath her drawers, she tensed.

"Trust me, Mercedes," he said against her mouth.

His hand drew lazy S-shapes directly below her stomach. His soft kisses relaxed her until she didn't care any longer about propriety. She was beyond shock. With one hand, he nudged her thighs apart while he licked and nipped down her collarbone to her breasts. With his other hand, he followed the curve of her stomach until he reached the curling hair there, then slipped lower still.

"Ah, Mercedes, you're so soft, so moist."

A gasp left her lips. She seemed to dissolve under his touch and opened her legs wide, wider still, having no power left to do otherwise. The pad of one finger touched, circled, caressed. Mercy swallowed. A small moan escaped her lips and she realized she was short of breath. The magic of his hands took the very air from her. She was caught in the vortex of his touch, drowning deeper and deeper with his circling fingers.

"That's it, love. Flow for me. Let me feel your passion."

He pulled down the lace of her corset and his mouth closed over the tip of one breast. He sucked gently as one finger eased inside her, not a violation but a loving touch that cherished, withdrew, then returned to bring her greater pleasure.

She closed her eyes, now laughing, pressing toward him. It was everything Kate had said it would be, and more. So much more. Yes, this was worth the risk, to know that this could exist . . .

Rey heard her laughter, found it just as startling as her threatened tears—and just as moving. He laughed with her, then whispered as he tongued her nipple, "Slowly, my heart. We have all night, after all."

"Yes, I know." She bit her lip when his finger delved deeper, withdrew. "Slow and steady—Ah!"

The current he'd created swept over her. She couldn't breathe, didn't want to. She floated, suspended in time, then eased back to the surface with the pulse that softly squeezed her muscles around his finger.

"Perhaps not too slow this first time," he whispered.

Mercy lay back against the cool counterpane, her eyes closed, then huddled against him. She reached for the curling hair covering his chest, found his nipple, and repeated the rhythm still humming inside her with the stroke of her finger against the hardened nub. She smiled when she heard his heart pick up its beat beneath her ear.

Suddenly impatient himself, Rey sat her up and undressed her, leaving her in a pool of silks, then tossing the clothes to the foot of the bed. Kneeling on the bed facing her bare back, he reached and cupped her warm breasts in his hands. He heard her sharp intake of breath and kissed her neck, tasting the salty skin with his tongue. The circles he made with his fingers crept closer to the center of her breasts until he reached her nipples. He rolled the hardened tips and heard her breathing grow more strained. He pulled her against him, then lay her on the bed and rolled on top of her.

Her eyes were closed, her lips parted. She looked so sensual on the counterpane, he grew painfully hard against his trousers just watching her. Throwing his feet over the edge of the bed, he shucked off his boots and trousers.

"Slow and steady?" She broke into soft giggles behind him.

He turned back and glanced down at his erection. "Steady in any case."

Again he covered her, kissing her mouth, then sucking on her breasts—it was difficult to keep track of what he was doing. Her smell, her soft sighs, drove him, making him want to rush.

Mercy opened her eyes just as his lips closed over one

nipple. As if her body belonged to another, she watched herself stiffen, then release the tension with a languid sigh. She leaned back against the pillows as he continued to spin his magic. What he made her feel was a miracle, a gift. Every place he touched had in the past been a black memory of pain and humiliation. Now, he showed her with his caresses what she'd thought never to experience.

His lips traveled down from her breast to the skin of her stomach. He dipped his tongue into the hollow of her navel and she gasped, then laughed from the joy of passion that strung her body tight. She felt the cool breath from his mouth against her moistened skin. She looked up and found him watching her, propped up on his elbows.

He smiled, bringing a charming lightness to his eyes. "I don't think I've ever made a woman laugh so much in bed before." His hand reached between her legs. "Perhaps my technique needs improvement?"

"I'm ready to shatter from your touch," she whispered, bringing his mouth back up to hers. "I couldn't stand any improvements."

They rolled across the bed. The silk garments at the foot rustled to the floor and Mercy could imagine the state the material would be in. But when Rey lifted himself on his arms above her and aligned his hips to hers, all conscious thought stopped. Suddenly, despite the passion he'd given her, regardless of the magic they'd already shared, the fears resurfaced.

Rey stroked the hair from her face. "What's wrong, my heart? No more laughter?" His fingers grazed the reddened cheek she'd bruised against the mantel during her fight with Benoit.

"It's been a long time for me, Rey." Her hand smoothed over his bare shoulders, sinking her fingers deep into the muscles.

"For me as well," he said, brushing her lips with soft kisses. He smiled, then rolled to her side, holding her as he kissed the top of her hair.

"Are we going to stop?" she asked, almost afraid of his answer.

His face remained calm as he rubbed her arms. "Only if you want to."

"No, I don't want to stop. I can't."

He kissed her mouth. "Neither can I. I haven't been able to stop myself since the first day I saw you."

Mercy thought of the holdup on the River Road. She'd seen him first as Santana, a full day before he'd met Mercedes De Dreux. "I wanted you even before then, Rey."

He kissed her nose. "Such a romantic." Rey propped up on his elbows above her. Mercy heard a soft puff of breath that sounded remarkably like a sigh. "We should pause now, in any case. There's one thing we haven't discussed," he said, his expression turning too serious for her liking. "I don't want you to worry about my getting you with child. I am usually a very careful man. Though, you'd never guess it by my actions with you." He laughed, regret and a touch of self-derision mingled in his tone. "Still, in this one thing I'm usually very diligent. Unless you know of a better method, I won't spill my seed inside you."

A ripple of shock streamed through her. He was talking about preventing conception. She looked up and saw he was no longer smiling.

He didn't want a child.

A gift.

"But there is no need." The words came out in a rush, before she could even think clearly of what she was doing. Before she could change her mind. She hadn't dreamed of a baby when she'd fled Benoit's violence seeking Rey. But his concerns about her conceiving brought out a hunger she couldn't control. A child. A baby of her own. "I mean, there won't be any problem." She reached her arms around him and kissed him, trying to imitate his nips and licks, desperate to drive him to distraction with her touch as he'd done so skillfully with her.

At first, he returned her embrace, but soon enough he

pulled away. His eyes held her, the seriousness of his intent a heated ember in their depths. "It is of the utmost importance to me, that you not get pregnant, Mercedes. Under the circumstances, it would be disastrous not just for us, but the child as well."

Her heart squeezed and expanded painfully. A baby couldn't be wrong. She would love it. Take care of it. If he didn't want the child, she'd be parent enough for both of them. Like Carolina with little Rose. In a few months, Benoit would be out of her life forever. She and her baby would be safe. Rey's baby—a child that would have nothing of Benoit. A child that would carry Rey's goodness.

She looked into Rey's eyes. She'd suffered a miscarriage. Pascal wouldn't even speak to her. Within her reach was the child of a man she loved. And he was asking her to turn her back on that chance.

"There's no possibility of a child," she lied. "I'm barren."

His expression softened. "I thought perhaps that might be the case. I mean . . . you've been married so long. I'm sorry, Mercedes. Truly I am."

His sympathy sliced through her, making her betrayal even more villainous. Before he could see the lie in her eyes, she kissed him. "Please, don't worry," she said. "Just make love to me."

Again, his hands worked her to a fever pitch of desire. When he brought them together, he entered her with slow, teasing motions that could never intimidate. He made her want to explode, fracture with the power of her need as his body rocked against hers. And then she did. It came in wave after wave. She'd never experienced anything so beautiful, until she looked up and saw Rey tense above her. On his face, she could see him reach the very pinnacle she'd just left before he threw back his head and collapsed over her.

Minutes later, his mouth found her. Their breaths combined softly as her hands caressed his shoulders. Even in her fulfillment she thought of the one thing that marred her joy.

He didn't want a child.

And she wanted one so very much.

She closed her eyes as they filled with tears. So be it. Santana would steal again.

Chapter 12

Her knees tucked under her arms, Pascal sat on the hillside staring up at the sky. The crisp night seemed like no other. And it wasn't. Tonight, she'd become a woman. A *desirable* woman. A woman Harlan had wanted to kiss.

The starlight blended with moonshine to make everything around her sparkle. Her eyes closed, she thought again of her waltz with Harlan. Her head dipped back and forth to the pulsing beat in her head. It wasn't the warmth of her pelisse she imagined as she hugged her arms around herself, but Harlan's hands as he held her.

She rose, swaying with the music, then twirled in a circle that became a race past the house and across the river road. Climbing up the grass levee, she watched the dark waters of the Mississippi. The light of the moon shimmered off the ebony surface, catching eddies in spiderweb patterns on the water. With her fingers, Pascal traced her lips, recalling his kiss.

She hadn't even needed the love potion. Quite incredibly, Harlan Everard had *wanted* to kiss her, to hold her in his arms, even without the aid of Lena's magic. Pascal's heart swelled with the memory of their parting just a few hours ago. After she'd heard Mr. Parks tell another guest that he and Harlan would soon be taking their leave, she'd searched Harlan out. She'd wanted to say her farewells alone and urged him onto the balcony. For a moment, she thought he might kiss her again. She'd been devastated when instead he'd jammed his bowler hat back on his head, as if angry, then marched for the French doors. But her disappointment lasted only as long as it took Harlan to stop, mumble a curse, and return to take her in his arms for a lingering kiss.

Almost two hours had passed since he and Mr. Parks had left for Bizy. For half that time, Pascal had stayed outside, reliving the enchanted evening through her memories. Now, she wanted very much to share the magic with someone else. Skipping back to the house, she sneaked through the back door and ran upstairs to her room. She threw her coat on the daybed and reached for the door linking her room with Ling Shi's. After a perfunctory knock, she clasped her fingers around the door handle, ready to dash inside.

The sound of crying stopped her. Pascal frowned and leaned forward to listen. Her heart rammed into her throat when she heard her father shout in French for Ling Shi to shut up.

All thoughts of her lovely evening vanished as Pascal slammed the door open ready to defend her friend. But the sight that met her eyes made it impossible to move. Ling Shi sat on her bed, slumped against the headboard. She clutched the coverlet around her stomach, under her bare breasts. Though shadows shrouded the room, a lone lamp on the bedside table granted a meager light. Pascal could see her friend was sobbing and lay naked beneath the sheets.

Standing at the foot of the bed, her father watched Pascal. His shirt was unbuttoned at the neck, as if he'd been in too much of a hurry to bother with the last few buttons. He held his coat and neck cloth in his hands. In that fleeting moment, Benoit De Dreux spared his daughter the most attention he'd granted Pascal in her sixteen years of life. His dark eyes flickered with some emotion that appeared strangely like regret before it was snuffed out and his gaze swung back to Ling Shi. The whimpers from the girl on the bed instantly quieted.

"Go back to your room," he said to Pascal, shrugging on his coat.

"H-how could you?" Pascal whispered.

He didn't answer her, just looped his cravat around his neck and began to tie it in place.

All the fine emotions of the evening withered inside her as she watched her father casually prepare to take his leave. All her life she'd dreamed of his love, had vied for his attention, begged for it. And this was the man she'd tried to convince to love her? A culprit who would take a seventeen-year-old woman—a girl less than a third of his age—and force himself on her? She thought of her kiss with Harlan and how carefully he'd held her, as if she were more fragile than Dresden china, then looked at Ling Shi. Fear flickered in her friend's eyes as she glanced from Pascal to her father. Pascal looked closer, focusing on her friend's arms, her breasts. Quickly, Ling Shi hoisted the coverlet to her neck, but not before Pascal saw the bruises.

He'd beaten her.

The realization robbed Pascal's breath. She almost doubled over with the shock of it. "You h-hit her?" she whispered. "You hurt Ling Shi?"

She flew at him, punching her fists against his chest, kicking his shins. "You monster. You evil, *evil* man!"

Benoit tossed Pascal away. Ling Shi screamed. Pascal scrambled to her feet and drove at her father. This time, he caught both her hands and pushed her against the wall, pinning her there.

"Forget what you saw, Pascal. It has nothing to do with you."

"She's my friend!"

"She's nothing but a servant."

"No! She's my dearest friend and you hurt her. You're not to touch her." Pascal struggled to get free, kicking her father. "You're never to touch her again or I'll . . . I'll shoot you. I swear I will!"

He threw her across the room with enough force to send her crashing against the footboard. The air left her lungs in an audible whoosh. She hit the post of the tester bed and fell on her hands and knees on the carpet. The lights flickered and Pascal blinked, trying to orient herself. Ling Shi's strangled cry echoed behind her.

Pascal seized the post and struggled to her feet. She had to stop her father. She had to make sure he would never hurt Ling Shi again. She staggered toward him, until Ling Shi pulled her into her arms, holding her against her naked body. Pascal could hear Ling Shi begging her to stop, to leave things be.

Pascal tried to focus. Her father's image swam before her. "You're my father," she whispered. "How could you hurt my best friend like this? How could you be so bad—"

"You will forget what you saw, Pascal," her father said with his hand on the door. "It never happened. Do you understand?"

"You bastard!" she screamed. But even before the echo of the words died, Benoit De Dreux disappeared into the hall, uncaring of her opinion as he had been all her life.

For a moment, Pascal thought she might be ill. Her father. Her father abusing Ling Shi. But then Pascal remembered the girl beside her. She stood and helped Ling Shi to her feet, guiding her friend back to the tester. Ling Shi needed Pascal to be strong now.

On the bed, Ling Shi shuddered with sobs as she pulled away from Pascal and struggled to put on her dressing gown. Her eyes—dark mysterious eyes that Pascal had always thought wonderfully exotic—were swollen from tears. The lamplight shimmered off the rivulets of moisture on her high cheeks.

Pascal thought of all the beautiful emotions of the evening. Of Harlan and his sweet kisses. Of his arms around her as they'd danced and how he'd smiled at her, making her heart expand with joy. Then the images disappeared and all that was left was Ling Shi, huddled in the corner of her bed like a frightened animal, fresh tears running down her face.

"Don't hate me, Pascal," Ling Shi whispered, clutching the dressing gown at her throat. "Please, do not hate me for this."

"Hate you?" The statement seemed so ludicrous that for a moment, Pascal did not realize her voice sounded angry. She wrapped her arms around Ling Shi, inhaling the familiar scent of jasmine that had always made her feel safe and loved. "How could I ever hate you? You're my best friend. I love you, Ling Shi. Don't you know that?"

For the first time, it was Pascal who comforted Ling Shi as the girl wept against her shoulder, repeating her pleas that Pascal not think ill of her. Pascal rocked her, making hushed *shhing* noises. "He forced you, Ling Shi," she said, the venom returning to her voice. "There was nothing you could do to stop him."

Ling Shi gazed up at Pascal with wide eyes. "Pascal, don't—"

"How could he do this to you?" She stroked the red mark on her friend's cheek. "He beat—"

The horrible thought flickered inside her. Ling Shi alone all those nights Pascal had ridden with Santana. Ling Shi complaining of her stupidity for not lighting a lamp and stumbling against her night table. There had always been an explanation for the bruises.

"How long has this been going on?" Pascal asked in a deadened voice.

Not looking at Pascal, Ling Shi whispered, "Not . . . long."

"I don't believe you."

"It is as your father said, Pascal. You must forget tonight."

"So he can keep doing this to you?" Pascal straightened on the bed and brushed a few strands of Ling Shi's hair over her shoulder. "Why didn't you tell me? I could have protected you."

"I would not want you to go against your father for me."

"You mean you don't think I *could* go against my father."

Ling Shi smiled weakly. "We are both powerless against him."

"That's not true!" She hugged her friend with all her strength, crying now for what she must have suffered. "Ling Shi, I won't let him touch you again. You can go away. I'll help you. I can give you money . . . anything you need." A plan formed as she spoke. "Doc Chiang! You and he are great friends. He's a wonderful person with a fine reputation. He'll help you."

"Pascal, I cannot go."

"Of course you can! Tonight. You must leave tonight. I'll get Murray to help us." She thought of the coachman faithful to her stepmother, often running messages to Kate and other mysterious errands. Surely, when she explained the circumstances, he would agree to drive Ling Shi into the city. "Once you're safely in town—"

"Pascal, I will not leave here, tonight or any other night."

Pascal stopped, staring at Ling Shi in surprise. "But why? He'll just keep . . . hurting you."

"You do not know your father as I do," Ling Shi finished in a whisper. Even in the faint light, Pascal could see her friend's fear. "He would be very angry if I left. Anyone who thwarts him would be in terrible—"

"You're afraid he might hurt me?" A rage fired inside Pascal. "You're going to stay here to be . . . beaten—abused, because you're afraid of what my father might do to *me*?"

Ling Shi placed a soft hand on Pascal's arm. "I do not believe your father would turn against you, Pascal. Not in the way you imply. You are his only child. But sometimes, your father . . . you should do as you have always done

—cross his path as l-little as p-possible." Ling Shi's voice choked. She met Pascal's eyes. "I cannot leave you, my friend. It would break my heart to know you are here all alone."

With painful clarity, Pascal realized the sacrifice Ling Shi was prepared to make. How often had she complained to Ling Shi that only she loved Pascal? That, without Ling Shi, she would be desperately unhappy and alone? What a horrible life her friend had condemned herself to for Pascal's sake. And though a desperate voice inside Pascal cried out, *don't leave me Ling Shi*, a nobler part commanded her to make things right.

Pascal took up Ling Shi's hand. "You have to leave. I don't want you here."

The sorrow in Ling Shi's face pierced Pascal's heart. "But I thought . . . You said you did not hate me."

"No! Never that."

"You're not a-ashamed of me?"

Again, Pascal hugged her, letting her know how much she cherished their friendship by her tight embrace. "You are the dearest, bravest person I have ever known, Ling Shi. But if you're not gone by morning, I'll confront my father again and again, until he's forced to let you go."

"Oh no! You must not."

"I will, Ling Shi." She sat back, releasing Ling Shi's shoulders, watching her with deadly earnest. "You know I will. But if you go now, you have my promise that I won't seek him out. I'll stay out of his way, just as you said to do."

"Oh, Pascal."

"It's for the best, Ling Shi." Pascal held back her tears only through sheer dint of will. Inside her head, she screamed how much she needed her friend and how she would miss her. But she dared not voice her feeling aloud. She would only make Ling Shi's parting more difficult for both of them. "Now," she said gently, "should I help you pack?"

Ling Shi shook her head. A desolate expression shadowed her eyes. "I shall be ready shortly."

While Ling Shi packed her things, Pascal ran to her room. She wanted to collapse into tears on the bed, but instead she threw open her dresser. In the back of the bottom drawer, wadded up in a handkerchief were a pair of emerald earrings with a matching necklace and bracelet. The beautiful set had once belonged to her mother. The jewelry and a shawl was all Pascal had to remind her of the woman who had given birth to her. Without a second thought, she took the necklace and earrings and added it to a small stash of money she kept for indulgences. Then she sat down at her escritoire and scribbled out a heartfelt note.

It didn't take Ling Shi long to be ready. With the coachman to help them, the two crept outside carrying her valise to the waiting carriage. Swallowing back the knot in her throat, Pascal slipped the note with the jewelry and money into Ling Shi's bag as Murray helped the Chinese girl into the carriage. Later, Ling Shi would find her message. The letter explained how it tore Pascal's heart to see her friend leave, but surely Ling Shi could understand that she could never live with the guilt of what Ling Shi must endure to stay by her side.

Pascal walked back around to the carriage door. She climbed up and sat across from Ling Shi, who watched her from beneath the veil of her hat. Without a word, Pascal hugged her quickly and turned for the door. Ling Shi grabbed her arm, stopping her. "Pascal," she said in a strained voice. "Is this truly what you want, dearest friend?"

Pascal looked back. With a brave smile, she gave Ling Shi's hand a squeeze. "It's for the best." Turning away before her friend could see her tears, Pascal dropped down from the carriage and closed the door. She told Murray to take Ling Shi to Doc Chiang's, instructing him to stay and make sure that Ling Shi was safe. As the carriage sped down the drive, she waved her final good-bye.

Now, she was truly alone.

Mercy stared down at the moon-polished hair on the pillow beside her. The Silver Fox. The name certainly suited, she thought. He was a unique man, clever, and no doubt cunning when the circumstances called for it. But now, with his dark lashes feathered to rest against his skin and a slight smile tugging at his lips, he looked far removed from their dangerous game of intrigue. In his sleep, he showed only a tender lover. Mercy raised her hand, tempted to tease the small dimple on his chin, but decided not to disturb him. Lifting the arm he'd anchored across her chest, she edged off the bed.

He tightened his arm around her. "Don't leave," he whispered, his eyes still shut.

Mercy settled on the pillow with a sigh, then gave in to her desire to trace a path across the dimple to his mouth. "I thought you were asleep."

He nibbled on the tip of her finger. "I'm a light sleeper. And," he said, smiling as he opened his eyes, "I hesitate to say it, but I'm not used to sleeping with someone in my bed."

"That's not a bad thing to admit," she whispered, his words warming her. "It makes me feel rather special."

Rey pulled her face close, thinking of his words to Mac. *Do you know how many years it's been since I've fallen asleep holding a woman in my arms?*

He caressed her lips persuasively until her mouth opened and Mercy lost herself in his kiss. "You have no idea just how special," he whispered.

But before things could progress, he felt Mercy retreat. "I really must get back, Rey."

He studied her, seeking answers in her soft brown eyes. "To what, Mercedes?" He touched the red mark that still marred her left cheek. "To Benoit and more abuse?"

"Don't."

"Stay here with me," he said. "And I'll never let him hurt you again."

The pledge surprised Rey. It was an incredible promise for a man whose wife had died as a criminal's pawn. *What makes you think you can protect anyone? You failed Sophie. What about your mission here? Sotheby and De Dreux?* But his haunting voices seemed distant, their power silenced by the woman in his arms. Mercedes, the mere sight of her in the beginning, and now so much more, had sent him wildly beyond the regulation that had shaped his life the past five years. He should have paid more attention to those first trivial transgressions, he thought: the smoking, the drinking, both activities he'd given up in atonement for past wrongs. He should have seen them as guideposts for what was to come. Now, like some knight-errant, he offered his protectorship to the wife of a man he'd sworn to bring to justice. And Rey knew with a certainty that he would protect her, if she allowed it.

Mercy blinked back tears. She hadn't been wrong that night she'd confessed love's possibility to Kate. She'd wondered, of course, these past days, if her words had been fanciful or insightful. But no other emotion could describe her feelings for this man—not just someone whose touch brought magic. She knew what he risked by offering a haven to the wife of the man he investigated.

She answered him first with a lingering kiss, a celebration of the love she held for him. Threading her fingers through the incredible silver hair, she shook her head. "No, Rey. I don't need protecting. What happened last night with Benoit is . . . rare."

"And if it happens again?"

She touched his lips, smoothing back the angry lines with her fingers. "I promise I'll come to you immediately."

He grabbed her wrist and kissed her palm, then fiercely embraced her, as if he planned to change her mind with actions rather than words. But little by little, with a gentle stroke, a staying hand, Mercy pulled away and left his side. As she dressed, Rey watched her from the bed and there was a haunting ardor to his gaze reflected in the wardrobe mirror before her. She wet her lips and held her corset against her. "I need your help." She lifted the hair over her shoulder, presenting her bare back.

She heard the bed ropes, the pad of feet on the carpet. But instead of fastening her corset, his warm hands glided beneath the material of her camisole and cupped her breasts as he kissed her neck.

Mercy leaned back against him. "That's . . . not . . . helping."

"It's helping me."

Mercedes giggled, then turned in his arms, releasing her hold on the corset. Her hands traveled up the muscles of his shoulders and she buried her fingers to his scalp. Passion unfurled inside her tempting her to forget the coming dawn.

"Don't go," he whispered. "Not yet." He stepped backward toward the bed, pulling her with him as they kissed.

Mercy stopped. "I must." She stroked his lips with hers before meeting his eyes. "Please, don't try to persuade me otherwise, or against my better judgment, I might stay."

With a look of utmost reluctance, he gave her one final kiss before fastening her underclothes and then her dress. By the time she held her pelisse draped across her arm, he'd made arrangements for a servant to bring his carriage to the front door. Leaning against the clothespress, wearing only his trousers and smoking a cigarette, he said, "I want to be with you again. Soon."

She hesitated as she looped the pelisse over her shoulders. She buttoned the frogs of her coat to give herself something to do rather than answer his question. "I—" She sighed, refusing to lie by giving excuses. "Please, Rey. Let me pick the time."

He didn't respond, just smoked the cigarette. His was the face of a man trained to wait out opponents. Certainly, that stoic regard must have garnered many a concession in the past. But at the moment, Mercy had few choices left.

She walked toward him, halting just half a foot in front of him. She placed a gloved hand on his chest. Leaning forward, she stepped up on tiptoes and placed a kiss on his cheek. "I'll let you know when I'm able to get away."

Rey dropped his cigarette to the floor and swept her up against him. His mouth on hers left her breathless and wanting, letting her know that he had the power to change her mind. He didn't release her until the tight muscles of her arms became supple, granting her compliance. In the end, it was he who stepped away.

"If anything happens. If he even threatens you, Mercedes, you're to come to me immediately. Your word on that."

"Yes, Rey. I promise."

Less than an hour later, Mercy climbed the stairs to her room at L'Isle des Rêves, tired but wonderfully satisfied. At long last, something good had come of Benoit's torments. Running from him, she'd experienced the beauty of her love for Rey. Now she could understand why she'd risked so much to experience their tender union.

But you lied about the baby. Mercy stopped, clutching the mahogany banister. Slowly she climbed up the next step. *He was adamant . . . no children. And you lied.*

She closed her eyes. Unconsciously, her hand dropped to her stomach. She could almost picture herself swollen with his child. A baby girl of her very own. Not Benoit's offspring—not even hers alone. But the child of a man like Rey. His child would never be stillborn. His baby would be a gift beyond comprehension.

Yes, she'd lied, she answered her conscience, briskly taking the last step and heading down the hall to her room. And she'd do it again. And again. She wanted his child that much.

Mercy dropped her chin to her chest as her fingers closed around her doorknob. Once, just *once,* she'd like to experience joy without guilt. What would it be like, she wondered, not to have to lie and cheat and steal for every miserable scrap of happiness.

With a sigh, she opened the door, thankful for the privacy of her own wing. The freedom to do as she pleased had been the most difficult concession she'd earned from her husband after her miscarriage. But now that she'd actually been unfaithful, she would take extra precautions to make sure Benoit failed in monitoring her comings and goings. It helped that the household staff was loyal to her. A man as hard as Benoit did not earn personal devotion and his paid spies had always proven inept against her network of servants.

When she entered her room, the first thing she noticed was the darkness. Mercy frowned, releasing the door handle. Her personal maid always made certain a light burned while she was out. She glanced at the opened window as she removed her gloves. Another anomaly. Tossing her coat on the bed, she found a twisted piece of newspaper, one of many spills kept in a metal cup on the mantel, and lit the taper with the embers in the fireplace. She touched the rolled-up newsprint to the lamp's wick until its glow filled the room, then snuffed out the spill and returned the unused portion to its canister. She turned around.

In the room's corner, Pascal waited silently on the blue satin chaise.

Something was terribly wrong; Mercy sensed it immediately. Pascal sat motionless, almost despondent. There was no light to her eyes. They appeared glazed as they watched Mercy. All thoughts of their last confrontation fled, as did Mercy's anguish over the week of silence she'd endured. Pascal needed her.

"What's happened, Pascal?" Then, in a moment's insight, "Is it Mr. Everard? Has he hurt you somehow?"

The girl shook her head. She blinked her eyes rapidly and gazed up at the plaster molding of the ceiling. One foot made lazy circles on the Belgian carpet. She dropped her head and focused there as she asked, "Did Santana make a run tonight?"

In her stepdaughter's eyes, Mercy saw a beaten child waiting for a final blow. "No, Pascal," she said gently. "Not tonight."

There was a glimmer of relief, pitifully brief. "I thought because you weren't here—Mr. Parks?"

She drew closer to the wounded girl on her chaise, thinking of her answer carefully. "Yes," she said. She'd kept so much from Pascal already. "I was with Rey at Bizy."

Pascal nodded, as if everything made sense to her now. She looked out the window past Mercy, toward the levee. "I'm glad."

The vehemence in those simple words made Mercy hurry to her stepdaughter's side. Rey must have felt this way when Mercy entered his salon, frightened and damaged from Benoit's attack. Following his example, she knelt down in front of Pascal. "Tell me what happened."

Pascal shook her head. "Never mind about that. I wanted to ask you something. It's . . . important."

Mercy took Pascal's delicate hand between hers, surprised even as she executed the gesture that Pascal allowed it. "Anything."

"I wanted to know—" Again, Pascal glanced out the window. She slipped her hand from Mercy's and dropped it to the skirt of her ball gown. She worried the material between her fingers. The pose brought back an image of Beth, twisting Mercy's heart as tightly as the satin wrung in Pascal's lap. How many years ago had Beth, a girl almost Pascal's tender years, fumbled with the hem of her tattered rags in that cold London alley?

"I wanted to hear what my father has done to you."

Pascal's strong voice banished the past. Mercy sat back on her heels. *Benoit.* She should have known.

"How has he hurt you?" Pascal asked. "It must be something terrible for you to hate him so much. I mean, to dream up Santana and steal from him. It is my father we've been stealing from, isn't it?"

The unexpectedness of Pascal's questions left Mercy speechless. She'd never wanted Pascal to know about her father, had worked hard to keep that knowledge from her. "I thought you didn't know," she said at last.

"That Santana stole from father?" Pascal shook her head. "No, I didn't even guess, until today. That was rather cabbage-headed of me now that I think back on it. I mean"—she seemed to concentrate as she spoke—"I knew we were stealing from one of Gessler's cronies. My father owns the constable, lock, stock and barrel. And of course, Father was absolutely rabid whenever anyone brought up the subject of Santana—" Pascal stopped, as if realizing she was babbling. "But I guess I wasn't thinking clearly at the time." She straightened on the chaise, instantly looking years older. "Is it the girls you wanted to help? He kidnaps them, doesn't he? He's a . . . a white slaver, just like in the books. Or has he done something to you as well? I know my father can be very evil."

"Oh, Pascal. I'm so sorry—"

"Tell me. I want—I *need* to know the truth." And when Mercy said nothing, Pascal's fingers dug into her arm. "Don't you see?" she whispered. "I have to know what kind of monster my father is. I want to understand"—Pascal struggled over her words, as if her throat had grown too thick to speak—"to understand . . . why you and everyone I've ever known"—a choked sob escaped; she buried her face in her hands—"why everyone hates me!"

Mercy sat down beside her and gathered Pascal into her arms. "Shhh." She rocked her, feeling her pain, despising Benoit. "I don't hate you, Pascal. I never could. No matter what happened between us."

Pascal broke Mercy's grip. "Don't lie! How could you not hate me? I know he's hurt you very badly. My father is evil. I know he's capable of the most vile acts . . . and I'm part of him. I am *his* child."

Memories flashed through Mercy. Benoit baiting her, screaming at her that she was nothing, a whore, a slut, mud he had molded into gentle womanhood. Benoit's eyes as they flashed the evil venom of his hate when he'd beaten her that last time, then shouted that she was a failure for miscarrying their child after his brutality. And Benoit's vile little smile when she'd held her first gun, awkwardly, unaccustomed to its weight, and aimed at his heart —until he'd taken it easily from her grasp saying she could never destroy her creator, her god.

It had taken years to fight his image of her, years of convincing herself that he was wrong, that *he* was evil, not Mercy. A ballad of Robin Hood, read in bed while she recovered from her miscarriage, a pure red rose, and a mask of feathers had come together to create Santana Rose, a woman strong enough to fight him. But even now, in those desperate moments of darkness, she still wrestled with the voice inside her that argued he might be right— that Robin Hood was only a myth, and no good person would steal for the sake of justice.

Mercy focused on the eyes of the child before her, the girl who now condemned herself for the very flaw Mercy had fought the past ten years. Benoit's creation. His child.

"He hurt Ling Shi." Pascal spoke the words as if they were her final condemnation. Her face screwed up with shame and held-back tears. "I had to send her away because he was hurting her."

Mercy gathered Pascal back into her embrace. The girl buried her face against Mercy's neck as she'd done when Gessler's men had stalked them in the swamps.

"I saw him," Pascal wept. "He was in her room. He'd hit her. He'd forced himself on her. And it wasn't the first time."

Mercy knew immediately what horrible scene Pascal had walked into. Her father was a man who sought his pleasure in the pain of others. That he found solace for aging in the arms of girls half his age Mercy might suspect, but never that he'd choose his daughter's sole friend as a victim. Mercy shut her eyes against the horrible image. Dear God, that Ling Shi should have to endure Benoit's degradations. And Pascal a witness to it all.

She held Pascal with a strength that let her stepdaughter know Mercy could never hate her. She knew of only one remedy that could banish Pascal's nightmares.

"We can't help who our parents are, Pascal," she whispered against the red locks. "My mother was a prostitute. She didn't even know my father."

Pascal stiffened, then leaned back to look at Mercy in surprise.

"I was one of those women, Pascal," she explained, brushing back a curl of Pascal's hair. "The ones we take from Gessler's men in the swamps. Twelve years ago, your father was young enough to search for the girls himself. He discovered me in London, living off the streets. But instead of a bawdy house, he sent me to the country and paid to have me schooled on how to become a lady. His grand experiment, he called me. I guess he felt he succeeded well enough. Two years after he found me, he forced me to marry him. Everything you know about me, my illustrious family, my aristocratic roots, it's all a lie made up by your father. My mother was a whore."

"That means nothing," Pascal argued hoarsely. "Kate, all those girls we help, they aren't bad. But my father—"

"Listen to me. You are nothing like Benoit. You could never do the things your father has done. His mind is twisted." She thought of Benoit's black blood, a secret heritage Mercy was almost certain Pascal was unaware of, and chose her words carefully. "His family rejected him, long ago, for something he could never change. It did something to your father. It made him want to hurt people, like he was hurt." Mercy wiped away a tear gliding down Pascal's cheek. "You are his victim. Just like Ling Shi. Just like the other girls. Never think of yourself as anything else."

"At school," Pascal whispered, "here at home with you, all the things I've done . . ."

Mercy pressed a finger across Pascal's lips and shook her head. "Think of the swamp, when Gessler's man would have shot me. You saved me, Pascal. You saved my life."

A light of hope flickered in Pascal's eyes.

"And tonight. With Ling Shi. You said you sent her away. You helped her, didn't you? You made sure she would be safe from Benoit, even though it must have hurt you terribly to see her go?"

Pascal nodded. Fresh tears welled in her eyes.

"Are those the acts of an evil person, Pascal?"

A fragile smile turned one corner of her mouth. She launched herself against Mercy, holding her like a lifeline. "No. No, they're not."

"And in those dark moments when you think differently," Mercy continued in a low voice, "you'll come to me? We'll be friends now. There's no need to hurt each other anymore."

Pascal nodded against her shoulder. "I would like that, very much. I—I need a friend."

"So do I," Mercy whispered. "So do I."

Ling Shi dropped the leather satchel on the doorstep of the boarding house and glanced back at the carriage driver. She'd tried to convince the man to leave her at the St. Charles Hotel for the night, afraid to disturb Chiang at his boarding house at this early morning hour—and ashamed, she admitted, deeply ashamed that he should again see her at her lowest moment. But the driver would not hear of a change in plans, even after she'd assured him that she had enough money to pay for accommodations. Now Murray waited atop the coachman's boot for her to knock on the door. Resigned, Ling Shi took up the brass knocker and banged it loudly.

Each knock struck through her, increasing her humiliation, until the door creaked open. A woman dressed in a wrapper, her nightcap askew over white corkscrew curls, peered into the darkness with her candle.

"Gott in Himmel," the lady exclaimed, holding a hand to her bosom. She straightened the spectacles perched on her nose and narrowed her pale blue eyes on Ling Shi. "Vat do you vant?"

"Please, madame." Ling Shi glanced back at the driver. "I wish to speak with Doc Chiang."

"Herr Doktor Chiang? *Es ist drei Uhr.* Three in the morning! You have a medical problem?"

Ling Shi could feel the spots of color on her cheeks. "No, nothing like that. I know it is a great imposition, but he is a friend of mine . . ." she finished weakly. Focusing on the toes of her slippers, she added, "I have nowhere else to go."

When Ling Shi looked up into the older woman's face, she saw concern in the pale blue eyes behind the wire spectacles. Ling Shi turned away, knowing that any sympathy would release a flood of tears.

"Kommen Sie." She waved Ling Shi inside, taking up the satchel on the doorstep and guiding her to the parlor at the entrance. "You vait *hier.* I come back with *Herr Doktor."*

Ling Shi sat miserably on the horsehair sofa. Not since the day she'd come into town to seek an end to her pregnancy had she felt so empty inside. She'd known the moment Monsieur De Dreux walked into her room this night would be a nightmare. And, if she were honest with herself, she also knew that sooner or later Pascal would discover her relationship with her father. But still, the knowledge did not ease her heartache over the horrible night and the painful parting.

Doc Chiang scrambled in, his hat and medical bag in hand. His coat was only half on and he shouldered on the other sleeve while pulling out his long black braid of hair from beneath. When he saw Ling Shi, he immediately stopped, then nodded at the landlady who watched curiously from the door.

"It is all right, Mrs. Bruckner. I know the lady well. If we could perhaps have a few moments?" he asked.

"*Herr Doktor,* this is highly irregular."

"Yes, I know. I've been a trial to you from the beginning, Mrs. Bruckner, with all my nightly comings and goings. But as you know, it is all in the name of medicine."

This final statement seemed to pacify the lady. "*Ja.* Of course, *Doktor.* A medical man has many responsibilities." Mrs. Bruckner's frown vanished and she gave them both a motherly smile. "I come back in a few minutes, *doch?*"

"Thank you, Mrs. Bruckner."

Shaking her head, Mrs. Bruckner left Doc Chiang and Ling Shi alone. He dropped his hat and bag on the sofa and sat down beside Ling Shi. His gentle hands came up to her face, finding each hurt, every bruise, with the accuracy of experience. "How could this man do such a thing?" he asked, almost to himself. "It is he that you are running from, is it not?" he asked as he reached for his medical bag.

"Yes," she answered almost inaudibly.

"Ling Shi, listen to me. You must never return. He will hurt you. Perhaps next time—"

"I have left for good. That is why I am here."

"Do you mean—"

"Please, let me explain the circumstances"—she met his eyes for the first time—"before I lose my courage."

She saw a spark of hope in his eyes as he nestled her hand in his. Looking down, Ling Shi took a deep breath. "Chiang, you know everything about me. How I came here to New Orleans and why I stayed. You even know the darkest secret of my soul . . . about the child . . ." His hands squeezed hers, giving her the courage to go on. "We have been friends—"

"The best of friends, Ling Shi."

She nodded. "If knowing what you do about me, you still want us to marry, then it is my wish as well."

For two heartbeats, Ling Shi held her breath. She waited in agony for his response.

"You have made me a very happy man, Ling Shi."

At his whispered words, she could no longer hold back her tears. They fell to betray her. Doc Chiang lifted her chin. "What is it, dearest one? I tell you how happy you make me, and you cry? And do not try to convince me that these are tears of happiness."

"No. They are tears of shame." She steeled herself, not wishing to mar her confession by crying. "To come to you in this manner when you have treated me with nothing but kindness. I will not lie to you; I take advantage of your generous heart. You are a good man. You deserve the truth. I came here tonight only because L'Isle des Rêves is no longer a safe place for me and I have nowhere else to go."

Ling Shi waited, expecting the condemnation she deserved. But instead of anger, Chiang gave her a warm smile. "When a smart man finds his golden treasure on his doorstep, he does not question how it got there, Ling Shi."

"But—"

"You worry too much, dearest one. Tomorrow, things will look brighter." He stood and guided her to the door. "Let us get you settled for the night and worry about the details of our marriage in the light of morning."

He opened the door to find Mrs. Bruckner waiting in the hall. With great pride beaming on his face, he pulled Ling Shi forward. "Mrs. Bruckner, I would like you to be the first to know what a lucky man I am. Ling Shi has consented to be my bride."

The lady's face lit up, reflecting the happiness in Doc Chiang's own expression. "Oh, *Herr Doktor,* how happy I am for you." She switched her smile to Ling Shi. "And so lovely too. *Kommen Sie,* we find a room for you, *ja?*"

With Mrs. Bruckner's help, Ling Shi soon settled into a

small chamber across the hall from Doc Chiang. The entire time he'd tended to her minor wounds, Chiang had spoken of his plans for a special home together and how Ling Shi could take over his lazy assistant's position at the apothecary. They could marry across the river in Gretna, the banns not being necessary in Jefferson Parish. When he left her alone to prepare a special sleeping potion in the downstairs kitchen, Ling Shi looked about the room. Though the chamber appeared cheery, with chintz curtains and a plant in a pot near the window, she couldn't help feeling lonely here. Pascal would not be in the room adjacent, as she'd been for half of Ling Shi's life.

Sniffing back her tears, she opened her leather satchel on the bed, thinking to retrieve her night rail and wrapper. The first thing she saw was a sheet of Pascal's stationery. When she carefully picked up the note, she saw the bundled handkerchief beneath it.

Ling Shi opened the letter, her heart pounding in her throat until she read the bold dark script. Tears glided from her eyes as she scanned the words of love. Pascal did not hate her, as Ling Shi had secretly feared despite her friend's assurances. Ling Shi closed her eyes as she read the last line.

Know that you have been mother and friend, sister and confidante, and that I will always love you.

Ling Shi folded the letter and untied the handkerchief to find the money and jewelry mentioned in the note. It eased her pain to know that Pascal cared for her. She tried not to see tonight as a sad ending, but rather to accept the good it heralded. Pascal had grown up. This night, she had put the needs of another before her own. Certainly, such a girl would soon make new friends and find others who would care for her as deeply as Ling Shi. Yet, despite the logic of her thoughts, the note and jewelry also brought a deep sadness.

At the knock on the door, Ling Shi called out to enter. Doc Chiang came in with the tea he'd made for her. "You drink this, and soon you will get the rest you need. By morning, you will feel much better."

"Thank you," she whispered, taking the cup from his hands.

He glanced at the jewelry on the bed. Immediately, a look of grief crept into his eyes.

"Those emeralds are very fine. Much better than the simple trinkets I gave you."

"It is not what you think, Chiang."

He set down the tray and sat down on the bed beside her. "Then be so kind as to explain."

"It's a dowry of sorts. From Pascal. Not from—"

"I understand," he said, cutting her off before she spoke Monsieur De Dreux's name. "I'm a foolish old man, Ling Shi. Drink your tea, before it gets cold."

Chiang watched as she finished the herb tea then handed him the cup. He seemed to linger, staring down at the tiny porcelain as if wishing to say something more. At last, he placed the cup on the nightstand. "I want you not to worry," he said. "I know that it will not be easy for you and I to have a real marriage. Certainly you have very bad memories. It will take time for you to recover from your experiences. I want you to know that I am a patient man."

His kind words combined with Pascal's message of love tore through her reserve. Ling Shi turned away as she cried, "Dearest Chiang, how could you understand what it is like to care for a man, as I do for you, but to fear those feelings? I want to touch you, and I cannot. I have often thought of your arms around me, only to have fear crush my thoughts from my mind. I do not want the ugliness that has haunted me at L'Isle des Rêves to follow me to my marriage. Do you not see clearly I am flawed? I will never be a proper wife to you, as you deserve."

"Ah, Ling Shi. How it warms my heart to hear that you see me as a man as well as a friend. It is a start, no?"

She kept her face away. "Chiang, what you desire may not be possible."

He pulled her around to face him. "I have dedicated my life to healing, Ling Shi." He gave her his warmest smile. "Do not underestimate the power of my love."

Chapter 13

Rey swayed with the motion of the landau, watching De Dreux seated across the carriage from him. Strips of moonlight beamed through the two windows like patchy stage lights, spotlighting De Dreux as he smoothed his pencil-thin mustache above a semblance of a smile. From the top of his beaver hat and double-breasted frock coat to his fawn-colored spats, the planter appeared the perfect gentleman—as manicured as a well-tended English garden. De Dreux's polish, his urbane air, seemed to place him above common violence against a woman, but Rey wasn't fooled. His years as a lawman had taught him that, at times, evil came in neat, rather elegant packages.

Rey glanced at Harlan seated beside him. The Pinkerton extended his legs across the narrow carriage floor, crowding De Dreux on the seat opposite. For once, Rey ignored the tension between Harlan and the sugar baron, his thoughts fixed on the problem that had plagued him the past four nights. Too-familiar questions sounded in his head with the rhythm of the horses' hooves clamping against the crushed shell road, threatening his concentration for the meeting with Sotheby ahead.

Why didn't she leave De Dreux? From the sound of it, their relationship didn't even reach the legitimacy of marriage of convenience. Was it the scandal of divorce that stayed her? The money? Either factor held more than sufficient cause. Yet, he refused to believe it of her. Not Mercedes.

Something more than security and social standing kept her at De Dreux's side. Rey had watched her during the dinner party four nights ago, had seen how she'd allowed others to preen and boast while never participating in their peacock discussions. Time and again, she'd nod and grant each puffed-up society dame a smile that held too much mischief to be in step with the *beau monde*'s priorities. And De Dreux. From the first night Rey had arrived at L'Isle des Rêves, she'd baited her husband without consideration to appearances. Even the night the bastard had struck her, she'd fled to Bizy, gambling that her absence would go undiscovered.

Her motives for remaining in her loveless marriage more than fascinated Rey as he faced De Dreux in the moonlight. They obsessed him almost as much as the woman herself. For years he'd thought of nothing but Sotheby. Now, even in the middle of strategy sessions with Harlan and Mac, his mind wandered at odd moments to Mercedes, the softness of her lips, the warmth in her eyes, and the release she offered, an oblivion so profound it could blot out his dark memories, if but for a moment.

Bewitched by a married woman—haunted by desire for revenge. Which was the greater character flaw, he wondered?

Since the night Rey had spent with Mercedes, he'd made it a point to call on De Dreux each day to make certain she'd suffered no harm. He'd found her cool and elegant, attending to him and her husband as any experienced hostess might. It was sweet torture to watch her. They were never alone. Rey had waited for the promised message, but received only disappointment.

The past four nights he'd spent lying in bed alone, smoking a Choctaw, puzzling over the choices he'd made and those he still faced. So much for structure and the black and white rules Mac claimed Rey so fond of. Mercedes De Dreux had thrown him into a tangle of grays. He wanted her, like he wanted to walk, to eat, to breathe. She —a married woman—had somehow become essential to him. But it wasn't until last evening, when his body had grown hard just thinking of her and his heart had ached contemplating the sleepless and lonely hours ahead, that he'd surrendered to the question that condemned him most: What would it take to make her leave De Dreux?

What indeed.

Thou shall not covet thy neighbor's wife. The Bible verse ran over and over in his head.

The carriage hit a rut. De Dreux cursed, inconvenienced even by that slight jostle. Rey pictured Mercedes as she'd appeared that night in his salon, the bruise on her cheek, the red marks on her throat. How could any man, much less God, sanctify such a union?

"I read in the *Democrat* this morning," Rey said, his voice low and even as his hostility toward Mercy's husband joined forces with his plans to put the man behind bars, "that there's no doubt the governor will sign the bill outlawing the lottery."

"Jus' where does that leave us and the other investors, *m'sieur*?" Harlan added beside him.

Rey lifted his eyebrows a fraction of an inch. "If what the newspapers say is true, I imagine we're out of a hell of a lot of money. Wouldn't you agree, De Dreux?"

"You worry needlessly, *monsieur*." De Dreux's eyes glittered in the lamplight illuminating the New Orleans–bound carriage. "As I said before, the men I work with assure me that the bill will be stopped in the courts should the governor sign it into law. I am sorry this meeting was even necessary, that my guarantee has been insufficient for you."

"Blind faith has never appealed to me," Rey answered dryly. "I'm willing to take certain risks, you understand, for the kind of return you're promising. Calculated risks—not foolish ones."

"*Mon Dieu,* man. 'Bout time we get more for our money than jus' words," Harlan added.

De Dreux's eyes shifted to the younger man. The corner of his mouth slipped downward in thinly veiled distaste. "How fortunate that we were able to schedule this rendezvous then, to put your fears to rest."

"And why all the secrecy?" Harlan pressed. "Don't trust us much, do you?"

"Oh, I wouldn't let our host's caution disturb you," Rey answered, letting Harlan play the role of adversary while he acted the part of diplomat. "I quite understand the need for discretion. But I must admit, De Dreux, a secret location, mysterious solutions in government, a silent partner—it reads a bit like a bad penny novel. I have reservations about the funds already invested, and even less desire to hand over more as you've requested."

"It won't be long until we reach town, *messieurs,*" De Dreux assured them. "Soon, all your questions shall be answered and your concerns put to—"

A high-pitched squeal hissed outside, rising in an eerie crescendo. *The brakes,* Rey thought, just as he was slammed back against his seat. Harlan grabbed the arm rail. De Dreux tumbled to the floor. The smell of burning wood and leather filled the carriage compartment. Gunshots and curses from the direction of the driver's boot peppered the air outside. The landau pitched wildly, tipped on two wheels, careened off the road.

With one hand looped through the leather strap, Rey grabbed his Colt and flipped back the curtain. He couldn't afford for anything to go wrong. Not tonight. Not when he was mere miles from confronting Sotheby. But almost as if the past moments of inattention could curse his mission, Rey knew something had indeed gone very wrong. A broken axle or wheel rim didn't account for the gunfire that echoed off the swamps as the coach lurched to a stop. He scanned the road, searching for what his gut told him he'd find soon enough.

Up on the levee, the moon silhouetted a rider mounted on a midnight-black horse. Her cape billowed around her, ebony wings that reflected the character of her birdlike mask. A pair of Smith and Wessons smoked at her sides.

"I don't believe it," Rey said under his breath.

"What is it, *monsieur*? What do you see?"

More shots blasted overhead. De Dreux shouted and ducked back to the carriage floor. Harlan joined Rey at the window, his gun in his hand. Behind them, hoofbeats rolled like approaching thunder.

Harlan strained to see over Rey's shoulder. "*Tonnerre!* It's not . . . ?"

Rey cocked his pistol. "Santana Rose."

"*Merde!*" Harlan punched the leather-padded wall.

Behind them, De Dreux staggered to his seat. Still watching the figure on the levee, Rey said, "So much for Gessler's patrols."

"The bandit appears beyond his capabilities," De Dreux answered in a thin voice.

"To say the least," Rey finished.

The powerful horse reared on its two hind legs. Santana pulled back on the reins, leaning forward, one with the horse. Both mount and rider sped down the levee toward the coach. There was a disturbing beauty to the picture they made. An annoying sense of admiration swelled inside Rey for the rider's skill—an opinion he revised as he thought of his meeting with Sotheby. Thanks to Santana, his confrontation with the counterfeiter might never take place.

"*Tout le monde, dehors!*" a familiar voice called from outside, instructing the men to disembark.

"Damn you, *ma belle,*" Rey swore to himself, falling into the bandit's native language. "I don't care what it takes, but this is the last time you thwart my plans."

He glanced back at De Dreux and Harlan; both appeared to be waiting for instructions. If he and Harlan were alone, Rey would be sorely tempted to shoot. But the sweat gleamed off De Dreux's forehead and the man's hands shook on the wolf's head of his cane. If Rey wanted to salvage this meeting, he'd have to make sure all three would be in condition to make the trip into town before Sotheby lost interest waiting for them.

"We can't let her take us a second time, man!" Harlan said beside him, as if sensing Rey's thoughts.

"I do not want trouble," De Dreux whispered. "Perhaps if we simply do as she says?"

Rey watched De Dreux take out his handkerchief and swab his brow. Where was the brave gentleman now, Rey wondered? The one who'd sworn—from the safety of his dining room, of course—to see Santana behind bars? Again he pictured the bruise on Mercedes's cheek. Apparently, unarmed ladies were more to De Dreux's liking.

"We have no choice but to do as she says," Rey answered, swallowing back his disgust for De Dreux. "God willing, we'll be on our way soon enough with only our wallets missing."

Rey swung open the carriage door and tossed his Colt to the ground before jumping down the step to the road below. Harlan and De Dreux followed, their arms raised high in the air. The bandits searched for weapons, leaving Rey mildly surprised when the knife sheathed inside his boot—a precaution he'd taken for tonight's meeting— went undetected. Clearly, Santana's men were accustomed to civilians and took no measures against subterfuge. Even if her men had found the one weapon, Rey had others at his disposal, hidden in places sure not to be discovered, but the knife in his boot was the most easily accessible and he was glad to feel it snug against his calf as the mounted bandits circled them, herding them like cattle away from the coach.

At the head of the motley group waited Santana atop her midnight-colored horse. Hair as black as her form-fitting clothes cascaded down her caped shoulders. The characteristic crimson mask crowned with feathers disguised her face. She controlled her powerful mount with her knees, keeping her hands free. She held her two pistols trained on the gentlemen and their driver.

Rey took a step toward her, making himself her primary target. "I wish I could say it was a pleasure, Santana, but to be honest this is getting to be a bit of a bore. Surely there are others you can harass on these roads besides myself and my companions?"

Beneath her mask, a smile blossomed in the moonlight. The sight of it brought a disturbing warmth through Rey. As he stood on the moon-drenched road, surrounded by bandits waving guns, he experienced an emotion quite inappropriate to the circumstances. Desire. Hot, sweet, and achingly familiar.

He mentally shook his head, concentrating on the reality of Santana Rose rather than the memories she invited. Caught in currents of the breeze off the river, her ebony hair waved like a banner. With the light wind came the strong scent of roses so unlike the delicate lavender fragrance Mercedes used. Dark eyes, surely a deeper shade than ginger brown, flickered behind her guise. He recalled his powerful response to Santana that first time they'd met on this very road; blamed it for the moment's confusion. *But that was before Mercedes,* his conscience protested. Before he'd held her, kissed her, made love to her. For five years he'd never even considered involving himself with a woman—only to risk everything for Mercedes. She was no fickle choice.

Surely, he couldn't desire both women.

"Bonsoir, monsieur."

The perfect French accent and singsong, breathy voice shattered the image of Mercedes, as did Santana's familiar grip on her pistols. "You made me such a tempting offer the last time we met. Have you forgotten so soon, *mon chou*?"

She spoke softly, as if she whispered a playful coquetry meant for his ears alone. Her teasing tone had the opposite effect from what she'd intended. Rey's ardor died instantly as the woman before him became her own distinct entity rather than a shadowy reminder of Mercedes.

"I did say another time, did I not?" Her words had an edge of feline purr. *"Vous,"* she called to Harlan, De Dreux, and their driver, ignoring Rey. Her smile vanished as easily as a flame doused between two fingers. "My men will escort you down the road. Do not even glance back at the carriage, *vous comprenez?"*

"We're not leaving Rey. *Mon Dieu, non."* Harlan stepped forward. "Not on your life!"

Rey's survival instinct snapped alive like the trigger of a pistol cocked into place. He glanced at his Colt on the ground, estimated his chances of reaching the gun before the bandits fired on his men.

"A step back, *s'il vous plaît,"* Santana said. She gestured with one Smith and Wesson, wagging the barrel in a sweeping motion. Both Rey and Harlan obeyed, widening the distance between them and Rey's weapon.

"Le monsieur et moi," Santana added, addressing herself to Harlan and De Dreux, "we have unfinished business." Her teeth gleamed white in the moonlight, but this time there was no resemblance between her and Mercedes. "Do not worry so, little man," she said to Harlan, making him turn two shades of red. "No harm will come to your friend if he follows instructions. But any brave attempts at rescue"—she shook her head, pursing her lips in a disapproving pout—"would not be well met."

"It's all right, Harlan," Rey said. He had no idea what the lady bandit had in mind, but he was focused now. He needed to salvage the meeting with Sotheby. He turned to look at Harlan standing beside him. "There's a lot at stake here." Fixing his gaze on his partner's, Rey added, "I trust you will look out for my interests in my absence."

Understanding pulsed between them. Though he and Harlan had worked together but a short time, Rey sensed the subtle communication he'd shared with Mac in the past.

"You're crazy," Harlan whispered. *"Complètement fou."*

Harlan's steady expression and the tone of his voice spoke as clearly as words—if possible, Harlan would carry on with the meeting in Rey's stead. "I'll be fine, Harlan. Just take care of business."

"Enough!" shouted Santana. *"Departez!* Move now!" The grin that followed took the sting from her words. "And kindly leave your wallets behind."

When the two gentlemen and their driver started down the River Road, with one of her henchmen following close behind, Santana dismounted. Each step she took swung her hips, the prominent gun belt exaggerating the motion as she sauntered toward Rey. Her guns leveled on him, she said, "You wished for privacy at our last meeting, *monsieur.*" She nodded toward the landau behind him. "Step inside the carriage. I plan to be more accommodating this time."

Rey watched the dark eyes hidden behind the jewel-rimmed slits of her mask, calculating his chances of leaving this encounter alive. This was no random meeting. She'd singled him out. And he certainly didn't believe she had sexual designs on him as she'd teased. Now, even her motive of robbery for profit appeared in doubt. Seeing little choice, he returned her suggestive smile. "I look forward to it, Santana."

He mounted the carriage. Behind him, Santana instructed her man in French before joining him and dropping to the seat opposite Rey. He could hear one of the bandits climb the landau to the driver's seat. With a sharp whistle, the new driver steered the carriage around and drove the horses, hell-bent for leather, in the direction opposite the city.

Rey seized the padded leather to keep his seat in the reeling carriage as Santana braced her shoulders against the cushions. Spurts of moonlight flashed through the windows, igniting the metal of her revolvers. Soon enough, the carriage tilted back, swaying off the road, the uneven ground testing its steel springs.

For once in her life, Mercy was exceedingly happy for her leather gloves. Sweaty palms had never been an occupational hazard she'd suffered. But as she held her fingers tight around the handles of the two Smith and Wessons, she knew she never would have kept her grip without the leather's protection.

Meeting Rey's gaze across the carriage, she sensed even greater challenges to her composure ahead. Again, she questioned her decision to ambush Benoit's carriage. Though she'd been terribly shaken by Rey's exposure to Sotheby, she'd analyzed the evening in great detail over the last weeks and determined Rey's identity was safe enough. His prone figure on the carpet at Kate's couldn't possibly subject him to the danger she'd imagined, not with his hair stuffed securely inside his hat with only a stray strand or two to betray its distinctive color. No, she'd certainly overreacted. Yet, despite what time and logic had done to wear away her concerns, an insistent voice urged her to act when she'd intercepted Benoit's missive to Sotheby setting up tonight's meeting. At the last possible moment, when she'd left herself no option other than this half-cocked plan, she'd gathered her forces and sought out the carriage bound for New Orleans. Now, watching him through Santana's mask, she wondered at the wisdom of her method.

His clear green eyes glanced down at her pistols, then rose to meet her gaze once more. His lips shaped a cool smile. "An abduction?" He settled back as he crossed his arms over his chest. "How charming. I've never quite inspired a kidnapping."

Mercy could feel the tufting buttons digging into her shoulder blades as she leaned against the squabs and forced a cocky grin. She suppressed all tender emotions for Rey, ruthlessly shoving below her consciousness their last evening together. She had to think like Santana, *be* Santana. How would *she* react to Rey. In this carriage, behind this feathered mask, Mercy did not exist. For all the courage Mercy had earned fighting Benoit, only Santana could save Rey tonight. She dared not fall out of character now.

Like countless times in the past, her hidden self rose inside her, churning to the fore as a separate being. Slowly, Mercy's fears ebbed, replaced by the confidence characteristic of the lady bandit. Her muscles loosened, relaxing into genuine assurance. Santana wasn't in love with Rey. The situation she faced now would not concern the highway woman. It would merely challenge her.

She heard herself cluck her tongue in a teasing manner, saw Rey's smile tighten at the gesture. "I am sure," she said in her slightly accented English, "if *les petites amies* of your past had thought themselves capable, the ladies would have done as I have long before. But I am happy to be the first, *monsieur.*" She nodded her head in a slight bow of admiration. "You see, I find you very inspirational."

Placing one of her guns on the seat beside her, out of Rey's reach, she held the other Smith and Wesson steady as she grasped the top button of her shirt. She was Santana, a woman free to dare anything, a bandit capable of even tonight's bold escapade. She watched his eyes lower to where her fingers unlooped the top button of her shirt, saw them widen almost imperceptibly as she reached for the next.

Rey sucked in his breath. The shock of what she was doing ripped through him. Just as quickly, he held back an urge to laugh as he calculated how she could possibly accomplish what she appeared about to attempt.

"Perhaps I can make this all a bit easier, Santana. If you toss those guns outside I promise to be very obliging. Otherwise, I'm afraid I may not be *up* to the task ahead—I've never performed at gunpoint, you see."

She laughed, her relaxed pose that of an old friend enjoying a pleasant discussion, but her gun never wavered. "*Pardon, monsieur.* I'm afraid I have given the wrong impression." Rather than unhooking the second button, she pulled out a familiar gold chain from inside her shirt. Rey's St. Christopher medal followed, dangling from her fingers.

The chain fell between her breasts, sparkling with moonlight against the black silk of her shirt. "I merely wished to show you how taken I was by you at our first meeting. I kept this as a momento. But the thought of your performance intrigues."

The taunt of his St. Christopher medal ignited embers of rage that until that moment, Rey had kept carefully banked. It was all a game. The medallion, the abduction. A game that would cost him Sotheby. She was manipulating him, teasing him outrageously for her own pleasure while he sat powerless. But instead of the threats that itched to be voiced, Rey reached for the control that had saved his life on more than one occasion. He felt not anger, not desire, but cold chilling command. He had one purpose, one reason for action or words: get free of this bitch's web and return to Sotheby.

Whatever I have to do, Santana.

He smiled, but there was nothing pleasant about the curve of his lips. "It's a shame my many charms can't inspire you to put that down." He nodded toward the remaining gun. "I'm quite disappointed." His gaze lingered on the pale skin of her throat exposed by her unbuttoned shirt. "We might deal well with each other without them."

Santana's smile widened. Slowly, deliberately, she lifted one booted foot and propped it on the seat between his legs. "You inspire many things, *monsieur,* but not stupidity."

He glanced down at her boot. *Control,* he chanted mentally, keeping anger at bay. *Ice-cold control.* His eyebrows raised. He shook his head as if disappointed. "What a tease you are, Santana," he whispered as he met her dark eyes. Slowly, so she might stop him, he lifted one hand. His strong fingers trailed up the soft leather boot encasing her leg. He squeezed, then began to massage the muscles of her calf through the kid leather. "Shall I try to be more convincing then?"

She jerked her foot down to the carriage floor. A powerful emotion jolted Mercy to the surface, displacing Santana. Her hands shook. Not Santana, but simply Mercy sat across from Rey.

He'd used the same soft voice, the same smoldering expression of desire that had brought Mercy to his bed so many nights before.

But it's Mercedes he cares for! Not Santana. Me. Mercy.

Heat rushed through her as she realized what was happening. Dear God, she was jealous of herself.

Rey sighed and lounged back against the red moroccan seat. "You don't even find my offer tempting then."

"A great loss for me, I'm sure, *monsieur*," she said, a tartness to her voice she'd not intended.

"A great loss for us both."

Rey kept his eyes on Santana as the carriage slowed. Outside, her driver shouted to the horses. The carriage lurched to a complete stop. A palpable silence filled the carriage compartment.

"Ah," Santana said, breaking the stillness. "We have arrived."

Almost kicking the door open, she jumped down to the loamy ground and shouted in French for two men to cover Rey with their rifles. While she retrieved a rope from her saddlebags, the two culprits pulled Rey down to the ground, dragging him deeper into the grove of moss-covered oaks. Within minutes, his hands were tied in front of him and he was propped up against a barrel-trunked oak, seated in the dirt. He waited to discover what could possibly be in store for him here in the deserted roadside, not believing for a moment that all the bandits wanted was the wallet they'd taken from him. Yet, despite the danger, he felt only anger.

At last, Santana's men were all mounted and ready to leave. Santana sauntered toward him, one gun still in hand. In the other, she held her characteristic red rose.

She stood before him and stroked his chin with the velvet petals, the long stem allowing her to stay out of his reach. "We have a little fun with you, *oui, monsieur*?"

He thought of his meeting with Sotheby, the years of sacrifice now gone to waste. "I only hope to return the favor someday, Santana."

The rose stopped at his lips and she shook her head. Pulling the flower away, she crouched down beside him and leaned closer, her gun still between them. Rey caught her eye, held her gaze, smiled.

His bound hands shot out. Before she could fire, he clasped both hands around her pistol. His thumb reached the trigger, holding it in place against any possible pressure from her finger.

Her eyes behind the slits of the mask darkened. "My men would kill you before you fired a second shot."

"I'll only need one."

"To kill me?" She laughed. "But the barrel is pointed at you, *monsieur.*"

"At the moment."

"I do not wish to shoot you," she said quickly. "I will leave you here, unharmed. Do not force my hand." When Rey made no move to release the gun, she added, "You are angry, *oui*. But do you really wish to see bloodshed?"

"Perhaps I doubt you'd shoot me, Santana," he said. "Perhaps I think this is all a game, and I merely wish to switch my role from the mouse to the cat."

"An incredible gamble, *monsieur*"—she glanced at the revolver between them—"given the circumstances."

"I'm a gambler by nature."

"*Tais-toi,*" she whispered. He could hear the desperate edge to her voice. "If I cause you problems by my prank, I apologize now. In my defense I say you would tempt a saint, *monsieur*. And as we both know," she said, leaning toward him, "I am no saint."

As it had the first time, her kiss took him by surprise. With the touch of her lips, his control exploded as if between them they'd pulled the gun's trigger. Rey dropped his hold on the grip and twisted his fingers in her shirt, pulling her toward him, kissing her hard. His mouth attacked in a way his tied hands could not. It took perhaps minutes before he realized she struggled in his arms. One hand braced against his shoulders, wrestling him for release, the other still holding the gun. He let her go. She jumped to her feet. They both watched each other, their breaths coming hard.

She stepped away from him, almost tripping, her movements unsure, her expression wary. Twenty feet away, she lowered the gun, leaving it in the grass.

"Santana?" called one of her men. "Is there trouble?"

Rey stayed on the ground propped against the oak. But his muscles tensed for immediate action.

"*Non.* It is nothing," she shouted, her gaze never leaving Rey. She tapped the toe of her boot to the revolver on the ground. "For you, *monsieur*. I do not want to leave you here alone without protection. There is a small settlement a few miles north of here. The road is behind you."

"Your concern is quite touching, Santana."

She tossed the rose at his feet. "Until we meet again."

"You can bet on it."

"A threat, *monsieur*?"

"No." He glanced at the men on horseback waiting for her, then turned his gaze back to Santana. "A promise."

"Then I shall say not good-bye, but *à bientôt.*"

She saluted and walked back to her gang. Rey watched her carefully, thinking over her parting words. *Perhaps we'll meet sooner than you think, Santana.*

He saw her swing a leg up. When she urged her devil horse around, Rey made his move. He vaulted to his feet, racing to the gun. He dove to the ground, snatching up the pistol in his bound hands, and rolled. *Keep them guessing.* A moving target was difficult to kill. The instant he stopped, he propped up on his elbows, aimed.

He had two seconds, maybe three, before her men sighted him in the darkness and sprayed his prone figure with bullets. His finger curled around the trigger. He found his target.

The thrumming of his heart slowed. The strong pulse seemed to echo from the distance of a long tunnel. In the time between heartbeats, his gaze met the jeweled eyes, registered the seven clicks of her men's rifles, watched her lips form the word *no*.

The shoulder! Aim for the shoulder.

He pulled the trigger back, squeezing tighter . . . tighter. . . . Shoot! *Shoot!*

Rey dropped his gun to the ground, unfired.

"Au revoir, mon coeur." The words trailed in the distance with the sound of Santana's escape.

He shut his eyes, his chin resting on the wet grass as he listened to the waning sound of Santana's retreat. She'd called him, "my heart."

Four days ago, he'd said those very words to another woman.

When he looked up again, he could no longer see her. In the darkness of his mind, he replayed those last seconds. He could have done it. He could have fired. Shot her right out of the saddle.

More prudent to let her go, he told himself as he reached in his boot for his knife. *Too dangerous to shoot,* he counseled as he sawed through the ropes and gained his feet.

But that wasn't why he hadn't fired. And he knew it.

He turned back to the oak where she'd left him and snatched up the rose from the ground. When he pricked his finger on a thorn, he tossed the flower back to the grass with a curse. He shook his head and searched the ground for a second object.

Crouching down near the oak tree, Rey sifted through dirt and blades of grass until he saw a flash of metal. With a smile, he picked up the medal he'd snagged from her during their kiss. She'd never even felt the chain break as he'd pulled it.

Rey held the St. Christopher in his palm. "We'll meet again, Santana," he said under his breath. "And next time, I swear I won't hesitate."

Chapter 14

Mr. Russell's experiments fully demonstrate the simplicity of extraction, as well as the value of the residue of Saccharine that remained in the Bagasse after the most powerful expression . . .

Pascal blinked her eyes and focused again on the minuscule print of Bouchereau's *Country Directory for Business Men* opened on her lap. Rather than spending the evening worrying about Santana's holdup that night, Pascal had tried to distract herself by reading about sugar-making. So far, she'd found Bouchereau's technical expertise less than riveting. She forced herself to concentrate.

Mr. Russell's experiments fully demonstrate the simplicity of extraction, as well as the value of the residue of Saccharine . . .

She slapped the book flat onto the counterpane and propped herself on her elbows above it, attempting a more comfortable position on Mercedes's bed. More than ever, Harlan had pressed Pascal for details of her father's business.

Mr. Russell's experiments fully demonstrate the simplicity of . . . Mr. Russell's experiments fully demonstrate . . .

She flipped onto her back with a sigh, taking the book with her. She held it suspended above her, tilting the pages to catch the light.

Mr. Russell's experiments . . . Mr. Russell's . . .

"Oh, to hell with Mr. Russell's experiments." Pascal slammed the book shut, failing miserably in her attempts to ease her worries with Bouchereau's advice. She tossed the directory on the blue silk counterpane of the bed, vowing to slug through the tome later. How on earth these gentlemen planters got beyond the tiny print size, she had not a clue. She glanced up at the clock on the mantel place of her stepmother's bedroom. Nearly eleven o'clock. With a sigh, she returned to the activity that, between attempts to read about saturators and vacuum pans, had taken up half her night.

She paced.

Pascal pivoted on her foot and retraced her well-traveled path to the bed. This was just another holdup, she reminded herself. Nothing like their dangerous missions into the swamps to rescue the women her father smuggled into the country. Routine, Mercedes had called it. On the morrow, Pascal and Mercedes would return to St. Bartholomew's Orphanage with tonight's cache, nothing they'd not accomplished dozens of times without mishap.

But still, she worried.

Pascal flopped back onto the bed, thinking over the comforting words Mercedes had offered earlier that evening. Her expression as she'd swept Pascal's hair off her face had made Pascal's heart squeeze painfully in her chest. There had been love in her stepmother's eyes, in her touch—a mother's love.

Pascal's pulse did a funny skip as her thoughts turned to Harlan. She'd seen him almost every day since the night he'd kissed her. And though his easy charm was gone, she'd found something more genuine about his recent gruffness. At first, she'd thought that quite strange, but the more she considered it, the more she realized his curt responses were always followed by a reassuring touch, a longing glance, or some other sign of affection. It was more than she'd ever hoped for.

At the sound of the door swinging open, Pascal sat up. She heaved a sigh of relief when Mercedes walked in, looking reassuringly calm. Seeing Pascal, Mercedes stopped. Her features changed into a look of concern as she took off her gloves.

"You worried," Mercy said, stating the obvious as she placed her bonnet and gloves on the Duchess vanity. The picture of elegance, she wore a visiting gown made of pearl gray faille richly trimmed in dark crimson velvet. Pascal marveled over her appearance. No one would ever suspect this lady could be Santana Rose, a notorious highway robber.

"Well, maybe I was a little concerned," Pascal said skipping to her stepmother's side. Seeing Mercedes's disbelieving expression, Pascal sighed and gave in to the truth. "All right, I was frozen with fear. But I *tried* not to worry." She shook her head. "All this time, I thought it was awful riding with Santana. Waiting here—not knowing if something had gone wrong, if you needed my help—was twenty times worse."

With a smile, Mercy took Pascal in her arms and hugged her. "Thanks for caring," she whispered.

Mercy squeezed her stepdaughter tightly, allowing the warmth of Pascal's affection to comfort her. How different to hear Pascal's concern voiced gently, rather than shouted in threats. She held the girl back at arm's length. Her eyes glided from the tip of Pascal's artfully styled hair, to the toe of her black kid slippers. "You've changed Pascal. You've grown up." She heard the wistful note in her voice. Pascal was no child to mother and cherish as Mercy had dreamed of doing in the past. She was an equal, an adult— and a friend.

"Of course, I've changed," Pascal answered with a grin that showed her resilience against tragedy. "Love does that to a woman."

Mercy dropped her arms to her sides. "Harlan Everard."

"Don't say it that way! Like you've just discovered an outbreak of yellow fever in town. He's a wonderful man." Pascal walked to the window and peered outside. "He's good and kind. And beautiful beyond words. Not like . . ." Pascal glanced at Mercy. Her expression as well as her words instantly brought back the dark memories of four nights ago. "Is it horrible? Living with him? Does it really make it bearable because you steal from him?"

Another fraction of Mercy's pleasure cracked and chipped away. It would take two hands to tick off the half-truths and evasive statements she'd told Pascal. Her stepdaughter thought Mercy's forays against her husband simple revenge, a bane for the agony of being his wife.

"He's your father, Pascal," she answered in a gentle voice. "I think you know exactly how I feel."

Pascal nodded, acknowledging the similarities in their relationship to Benoit. She walked back to Mercy and buried her face in the niche between Mercy's neck and her shoulder. Mercy stroked the girl's back absently. As she'd planned, her response had both answered Pascal's question and withheld the darker truth.

Mercy shut her eyes as she held Pascal. As long as neither Pascal or Rey knew her true intentions, Mercy would always take their affection like a thief rather than a deserving recipient. And yet, she had no choice but to accept the wall of lies she'd built between her and the people she loved. In Rey's case, it was lie or lose any chance of happiness with him. For Pascal, a voice inside Mercy counseled against revealing all. Mercy's involvement with Sotheby, her plans to destroy Benoit's empire and leave him penniless, were her burden alone to carry. The man she planned to destroy was Pascal's father. His daughter should not be an accomplice to that destruction, even a silent one whose only participation was failing to warn her father because she loved her stepmother.

Her hand crept to her neck where she normally wore Rey's medallion, then dropped back to Pascal when she remembered she'd lost the St. Christopher on the River Road. She felt the loss as deeply as her falsehoods.

Pascal stepped back and gave Mercy an energetic smile. "Guess what I'm doing tomorrow?"

"What?" Mercy asked, her spirits lifting with Pascal's enthusiastic tone.

"I'm taking Harlan hunting, just as I promised."

Mercy frowned. "Mr. Everard again."

"Mr. Everard *always,*" Pascal answered happily.

"He's a good deal older," Mercy warned, "more experienced—"

"You mean you think he's toying with my affections?" She clapped her hands in front of her and laughed. Then her smile turned a bit melancholy as she shook her head. "You sound just like Ling Shi."

"You miss her terribly."

Pascal nodded. "She sent a letter yesterday returning my mother's emeralds and saying she married Doc Chiang in Gretna. I wish I could have been there to see her." Pascal stepped back to the bed and sat down. "I know she's happy now. That's all that matters."

When Mercy joined her, Pascal laid her head on Mercy's lap, smiling again. "Don't worry so about Harlan. He's a wonderful man. He makes me feel so special. I'm not a child, after all." She glanced up, looking endearingly childlike despite her words. "And honestly, I would give anything to experience the joy he makes me feel. You understand that don't you?"

Mercy thought of the letter she'd stolen as Santana, then pushed away her doubts about Everard as she watched Pascal's delighted expression. There was no need to poison Pascal's happiness with her suspicions. Mercy had no evidence that the Pinkerton's attentions were not heartfelt, and, indeed, over the past few days, she thought she'd seen a marked change in the cocky gentleman. Everard appeared to have fallen for Pascal's charming innocence. And why not? Her stepdaughter was a beautiful girl and certainly deserving of his regard.

Mercy clasped Pascal's hands in hers, watching this bit of budding womanhood with wonder. "Yes, I understand your feelings, Pascal. I know all about men who turn women's heads with their fine talk and good looks." She gave Pascal's hands a squeeze. "But sometimes, it's not wise to share your heart so freely. Even in love, caution can be important." Having given her advice, Mercy rose, pulling Pascal up with her. "Well, now that you're satisfied that I'm safely home, it's off to bed. You'll need your wits about you if you plan to impress Mr. Everard."

"I've done nothing but read for the past two days. I plan to dazzle him with my knowledge on the game in this area —and perhaps something more," she said coyly from the door. "I have this absolutely stunning outfit. At the *very* least . . . I plan to take his breath away!"

She spoke as if Mr. Everard's admiration were a *fait accompli,* making Mercy smile.

"Good night, *maman.*"

Mercy watched the door close softly. *Maman,* Pascal had said. The sound of the endearment, given with love for the first time, echoed in Mercy's ears. In one night, Pascal had opened her heart, exposed her soul, and stood ready to give Mercy her complete love and devotion. And how Mercy wanted it. But rather than accepting what was freely given, she would earn her stepdaughter's admiration. She would make sure the girl had everything she needed for the rest of her life. From now on, Pascal was *her* daughter, not Benoit's.

To that end, Mercy thought of her plans to keep Benoit from injuring Pascal ever again. She wouldn't allow Pascal to remain Benoit's victim. She'd already spoken to Benoit about Ling Shi. Though he'd not sounded a bit repentant, he'd at least agreed not to seek the girl out again. And Mercy had succeeded in gaining her stepdaughter greater freedom, forbidding one of Benoit's stooges from becoming Ling Shi's replacement. It didn't make up for her lost companion, but perhaps it made the loss a bit easier.

Mercy sighed as she remembered Ling Shi. She still felt responsible for what had happened to Pascal's friend. To think that Mercy could protect countless strangers, but had failed to stop Benoit's abuse of the girl in her own home. Never again, Mercy vowed. She had spoken with Kate, who had more experience in such matters. Kate said she knew a woman who could curb Benoit's strange, violent urges. Through Gessler, Kate hoped to introduce Benoit to her at Catalan Kate's.

Mercy sat down at her escritoire intending to write herself a few notes. Within minutes, she cradled her head in her hands, tired to the bone. After she'd left Rey, Santana had delivered one of Sotheby's filthy bribes. Just dealing with the man and his cronies made her feel soiled, but she was willing to play his delivery girl for his help against Benoit. Thankfully, the next transfer wouldn't occur until next week. She'd been able to leave the burlap bag of money in the clothespress at the *pied-à-terre*.

In her mind, Mercy again saw Rey, aiming the pistol between his bound hands. He'd wanted to fire, almost had. But though shocking, that hadn't been the incident that disturbed her most. His camaraderie with the highway woman had been a problem she'd analyzed since she'd left him at the roadside. How easily he'd fallen into Santana's sensual banter. Had he thought to disarm the bandit by playing her game? That would explain his passion. Or had he simply responded to the kiss of a woman he desired?

That would explain things quite differently.

From the drawer, Mercy pulled out a clean sheet of vellum. She penned her message quickly, before she changed her mind.

Quite suddenly, she needed to know the answers to her questions.

Rey slammed Bizy's back door closed. "Mac! Get the hell down here."

At the top of the steps, MacAfee appeared. "Yer back!" He scrambled down the stairs, one hand on the banister, meeting Rey halfway. "Thank the Lord . . ."

Rey passed him without a word, without even a glance, the lines of his face etched like sculpted granite. Mac turned on the balls of his feet and started back up the stairs, following Rey into the salon. Once inside, Rey stripped off his hat and coat and flung them with uncharacteristic negligence onto a chair. He poured himself a bourbon and dropped into the settee.

"Harlan sent a note," Mac said, picking up the jacket and folding it over his arm, noting the dirt, the torn sleeve. "He's got Gessler and his men patrolling the swamps for ye and Santana. I thought I should stay put in case ye made it back to Bizy."

"Did he meet with Sotheby?"

"That he didna say."

Rey turned the glass in his hand. His knuckles turned white around the cut crystal. "Damn that woman."

Rey focused on the flames battling behind the grate as he sipped his drink. Mac recognized the expression. Something was definitely brewing inside that fair head, something Mac didn't want to disturb. When Rey finished the whiskey, Mac took the tumbler out of his hand, afraid the glass might break under the pressure of Rey's grip. Once relieved of his fragile burden, Rey slammed his fist on the upholstered arm. Mac winced, thinking the blow must have hurt.

Rey jumped to his feet and paced to the fireplace. "Something must be done to stop her, before she ruins everything—if she hasn't already." Rey looked back at Mac. "I was so close to meeting Sotheby—minutes from town when she ambushed the carriage. Thank God she let Harlan and De Dreux go."

Mac dropped Rey's coat on a chair and dogged Rey's steps to the hearth. "But why? Why would she take ye and not the rest?"

"Who knows what her motives are? A prank? Malicious mischief? She dumps me in the swamp, but at the same time, makes sure I can get away unharmed. It makes no sense."

Rey braced his hands against the mantel, staring into the flames. The woman was a menace—a menace he'd allowed to escape. But let her come near him again and Rey swore he wouldn't hesitate. Woman or not, he would shoot her right off that black devil horse of hers if he had to. He shook his head, pushing off the shelf and turning to face Mac. "I can only hope Harlan had the sense to meet Sotheby without me."

"We'll know soon enough," Mac said. "The laddie's due back any minute."

Rey reached inside the pocket of his waistcoat, retrieving his gold St. Christopher. He wrapped the chain around his fingers and stared at the hanging medal.

"Ye got it back?"

A calculated smile curved Rey's mouth. "For once, I found Santana very obliging." He gathered the chain within his palm and pressed his fingers into a fist. "What have you learned at Kate's?" When the Scotsman didn't answer, Rey turned on him. "Come on, Mac. You've been there every night for the last week. Don't tell me you don't have any information. You're much too good an agent for that."

"I'm on the verge of something, and that's a fact," Mac hedged, not sure he wanted Kate linked with a woman who could inspire such anger from the normally cool-headed agent.

"I want Santana, Mac. I want that thieving bitch so bad

I can taste it. Next time, she'll be the one in for a surprise
—not me."

"We'll have her behind bars and out of our way in no
time," Mac seconded.

The sound of a door opening echoed up the stairs. Rey's
head whipped to the salon entrance. "Harlan."

He reached the landing just as the Pinkerton was halfway up the stairs. Harlan stopped and expelled an audible
sigh. "*Merci Dieu,* you're safe," he said continuing to climb
up the rest of the steps.

"The meeting?" Rey asked.

Harlan's smile instantly answered the question. A responding wave of relief washed over Rey.

"It went just like you said, Rey, *mais oui.*" Harlan
wrapped an arm across Rey's shoulder and guided him
back to the salon where Mac waited. "I slipped Sotheby
that counterfeit bill of yours and told him we were interested in more of the same." He stopped at the settee and
sat down, kicking his heels out and crossing his feet at the
ankles. "We're in the business of passing boodle, *mon
ami.*"

Rey's mouth turned into a grin of genuine pleasure.
"He bought it?"

"Hook, line, and sinker."

Rey sat down on the settee beside Harlan, sharing in the
energy of their triumph. "He actually talked about the
counterfeiting?"

Harlan nodded. "*Mais* yeah, man. Soon as he saw that
five dollar bill you gave me, he sent De Dreux out to find
one of his men downstairs. And I tell you what, when I
explained the banks you're acquainted with, the man
nearly drooled right there in his seat, him. When De
Dreux came back, the whole deal went right over his head.
Most of the conversation about ready supply of tens and
twenties was between me and Sotheby. He's willing to sell
as much queer as we have good bills to buy, I guarantee."

Rey glanced up at Mac, catching the Scotsman's eye.

He'd been right to trust the Pinkerton. "You did well, Harlan."

"I told you"—Harlan knitted his fingers behind his head and leaned back—"you need me."

The heavy bang of the knocker disturbed the air of celebration. All three men exchanged wary glances. It was almost midnight.

Rey watched Mac quit the room to answer the front door. Perhaps Gessler or De Dreux had come to check on his safe return. But a sharp tug at his sleeve turned his attention back to Harlan.

"Don't ever ask me to leave you like that again," Harlan said, his eyes bright, reminding Rey more than ever of Christopher. "I don't leave my man down. Understand? Silver Fox or not, I didn't know if I would ever see you again. And for one lousy meeting, *mon ami*, it wasn't worth the risk."

Rey couldn't help the responding grin. Suddenly, the night's debacle, even Santana, didn't seem so important. He pocketed the medallion he still held in his palm. "Oh, it was worth it, all right."

Before Harlan could respond, Mac came back into the room, carrying a folded piece of vellum in his hands. He handed the missive to Rey.

"It was delivered by De Dreux's driver."

His valet hovered over Rey as he flipped the paper around to see the handwriting on the outside. The beautiful script flowed across the paper in bold lines and dramatic curves.

"From De Dreux?" Mac asked.

The blood rushed from Rey's head. His heart flooded with it. "I don't believe so."

Rey broke the seal and read the words for which he'd waited so long:

232 Rue de l'Hôpital. Tomorrow night.

Chapter 15

Rey walked through the junglelike foliage of the garden leading to the *pied-à-terre*. Uncharacteristic of other homes in the Vieux Carré, the two-story building was set back from the street behind an enclosed courtyard. Keeping to the brick path, Rey bent low to avoid the low-hanging branches of a lush magnolia laden with trumpet vines. At the base of a wooden stairwell, he stopped and stared up the whitewashed steps leading to the front door on the upper gallery.

A light shone in the French windows, a sign of welcome. The darkened figure of a woman, her hands clasped in front of her, paced the length of the room. Rey watched Mercedes's silhouette pivot and retrace her steps. He turned away, focusing on the gas lamps at the base of the courtyard. It was approaching ten o'clock. The music and voices from the taverns on Bourbon Street were a faint whisper on the breeze as the city's population prepared for Mardi Gras in two weeks time.

Leaning against the rail of the stairs, Rey reached inside his coat for a cigarette. He stared out at the quiet darkness of the street beyond the gates, taking in the calming effects of the tobacco. A lone dog scavenged the street and sniffed judiciously at the cast-iron gate before moving on. Rey took another pull of the Choctaw and admitted for the first time that his feelings for Mercedes involved something other than obsession.

If he walked up those stairs, he risked more than rousing De Dreux's suspicions. He risked his heart.

He was falling in love.

Rey stared at the burning tip of his cigarette as if it held his answers. Five nights back, when he'd drifted off into a light sleep with Mercedes in his arms, he'd never been so close to the peace he sought. But love. Rey had loved only one woman in his life. And nothing had hurt as much as losing Sophie.

Rey drew on his cigarette and exhaled a stream of smoke in a half sigh. He hated the fact that she stayed with De Dreux, that each night he worried she might again show up on his doorstep, beaten and bruised. And, he hated himself for allowing it. But as long as she refused to leave her husband, Rey felt powerless to help her. Mac had likened Rey's desire for Mercedes to his affair with Leticia—but nothing could be further from the truth. With Leticia, Rey had always been in control. Even in the end, it was he who'd finished the affair when he'd realized Leticia truly cared for him. With Mercedes, nothing seemed within his control.

He glanced up at the top of the stairs. Mercedes stopped pacing and pushed back the curtains. The darkened outline of her body showed clearly through the window. She seemed to watch him. Slowly, she raised her hand and waved.

Five years, Rey thought.

Five lonely years.

He tossed his cigarette to the cobblestones and gripped the whitewashed railing. Climbing the steps, he acknowledged that the time for caution had long since passed.

When he reached the loggia, Mercedes waited outside. She took his hand and drew him over the threshold with a smile. She shut the door behind her and leaned back against it, a bit breathless. "You came."

"Did you think I wouldn't?"

"The thought occurred to me."

Rey shook his head. "I couldn't stay away. And I'll never believe you thought otherwise."

"I hoped," she answered softly. "Here, let me take your hat and coat."

She fluttered about him with charming enthusiasm. A seed of happiness grew inside him just watching her. He saw no servants. They were alone in the small salon. She wore an emerald silk wrapper, and her hair tumbled down in a curtain of gilded browns. Her eyes shone with reflected firelight as she poured a brandy and handed him the glass. She was an extraordinarily beautiful woman—but it wasn't her appearance that made him ache to hold her. With startling clarity, he realized her attraction. She didn't offer just a momentary oblivion from his dark memories. To Rey, she represented giving when he'd known only loss. A companion where there had been only loneliness.

Her hands smoothed down her silk wrapper and she watched him anxiously. Her nervousness made her seem younger, as did her expectant expression. Rey sat down on the courting couch, feeling the familiar tension overtake his body as he leaned against the gold bolster.

"Don't you care for brandy?" she asked, glancing at his untouched drink.

"I like brandy fine." He placed the glass on the polished table before him and reached for her hand, pulling her down across his lap. "But I like you much better."

He nuzzled the warm skin of her throat, the heat of his desire almost painful as he touched, tasted. Memories of their night together flooded him, making him even more eager. Mercedes drew her arms around him and leaned her head back, displaying the sensitive curve of her throat. When he kissed beneath her jaw, she laughed—a deep throaty sound that rang hauntingly familiar.

Instantly, his kisses stopped; Rey drew back.

"What's the matter?" she asked.

He studied her face, her eyes, her lovely hair. *All light as an angel's.* "Nothing," he said, returning to the skin that smelled of lavender. Damn all! That blasted bandit was beginning to haunt him.

When she giggled a second time, the enchanting sound was uniquely Mercedes, making him recall the first time they'd made love. He watched her with a smile. "You always laugh when you're with me. Is my lovemaking so funny?"

A becoming flush warmed her cheeks. She held her lips pressed together, as if she were fighting back another giggle. "You're tickling me."

"Tickling?" He reached up and stroked the raised peak of her breast clearly defined against the silk of the wrapper. "Nothing more?"

Her tawny eyes darkened, their black centers expanding to leave only thin bands of gold. "Definitely more." An almost frightened expression crossed her face, but before he could be certain of the emotion, she hugged him. "Oh, Rey. I'm so very happy you're here."

"So am I, Mercedes," he answered, holding her tighter. "So am I."

Rey picked her up in his arms and carried her to what he guessed would be the bedroom. He kicked open the French doors and took her into the darkened chamber. Shadows created by the fire and one oil lamp danced across the walls and the counterpane of the tester bed with carved mermaid bedposts. Slowly, he released her, enjoying the sensation of her body gliding down his before her toes reached the carpet. As her breasts grazed his shirt, he kissed her lips, coaxing them to part. He smoothed his hands over her buttocks and cupped the firm curves in both palms, squeezing. A low moan eased past her mouth into his. Guiding her closer to the fire, he pulled the ties of her wrap open. When his fingers met bared skin, he stopped. She was naked underneath the silk.

Their eyes met. The pink color of her skin deepened. "I thought perhaps . . ."

"You thought right."

He pressed her toward the fireplace, urging her back against the warmed wall near the hearth. Mercy seized the mantel with one hand; the other she spread against the French wallpaper's pattern of twined lilies and vines, supporting herself as Rey opened the lapels of her robe. He inched the material apart, savoring the unveiling like the unwrapping of a prized gift. With each teasing graze of cool silk against her nipples and stomach, a frenzied energy charged inside her, building until she shuddered. The wrapper hung precariously from her shoulders. Its folds swept against the full curves of her breasts, as caressing as fingers.

Rey stepped back. Mercy could see his aroused state outlined against the black wool trousers. He watched her, his hands holding her shoulders against the lilies and their climbing vines. The hunger in his expression made Mercy reach to close her gown; it seemed too much, too great to satisfy. But he stilled her hands, keeping her in the warmed niche between the mantel and wall, her robe draped open.

He lowered his gaze to her mouth, her neck, her shoulders . . . lower. His very look seemed to cherish and heat. Following the line of his vision, Mercy glanced down at herself. She'd never stared at her breasts before and it seemed almost indecent to examine herself—but the sight of Rey's hand closing over her breast captivated her. Her skin gleamed pale in the firelight, contrasting against Rey's tanned fingers. As she watched, his thumb stroked her nipple. The skin tightened, blushing from a pale peach hue to a dusky rose. She saw his head lower; his lips close over her nipple. "Beautiful," he whispered.

Rey circled the peaked center with his tongue then sucked gently. Her whimper relaxed into a sigh as he eased the pad of his thumb over her other breast.

"That feels so wickedly nice," she said.

He rolled the nipple between his fingers. "You haven't even begun to feel wicked, dear heart."

Her eyes were closed, her lips parted. She clutched the wood mantel at her side while her shoulders braced against the paper garden of lilies behind her. The opposite hand seemed to stretch for the painted vines just out of her reach on the wallpaper. Rey kissed her neck and imagined them making love on a bed of flowers as he inhaled her scent. He tasted the salt of her neck, his teeth scraped across her breasts, then teased a path to the tender skin of her stomach. The amber glow of the flames shimmered off her body, bronzing her skin. He thought of honey, gold, warm, endlessly sweet. Slowly, one aching inch at a time, his mouth devoured her. He lowered to one knee, then knelt before her as he kissed the slight swell of her stomach. She was surprisingly muscular, yet soft, like the heated silk wrapper. And incredibly desirable.

Rey looked up. A backdrop of pink and white flowers and firelight crowned Mercy's head. Her eyes remained heavy-lidded, her mouth moist. He rested one hand on her breast; her pulse beat against his palm. Her shiny white teeth ate at her bottom lip as he stroked her. With his other hand, he trailed small circles, outlining a rib, the tempting dip of her navel. At her thigh, he spread his hand until he brushed her soft gilt curls. Using the strokes of a painter, he felt the creator, transforming this lady into passion as his fingertips wandered through the curls in lazy S-shapes. If he were as talented as Renoir this would be the image of ecstasy he would paint.

He imagined his finger a soft sable brush, a painter's tool, and eased beyond the curls to her center. A low moan escaped from Mercy as he tested the flesh. His strokes followed the pulse tapping against the pad of his finger. He heard her breath catch. He looked up. There. On her face. Her expression. Passion in all its glory. Suddenly, he didn't want just to witness her desire. He wanted to be consumed by it.

He eased her legs apart with both hands, spreading her wider until he saw her, the pouting flesh, very pink, like the center of a bud rose. He kissed her, his mouth closing over her as his tongue covered the tender petals. Her breath came in short gasps. Her hands dug into his hair. She slid down the wall of flowers, her emerald wrapper pooling around them as he followed her to the floor. With his hands on the inside of her thighs, he kept her legs open to him as his tongue circled the delicious flesh, searched gently inside, followed her rhythm, increased it.

"Stop."

"You mean don't stop."

"Rey . . . I can't—"

"*Hmmm,* you can. And you will. Soon, I think."

She tensed; her hips arched off the floor. The expression on her face was everything he'd hoped and more. It made him hurt just to watch her. She shuddered, her release doubling the excruciating tension inside him, then collapsed against the carpet.

Rey listened to the clock ticking on the mantel place above them, to Mercedes's breathing, the crackle of the fire. He shifted, leveling himself over her. Her eyes fluttered open and her smile blossomed with the heat of her satisfaction. She pulled Rey into her arms and kissed him. Her very touch was an offer of thanks. He smiled. "I feel the same, dear heart," he whispered.

Rising to his feet, he picked her up and carried her to the bed. He planned to show her so much more.

He began to fling off his clothes, practically tearing off a few shirt buttons when a suspicious giggle made him look up. Mercy sat with her back against one of the mermaid carved bedposts, her robe negligently closed so that one thigh, shoulder, and most of her breasts were exposed. Hair spilled around her face, burnished by the fire behind her. She covered her mouth with her hand, but he could still see the edge of her smile. She glanced pointedly at each article of clothing strewn about the room, his jacket on the counterpane, his waistcoat tossed on the cane chair, his boots thrown to the floor. She raised a brow. "Slow and steady?"

Rey dove across the bed and grabbed her ankles. Peals of laughter filled the room as he dragged her beneath him on the bed. "No, Rey. Stop!" But he was laughing too, enjoying the exhilarating swells that had been absent from his life for too long. Mercy sat up, nipping at his lips and chin between kisses and giggles as Rey slipped the robe from her shoulders. And then the laughter stopped and they both watched each other. Mercy's lips were bruised red from his kisses; her eyes shone dark. "Again, Rey," she whispered, her hand closing over the wool covering his erection.

He cast off his shirt. Mercy unfastened his trousers, pushing them past his hips and down his legs as Rey kicked them off. He eased her back onto the quilt, feeling himself engorge impossibly more with the sight of her. Her eyes never left his steady gaze as she wrapped her legs around him, drawing him closer. The sweet touch of her mouth fired him, making him too hungry, and he pulled back, trying to gain control.

His Saint Christopher medal swung from his neck between them, brushing her skin. At its touch, her eyes opened wide, as if with surprise. Catching his glance, she took the chain and pulled gently, bringing him back into her arms.

The minute he entered her, he felt complete. For this, he might risk anything. To feel himself deep inside her, her sweet breath on his mouth, her breasts crushed against his chest. She could shut out the memories. She could make him happy. *Giving when he'd known only loss. Companionship to fill the loneliness.* Her thighs against his hips urged him deeper. Her soft hands clutched at his back, communicating urgency. She delivered a fantasy he'd never known he desired. It was there in her touch, her hungry mouth, and her whispered words that repeated, "I love you. I love you, Rey," so deliciously in his ear. With a cry, he felt his seed pour inside her as she reached her peak, contracting around him. Rey squeezed Mercedes tightly, clinging to the wave of peace.

He lay perfectly still, his head resting between her breasts, listening to her heart's slow satisfied beat. A sigh passed her lips. She pulled his face up to meet hers. "Thank you." She kissed him gently on the mouth, a gift as tender as her words. *I love you, Rey.*

Her fingers laced through his hair, twisting a strand, then stroking it back. Rey felt himself drifting off to sleep when she picked up his St. Christopher medal and gave it a playful tug. "This is new."

"Hardly. It's almost as old as I am." He grinned. "But you've never seen it before. The clasp was broken. I had it fixed this morning."

"A religious medal." She smiled, dropping the chain. "Are you a religious man, Rey?"

The first shadow fell on his pleasure. "I'd say not religious enough. I believe the Church would term this the 'Fine Art of Adultery.'"

She shook her head, her eyes serious. "For me"—she traced his lips with her finger—"this is the fine art of salvation."

He took her hand and kissed her palm. "Mercedes—"

"I love you, Rey. With all my heart." Her voice rang strong. There was no questioning the feeling behind her words. "That can't be wrong."

She offered up her love so sweetly. It was there for the taking—happiness spread like a bacchanalian feast. The prior night's question came back to tempt him: *What would it take to get her to leave De Dreux?*

"Then don't go back to him, Mercedes," he said, giving in to what he desired most. "Stay with me. Divorce Benoit." And because it felt right to say it, "Marry me."

Mercy closed her eyes, feeling her past swallow up her joy. For once, life offered her something other than grief and loneliness, and because of Benoit, she was powerless to accept it. She was his pawn, no better than a slave. Until she could destroy his power to harm Laura and Beth, she couldn't afford the luxury of what Rey offered. Of all the things Benoit had done, this was perhaps the most painful.

"I can't," she said, glancing away. "There are reasons you can't even begin to understand . . ." *The things I've done, Rey. You would never want me if you knew.* "Benoit would never allow me to divorce him."

Mercy waited on the coverlet. Now surely he would leave her. She would be alone again. It was for the best, she told herself. He'd risked so much for her already, never knowing the lies she'd told. But just as she had when he'd asked about the possibility of a child, Mercy found the prospect of losing the small slice of happiness she'd carved for herself intolerable. Before she could think better of her actions, she turned back to Rey, hugging him, kissing him. "Please, tell me it's enough just to be together like this, Rey. Let it be enough."

He barely held her, at first only receiving her embrace. But then his arms pressed her against him, almost hurting her with the strength of his grip, and he whispered, "It's enough, Mercedes . . . for now."

"I love you, Rey," she said, giving him the only truth she could offer. She buried her face in the warmth of his neck. The curly hair covering his chest tickled her mouth. "You're like a dream come true." She thought of the ballad she'd memorized those many years ago. Perhaps Mercy would never reached Robin Hood's chivalry, but Rey certainly would. "You remind me of those heroes in the old poems."

"Hero?" He pulled her to arm's length, laughing. "You are mad."

" 'Attend and listen, ye gentlemen, that be of freeborn

blood; I shall tell you of a good yeoman, his name was Robin Hood.' "

Immediately he frowned, his expression far from pleased. "You can save that little comparison for your Santana Rose."

Mercy's pulse took an odd jump when she realized her mistake. "All right," she said, quickly correcting herself, "then, the Celtic hero, Tristan."

"Now that seems more appropriate, considering he slept with his uncle's bride."

"No, not that." She took his hand between hers. His fingers extended a good length beyond Mercy's. "He saved the damsel in distress."

He watched her for a moment. "But I haven't saved you, have I, Mercedes? You're going right back to the dragon's castle, aren't you?"

She laced their fingers together and looked up. "For now," she said, repeating his words to her.

Rey released her hand and reached behind his neck to unclasp his gold chain. When he placed the medallion around her neck, she asked, "What are you doing?"

"When my mother gave me this medal, she said that if I looked at it each day, St. Christopher would keep me safe. She thought it was the perfect medal for a child. But I think it's just as appropriate for a damsel in distress. It's yours, Mercedes. If you ever need me, send this to Bizy."

"And you'll appear and slay the dragon?" she asked, holding the medal in her hand.

"Something like that." He grinned. "You know, when you're like this, smiling, joking, you don't seem at all like a Mercedes. It's such a stiff, formal name. Fit for a novice."

She looked around the tousled bed and her naked state. "I'm hardly that."

"Thank God." He rolled on top of her, laughing with her, kissing the breath from her. "I like you just the way you are. My angel of mercy." He sat up, stroking her face gently. "That's what I should call you. Mercy. Sweet, sweet Mercy."

With the sound of her real name, Mercy felt her throat tighten. *Mercy.* Not since she'd left Laura and Beth had anyone called her that. With a little shock, she realized she'd never even heard the name said out loud since she'd left that cold London alley. Until now.

"You're right," she said, her voice straining past the lump in her throat. "Mercedes isn't the right name for me, at all." *That's a name Benoit created, a woman he made up.*

Rey stroked back her hair with a tender expression in his light green eyes. "Will it be Mercy, then? Or Madame Seductress?" He caressed her lips playfully with his thumb. *"Chère?"* His head dipped down to hers. His tongue traced her mouth. "My heart?"

Mercy leaned into his kiss, blinking back her tears. "Mercy will do just fine."

Mac felt the mattress shift with Kate's weight. He almost reached across to anchor her back to his side, but something about her movements, the slow steady inching across the sheet, made him wait. What was the lass up to? Then he heard it, the soft knocking at the door.

Mac lay still as Kate crept off the mattress and dressed in her wrapper. When he sensed she was at the door, he cracked open one eye. She was watching him, as if trying to decide if he were still asleep. Then she eased the door open just wide enough to scoot through and soundlessly close it behind her.

Mac jumped to his feet. He'd seen the lass's guilty glance. She was up to something.

As skillfully as Kate, Mac cracked the door a slit. Pressing his ear to the gap, he heard Kate talking to her man. Jean Claude, was his name. A young good-looking Frenchy who saw to almost everything for Kate. Mac listened.

"Gessler's drunk as a weasel downstairs. He's asking for you. I told him you were out."

"*Gracias,* Jean Claude. I do not think I could stomach *el gordo* tonight. Give him anything he wants. On the house."

"I already have . . . and it seems your tempting figure isn't the only thing that makes our good constable run at the mouth."

Mac felt a white hot blade of jealousy rip through him at the youngster's casual measure of Kate's shapely figure, but he pushed his feelings aside when Kate answered, "Another run?"

"Yes. Tomorrow night. Just like always. Barataria to the Little Temple. Gessler's taken heart from the fact he almost caught Santana the last time. He's doubling the guard. De Dreux's pressuring him more than ever to bring Santana in."

"And the cargo?"

"Same as ever."

"*Dios.* If I tell her about this, nothing will stop Santana from going to the swamps."

"And why should it, Kate? It's a simple job. Typical of Gessler. He's planning his ambush south of the Little Temple, just beyond Little Lake, thinking she'll be waiting there like the last time. All she has to do is meet them farther down the bayou."

"You're *loco,* Jean Claude. Santana almost found her head in a noose the last time."

"So have her intercept them nearer to the bay. The boats always unload at the same cove. This time, we could be waiting west of the Manila village—catch them before they ever reach Bayou St. Denis, much less Little Temple. It's a fine spot, with plenty of inlets and waterways for escape. Why not wait for them right at the mouth of the swamps?"

"*A lo mejor.* It might work."

"Of course, it will work. Remember who we're dealing

with, Kate. For God's sake, a catfish has more brains than our constable."

During the silence that followed, Mac's thoughts reeled. Kate wasn't just passing on information to the lady bandit. She was involved up to her finely plucked eyebrows in Santana's business.

"*Ay Dios,* Jean Claude. I do not have a good feeling about this. But I will tell Santana. Your plan is good."

The door closed and Mac raced to the bed. When Kate came in and snuggled next to him, he gave the lass his back. To think he'd defended her to Rey. But then, he heard her sigh as she inched closer, felt her persistent hands that seemed to say she needed him, and the anger inside him softened. He sighed, turning over to kiss her.

He'd leave being perfect to Rey.

"Christopher."

Rey's voice reached beyond Mercy's warm haven of sleep. She tried to ignore the sound. She was dreaming. She held Rey's baby in her arms; Rey stood over them, watching her and their child proudly—

"Not Christopher."

The urgency in those two words woke Mercy. She sat up and turned to Rey. Beside her on the tester bed, he tossed his head and mumbled, in the grip of his own dream. "Let him go!"

There was such anguish in his voice, Mercy became concerned. She shook him, hoping to wake him from his nightmare.

Rey jerked upright in the bed, his breath coming in heavy gasps. He glanced at Mercy, then shut his eyes, falling back against the pillows as if just realizing he'd woken from a nightmare and his imagined demons could not hurt him. Mercy rose and walked to her clothespress to retrieve a handkerchief. When she opened the drawer, the first thing she saw was Sotheby's burlap bag filled with his bribe money. Grabbing a linen kerchief, she slammed the drawer shut, closing her mind to the painful reminder of her lies to Rey. Now was not the time to think of such things.

She poured water into the washstand and dipped the linen. When she climbed back on the tester, she wiped Rey's brow with the moist cloth. "Better?"

He nodded and scanned the room. "What time is it?"

"Close to three in the morning."

Taking the handkerchief, he tossed the cloth on the bed stand. He pulled her into his arms, seeking the comfort of her touch. "Will this be a problem? Your staying here for the night?"

"No. Benoit and I fought this morning over Pascal. I told him I would be staying in town tonight. He doesn't expect me back until later today."

Still holding her, he said, "I hate to think of you taking chances. That he might hurt you because of me."

"He won't, Rey. Truly." She searched for something to allay his fears. "I've explained to you about Benoit, about our marriage. I often stay in town. He won't think anything suspicious of my doing so tonight."

He looked so tired, Mercy ached in sympathy. His eyelids lowered, the stroking of his fingers at the back of her head slowed, but she could see from his expression he would not fall back to sleep easily. Too much of his nightmare remained in his unfocused gaze. "Did you know you talk in your sleep?" she asked.

His muscles beneath her palm tensed. She knew he was alert, yet his eyes drifted open; the lazy strokes in her hair continued. "Did I say anything interesting?"

"You were calling for someone. Someone named Christopher."

He relaxed against the cushions. "I was dreaming about him. A bad dream."

Mercy edged closer. "Who is he?"

"Christopher?" He seemed lost in thought, as if he found her question difficult to answer, then sat up against the pillows. He pulled her around to face him. His eyes looked very serious. Very sad.

"Christopher is my son, Mercy."

"Your son?" Her voice sounded faint, not her voice at all, almost childlike. Of course. He'd been married. It made sense. And yet, it hurt to think of him with a child, not her child, but someone totally separate from her—from her love for Rey. And to remember that he'd made it very clear he would not allow her a baby of their own. . . .

Mercy pushed back her resentment, knowing she had no right to it. Rey's hands caressed her hair, the touch light, distracted. As she'd done all her life—with Laura and Beth, the orphans at St. Bartholomew's, with Pascal—Mercy sensed his pain. Tentatively, she touched the dimple of his chin, then cupped her hands around his face and kissed him lightly on the mouth. She nestled into the curve of his arm. "It must have been a terrible dream," she said, believing it might help him to talk about it. "You sounded so sad when you called his name."

He frowned as if struggling to remember, or perhaps hesitating to recount his tale, she couldn't tell which. When he said nothing, she turned his face to look at her and whispered, "Tell me, Rey."

He watched her with eyes filled with a terrible sorrow. She could see he wanted to share the burden of his dream, even as he held back his confidence.

"Tell me," she urged.

His fingers curled around the strands of her hair and slowly tightened into a fist. "I dreamt he was on a boat with his mother," he said, his voice barely above a whisper. "I was on another boat, very far away. I was trying my damnedest to reach them. I had to get there quickly. Before . . ." He shook his head; his fist relaxed into an opened palm on the coverlet. "But the more I struggled, the farther the current carried us apart. And then . . ."

"And then what, Rey?" she asked, seeing he would not finish.

Again, his fingers played with a long strand of her hair. He focused there, as if it took all his attention. "The boat exploded," he whispered. "And they were gone."

The shock of his dream silenced her. She didn't know what to say. To experience something so terrifying, even in a dream . . . "What an absolutely horrible nightmare." She hugged him, trying to make up for the inadequacy of her words by the caress. "But it was just a dream. It didn't happen—"

"No . . . not exactly like that, anyway."

Mercy's heart stopped. *Please God, no.*

"Only to my wife. Christopher was nowhere near the boat when it exploded."

There seemed no air in the room. She couldn't move. She could only sit there, staring at him stupidly.

"Sometimes," he continued, "I see them, leaning over the rail, beckoning to me. Sometimes, everything is foggy and I only hear them screaming for me to hurry. But I never make it in time."

Mercy closed her eyes against the image so vividly painted by his words. The tragedies in her life suddenly paled. An itch, a scratch—nothing compared to the gaping wound Rey had just described. To watch a loved one die in such a brutal fashion . . . she remembered the look on his face when she'd held his wedding band during the holdup, his expression at dinner that first night when he'd mentioned his wife. So much pain. *No wonder. No wonder.*

"I'm so sorry," she whispered. She turned her face up to his and kissed him. "But it wasn't like that," she said, searching for words to console him. "It wasn't your fault. These steamboat accidents, the passengers don't even know the engine is going to blow. She didn't suffer, Rey. Don't think about her suffering."

His mouth stopped moving beneath her kiss. She pulled away and glanced up at his face. His normally clear eyes looked haunted by an emotion she knew well: overwhelming regret. She realized then the scenario she'd just cre-

ated had nothing to do with his wife's death. She thought
of his occupation—an agent working for the United States
government. A man who led a perilous life. A lifestyle that
might place a loved one in danger.

"Don't blame yourself, Rey." The words fell from her
lips, weighted by their inadequacy. "What good does it do
to blame yourself?"

The terror of that day flooded Rey. He barely heard
Mercy's words of comfort. The empathy in her voice—the
tone of a woman who knew the agony of surviving—hardly
registered. He could still see himself, screaming at the
ship's captain as their boat fought the waves. Watching
Sophie urge him closer, smiling with relief at seeing him—
until her image was extinguished by a blinding flash and a
deafening roar.

If he'd only reached her in time. Why hadn't he reached
her in time?

Soft fingers caressed his cheek. A gentle pressure
turned his gaze back toward Mercy, away from his nightmare questions. There were tears in her eyes.

"Tell me about your son, Rey."

A single teardrop slipped down her cheek, but her smile
denied she was crying. She appeared to have an unfathom-
able tolerance for pain; as if she would carry the burden of
it for him if he allowed her. That expression had drawn
him from the first. There'd been such delicious sympathy
in her eyes that night they'd met. He remembered he'd
thought she was a woman familiar with life and its disap-
pointments. A woman strong enough to share the suffering in his soul.

Rey's heart slowed, approaching a normal pace. Mercy
slipped down on the bed, pulling him beside her.

"How old is he?" she asked, cuddling into his side.
"Does he look like you?"

He saw Christopher's face. It had been months since
he'd seen his son's features so well defined in his mind.
He'd been afraid he was forgetting . . . but now he could

almost reach out and touch him. Christopher. He still had his son.

"He looks a lot like me," Rey said. "Except for his eyes. They're blue. A very dark blue."

"Like Mr. Everard's?"

"Yes," he answered, relaxing beside her. "Just that color. We always wondered where he got those eyes. No one on either side of the family has eyes quite so blue. And of course his hair is dark—the way mine used to be."

"When did it change color?" she asked, twining strands of it through her fingers. "Were you a white-haired young man the girls whispered about, so handsome and striking with your silver locks?"

He turned on his side to face her. The terror of his memories lost some of their bite and he found he was able to speak without the heartache of the past. "It changed after my wife died," he said. "It took a month, maybe two, to look like this."

Her eyes were a sweet golden brown, like the sugar candy peddled on street corners in town. At his explanation, they filled with compassion. Her fingers continued to tease his hair. He closed his eyes, relaxing with the rhythm of her strokes.

"How old is Christopher?"

"He's six, soon to be seven." He smiled, concentrating on his son. "And loves fishing, dogs, and bicycles." He thought of the red safety bicycle he'd ordered for Chris's birthday. "He has this smile that gets him anything he wants—"

"With a dimple here." She touched his chin. "And another here." Her finger moved to just below his left cheek. "And what a wonderful smile it is."

He opened his eyes. "I hadn't realized."

"About your smile? I think you described it perfectly. The kind that gets you anything you want."

"Hmm," he said, accepting her kiss. He felt better, now.

The haunting devils were almost behind him. His palm covered her breast. "One hopes."

Mercy stilled his hand. Holding his wrist, she pulled his hand from her breast, then laced their fingers together. His pale green eyes watched her, waiting for an explanation.

"I suppose you miss him terribly?" she asked, hoping that he would confide in her, that with her help he might stop running away from the ghosts of his past. "How long has it been since you've seen him?"

His eyes shifted to the drapery of the tester behind her. The length of his silence made her wonder if he would answer. "Too long," he said at last. "I saw him at the station between trains a few months ago, but it's been almost a year since I've stayed in Boston for longer than an hour."

She nodded, as if expecting his answer. She knew what kind of man he was. He wouldn't leave his son for so long without reason. And she knew instinctively that she could help him face that reason. "Do you think," she began, hesitating, knowing that what she asked would be painful to accept. "Do you think perhaps that you . . . you stay away from him because . . . because of what happened to his mother?"

Rey turned away, but she reached out and stilled his face between her hands.

"I only say that because I did the same, Rey. With Pascal. For the longest time, I denied myself her friendship because of Benoit. She looks so much like her father . . . she reminded me. With your wife. Perhaps, because of her death, and Christopher being her child . . . it brings back the memories."

Rey's heart pounded in his chest as her words evoked emotions he'd rather not face. He loved his child. He'd loved no one in his life as he adored Christopher. And yet, what Mercy said contained a frightening grain of truth. Since Sophie's death, he'd spent more and more time away, searching for Sotheby. He thought of his son's letter. *It's all right if you miss my birthday.* Recalled the guilt that had struck him as he'd read those words. And still he stayed away, making no plans to return home until he had Sotheby behind bars, ignoring the voice inside him that told him what he did was wrong.

"It's not that he reminds me of her death, Mercy," he said, struggling to put into words the fears that plagued him for the past five years. "I feel responsible," he said. "She was his mother, and I feel responsible."

"For her death?"

A long silence, then, "Yes."

The ferocity of her embrace startled Rey. His hands hovered over her, overwhelmed by her emotion and the feelings she evoked inside him. He wanted her to take away his grief . . . he wanted to protect her from it. Finally, he cupped her face in his hands and raised her face to his. There were tears in her eyes. "Don't cry, my heart. Not for me."

"The ones that are left behind always feel responsible, Rey," she said gently, blinking back her tears. "Your guilt can poison you, destroy your relationship with your loved ones. Don't let it stop you from being a father to Christopher. He needs you. And you *need* him. Allow yourself that happiness. If not for yourself, then for your son."

Rey held her gaze. Such simple words she'd spoken—*I forgive you, Rey. Forgive yourself.* If only forgiveness could come so easily: a loving woman granting absolution like so many verses of a rosary. He brushed back her tears, kissed them from her lips. Perhaps, if he could stop blaming himself for Sophie's death, it would all disappear—the burning desire for revenge, the images of his bullet piercing Sotheby's heart. Then he could take Mercy back to Boston and return to his family, be a real father to Chris. But no matter how much Mercy loved him, the past was his cross to bear. For now, he would settle for Sotheby's destruction to earn back his self-respect. To earn back his son.

He looked down at Mercy in his arms. She watched him expectantly. For Christopher's sake, she'd said. If only it could be possible. But even for his son, Rey couldn't overlook his guilt.

He tucked her against him, holding her. There'd been a deep sadness in her eyes, as if she'd sensed he could not follow her words of advice. It squeezed something in his heart to know she cared so much. Mercy seemed the only joy he could allow himself. If not total absolution, certainly she was a reprieve from his purgatory.

In the darkness of the room, he kissed the top of her head and whispered, "I love you, Mercy. I love you."

Chapter 16

Rey left his mount at Bizy's stable, the same smile on his face that had traveled with him since he'd left the *pied-à-terre*. Memories of his night with Mercedes lingered, buoying his spirits. He thought of his name for her: Mercy. That's what she was for him—what she had brought him.

No one had ever touched him as deeply, not even Sophie. He'd loved his wife dearly, but they had been so young when they'd married. Their lives had been simple, without the least hardship. Sophie's parents had given them their brownstone on Beacon Hill. Rey's father had stepped aside as president of the family bank, granting his oldest child the coveted position. A fine son had been born a little over a year after their wedding. They'd never experienced tragedy. But Mercy understood the abyss Rey faced each day, carrying the burden of Sophie's murder. Their night together had opened, and soothed, the wounds of his past.

Crushed oyster shells groaned beneath his boot heels as he walked the path. Up ahead, Bizy's plantation house lay shrouded by a tangle of ancient oaks. The late morning sun filtered through their branches to light patches of grass. Rey thought over the letter he would write to Christopher. All his instincts told him they were on the verge of apprehending Sotheby. And with the man's arrest, Rey would earn a second chance with his son.

Taking the stairs to the main floor, he called for Mac,

thinking of how to explain his long absence to Chris in his letter—then deciding to wait until he held his boy in his arms. He pictured Mercy in Boston beside him, free at last to follow her heart after Rey arrested De Dreux as Sotheby's accomplice. For now, Rey would write Nan that he would hurry his work and return home, not in time for Chris's birthday but certainly soon thereafter.

Rey shouted Mac's name again, heading for his room, then stopped when he heard no response. Odd. Mac was always on the alert to Rey's comings and goings.

Glancing in the salon, Rey found his valet lounging on the settee—oblivious to his entrance and deep in thought. Rey frowned. Few times in the ten years he'd known John MacAfee had he come upon the Scotsman unawares.

"Mac?"

His friend's glazed eyes blinked to attention. "You're home." He rose slowly. His face and his movements showed that, like Rey, Mac had had a long night. "I've been waiting for ye. I have the information you're wantin'. Seems Gessler's bringing in new cargo for De Dreux through the bayou. Kate's man is lettin' Santana know about the details."

Santana Rose. Rey felt as if he'd slammed into a wall of moist Louisiana heat. His satisfaction for the evening dissipated. Contempt for the highway woman simmered to boiling, straining like bottled steam as he pictured her masked face taunting him. He couldn't even kiss Mercy without the robber woman haunting him. Tender thoughts and blissful memories lifted away like a curtain of fog, leaving only one consideration center-stage: Santana's capture. Her games had cost him his meeting with Sotheby. If not for Harlan, all would have been lost that night.

"And you know the details surrounding the shipment?" Rey asked.

"Aye. I got the lot by plastering me good ear to the door. It's a plum set up. She'll not be expecting us to interfere."

Quickly, Rey weighed the costs and benefits of pursuing the bandit. If all went well, Sotheby would soon be behind bars—unless the bandit interfered again. Who knew what mischief the highway woman could cause Rey. He needed her out of the way. "With a bit of luck, we'll have her."

"Aye. Like a cock on its dunghill."

Rey frowned. Mac's tone was far from jubilant. His valet's expression placed him a hundred miles away.

"All right, Mac. What is it?" Rey asked, knowing his man well enough to see something was amiss.

"Och, it's the lass at Catalan Kate's." Mac sighed. "I've been thinkin'. You're going to be wantin' her as well as yer robber lady."

"If she's involved . . ."

"Oh, doubtless Kate's in it. Right down to those fancy buckle shoes of hers. But I've been wondering if there wasna some other way to deal with her."

"What are you talking about?"

"I'd hate to see her jailed."

Rey stared at Mac in disbelief. "You're protecting this woman?"

"Looks to be that I am."

"Are you crazed? She's harboring criminals. A woman like her must be stopped."

"I've been spendin' a fair bit of time with Katie, sir, and I don't quite see her in that light."

Katie. The diminutive, spoken with such familiarity, stole the condemning words from the tip of Rey's tongue —as did the generous display of emotion on Mac's face. "You're in love with her."

The whiskered chin jutted out. "Love her or not, it's a fact I don't want to see her in jail, ye ken?"

"I don't believe it." Rey paced on the threadbare rug. The last of the finely tuned rules of his life teetered on a precipice, threatening to go the way of other principles he'd abandoned since he'd arrived in New Orleans. "Dammit, Mac. She's one of Santana's own—and who knows what other villains she grants safe harbor. She could be involved with Sotheby himself! It's not up to us to decide the fate of criminals. We can't just point a finger and decide this one we turn in, that one we don't. We leave that to the lawmakers and the courts."

"Aye, but I'm thinking those lawmakers ain't always got the right of things—not if their laws say my Katie's good for nothing but jail."

Rey stared at Mac, dumbstruck. But even as Rey's anger threatened his control, he realized a good portion of his rage was misdirected. It wasn't Mac who'd let Santana escape when he could have shot her out of her saddle. Nor was it the Scotsman who'd entangled himself with De Dreux's wife. Yet, for reasons Rey did not understand, it seemed vital that he keep Mac from making his same mistakes—as if by saving his friend from the purgatory he'd entered, Rey might make up for his own trespasses.

He advanced on Mac and grabbed the Scotsman by both shoulders. "We're lawmen, Mac. It's not our choice whether Kate goes to jail. We hunt down criminals. That's our job. For the love of God, man. We took an oath to the office we serve."

Mac shrugged off his hold and shuffled back two steps. He turned his back to Rey. "I canna betray Katie."

"But you *can* betray your beliefs?" Rey spun Mac around to face him. "You've dedicated just as many years as I have to putting criminals behind bars. You've made just as many sacrifices. Justice, Mac. It's a simple concept. If we didn't honor it, where would we be? What would the past five years be about?"

A empty silence followed. Mac's expression remained just as stubborn as ever.

"Could you really," Rey asked, "after all this time, care for this woman? Knowing what she is?"

Mac dropped his chin to his chest. After a moment, he slanted a look up at Rey.

Disappointment, clear and condemning, shone from the Scotsman's eyes.

Rey stood stunned by the older man's disapproval. He watched Mac straighten his waistcoat and square his shoulders. His companion's clear brown gaze fixed on Rey.

"That's about what I thought ye'd be sayin'. Well then, I got no other choice. I'll marry the lass."

The breath left Rey's lungs. "Marry?"

"Aye. Ye let Kate go, and I'll make sure that, as my wife, she stays on the straight and narrow. That seems justice enough for me."

"You're mad."

"I'm thinkin' the same, sir. But t'was the only thing I could think to do. She'd be my wife then, ye ken, and I'm betting anything of mine ye'd protect."

"You're forcing me to conspire with you to let this woman go?"

"I've no choice, Rey." Mac's strong Scottish burr almost overpowered the words he'd spoken so softly. "I'm verra sorry."

Anger and the pain of betrayal tumbled inside Rey's gut. He opened his mouth, ready to dole out his rage. But Mac stood before him in his shirtsleeves, the stitches of his waistcoat straining against the muscles of his hunched shoulders. His hands hung down to his side; his mustache drooped—both weighed down by seeming regret.

Mac. The man who'd pulled Rey bleeding from the trenches during the war. The man who'd fed him like a baby while Rey recovered from a fever brought on by an infected gunshot wound. Mac.

Slowly, sweetly, the image of Mercy crept into Rey's consciousness. He could feel the touch of her arms around him, almost hear his voice as he asked her to leave her husband and marry him. He understood the powerful emotions that held his friend. But a criminal, a woman so clearly undeserving of Mac's esteem . . .

Rey placed his hand on Mac's shoulder. "What can I do

to stop you from committing this . . . this . . . disaster? Don't marry her; we'll work with her, offer her a deal if she tells us who she works for—"

"I've already thought of that, and Kate doesna strike me as a turncoat. It's marriage, I'm afraid. As ye said, Rey—I believe in justice. If I keep her out of jail, it's my obligation to watch over the lass for the rest of our lives. As my wife, I'd have control over what Katie does." There was a hard gleam to his eyes. "By my soul, t'would be as good as jail for the lass."

Rey thought of his own proposal to Mercy—then dismissed the comparison. Mercy was no criminal. Nor was she responsible for her situation with De Dreux. She didn't have a real marriage; she was a victim of abuse. "It's a mistake, Mac. A woman who runs a brothel, harbors criminals—"

"Circumstances make people do strange things. That doesna make them bad."

Indeed, Rey thought, turning away. But he kept any further opinions to himself, seeing that he would not sway Mac. He grabbed up a decanter of whiskey by its throat and poured himself a shot despite the early hour. "It's your decision, of course. You'll do as you please, in any case." But the idea of Mac marrying so nefarious a woman rankled. In a way, Rey felt responsible, having sent Mac to Catalan Kate's in the first place.

Falling into the tapestry armchair with his glass in hand, he reached inside his coat and retrieved a cigarette. He searched his mind for a safe topic of conversation to ease the tension between them as he placed his glass on the table and struck a friction match.

"Do you know where Harlan is, by any chance?" Rey stopped in the middle of lighting the Choctaw. "Wait. Forget that. You don't have to tell me. He's at L'Isle des Rêves, isn't he?"

"Seems the womenfolk there have a powerful attraction." Mac nodded his head toward Rey's whiskey and cigarette. "Never did ken moderation, did ye, Rey? It's always been all or nothing for ye."

Rey flushed, knowing Mac referred to more than his picking up of old habits. Ignoring the heat in his face, he leaned back against the floral *gros point* of the armchair. "I would hope, given your own circumstances, I'm in no peril of one of your fine sermons."

"Nay. No sermon. The heart can make a man do strange things, and that's a fact." Mac paced to Rey's side, his expression thoughtful. "I'll admit to being skeptical about the Missus, and sad she's not free to marry ye. I told ye before, I wished you a birn of bairns. And I'm not above mentioning the kirk's laws to switch yer path." He shook his head, sending his shaggy curls brushing against his beard. "But bless me if I've never seen ye happier than when yer with her. It's only afterward that you're looking like ye've made a miserable error of life, with yer lip hanging down to yer shins—or worse, pacing the night"—he glared at the whiskey glass—"drinking and smoking the day through."

"It's not Mercy that's driving me to drink right now, Mac," Rey said meaningfully. He tossed back the whiskey in one swallow.

Mac snatched the tumbler from his grasp. He grunted something that sounded suspiciously like "cockerel's cackle," apparently finding Rey's response unworthy of further reply. Rey glanced away from his friend's somber countenance, experiencing a bit of melancholy himself. What a predicament they'd placed themselves in. Rey in love with De Dreux's wife. Mac planning to marry a brothel owner and likely criminal.

Rey stretched his legs out, crossing them at the ankles. "I'm happy to hear I have your good wishes for Mercy and myself, Mac. But I can't say the same for Harlan and De Dreux's daughter," he said, steering the conversation back to the original topic.

"It's clear he has a grudge against the father. Ye think he'd hurt the girl?"

"I'm inclined to believe he wouldn't—but why tempt fate? Send a message to get his able body back here." Rey studied the smoke pluming from the Choctaw in his hand. "I can't blame him for taking an interest in her; she follows him about like a love-starved puppy. But I sincerely wish he'd never encouraged her in the first place." He looked up at Mac. "When is Santana set to make the take?"

"Tonight."

"Tonight," he repeated with the determination of a man intent on at least one victory.

Harlan lay on a bed of flowers as Pascal stroked his lips with the petals of a daisy. The late morning sun warmed his face as he lounged on the hillside—but nothing heated him as much as the thoughts coursing through his mind, *mais* sure. Beneath hooded eyes, his gaze drifted up the gauntlet of temptation dressed in muslin and lace. Following the gentle flare of her hips that dipped at her waist, he imagined his hand closing over the swell of her young breast . . . Harlan closed his eyes firmly, blacking out *that* thought. He'd be making a muck of things before he knew what's what if he wasn't careful. He called up the sobering image of her father to deflect *la petite*'s charms. He almost mouthed those sweet words, "you're under arrest," to the image of De Dreux in his head—

The soft touch of her lips shocked Harlan out of his vision, making him jerk up on his elbows, away from Pascal's kiss. Pascal watched him quietly, the daisy's stem now bent so that the flower drooped over her grasp.

"I don't think a simple kiss deserves such a scowl, Harlan."

He rose, brushing the grass from his pants and forced himself to give her a lighthearted grin. "Me? Scowling over a kiss? *Jamais, petite.*"

Taking her hand, he helped her to her feet and pulled
her into his embrace. He told himself the kiss he gave her
would wipe away any ill feelings that might later develop
into suspicion. That's what he told himself. But damn if he
didn't enjoy just touching her. She smelled like the grass
and flowers they'd spent the lazy morning picking and
tossing back at each other. And when her breasts crushed
against his chest, and her lips parted beneath his, Harlan
felt hotter than a moss bed in summer.

"Mr. Everard. Mr. Everard!"

The sound of his name echoing from the house jolted
them apart. They turned to watch one of the house servants running toward them, waving a note in her hand. It
wasn't often they were interrupted. Harlan wasn't quite
sure how *la petite* managed to get away unchaperoned.
Pascal always smiled with sweet mischief when he asked
and said that she had her ways. When the servant reached
them, Harlan read the message quickly. "Looks like I'm
needed back at Bizy."

"I was hoping we could have a picnic," she said, disappointment clear in her voice. "I thought maybe—"

"Work calls, *mon chou.*"

"Oh, of course." She looked to the tips of her shoes. "I
shouldn't keep you."

Pascal dismissed the servant, instructing her to have
Harlan's mount brought from the stables to the front
drive. As the maid scurried back to the plantation house,
Pascal stared at Harlan, her expression both hesitant and
expectant. Harlan tried his damnedest to clear the heat
she created from his mind. Imagine, a sugar baron's
daughter carrying on for a poor Cajun like himself. With
his finger he traced her lips. If not for De Dreux . . .

He dropped his hand from her mouth. *Tonnerre*! If he
didn't get a hold of himself, this little bit of womanhood
no taller than a whooping crane could make him forget his
plans against his enemy. He took a step back, then turned
and started up the hill toward the house, fortifying his

defenses. By the time Pascal followed beside him, he was again focused on his mission.

"What's wrong, Harlan?"

"Mais nothing, *chou."* He stared at the cane fields above the house. "Your father got any new plans to increase production? Seems like he's planning a big crop this year, him."

Pascal's slender shoulders visibly slumped under the lace scarf she wore. "My father, always my father." She gave Harlan a sad smile. "Sometimes I think you're more interested in my father than me, Harlan."

The accuracy of her statement left him momentarily speechless. But then he grinned shrewdly and said, "Your father's very wealthy, *petite.* Maybe I jus' admire him. I might want to be like him—"

"No! Never!" Pascal spun around and threw her arms around Harlan, hugging him for all she was worth. "You're nothing like my father!"

"Mon Dieu, chère." He lifted up her chin and stroked the dark red curls from her face, startled by her vehemence. "It's all right. I didn't mean anything by it."

"I love you, Harlan," she said in a heartfelt voice that choked something up inside him. "Just the way you are."

Her dark eyes sparkled with the love she'd just declared. *Dieu,* it was so seductive, all that undying devotion she offered so sweetly. So hard to resist. To think, he could fall for De Dreux's daughter.

"You don't like your father much," he whispered, wanting despite himself to separate the two of them in his mind.

She didn't answer immediately, just tightened her hold and nuzzled against his chest. "I know he's my father. I shouldn't speak ill of him, but—" Her head dropped back and she stared up at Harlan. "He's horrible." She said it like a confession, as if she believed herself tarnished by the very words. "You have no idea what he does for his wealth

. . . what he's willing to do. The people that suffer because of him."

Harlan couldn't believe his ears. He almost laughed out loud, he was struck by such a powerful sense of relief. She knew. She knew what a demon De Dreux was. And she hated him for it.

"There's *nothing* laudable about my father, Harlan. He's an evil, evil man. He doesn't care who he hurts to get what he wants."

There was an edge of desperation to her voice, as if she needed to convince *Harlan*—the man who'd suffered at her father's hand—that De Dreux was a devil.

Pascal looked away, as if she couldn't meet his gaze anymore. "Do you still like me?" she asked in a very small voice.

He tipped her face back up to him, touched that his opinion should matter. But it worried him that *la petite* could believe herself sullied by her father's crimes. "You're not responsible for your father, Pascal." Even as he defended her, Harlan knew his words were intended just as much for himself as for the girl he held in his arms.

"But, I live off his money. It buys my clothes, my food, and . . . oh, Harlan! If you only knew half of what he's done. I've been so frightened that if you ever found out you wouldn't like me anymore. I'm his daughter. His flesh and blood."

Harlan crushed her to him. "Hush now. You can't help that." *No, she can't Harlan.* "You're all of sixteen. And don't remind me that you'll be seventeen next month, you're still in no position to do anything but accept his money." *That's right, Harlan. She's not her father. You can't blame her for De Dreux.*

Harlan lowered his mouth to hers and kissed her. "Promise me, you'll never think bad of yourself because of your father, *petite*," he said, vowing to do the same.

She laughed shakily. "That's what . . . my friends say." She filled her lungs as if the heavy moist air of the morning were an elixir to heal her fears. "But sometimes"—she sighed, shaking her head—"it's so hard."

He saw it then, the burden she carried as De Dreux's child. It made him angry—angry at De Dreux for hurting yet another person Harlan cared for, angry at himself for ever thinking of using Pascal as a weapon against her father. He squelched that thought. Right now, he couldn't think of the more complicated implications of what he'd learned. He just wanted to hold her and believe that for him and *la petite* there might be more than painful memories and revenge. But one thing was sure, Rey had been right all along. It was wrong to use her.

"*Allons, chou.* We should be getting back," he said, thinking that he had a lot to unravel in his mind. And he needed to be away from Pascal's soulful eyes to concentrate.

"Will I see you tomorrow?"

The blinding happiness in her eyes made Harlan's smile. He tapped his finger against the tip of her nose. "Jus' try to keep me away."

When they reached the drive, Pascal watched Harlan walk to where a servant waited with his horse. As he rode away, she picked up her skirts and ran down the drive, waving good-bye. She watched until he disappeared on the horizon, then glanced down at the daisy she still held. She'd meant to give him the flower. It was miserably wilted now. She decided then to pick him an entire bouquet of daisies!

Pascal drifted down the road, plucking the petals from the flower, deep in thought as she relived their kisses and Harlan's reassurances. She took off her scarf, the promise of the day's heat already becoming burdensome. She'd told Harlan about her father and not once had he looked at her with the revulsion she'd feared. Of course, she hadn't given any details about her father's heinous crimes, but she sensed so much compassion in Harlan. She believed him when he said he wouldn't blame her.

Out of the corner of her eyes, she caught sight of a dark blur. Pascal looked up and saw Lena Larouse waiting for her at the end of the drive. A thread of apprehension twined through Pascal as the voodoo priestess waved. Pascal raised her hand to answer the greeting. But when Lena beckoned her over, her good spirits faltered completely. She dropped the daisy and walked down the crushed shell path to meet the woman, her scarf practically dragging on the grass behind her.

"I saw your man, Pas-cal De Dreux," Lena said when Pascal reached her side, "and I'm glad dat potion worked for ya. I got more where dat come from."

"I didn't have to use it after all." Pascal smiled. "Harlan liked me without the potion."

Lena's gold eyes narrowed shrewdly. "Ya didn't give'm da potion? Ya sure, Pas-cal De Dreux. Ya sure dat boy love ya true?"

Instantly, Pascal had misgivings. Harlan had never spoken of love. But then she remembered his words and his gentle touch.

"Well, it doesn't matter," she said more to herself, though she'd spoken out loud. "He cares about me, that's all that's important. He comes over almost every day."

"But my potion can make him love ya. Make him love ya somet'ing fierce."

Pascal shook her head. "I love him, Lena. It's enough."

"Enough is it?" A sly look crossed her eyes as if she could guess the darkest longings in Pascal's soul. With a cackle, Lena said, "You come by and let Lena know when it's *not* enough, Pas-cal De Dreux."

Mercy stared at the black ink squiggles marching across the parchment, her pen perched useless in her hand. She had to write Kate back and let her know all was set for tonight. Benoit would be in town—most likely for the night. On Gessler's recommendation, Benoit was to meet Teresa, a woman Kate guaranteed would know how to control her husband's prurient interests. Jean Claude had the men on alert. Still, it was difficult to concentrate on Santana's business. Mercy's thoughts kept returning to Rey.

A confusing mixture of dread and giddy happiness twisted inside her, doubling her unease about tonight's impromptu raid in the swamps. Last night had soothed any doubts she'd had about Rey's true feelings for her. He loved her, had even asked her to marry him. And she knew what he risked by that proposal. For the short hours they'd spoken about his son and he'd held her, making sweet love to her, she'd been able to forget—forget that she lived a lie and the woman Rey loved didn't exist.

She cradled one hand against her stomach, trying to soothe the ache caused by her nerves. But as her hand pressed against the stays of her gown, her stomach took another flip-flop. She could very well be carrying Rey's child. Like his love, a baby would be another part of Rey she'd taken like a thief.

Anything good in your life you've had to steal, Mercy—but you can't keep stolen love.

She closed her eyes. She reached up and touched the St. Christopher medal hanging from its chain around her neck. As skillfully as Santana had taken the medal during their first encounter, Rey must have retrieved it when he'd kissed Santana after his abduction. How ironic that he should choose to gift the medal to Mercy last night. He'd meant it as a token to keep her safe. But Rey was a lawman, a man of honor who would certainly condemn her actions as Santana. If he ever discovered her identity, would he be the first to turn her in?

Mercy shuddered, picturing, not Gessler, but Rey's beloved face as he held his gun trained on her and announced she was under arrest.

You can't keep stolen love.

A sharp knock rapped behind her. The sound of the door swinging open followed. Mercy turned from her writing desk, tossing a sheaf of blank paper over the message she'd been writing Kate. When Pascal walked in, Mercy let out a sigh of relief, but her ease was short-lived. Pascal's smile stiffened. She was staring at Mercy's desk. Kate's note lay at Mercy's elbow, carefully folded and waiting for a response. Of course, Pascal would recognize the distinctive stationery.

"Another run," came the flat, knowing voice.

Mercy cursed herself a thousand times for the hurt look on Pascal's face. "I have to go, Pascal. Please, understand."

The girl nodded, but her dark searching gaze remained steady on Mercy. "Another shipment of girls?"

"Yes."

Pascal's slim shoulders trembled. "Oh, Mercedes. How can I let you do this alone?" Her voice was a whisper, her eyes, large. "Without me to protect you?"

Mercy stood and walked to Pascal, taking her into her arms. She breathed in the fresh clean scent of the outdoors that would always remind her of her stepdaughter. "I'm not giving you a choice, Pascal."

"But the swamp is so risky. The last time, Gessler almost caught—"

Mercy pressed a finger across Pascal's lips. "Not one word about failure. I have Jean Claude and the men to help me. Kate has all the information. I'm ready for Gessler this time. I won't be careless."

"Don't go, Mercedes," she pleaded. "Please, not tonight. I just know something's going to go—"

"Stop it!" Mercy shook Pascal, then hugged her quickly, shocked by her harshness. "I'm sorry, Pascal. I must be a little spooked myself about tonight. If it weren't for the girls, I'd like nothing more than to stay here with you." She sighed, still holding her stepdaughter. "Perhaps it is time for Santana to retire," she said almost wistfully.

Pascal bounded back from her arms and looked up at Mercy. "You mean it? You'll stop?"

Mercy thought of her plans against Benoit. Soon, very soon, Sotheby would take the last of Benoit's funds. With his demise, there would be no more shipments of bedraggled women, drugged and bound—no money to search out and threaten Laura and Beth in far-off London. Then perhaps, just perhaps, Mercy could put her past behind her and start a new life. "Yes, Pascal, I'll stop. But not tonight."

Pascal gave her a quick hug, obviously happy to win her concession. "I truly will worry tonight. You must promise to let me know the second you arrive safely."

"Come to town with me, then. We'll stay at the *pied-à-terre*. You could visit with Ling Shi . . ."

Pascal shook her head. "Harlan might be over early tomorrow. I don't want to miss his visit."

Mercy quelled her unease over the Pinkerton agent. By now the young man had certainly discovered Pascal had no information about her father, and even less influence over Benoit. Mr. Everard's continued visits must be sincere. "All right, Pascal."

Pascal squeezed Mercy's hand. "Take care, *maman*."

Bathed in moonlight, Pascal sat staring at the cypress and black willow branches cresting the grassy slope of the levee. She'd passed a lazy afternoon by herself, dreaming of Harlan's dear blue eyes and crooked smile. What she and Harlan shared made it seem possible that she could be good—nothing like her father. Not only was she capable of giving love, but Harlan seemed to care for her deeply. Surely, if she were bad, that wouldn't be possible?

Perhaps Mercedes was right, Pascal thought. She was only a victim of Benoit De Dreux.

Her father, the white slaver.

White slaver. An evil, evil man.

Doubts crowded in. Mrs. Beasley's ever-sophisticated voice boomed in her head, telling her she would never amount to good. And with her doubts crept in fear for

Mercedes. She would be with her men now, waiting in the swamp. Pascal glanced up the road. Perhaps she should have gone with Mercedes and waited for her at the *pied-à-terre*. But she'd wanted so much to be here if Harlan should visit in the morning.

She thought of the flowers she'd planned to present him on the morrow. It was dark now. She'd be expected in her room soon; she'd just finished dinner in the kitchen. But then she thought of how romantic it would be if Harlan should find a bouquet of flowers waiting for him on his doorstep first thing in the morning. He would guess immediately who'd left them. In no time at all, he would come to L'Isle des Rêves to thank Pascal.

Pascal jumped to her feet, a smile on her face for her daring. Gathering her skirts, she ran up the hillside back toward L'Isle des Rêves, and stopped to pick an enormous bouquet of daisies in the moonlight.

Twenty minutes later, Pascal rode up Bizy's drive from the River Road. She almost laughed as she thought of how ingeniously she'd snuck Phoebus past the groom at L'Isle des Rêves, who was even now out in the fields searching for the prized stallion Pascal had let loose. She'd excused Thelma for the night, telling the maid she wouldn't need her help to undress later. Her father had gone into town—not that *he'd* ever notice Pascal missing. If she hurried, Pascal would only get a dark look from poor Frank for letting her father's favorite mount out of the paddock.

Turning down the drive, she saw Bizy up ahead and frowned. By the light of the moon, the plantation looked terribly run-down, but she couldn't be sure. Must be shadows, she thought, staring at the twin staircases leading to the main entrance on the second floor. Renovations should have been finished by now. But as she drew closer, she saw that indeed, the plantation house looked little better than the run-down house she'd passed on occasion. She handed the reins to a boy in the stables and headed toward Bizy, the bouquet of daisies filling the cradle of her arm. Perhaps she could help Mr. Parks and Harlan get things into better condition. She could certainly lend some advice on servants or craftsmen in the area.

She dashed across the lawn, hoping no one would catch her leaving the flowers on the front step. But as she climbed the stairs leading to the main gallery and front entrance, she heard the door opening. Immediately, she spun on her heel and jumped down the first step to the ground.

She hid behind a pillar and clapped her hand over her mouth, muffling a childish giggle, giddy with her own boldness. She could hear Harlan addressing a man who answered with a deep brogue. Oh, why did she always act on her impulses? Arriving at a man's doorstep, unchaperoned and uninvited, *was* a tad forward, even for her. She looked down at her daisies. But it would be so romantic to leave the flowers. And she had to put them near the front door for her gesture to work. She decided then to wait and see if the two men returned inside. It was just after the dinner hour. Perhaps they were merely taking in the evening breeze on the gallery facing the river; the afternoon had been one of those unbearably muggy days.

She heard Harlan and the other man walking down to the opposite end of the gallery, away from her. Biting her lip, Pascal followed the sound of their voices. It was best to keep track of the two, lest they catch her unawares. When she was directly beneath them, she settled down to wait. For now, she would listen to her beloved's deep voice with its soft Cajun accent, dreaming of his delighted expression when he saw the flowers.

Harlan stubbed the toe of his boot against the gallery rail, still uneasy over his outing with Pascal that morning. He held his face up to the breeze coming off the river. The dinner he'd just finished sat none too well in his stomach. "I'll be glad to get this Santana business out of the way, Mac, *mais* sure. I've said from the first we should concentrate on De Dreux." The sooner her father was behind bars, the quicker Harlan could be truthful with Pascal.

"Ye can stop yer keening to me, lad. T'was not my decision."

"The plan was to bring Sotheby and De Dreux down with the lottery scheme—that's what Robert Pinkerton hired me to do, not to go running around the swamps hunting down Santana Rose," Harlan said, taking out his frustration over Pascal on Mac. He'd spent the afternoon mulling over the coil he'd found himself in. He had to put her father behind bars, and yet, he'd grown very fond of Pascal.

Mac shook his head for Harlan's impatience. "Now dinna go redheaded on me, lad. After tonight, ye'll get yer wish. T'ain't you out there mucking around the swamp, anyhow, but Rey. He said we needed to make sure that bandit lady didna upset our mission again. You and I know she's sure to slip through Gessler's not-so-nimble fingers. The plan I overheard Kate and the Frenchy discuss for tonight—"

A gasp sounded from below. Both men raced to the stairs in time to watch Pascal De Dreux running toward the stables. With his heart in his throat, Harlan glanced down to where she'd been standing. In the moonlight, he saw what looked like a bouquet of daisies crushed in the dirt.

She was bringing me flowers.

Beside him, Mac muffled a curse and started down the stairs. Harlan seized the railing and braced his arm in front of the Scotsman.

"I'll take care of this, Mac."

"The hell ye will."

"She'll keep quiet for me. I know she will." When Mac moved to step around Harlan, he added, *"Mon Dieu,* Mac. What she heard . . . it sounds so bad. The explanation— the truth—it should come from me."

"The lass could be going to warn her father! If De Dreux gets wind of this, Rey's in trouble."

"Tonnerre! She's not running away to warn De Dreux! She loves me, Mac. *La pauvre* told me so this afternoon." He pointed down to the daisies. "She was bringing me flowers, man. She overheard me talking about her father and now she's thinks I used her to get information on him."

Mac looked down at the crushed daisies. A look of sympathy softened the Scotsman's expression. With a sigh, he rested a hand on Harlan's shoulder. "And were ye not using the lass fer just that?"

He stared over the railing to the stables where Pascal was mounting her horse. *"Oui,"* he whispered. Just that afternoon Pascal had questioned his interest in her father. Now she would know her suspicions were right. A heavy despair settled in Harlan's heart. "Rey warned me not to use her. He said someday I'd have to face the pain of betraying her."

"Did he now?"

Harlan nodded. "But God's truth, Mac. I never knew it could hurt this much."

Chapter 17

Pascal pressed her heels into Phoebus's side. She held both hands curled around the leather reins, fingers knotted in the mane, nails biting into the skin of her palms. Her leg tightened against the pommel of the sidesaddle. Faster. *Faster!* She risked a glance over her shoulder, saw nothing but a dark green blur of sugarcane and oaks in the moonlight. But she knew he was there, urging his mount to catch her. She could hear him shout her name. *Harlan, my beloved Harlan—who never loved me at all.*

Pascal blinked back her tears, shutting out the horrifying truth as she raced past the avenue of moldering slave cabins. She couldn't think about that now, about Harlan and the reasons he might have for courting her—the daughter of the man he was investigating. She had to get to Mercedes. Had to warn her.

She leaned forward, as close to her mount as the sidesaddle permitted, whispering to Phoebus in hushed desperate pleas. The moon was almost full. She could still see well enough. But her safety was the least of her considerations. *Fly, dear Phoebus. Fly.* Mercedes needs me.

Off the road! Pascal urged the horse down cane fields. The air smelled of moist earth kicked up by Phoebus—or was it the scent of her fear? The knee-high cane slashed against her boots, ripped her skirt. Her horse stumbled; Pascal checked their speed. She couldn't afford a lame mount.

"Pascaaal!"

Dear Lord, so close! How had he gained on her so quickly? Her glance darted ahead, sighted a grove of ancient oaks, temptingly near. She might lose Harlan in the trees. Go Phoebus. *Go!*

The moon had turned the field into a swamp of shadows —deadly. One misstep . . . Pascal blinked back tears, focusing on the patterns of light and dark, guiding Phoebus. Harlan's shouts grew stronger, nearer. The trees, she had to reach the trees! *Two hundred yards.* Phoebus hurtled the last cane row. She could hear Harlan's mount struggling through the cane behind her. Careful of the ditch! *One hundred yards.* She skirted a clump of hackberry, jumped a plank. *Fifty yards.* Horse's hooves pounded at her side. Hurry!

An arm whipped across her stomach. The breath left her lungs in a great *whoosh*. Harlan yanked her across his saddle, holding her waist against him as he slowed his mount.

"Dammit, *petite*. Sit still or we'll both break our skulls."

Pascal gulped air, trying to dislodge the arm cutting off her breath. Terror gave her strength. They'd overheard Kate; they knew about the plan. She had to warn Mercedes!

"Zut alors!" Harlan cursed as he managed to dismount, pulling Pascal down with him. The minute they hit the ground, Pascal kicked back, leveling a blow to his shin with the heel of her boot. Harlan stumbled. She connected a second time, then again. Harlan twisted to the side. Pascal reached over her shoulder. The tips of her fingers grazed his neck; she dug in her nails.

"Ahhh! *Mon Dieu*." Harlan shoved her hand away as she clawed his skin. The second he released her, Pascal bolted, charging for the patch of bearded oaks.

Harlan tackled her to the ground, catapulting them into a slide. Pascal tasted dirt. Stones scraped her palms. She scratched at the ground, trying to slip out from under

Harlan. *Mercedes!* He grabbed her hips and flipped her on her back. Pascal fisted both hands, threw punch after punch. Catching her wrists, Harlan straddled her and pinned her hands over her head.

"Stop fighting me. I can explain about your father."

"I hate you, Harlan Everard!" *That's it, Pascal. Concentrate on his betrayal. Don't let him know about Mercedes.* "You used me!" But the tears that came were real. Her pain burned in her chest like an ember. "You're investigating my father! You used me to try and get information about him."

"Let me explain."

"All those questions! Do you know much about the workings of L'Isle des Rêves? Did the shortage of labor hurt you?" The ache strained to be voiced, past the tears and the choking thickness in her throat. *I thought you cared about me. You made me believe I was worth loving.* "I spent hours trying to answer those questions. Reading book after boring book, talking to the plantation manager. But that's not what you wanted at all—"

His lips smothered her words. Pascal tossed her head from side to side, avoiding his mouth. She screamed for him to stop. His kiss seemed the greatest treachery. But Harlan wasn't listening. He'd cuffed both of her wrists in one hand. He used his free hand to steady her face for his kisses. With a muffled cry, Pascal bit down, hard.

Harlan pulled back with a curse. Still holding her wrists, he touched his bottom lip with his fingers. "You drew blood."

"I wish I had something more deadly than my teeth!" she screamed. "I wish I had a gun!"

His eyes grew wide; his mouth fell slack—as if her vehemence startled him.

"What did you think, damn you?" she shouted. "That one kiss and silly little Pascal would melt?"

"I thought you loved me," he answered with a gentleness that cut deep.

Tears filled her eyes. "You've torn my heart in pieces, Harlan. There isn't enough of it left to love you."

She turned her head away when the moisture slipped down her face, unwilling to let him see. When he touched her cheek, the sobs burst into harsh, ugly sounds, shaming her. How dreadful and pathetic that she would still want him to hold her and comfort her. How perfectly horrible that despite his betrayal, she still needed his love.

"I've had my share of heartbreak, *petite*," he said in a low voice. "And I know that no matter how much we wish it, you can't break a heart so much that you don't care. Look at me, Pascal. Tell me you don't care."

His free hand guided her face back to his. Pascal kept her eyes shut, refusing to see his beautiful face in the moonlight, the eyes so blue it almost hurt to look at them. But when his lips touched hers, she let him kiss her. *Think of Mercedes,* she told herself. She pressed her mouth to his, as if forgiving him. Her sobs calmed to soft whimpers. For Mercedes, she must do this. Harlan moaned at the back of his throat when she soothed the skin she'd bitten with her mouth. Slowly, he loosened the manacle hold on her wrists, then released her, lifting her into his arms.

Harlan rocked her, his voice almost a croon as he apologized. Pascal allowed him to think he comforted her. Her body, she gave to Harlan—but her thoughts remained focused on Mercedes. And escape.

Harlan cradled Pascal to him, sending a silent thanks that she would at last respond to him with something other than anger. He would make it up to her—the hurt, the betrayal, everything. The words came out in an incoherent blur of Cajun French. He hadn't known, he whispered. Rey had tried to warn him, but Harlan had never guessed at the pain he'd seen in her lovely eyes or the ache he'd heard in her voice.

Her kisses became almost desperate as her arms reached behind him, stoking a fever in Harlan. This time, he held nothing back. There was no voice in his head warning him not to fall in love with his enemy's daughter. He murmured sweet words of praise to Pascal, encouraging her. He found himself the receiver of kisses as she urged him to the ground. He'd guessed right, he told himself, lacing his fingers through her hair, enjoying its silky texture. She loved him enough to help him fight her father. When she propped herself over him, one hand caressing the skin at his temple, he almost sighed with relief. Her touch became a long sexy kiss that robbed his breath and then—

Pain. Blinding pain.

Harlan reached for his temple. There was something warm and sticky on his fingers. Through half-closed eyes he saw Pascal rise and drop the rock she'd used to hit him. The moon behind her left her in darkness. He couldn't see her face. She stepped back, then spun and darted to the horses. When he glanced at his fingers, they were spotted with blood. He tried to form the words to tell her to stop. He rose slowly, shaking his head, trying to clear it. *Mon Dieu,* he still couldn't believe it. One minute she was kissing him, the next, she'd struck him. And now she was running away.

Harlan took two halting steps toward her. He had to catch up with her before she mounted her horse. That's when he saw it, not another shadow but a long black ribbon undulating toward him. It was a death he'd learned to recognize as a boy growing up in the bayous. He shouted, adrenaline giving him voice at last, then kicked out. Too late. He saw the flash of its white mouth. Fangs bit through the cotton fabric of his trousers just above his boot.

His next kick flung the snake deep into the sugarcane behind him. He was still woozy, but he knew soon enough he'd be senseless from something more deadly than the blow Pascal had delivered.

His leg folded beneath him. As he dropped to the ground, Pascal appeared beside him. She rolled up his pant leg, her breath coming in sharp panting breaths as if she were scared for him. Had she seen the snake? Would she help him now? Or had she lost her breath running. Running.

Harlan shook his head, losing his train of thought. The pain made it hard to concentrate. He looked up at Pascal. "A water moccasin, *petite*. Not good news."

She didn't answer. More tears filled her dark eyes, turning them liquid and hauntingly lovely in the soft light.

"I think . . ." he said, having trouble forming the words, "I think I'm going to die."

Pascal shook her head. She stood, backing away.

Harlan blinked, trying to keep her in focus. His leg hurt more than his head now. If he passed out, he had a horrible suspicion she would leave him, leave him there to the black cottony silence. He had to make her understand. Tell her what to do, how to help him. He licked his lips. "Pascal," he barely formed the word, "don't . . . leave . . . me here. . . ."

She kept backing away, shaking her head. *Que diable!* Didn't she understand? He was going to die if she didn't help him. He had to make her understand.

"I know he's your father," he said, marshaling his energy for one last plea. "But don't choose him over me. Help me, *petite*. Don't let me die. He's bad, real bad; you told me so yourself. You don't know. I had . . . I had . . . good reason for what I did. Please. Don't let me die. . . ."

"You don't know what you're asking of me!"

Why was she shouting at him? And crying, she was crying. But she wasn't walking away anymore.

"Oh, Harlan, you have no idea what you're asking me to do!"

There was such misery in her voice, Harlan couldn't understand it. Just this afternoon, she'd said how much she hated her father. And now, all this anguish . . . it made him feel bad, almost as bad as the poison in his veins. *You were wrong, you sonofabitch, and it's going to cost you your life.* She's choosing her father. But he could have sworn, he would have bet his life . . . Harlan managed a weak laugh. *You jus' did, fool! Bet your life and lost!*

But then she was kneeling beside him, holding him up. He reached out to touch her, but his arm was heavy, too heavy to lift.

"Oh, Harlan," she sobbed in his ear, "You don't know what you're asking me to choose. Don't make me choose. Please God! Don't make me choose!"

Rey waited out on the shores of Barataria Bay with Gessler's men. The moon poured over the long expanse of sand, bleaching it white as the ship reached the cove. It seemed so arrogant, smuggling goods by the light of the gibbous moon—but then De Dreux had nothing to fear from the law, not with Gessler supervising the patrols. In no time at all, the men began to unload their goods for transfer to the smaller boats that would be poled up the bayou to Little Lake and beyond.

When Rey saw what cargo the ships carried, the old sickness crept into his heart. He watched as a group of twelve women were herded like animals toward the dugouts. "De Dreux deals in white slavery?"

At the constable's nod, every fiber of decency inside Rey drove him to forget his plans for Santana and pull his Colt on Gessler and his men. For a moment, he allowed himself to fantasize about rescuing the girls, but he was only one man. Even if he told Gessler he was a government agent, he doubted the constable would aid him in releasing the women. Gessler was in too deep with De Dreux. More likely than not, neither Rey nor the girls would leave the swamp alive.

Rey forced himself to watch the bedraggled women, their clothes hanging in tatters, their hands tied with ropes, chaining them together as they struggled aboard the boats. He wondered if he would ever become numb to this aspect of his job—witnessing crimes, at times participating in them in order to catch the ring leaders. When one girl, a child really, fell to her knees, crying pathetically as two men hauled her to her feet and dragged her forward, he could bear it no longer and looked away. His arm pressed against the barrel of his gun in his shoulder holster.

Beside him, Gessler nudged Rey in the ribs. "Interested?"

Rey shook his head, forcing his smile. "Not to my tastes."

Gessler shrugged, then instructed his men to forge ahead.

Following Rey's plan, Gessler's men crept into position, some by foot, others by boat, covering the different channels from which Santana might launch her attack. All were instructed to use the utmost discretion; no one was to alert the waiting bandits. Rey himself had reconnoitered the area earlier. And though he'd found no sign of Santana and her gang, he was certain they would attack before the boats reached the Manila village, just as Mac had overheard at Kate's. Santana believed Gessler's men were waiting at the Little Temple. She would want to intercept the shipment of women well before they reached that site. Rey would have done the same in her place.

Rey and Gessler boarded the last boat, a dugout made of cypress, and the vessel eased into the duckweed-clogged waters of the bayou. Rey scanned both shores for signs of ambush. Each foot they traveled, the branches stretched closer, moss and vines hung nearer, forcing him and the others to duck beyond their reach. Within minutes of leaving the cove, it seemed as if the caravan of dugouts was flowing into the mouth of an enormous beast. The rhythm of crickets, frogs, and cicadas throbbed like a heartbeat. Tendrils of gray moss dripped like tangled hair. Arthritic branches grasped across the water, reaching. Molasses-colored water oozed past tumorlike cypress knees. The

swamp was alive, a living, breathing thing to be respected
—and feared.

Barataria. The notorious pirate, Jean Laffite, claimed
the swamp's name stood for deception. Surrounded by its
dark and sinister beauty, Rey tended to agree. Their dugout wended around gum trees sprouting offshore. Felled
logs floated like alligators—and Rey knew there were
plenty of the predators here, submerged and waiting. He
wondered how they would ever find Santana within the
thick jungle foliage without first becoming alligator bait.

"I hope your man was right about his information,"
Gessler whispered after twenty minutes of uneventful
travel. "I'll be mighty disappointed to lose this cargo. I was
sure to get her at the Little Temple."

"Let's just wait and see, shall we?"

"Funny how she always gets away, like she knew we
were coming," Gessler continued, confirming Rey's opinion about the man's dull wits. The constable hadn't a clue
Santana had spies. "And the girls she takes . . . I always
keep an ear open to new blood being offered in the market, but I never hear nothing. Must take them out of state.
There's plenty of demand out west."

Rey surveyed the moon-brightened surface. "So I've
heard—"

Men shouted ahead. Their cries were followed by the
high-pitched wails of women screaming. *Santana.* Rey signaled for the boat to be poled to shore. Gunfire erupted,
hammering through the swamp. He leapt onto a felled
cypress, wove from one trunk to the next before hitting the
ground running. He shouted back to Gessler to circle
around the side opposite.

Rey hurtled palmettos, swept past moss curtains. His
breath thundered in his chest. The muscles of his calves
ached as he twisted right, left, then right again, cutting
through the maze of oaks, cypress, and flaming red maple.
He waded ankle-deep in swamp water, praying he

wouldn't stumble across an alligator, then sprinted when he reached solid ground.

Someone broke through underbrush to his left. Rey dove behind the trunk of a willow, keeping his body flush to the barked surface. A small band of masked men, led by a familiar caped figure, crashed through the knee-high swamp grass. Two girls stumbled in their midst, their hands tied at their wrists. The group passed inches from Rey. Crouching low, he followed in their wake, the considerable noise of boots pounding leaves and fallen branches masking his own movements.

The group of twelve ran as if they knew every curve, every path, of the swamp-forest. Rey tracked them, at times running parallel with the troupe of criminals and the women they prodded forward. Only a thin screen of vegetation stood between him and Santana. When they reached a narrow channel lined with pirogues, Rey waited behind a clump of hackberry, listening to Santana instructing her men in French.

She stood mere feet from his hiding place—and he could do nothing. In his mind, he cursed Gessler. Where the hell were the men Rey had stationed for this very spot? Beyond frustration, he took the Colt from its holster, checked the rounds, and pulled back the hammer as he listened to Santana's excited whispers. She ordered her men to disperse while she stayed with the last boat waiting for stragglers. Gessler's men had them outnumbered, she said; it was too risky to take more women than the two they'd rescued. *Rescued?* Odd term for looting, Rey thought cynically. One henchman argued vehemently to stay behind with Santana, a suggestion she rejected. No, the arguer was to lead her men to a safe spot, she commanded. She and the last of their number would join them shortly.

Rey pulled back a clump of leaves with the back of one hand and watched the men scatter as Santana waited on the moonlit shore. The sound of Gessler's pursuit was a dim noise in the distance. Rey could imagine the constable's men struggling through the tangle of vines and palmettos, fearful of alligators and other predators that claimed the swamp as their home. He wouldn't lay odds on them reaching Rey in time. With Gessler at the lead, they were probably running around in circles. It would be up to Rey to capture Santana Rose.

Two pirogues pushed off, disappearing into the bayou. When the third boat poled away from shore, taking the two weeping girls and leaving only Santana, the highway woman's head jerked up, as if hearing something. Her gaze darted back to the last pirogue; she took a step toward it. *No dammit,* Rey thought, *she'd not escape him this time.*

Rey broke through the brush into the clearing. Santana's black cape swung outward, whipping around her body as she faced him. Her mouth opened below her feathered mask, her only sign of surprise. In her hand, she held her gun aimed directly at Rey. He tightened his grip on his revolver.

"Departez rapidement," she ordered the man inching back toward shore in the pirogue with the women. Her eyes on Rey, she didn't even check to see if her command was obeyed. But her man didn't hesitate. The last pirogue disappeared down the bend of the channel as Santana presented a wide smile.

Her tactics stunned Rey. They were alone now, evenly matched. It was a guess whose men would arrive first—the stragglers she'd been waiting for or Gessler's. Rey frowned. Did the woman care more for the possibility of profit than she did her own life?

"So, *monsieur,*" she said in her familiar husky voice, "we are at a standoff, *non*? Like duelists." She laughed quietly.

"You have a fondness for games, Santana—a fondness I don't share. But I think you've overplayed your hand this time. You're surrounded. If you want to leave this swamp alive, toss your gun to the ground in front of me."

"Surrounded?" Her teeth sparkled with moonlight. "I see only you, *monsieur.*"

"Give up, Santana. It's just a matter of time before the constable and his men arrive. They're heading this way looking for you now. You'll only make things worse if you fight."

She clucked her tongue, disappointed by his logic. "*Monsieur,* it is just as likely to be my men who arrive first. Why not allow each other retreat? Twice I have spared your life. I am willing to do so a third time if you walk away now."

"A generous offer, I'm sure—but I'll take my chances that our good constable gets here first."

As if on cue, Gessler's tenor voice rang clearly to their right, calling out Rey's name. "Over here," Rey shouted. "At the channel."

Santana edged back.

"Don't," Rey warned. "This time, I won't hesitate to shoot."

Mercy stopped her retreat, reigning in the terror that urged her to bolt. Santana's mask heated her skin. Its customary weight chafed, but she controlled the desire to rip it off. It was too late to tell Rey the truth, too late to stand before him, unmasked, as the woman he loved and explain the choices she'd been forced to make in her life. The nightmare vision she'd dismissed earlier that evening was upon her. Rey held her at gunpoint. All that remained were the three simple words announcing her arrest.

Gessler's shouts grew high-pitched, excited—the hound smelling the kill. She could just make out his command to head for the water.

"You are too much of a gentleman, *un gentilhomme.*" She heard the panic in her voice. Her accent sounded forced even to her ears. She licked her dry lips and glanced to her side. If she could just reach the grove of trees . . . but Rey stood between her and that avenue of escape. "You would not harm a lady, *monsieur.*"

"A lady?" There was a mocking edge to his voice. "I see only a common criminal."

The water lapped behind her. She took a step back, thinking to take her chances with the alligators. The shouts of men grew louder, nearer.

"Our kiss the last time we met told a different tale, *monsieur*. We are like kindred spirits. You will not shoot."

"Your final warning, Santana. Don't take another step."

She wanted to shout—you told me you loved me! *But no, that was another woman.* And then, she thought of their last encounter, when she'd kidnapped him, and how he'd held his fire when he could have shot her. Perhaps somewhere deep inside him he recognized Santana and Mercy were one in the same.

"No, *monsieur*"—she lifted her chin, forcing herself to believe her words—"I trust you will not shoot me."

"Don't be a fool, Santana!"

There was an urgency to his voice that told her he didn't *want* to shoot. But then the crashing palmetto fronds and men's voices grew too close for further study. Mercy turned to flee.

From the corner of her eye, she saw the burst of light reflecting off the water. The Colt's blast followed like the roll of thunder after lightning. Almost as if she were a witness rather than the target, she saw herself fall to her knees, grab her shoulder—and then she saw nothing, consumed by blinding pain.

She tried to focus. The world became splotches of green and amber. She blinked and looked up. Rey stood over her, studying her.

"You shot me."

Rey frowned. Her voice sounded odd, not Santana's at all. Devoid of its accent, it rang almost familiar. He kicked aside the gun she'd dropped, and kneeled down. He was just shaken, imagining things. Though he'd given her only a flesh wound, in truth, he'd not wanted to shoot.

The chaos of Gessler's troop tramping down bayou foliage and sloshing through shallow channels filled the night. "Over here, Gessler!" Damn the man. Would he ever show up? Rey wished the fools would hurry and find him before Santana's men did. "It's over, Santana," he said softly.

With her free hand, she reached out and seized his hand. Her breath came in short gasps. He'd been shot in the shoulder before and knew the pain she must feel. But when she dropped back into his arms, as if seeking his embrace, the trusting gesture astonished him.

"Rey," she whispered. "Help me, Rey."

The blood seemed to evaporate from his veins. For one infinitesimal moment—a second no longer than it took to catch his breath—her voice, her touch. . . .

"Mercy?" The word came involuntarily.

"Don't let them find me, Rey."

He pushed her away until he could look at her face. "It can't be. It's not possible."

He ripped off her mask. The wig dropped to the ground.

At the sudden movement, Mercy clutched her shoulder harder. "Dear God, this hurts," she said through gritted teeth.

He couldn't talk. This couldn't be happening. He studied the mask in his hand—his gaze shifted to the blood seeping through the fingers clutching her wound. Santana lay in his arms. A woman he'd hunted down. A criminal who dressed in men's clothing, with black hair and a blacker heart! It couldn't be Mercy he held. Shot, by his own hand.

"Please, Rey. Help me. Help me get away."

"No." He shook his head. "NO! It . . . can't . . . be."

Her eyes fluttered open, focused on his. "You said . . . you said . . . you loved me."

The darkness of the swamp seemed to close in on Rey. Gessler and his men were coming. Rey could hear them only yards away running to meet him. Coming for her. For Santana. For Mercy.

Santana is a criminal! a voice inside him shouted. But he couldn't allow Mercy to become Gessler's prisoner. *It's your job to turn her in.* He imagined Mercy, tied in ropes, like the women he'd seen on the shore.

You said you loved me.

The echo of those words left him no option.

He scooped her up in his arms, grabbing the mask and wig. He pumped his legs, almost falling as he ran. He hid her behind the hackberries where just minutes ago he'd watched her unnoticed. Gessler and his men broke through moss as Rey kicked her gun under a pile of vines.

"Where'd they go?" Almost comically, Gessler turned his head left and right, searching the clearing.

"They've escaped," Rey said. "I tried to shoot her down, but I missed. If you hurry, you'll catch them." Rey pointed down the bayou, in the direction opposite that taken by Santana's men. "Just follow the channel."

Gessler face split into a grin. "Good work, Parks." He turned to the men behind him and waved them ahead. "Com'on, men. We've got the varmints now!"

Pascal spit the blood on the ground, careful not to swallow the poison she'd sucked from Harlan's leg. The skin around the two puncture marks was terribly swollen and a dark deep blue, almost black. She glanced up at Harlan's face. His eyes were closed; his head jerked left and right, as if he were fighting off the pain. She could see that despite her efforts, the poison was in him, killing him slowly.

No, don't even think that. Pascal returned to the wound she'd made with Harlan's pocket knife, crisscrossing the two puncture marks, and tried to suck out more venom just as he'd instructed her to do. When she finished, she left the wound to bleed freely. She checked the strip of cloth she'd torn from her petticoat and wrapped around his leg just above the snakebite. They weren't far from the plantation, but she couldn't leave him here alone. She tried to pull Harlan up to a sitting position. He remained a dead weight.

"Harlan?" She slapped her hands against his cheeks. "Harlan talk to me, please! Harlan!"

His eyes fluttered open and Pascal's heart gave a leap of hope. *"Petite,"* he whispered. *"Tu n'es pas parti?"*

"No, Harlan," she answered, smoothing back the curls moist with his sweat. "I couldn't leave you."

"Aide-moi, petite," he whispered so weakly she barely made out the words.

"I'm trying to help you!" Pascal answered. He'd been switching from French, English, and a strange Cajun dialect she had trouble understanding. Pascal looked over to his horse. "Can you stand? Harlan"—seeing he'd closed his eyes again, she shook him—"Harlan, please." She couldn't control her choking sobs. "I can't lift you by myself! You have to help me."

"Oui," he answered tiredly, leaning up against her as he stumbled to his feet.

They staggered to his horse. Harlan rested against Pascal, panting, then almost toppled her over. She tried to shake him from his stupor.

"Fight, Harlan. Help me fight. I can't save you alone."

"All right," she heard him say. "All right, *petite*. Jus' give me a leg up."

Using all her strength, she hoisted him face down over the saddle. When she saw he would slip off, she mounted up behind him, helping him into a sitting position. She looked over to Phoebus nuzzling the ground. Her horse would either return to the stable or she would send someone back for her. Pascal linked her arms around Harlan, trying to keep him steady. Her skirts were hiked up to her knees. One hand on the reins, she kicked the horse to a slow walk, whispering prayers under her breath.

Chapter 18

Pascal grabbed hold of Harlan as he slumped to the side, nearly unseating them both. She leaned over him, forcing him down against the horse's withers and anchored him there with her arms. Barely able to glance up to make out their direction without falling, she prayed the horse's steady pace would take them directly to Bizy. Yet, each step that brought her closer to that goal added to her worries about Mercedes. Was she at this moment battling in the swamps against Parks and Gessler's men? Could she already be clapped in irons in the New Orleans jail house, or worse—dead?

She closed her eyes, trying to blank out the horrible images. She couldn't think about that now. She nuzzled closer to Harlan, comforted by the familiar scent of hair tonic and tobacco. Right or wrong, she'd made her choice back at the cane field. No matter what she'd overheard, no matter what dangers Mercedes faced, Pascal could never have left Harlan alone to die.

The horse's withers sloped downward. Pascal gasped, clutching fistfuls of mane. Her eyes flew open as their mount skidded down a ditch. She tightened her hold on the mane and Harlan just as she caught sight of the plantation's overgrown walk leading to Bizy. Visions of the paint-chipped house gave her strength and she managed to stop Harlan's weight from dipping sideways as the horse charged up the ditch onto level ground.

By the time they reached Bizy, tears of relief coursed down her cheeks. She guided the horse to the house, shouting for help. Two oil lamps lit the entryway, but there wasn't a soul in sight. At the steps, she jumped off the horse, thinking to find aid. No one had yet to answer her cries. Harlan tipped toward her and she tried desperately to keep him seated. He groaned and doubled over.

"Mon Dieu," he mumbled. "Feel so sick. Think I'm gonna throw up."

While he clung weakly to the horse's neck, Pascal held him in the saddle. His skin felt cold and clammy beneath her palms. His breath was just a shallow puff on her arm as she held him. *Please, God. Don't let him die!*

A man with red hair and a beard streaked with gray appeared at the doorway. He squinted into the darkness beyond the reach of the lamplight. The second he saw Pascal, his eyebrows shot up and he bounded down the steps. "Here now, what's happened?" he asked in the same thick Scottish brogue she'd overheard earlier.

As the Scotsman pulled Harlan off the horse, Harlan's eyes flickered open. "That you, Mac?" he asked the man holding him. Harlan tried to stand, but the minute the Scotsman released him, he fell to the ground. "Weak. So weak." He moaned.

The man he'd called Mac immediately grabbed Harlan under his arms and hauled him up the stairs. Pascal grabbed Harlan's feet to keep them from dragging. When she caught Mac's gaze fixed on Harlan's leg where the cutoff trousers exposed the black-and-blue swelling, she said, "A snake, a water moccasin, I think."

"Jesus, Mary, and Joseph," he muttered under his breath as he glanced down at Harlan's pale face. His brow furrowed, but the expression he gave Pascal in the lamplight granted her hope. There was strength in the depth of those eyes. A strength she suspected both she and Harlan would need before the night was over.

"Can ye manage his feet, lass, while I carry him up the stairs to his room?"

Pascal almost wept from relief. Here at last was the aid she needed. "Yes. But please, hurry. He needs a doctor!"

As quickly as humanly possible, she and the Scotsman hauled the weakened Harlan up the flight of stairs. Though she stumbled more than once, Mac never faltered. When they reached a sparsely furnished room, Pascal pulled back the counterpane on the bed and they settled Harlan beneath the sheets. While Mac sent for the nearest doctor, Pascal filled the basin on the washstand with water. Finding a cloth, she sat down at Harlan's bedside and wrung out the soaked cotton, then swabbed his brow.

Within the hour, Harlan had vomited what appeared to be blood. His pulse was a weak flutter. He couldn't seem to catch his breath. Pascal pushed back her looming fears of death, occasionally glancing at the man who'd introduced himself as John MacAfee, Mr. Parks's valet. The Scotsman continued to pace before the fireplace as Pascal bathed Harlan's forehead with the cloth. The clock on the nightstand hailed the hour as half past ten. Pascal thought of Mercedes. Certainly by now she would be in the swamps. Pascal tried to convince herself that Mercedes would escape Parks's trap. Hadn't she always beaten the odds? But then Harlan's body tightened, jerked. His arm flung out, overturning the washbasin. All concern for Mercedes vanished as Pascal leaned over Harlan, holding him with Mac's help until the convulsions passed.

She looked up at Mac. Tears brimmed her eyes.

"He'll make it, lass," the Scotsman answered her silent plea. "Don't ye worry."

The door opened and a servant led inside a pasty-faced man with a mustache and goatee. A fraction shorter than the stocky MacAfee, the doctor spared no time for introductions but swept off his top hat and immediately shooed Pascal from her place at Harlan's side. Pascal picked up the spilled basin and examined the man's dark coat and trousers, garb more appropriate for an undertaker than a doctor. His clothes combined with the man's pale skin, shriveled by age, made him an unlikely choice for a savior.

As MacAfee and Pascal watched, the elderly gentleman tested Harlan's pulse, then shook his head as he studied the black-and-blue wound on Harlan's calf. He fit his finger beneath the strip of cloth still snugly wrapped around Harlan's leg.

"You bled him?" he asked Mac.

"I did," Pascal answered.

Disapproval radiated from the small dark eyes behind his spectacles. "Immediately after the snake bit him, girl?"

"Yes."

"Good." He nodded, loosening the tourniquet, then removing it entirely. The doctor stood and reached for his hat. "God willing, you got enough of the poison out to save him."

Pascal glanced at MacAfee then back at the doctor. "That's it? Nothing more?"

The doctor's small eyes marched across her in scorching distaste. "Every five minutes, make him drink as much brandy as he'll take. That and the bleeding is about all that can be done."

"But is it enough?" MacAfee asked, stepping beside her. "Will the lad survive?"

"That's in the hands of God, I'm afraid." The man's gruff tone left no room for further questions. He donned his hat and stepped to the door. "There's nothing more I can do for him."

Nothing? A shiver of apprehension pulsed up Pascal's spine as she watched MacAfee lead the doctor out. She turned back to the bed. As she watched, Harlan began to thrash against the linens. She ran to his side, hugged him. She whispered in his ear soft words that she hoped would soothe him. The fear that welled up inside her—for Harlan as well as Mercy—bubbled to the surface, overwhelming her. Pascal dropped her head to Harlan's chest, burying her face in his nightshirt.

"Don't die, Harlan," she cried when the convulsions stopped. "Don't you dare die on me!"

"He's a strong lad."

Pascal twisted up, turning toward the door. By the light of the oil lamp, she could see MacAfee. His worried expression belied his comforting words.

"He could die from that snakebite!"

"Aye, but I'm bettin' the lad will pull through."

"And you're just going to sit there and wait to see if he makes it or not?"

His bushy brows rose in surprise. He shook his head, his expression sympathetic. "The doctor said it's in the good Lord's hands now. There's naught else we can do but pray, lass."

Pascal glanced down at Harlan. His eyes were closed. The lids looked like two bruises on his sallow face. She couldn't imagine just sitting by, waiting, not doing anything but giving him brandy to drink. She thought of Doc Chiang in town—but no, he was too far away. She'd never make it back in time to help Harlan. She took her beloved's hand, holding it tight. There must be something she could do! Something she could give Harlan to make him better. She'd read so many medical books that time she'd hunted for the recipe for knock-out drops for Beasley and her Beasties. She searched her memory for a potion or a treatment to stop the venom that so clearly poisoned his body. But what? The doctor said there was nothing. *Nothing.*

Even as the sentence echoed inside her head, Lena's near-yellow eyes surfaced, glittering in Pascal's mind with the promise of hope.

Lena. The voodoo priestess was known as a powerful healer. Could she make a potion that could cure Harlan?

There's nothing more I can do for him, the doctor had said.

Pascal shot to her feet. Finding her pelisse on a chair near the bureau, she flung it over her shoulders and headed for the door—straight into MacAfee's chest.

"Where do ye think you're going, lassie?"

"I need to find help for Harlan," she said, stepping around him.

His arm shot out, barring her way. "The doctor's come and gone."

"Not him!" Her voice rose from frustration. "I know someone else." She tried to push his arm away. She might as well have tried to uproot an oak.

"I canna let ye go, lass."

"You must!" Pascal insisted. "I might find a cure. Something that could stop the poison."

The dark eyes shadowed by his brows watched her with pity. "Ye canna leave Bizy, lass, not until the master returns. I know what ye overheard tonight about yer father. Ye maun stay here, lass. It's what Mr. Parks would want."

Pascal's heart pounded. The breath strained in her chest. He thought she was trying to escape to warn her father.

"I'm verra sorry, lass. Truly."

Pascal grabbed MacAfee's arm, digging her fingers into the rough cloth of his coat. "You don't understand. It's too late to help . . . never mind that. I know a woman. She lives in the swamps. Many people seek her remedies. She can help!"

"Don't let her go," came the raspy whisper from the bed. "Conjo, woman, Mac. No . . . good, conjo woman."

Pascal released Mac and rushed back to Harlan's side. "Harlan!" She brushed her fingers through his hair, smiling with the joy of hearing his voice after so long a silence. "I'm going to help you, Harlan. You remember the love potion." She laughed, a weak bubble of relief and embarrassment. "Lena can make cures too. I'm sure she'll have something for snakebites."

"Mac . . ." Harlan's eyes drifted open, then fell shut. "Don't listen . . . *c'est dangereux.*"

Pascal stepped out of her chair. The backs of her knees sent it tumbling to the floor as she stared at Harlan in disbelief. They weren't going to let her go? She raced desperately to Mac. "Listen to me! I must help him. I love him!"

"No . . . Mac. Don't let her . . ."

Her fingers tightened on MacAfee's arm. "When the snake bit him, I could have escaped. There's no way he could have stopped me. But I didn't. I brought him back here. Don't you understand? I can't let him die. You must let me help him."

MacAfee stared at Harlan, then slowly shook his head. "I always knew the lad would be trouble." His eyes rested on Pascal, evaluating her. She tried to put all the love she felt for Harlan in her expression. For Harlan, she would do anything. For the man she loved, she'd run any risk.

"Please!"

"All right." His shoulders slumped, as if relinquishing the weight of decision. "By my soul, I'm trustin' ye, lass. If I'm wrong on this, it's more than the lad who will suffer. But, I'm not often wrong and to tell the truth, t'ain't nothing else my heart will allow."

Pascal heaved a sigh of relief, then wrapped her coat tightly around her. "You won't be sorry. I'll be back within the hour."

Rey held his arms lightly around Mercedes in the swaying carriage. She rested on his lap, where he'd placed her. Her cape remained draped around them both like a blanket, just as he'd positioned it. He could feel her shoulders trembling against his chest—shock, he thought. And that was all he could feel, the things outside himself. The motion of the carriage. Her fingers curled around his arm. Her breath against his neck. Inside, he felt nothing. Nothing.

The coach pitched to a stop at the *porte cochère*. Rey dismounted, carrying Mercy in his arms. Throughout the trip out of the Barataria, he'd kept her near. He'd leaned her up against his legs as he'd poled the pirogue to the secret meeting place where her men waited, all of them accounted for including stragglers. He'd cradled her in his arms down the journey to the river. It was as if by concentrating on that one thing—keeping her by his side—he could avoid thinking about the hideous events of the night. When her men had protested his guardianship, he'd snarled for them to back off, acting like a threatened animal. He'd tightened his grip possessively, making Mercedes moan in pain. That's when he'd realized just how close he was to losing all control.

Be numb, he commanded himself. *Feel nothing. Don't think.*

Mercedes had quickly explained that Rey was there to help her. Her men watched him warily, but obeyed her. And after many assurances from Mercedes, they'd allowed Rey to take her to the *pied-à-terre* in town alone. Now, climbing up the whitewashed steps, swiveling past the servant who opened the door, he again held her gently, taking Mercedes directly to the bedroom.

"Get me hot water and clean bandages," Rey called to the black woman worrying her hands as she waited at the French doors of the bedchamber. "And a bottle of bourbon. Hurry."

Rey lowered Mercy to the bed. She groaned, wincing with pain. She'd refused a doctor, and he knew why. How would Madame De Dreux—a jewel in the crown of New Orleans society—explain her highway woman clothes and a bullet wound?

When the servant returned, Rey took the bourbon and instructed her to leave the water and bandages on the nightstand. Propping Mercy up with one arm, he helped her drink from the whiskey-filled glass. He forced his mind

to concentrate on each step. Hold her up, tip the glass—
slowly! Don't let the whiskey dribble past her lips.

After a few sips, she pushed back the tumbler. Her eyes
fluttered open, watching him. "Please don't hate me,
Rey."

He leaned back against the slats of the cane chair he'd
pulled to her bedside. He cupped the glass in both hands.

The simple statement was enough to shatter him.

Feel nothing? What a damn lie. Inside, he was dying.

"What did you think I would feel when I discovered you
were Santana Rose?" he asked in a surprisingly level
voice. "How did you believe I would react to your stealing,
not to mention playing cat and mouse with me? Or did
you hope I would never discover the truth? Dear God,
Mercy. I could have—" He looked away. *I could have
killed you; been responsible for the death of another woman I
love.*

The hot touch of her fingers on his had the same effect
as her words. He felt as fragile as the crystal glass he held.
He could break at any moment.

"I didn't want to lie to you. The other things . . . the
stealing. There are reasons for what I've done, Rey."

He nodded, as if he understood, but kept his eyes carefully focused above her head, staring at the mermaids
carved into the bedposts. He couldn't bear to hear Mercy's
voice coming from the mouth of a black-garbed villain.

"You hate me," she whispered. "I can see it in your
eyes."

The strap around his chest cinched a notch tighter. *If
only it could be that simple.*

"Save your breath, Mercedes." He placed the bourbon
glass on the nightstand. "You're going to need it before
this night's over."

Rey unwrapped the makeshift bandage he'd used to
stop the bleeding, then began unbuttoning her shirt. He
tried to regain his control over the situation. This wasn't
Mercy, he told himself. His fingers weren't brushing

against the skin of the woman he loved. This was another creature altogether. A scoundrel who would stop at nothing—hold innocent men at gunpoint, steal life savings, manipulate a man into falling in love—capable of anything if it suited her needs of the moment. When he reached the button directly below her breasts, her fingers on his shirt-sleeve stopped him.

Mercy's head turned, directing his gaze. She stared at the hearth where only yesterday he'd pressed her up against the wallpaper of painted lilies and made love to her. He remembered her on the bed afterward, her anguish as he'd shared his pain over losing his wife, Mercy pleading with him to forgive himself and allow himself a normal life with his son. How all that sweet emotion had moved him then.

Almost roughly, he angled her back to face him. He wanted to call her every foul name he could think of for the things she'd done. But his memories warred with his villainous image of the highway woman. He couldn't see Santana anymore, despite the black clothes. Only Mercy sat on the bed.

"I've ruined everything, haven't I?" she whispered.

Her phrasing, the slight lift in her voice at the end, made it sound as if she hoped he might deny her words. A cold knot formed in his stomach. He thought of all the times he'd convinced himself he'd seen understanding in her eyes. *God, how could I have been so wrong?*

"Do you hate me, Rey? Could even the tiniest sliver of your love survive tonight?"

"Shut up, Mercy," he whispered, very softly.

Rey finished unbuttoning her shirt, then pushed it back over her injured shoulder. With a light touch, he explored the puckered flesh around the bullet wound. Her features twisted in pain despite his care. The bullet had gone straight through the fleshy part of her shoulder. When he began cleaning the blood away, Mercy's body arched against the pillows. Beads of sweat formed on her brow. She bit her bottom lip.

Rey couldn't seem to keep his hand steady. Her pain weakened him. Just moments before, he'd wanted to hurt her for her betrayal. But now, he found it almost impossible to administer that pain even to save her life. He studied the puncture wound. No bullet fragments. Infection was the biggest danger she faced. He reached for the bottle of bourbon. He doused one of the rags with the liquor.

"Oh no, Rey. Not yet. I'm not ready—"

"Listen to me!" he shouted, just as shaken as Mercy by what lay ahead. "I have to do this. I have to clean the wound or you could get an infection and die. Do you understand?"

She nodded, but tears slipped down her cheek nonetheless. With her eyes brimming, she looked so fragile. He fought the urge to hold her and reassure her. *Santana Rose,* he reminded himself, searching for his anger. *Mercy and Santana are one and the same.* He recalled the flashes of desire he'd had for both women. How tormented he'd been by what he'd believed was his betrayal of Mercy, the only woman he'd loved since his wife. He'd been willfully blind, of course. He hadn't wanted to see the similarities, made excuses for them even as Mercy reminded him of Santana. She'd made a complete and utter fool of him.

But no matter how he tried, the anger couldn't douse his need to comfort her.

"Take my hand," he whispered. When she just looked at him, uncertain of the kindness she heard in his voice, he picked up her wrist and placed her palm on his. "Take it," he repeated, his voice more firm this time. "And when the pain hits you, I want you to squeeze. Squeeze hard. Until the only thing you feel is my hand."

Mercy nodded, watching Rey as if he were a sanctuary from pain. Even before the alcohol-laced bandage touched her skin, she braced herself against the burn of the whiskey searing out infection. In one swift motion, Rey dropped the cloth on her wound and poured the bourbon, soaking her arm and the bedclothes beneath. Agony ripped through Mercy, as piercing as the bullet itself. She thrashed her head against the pillows. Her fingers bit into Rey's skin, her grip so tight she knew she must be hurting him. His gaze remained fixed on hers, as if he were sharing her pain, experiencing it as she did. She thought she might pass out, but focused on Rey and the cool depths of his eyes. When he peeled away the cloth and used a fresh rag to scrub the wound clean, she was still conscious. She watched him as he packed the wound with strips of cloth moistened with whiskey.

"Rey, let me explain." Her chest lifted and fell in a ragged breath. "I'm not trying to make excuses, but there are circumstances you don't know about. If after you hear what I have to say you still feel the same, I'll accept that."

Rey looked only at her arm as he tied the last bandage in place. "By all means then. Explain."

"I never stole from innocent people. I stole from Benoit. Only Benoit. My husband and his cronies were the people who suffered at my hands."

"And that's why you held up my coach, Mercedes? Am I one of your husband's cronies?"

She thought of telling him what she knew, that he was an agent investigating her husband, but discarded the idea immediately. He was so angry at her, ready to lash out at anything she said. She didn't want to put him on the defense, as he'd so neatly placed her. Though in the swamp she'd been tempted to use Robert Pinkerton's letter to gain her release, even at her most low, she couldn't manipulate Rey. Not again.

"You came to New Orleans to invest with my husband. To me, you were one of them, Rey. By now you must know how Benoit makes his money. Those poor women. Almost everything I steal I give away. I make certain Benoit's dirty funds support orphanages, schools—good causes that help children. I told you about the baby I lost." Her voice choked. "It's important to me to help."

Rey studied Mercy. *Just the right pause,* he thought, *just the right tone.* Mentioning the child, of course, was pure genius. She sounded so sincere.

"Do you understand, Rey? I had to help."

"How could you ever think," he asked, his voice low, his eyes fixed on hers, "that I would ever believe a single word you have to say, Mercedes?"

She seemed to shrink from him. Her shoulders dipped; her back curved against the headboard of the tester bed, making her appear smaller, almost cowed. "What about the women in the swamp? You know their fate. You can't possibly think it's right to make slaves of them. Who would save them if I didn't? I take them in. I give them money. I get them back to their homes, or help them start a new life here if they choose."

"Or perhaps," he said, standing, putting distance between them, "you steal the poor souls Benoit kidnaps and recruit them for Catalan Kate's or some other brothel. How truly noble that would be."

She gasped. "You can't believe that."

"Why not, Mercedes!" he shouted, throwing the rag he held to the ground. "Why shouldn't I believe the worst? You lied to me."

"Have you always been honest with me, Rey?"

"Oh, please. Don't compare me to you. One night you kidnap me as Santana Rose, the next you make love to me as Mercedes. I never lied to you about my love! Your kisses, your very touch—everything—all lies. How you must have laughed to have me panting after you as one woman, knowing all along that I would make love to you as another!"

"I know it looks bad," she cried. "But it wasn't like that!"

"You want me to believe you are good and noble," he continued, his words pounding into her, punishing her, "like your hero, Robin Hood? All I see is the stealing and the lies!" He paced back and forth in front of the bed. "What other crimes have you committed, Mercedes? What other lies have you told me? Should I worry that you're pregnant? That you lied to me about that too?"

The careful lack of expression on her face cut like a knife. Her guilty silence rammed the blade deeper. He lost his train of thought. He couldn't move. *No, please. Not that too. I couldn't bear it.*

"Are you pregnant?"

He spoke the words with great control, the agent coaxing out the truth. Nothing in his manner showed his terror. But she must have sensed it just the same. She remained carefully silent.

"Even if you have never told me the truth before," he said, "this one time, you . . . must . . . not . . . lie."

She looked down to her lap and studied her hands. "I don't know if I'm pregnant."

His fingers curled into fists. He swallowed his breath. "But you could be?"

Shadows from the fire played across the room. The clock on the hearth chimed the hour. Rey waited, slowly dying.

"Yes. It's possible."

He closed his eyes; he couldn't face her. Her or the truth. He thought of Christopher, all his arguments with Mac. He couldn't have any more children. He couldn't accept that responsibility again. Not after Sophie. "I explained," he began. "I told you very clearly how important—" He stopped. Then laughed. How absolutely insane for him to try and make her understand how betrayed he felt, as if she cared? As if the woman who had used him, lied to him, stolen from him, broken the laws he'd dedicated his life to enforcing, could possibly give a damn.

"Rey, I wanted your child so much. I lost a baby. You couldn't imagine the pain, the loss—a loss I could never replace. I couldn't let Benoit touch me. I didn't want the child of a man I despised. But your baby . . ."

He turned on her with disbelief. "You thought to steal that too?"

"Don't hate me." She reached for his hand. "Please, don't hate me."

He pulled away, unable to bear her touch. He didn't respond to her desolate words. That could be a lie as well, executed as neatly as she'd duped him into loving her.

His face grew hot, burning. He had to get out of the room. He had to think, take control. He walked to the table, picked up the bottle of bourbon. "Drink as much as you can stand," he ordered, falling into the comfort of practical matters. "It will numb the pain. I'll be waiting outside."

She took the bottle in her good hand and downed a good measure. It took only a few moments for her eyes to become glassy. She gave him back the whiskey and he placed it on the nightstand, prepared to leave her until he saw what he mistook for intoxication were actually tears. One lone drop slipped down her cheek as she stared ahead, unseeing.

"I knew it couldn't last," she whispered to no one in particular.

In her voice there was a depth of sadness Rey had heard in only one other's voice.

His own.

Pascal showed no hesitation climbing the rotted steps to Lena's porch, not like the first time when she'd come for the love potion on that stormy night. Even as her fist hit the door, it opened. Lena's assistant stood at the threshold, the same predatory smile on her face as she signaled Pascal to come in. Again, Pascal had the uneasy thought that her visit was somehow anticipated.

Lena hovered over the caldron in the fireplace, her snake draped across her shoulders. The light of the fire reflected against her skin, accenting her sharp cheekbones and eyes in an almost diabolic manner. But rather than frightening Pascal, the death-mask face reminded her of Harlan's precarious hold on life, giving her the courage she needed.

"You said I should come to you if I ever needed help," Pascal said.

"Yes!" Lena's eyes flamed with reflected fire. "Tell me what you want, Pas-cal De Dreux."

"The man you've seen me with, Harlan. A snake bit him, a water moccasin. He's fighting the poison; I sucked out as much as I could immediately after the snake bit him—"

"He's dying."

She spoke with such certainty that for an instant Pascal forgot to breathe. "W-what?"

"Dat man is dying. I feel it."

"No!" Pascal backed away. "No! I won't accept that."

Lena slinked to Pascal's side; her fingers clawed into her wrist. "He needs magic. My magic, Pas-cal De Dreux. Only I can save him."

Pascal's pulse struggled against Lena's tourniquet hold. The priestess's fingers bit into her skin as if it were the snake's jaws that held her and not Lena's bony fingers. But instead of fighting, Pascal reminded herself that Lena was her last hope. "I can't let him die. Can you give me a potion."

"It's gonna cost you plenty."

"Anything!"

"Don't be too hasty, Pas-cal De Dreux, cause it ain't money dat I want."

"Anything!" Pascal repeated without hesitation.

Lena smiled, a cruel lift of her mouth. "Ya hear Si-mone? Our girl must love dat man somet'ing fierce."

"She love 'im, all right," said the younger assistant. "But I ain't sure it's enough to save his life."

Lena grabbed Pascal's shoulders, grinning like a demon. "I am, Simone. I'm very sure."

"Tell me how I can save Harlan," Pascal urged, wanting to leave as quickly as possible.

"I'll make ya a potion, Pas-cal De Dreux. A potion ya give 'im every hour. And a poultice for the bite. But I already give ya my magic free once."

"I'll pay any price."

"Me an' Simone, we got a fancy ceremony we planned fer da people at Pontchartrain. But we need someone to help. A girl young and pretty. Someone jus' like you."

An explosion of panic set off in Pascal's stomach like the Fourth of July. She'd heard about the voodoo ceremonies that took place at the lake on St. John's Eve. Often, the people who attended were never heard from again.

"I'm not gonna give ya not'ing until I got your promise."

Pascal swallowed. "I'll do it. You have my word. Just give me the cure."

"All right Pas-cal De Dreux. But even if dat man of yours dies, ya come when I send fer you. Ya understand?"

"Yes."

Lena cackled, lifting the snake by the throat and holding it just above her head. She twirled around the room until she reached her wooden table. She placed the snake on the scarred surface. It writhed around the bowls and bottles set there while Lena mixed her potion, murmuring incantations over the bowl. When she finished, she put every drop of the dark green liquid into a bottle and handed it to Pascal with a sack that smelled as if it were filled with strong herbs.

"Every hour, ya feed him a spoonful," she said pointing to the bottle. "Ya mix what's in da bag with strong liquor to make a paste and spread it over da bite." She reached behind her and retrieved a muslin bag tied at the top with a red ribbon and feather. "Then ya rub da bite with this gris-gris bag. That will draw da poison out and fix da swelling."

Pascal stared at the gris-gris with awe. The amulet was believed by many to hold great powers. Her spirits lifted with hope for the first time. "Thank you!" she said with heartfelt enthusiasm.

"Ya give him da potion and use da bag and dat man of yours will live." Pascal turned to leave, but Lena grabbed her arm and twisted her back to face her. "Either way, ya come back here. Dat's my price Pas-cal De Dreux. And wear a pretty white dress when ya come. I like my girls to wear white."

Lena's expression seemed to devour Pascal. The bud of happiness inside her expired. Lord in heaven, what had she just agreed to? She wanted to hand Lena back the cures, but immediately thought of Harlan hovering near death. For the first time since she'd fallen in love, Pascal realized just how much Harlan meant to her.

"I understand, Lena. I'll come. And I'll wear white. Just as you asked."

Rey sat next to the fire on the cane chair, his long legs propped on the footboard of the bed next to one enticing carving of a mermaid. He studied the sea nymph, a brandy snifter unsteady in his hand, thinking the design appropriate for a siren's bed. His gaze shifted to Mercedes. The sound of her ragged breathing seemed to rattle in his own chest. She'd been sleeping for the past hour, a combination of the bourbon and much needed rest.

Pushing off the bed, he balanced his chair on two legs and thought cynically of the talent he'd discovered he possessed. What a unique ability he had to make nightmares come to life. For the past five years, his wife's death had haunted his dreams. Would the unveiling of Santana Rose into the woman he loved replace those visions? Would he relive the night in the swamps, aiming and shooting, only to find Mercy dead in his arms? Or would it be Santana he'd see, caped and masked, swollen with his child as she trained one of her fine Smith & Wessons on him?

Circumstances make people do strange things. That doesn't make them bad.

"Oh, shut up, Mac." He was drunk enough to have spoken out loud.

He took another swallow of the Spanish brandy. A baby —dear God. Did he have to worry about that as well? She was married to De Dreux, a criminal, and now could be carrying Rey's child.

And you love her. Don't forget that, Parks.

No. He refused to believe it. He thought of all his warnings to Mac against Kate, a brothel owner and a criminal —dammit, Rey couldn't be foolish enough to love Mercy knowing who she was . . . or could he? What made him think he had even one ounce of control when it came to Mercedes De Dreux?

"Oh, for chrissakes, don't think of that now," he mumbled, downing the rest of the brandy. Half the contents spilled onto his trousers.

Rey sprang to his feet, cursing. He scanned the familiar room, looking for something with which to wipe up the mess. He remembered the clothespress where Mercy had retrieved a handkerchief the night he'd woken from his nightmare. He crossed the room, his thoughts returning to the woman on the bed. He hadn't determined what to do with her, only knew that he would take her to Bizy before morning. He didn't want her men coming here and taking him unawares, and he thought to talk matters over with Mac and Harlan before deciding anything.

Rey pulled open the drawer. The linens lay neatly piled on one side. On the other, handkerchiefs and scarves were shoved across what looked like a burlap bag. A prickle tingled up the back of his neck. Ignoring the handkerchiefs, he picked up the bag. He placed his brandy glass on the clothespress and slipped the drawstring open.

Inside lay stacks of bills banded together in thick packets. Money? Rey frowned, wondering if this were part of Santana's booty.

He glanced back to Mercy and thought of the story she'd relayed the hour before. She wanted him to believe she stole from De Dreux to give to women and children. She'd made stealing sound positively virtuous. Oh, she'd put herself in the best light, all right.

So why did he want so desperately to believe her?

Almost against his wishes, his agent mind riffled through the facts. She certainly had all the money she wanted from her husband. She lived in a fine house, wore exquisite clothes and expensive jewelry. She lacked for nothing that money could buy. Of course, she could have turned to a life of crime for the diversion, for the perverted thrill of breaking the law and escaping detection. Or she might know how close her husband was to losing it all. And then there was the motive of revenge. De Dreux did beat her, after all.

Or she could be just what she claimed, a woman seeking justice outside the framework of the legal system.

The latter explanation certainly fit the Mercedes De Dreux he'd fallen in love with, a woman who visited St. Bartholomew's Asylum for Orphans once a week without fail, who protected her stepdaughter as if she were the girl's natural mother when all she received were snide remarks from Pascal for thanks—a woman who had held Rey in her arms and consoled him.

Don't be stupid, Parks. Don't try to believe the best of her. Vigilante justice! he reminded himself. That kind of morality went out with her sainted Robin Hood. They had laws now, and men to enforce them.

The image of the girl in the swamps came unbidden; again, he saw the child crying and struggling as they forced her to board one of De Dreux's boats.

He carefully blanked the picture—a simple task given the amount of alcohol he'd consumed over the past hour. He took out one bundle of money and thumbed through it. More from habit than anything he saw, he slipped out a note for a closer look. Immediately, he knew something was wrong. The paper didn't feel quite right. He walked to the fireplace. Holding the bill to the light, his eyes scoured the lines made by the plate. He pulled out his wallet and yanked out a familiar five-dollar note, compared the two.

"Rey?"

He glanced up at the sound of Mercy's sleepy voice. His head was positively swimming. It couldn't be. It just couldn't be! It would be too bizarre. Impossible. Then again . . .

"Where did you get this money, Mercedes?"

She sat upright on the bed. The nightgown molded the fine curves of her figure he remembered stroking with adoration and love. The slim fingers of one hand rubbed the sleep from her eyes. But when she saw the bag he held, her hand stopped, then dropped to her lap. The muscles of her body seemed to tense. *Guilty as charged,* he thought.

"It's part of a business arrangement I have." There was a wary note to her voice. "Nothing more."

"Someone paid you this money?"

He could almost see the wheels turning as she evaluated just how much she should say. "I deliver the money. I'm a messenger of sorts."

"For Harrison Sotheby."

Mercy flinched. "How did you know?"

His laughter was loud and wild—and not quite sane. Mercy sat up against the headboard, lifting the coverlet closer as if seeking warmth from a sudden chill. She tried to ignore the pain in her shoulder, worried now as she watched Rey doubled over with laughter, wiping the tears from his eyes.

"Oh, this is rich. Even I couldn't have dreamed this up. I haven't the imagination."

His laughter stopped just as abruptly as it had started. Mercy saw the empty glass on the clothespress. She wondered how much he'd drunk. And then his pale green eyes focused on her with such keenness that she knew she couldn't be foxed.

"You're a passer," he spoke as if the strange term had meaning to her. When she didn't respond, he added, "You buy and sell queer. Boodle."

Mercy said nothing, completely unfamiliar with the words.

Rey came to her bedside. "Don't tell me you don't know? It's counterfeit." He threw the bill he'd been holding on the coverlet. "Fake. But the best of fakes. Definitely Sotheby's work."

"Counterfeit?" she repeated. "But that's not possible. I pay—" Mercy sucked in her breath. But of course. Sotheby was buying off his men in government with counterfeit money. It made perfect sense. He paid crooks with crooked goods. Even if they discovered his ruse, no one would complain. Who would suggest to the police that their influence in legislature had been bought with illegal tender? Even if they discovered his game and complained to Sotheby, he might well convince them to keep their mouths shut or face the consequences of their own illegal acts.

And Santana Rose had been Sotheby's delivery girl.

"This money has been flooding the state." The light from the lamps accented Rey's eyes. A bright yellow flame burned in the normally clear green centers. "Have you any idea what counterfeit does to a country, Mercedes? It ruins the money supply. Destroys the confidence of the people in its value."

She closed her eyes, hoping to shut out the truth as easily as the look of hate on Rey's face. Even as she'd delivered Sotheby's money, she'd always justified her actions because she'd thought her participation benign. What Rey described was far-reaching, malignant, even lethal. Sotheby had used Santana Rose, the feared highway woman, to intimidate others into accepting and distributing his illegal money.

"Do you know what the United States government does

with counterfeiters? They consider them traitors. On a par with those who commit treason."

The condemning facts cut deeper into her conscience. Lord in heaven, what had she done?

"Tell me about Sotheby," he said. "Tell me everything."

Mercy nodded, realizing she had made a grave error. In her desire to stop Benoit she'd joined forces with Sotheby, knowing full well the man's diabolical character. Hadn't Kate warned her on countless occasions? But she'd wanted so desperately to have the means to destroy Benoit, she'd turned a blind eye to it all, making her pact with the devil.

"I deliver the money as Santana Rose," she said. Barely able to hear her own words, she cleared her throat and continued in a stronger voice, "To politicians and the like. Men with influence in the government who can help Sotheby. He never said, of course, but I always assumed the money I delivered were bribes."

Rey studied her. His was the face of a man familiar with the roles of both judge and jury. "I've been in the banking business for many years, Mercedes. Like many bankers, I'm well acquainted with counterfeiters. I know a lot about Harrison Sotheby. Do you have any idea what kind of man he is?"

"I didn't know the money was counterfeit, Rey. I swear it. I only did it because . . ." All her reasons suddenly seemed so weak. Excuses. Her past, Laura and Beth, none of these things could matter to the agent before her.

"Why, Mercy? Tell me why."

Mercy sunk back against the headboard. She concentrated on the throbbing of her shoulder, almost relishing the pain. "Benoit," she said, choosing to admit her failing rather than justify herself. "I did it to destroy him. It would have taken me years to bankrupt him as Santana. I might have been caught before I succeeded. Sotheby is well known in the Louisiana Lottery as an influential man. The lottery, the June fifteenth drawing—"

"It's not fixed." He was staring at her as if seeing her for the first time. "It's just a scam to bankrupt your husband."

"I knew he loved to gamble—"

"That he'd take the bait."

"Yes."

"Brilliant." Rey shook his head. "It's ingenious. He'll be ruined—already is. All the money he's sunk into the venture, his and mine, is lining Sotheby's and your pockets."

"Not my pocket, Rey. It was part of my deal with Sotheby that he keep all the money. And I was going to make sure you were paid back from my own funds. I swear it. I only wanted Benoit stopped."

Rey dropped down into the cane chair at her bedside. He stared, his gaze unfocused, at the fire. "I can't even begin to tell you how many people will be hurt by the money you've helped pass. The farmer's wife who discovers the bills she was paid at the market for her goods won't be accepted by the bank. The tailor just making ends meet who now has nothing to show for his labor but worthless paper." He shook his head, as if the staggering number left him numb. He turned and examined Mercy. His evaluation made her doubly miserable for the disappointment she saw in his eyes. "Can you imagine the number of victims who'll end up with useless boodle thanks to you, Mercedes?"

"I didn't know, Rey. Benoit is such an evil man," she said, trying to defend herself, but drowning in her guilt. "I did it for the girls. I wanted so much to help them. I thought the end justified the means."

In the flickering light, Rey's hair shone pure white. His fire-lit features looked more than ever like an avenging angel's. "The end justifies the means?" he asked softly, almost matter-of-factly. "Do you still believe that, Mercedes? Because, if you do, let me explain what that kind of reasoning leads to. Those women you help—the ones your husband kidnaps—do you know who buys them? Do you know who gives Benoit De Dreux the money to inspire more shipments. Sotheby—the very man you've helped."

Mercy shook her head. *No, it can't be.* A black void opened before her. She could almost smell the ship's hold where she'd woken twelve years before, Benoit's captive. She could see his black predator's eyes assessing her, as they'd done so many others. Her hands on the counterpane began to tremble. "No! NO!"

"Ironic, isn't it? You steal the money from De Dreux to stop the shipments, then hand it back to Sotheby who finances your husband's smuggling. Oh, and I'm sure he supports many more smugglers than just De Dreux." Rey leaned forward, closer to her. "Think of all the money you've given him." His words wrapped around her with the tension of a hangman's noose. "Now imagine how many expeditions it will finance. How many women will that money buy into the very misery you've tried to save them from? Can you find them all, Mercedes? Can you save all of them?"

She wanted to scream he was wrong. What he said couldn't be true. But the words stayed choked in her throat because no matter how much she wanted to believe otherwise, she knew Rey Parks, an agent for the United States government, would be familiar with Sotheby's crimes.

She shook her head. Someone was mumbling the words "it can't be true," over and over.

"You don't believe me?" Rey asked. "Then let me tell you something else that might sway you. I have a special interest in Mr. Sotheby. You might say that I'm on my own little quest for justice. I've followed his career quite closely for the past five years. And if I believed the end justifies the means, as you do, I would have killed him just as many years ago. He doesn't just bribe legislators, or pass boodle. He doesn't merely relegate his crimes to financing smugglers. He kills, Mercedes." There came a preternatural light to his eyes, as if their green depths were charged by the loathing in his voice. "Five years ago, Harrison Sotheby murdered my wife."

Chapter 19

Ling Shi rested her fingertips against the cool window-pane, then turned to scan the living room. Pillows covered the horsehair settee and its matching love seat. Beautiful jade carvings graced the side table and mantel over the fireplace. *Her home.* She smoothed back a crocheted coverlet on the armchair and smiled.

She looked beyond the parlor of the shotgun house Chiang had purchased the day they'd wed. She could still remember his tender and proud expression when he'd taken her there after their wedding ceremony the week before, the very day following her flight from L'Isle des Rêves. Even as she'd fretted over the expense, he'd assured her that he'd always had the money to buy the house but never the reason—until their marriage. It was a lovely home, painted pink with white trim and decorated like a gingerbread house. Like many other homes in the Vieux Carré, each room followed in perfect succession. It amused Ling Shi to think that, just as the term shotgun implied, if a rifle were fired from the front door, the bullet would indeed pass through each room to exit out the back door.

Ling Shi sighed, deeply happy. On evenings like this, when the world was peaceful and quiet and she had time to think over the past week since she'd fled Monsieur De Dreux, it was difficult to believe her good fortune. Her own house—just a few blocks from the apothecary where she worked as Chiang's assistant—a loving husband. Her hand dropped down to her waist. And now that she'd stop taking the powders against conception, she hoped soon to have a child.

Even as the thought of Chiang's son filled her with happiness, a shaft of doubt shadowed her joy. She glanced back to the world beyond the pane of glass. It seemed almost unfair that she should have so much when she considered the price Pascal may have paid for Ling Shi's freedom.

"Ling Shi? Dearest, come to bed."

At the sound of Chiang's voice, a thrill of anticipation tripped from her heart to where she still held her hand cradled against her stomach. She smiled at her response, thinking of the days long past when she'd thought never to feel passion for a man. She made her way to the bedchamber and hurried to the tester bed. As she pushed aside the mosquito netting, Chiang gathered her into his arms with that special gentleness uniquely his. The first night after their wedding, he'd shown Ling Shi that love could be experienced through the lightest touch and that desire need not be a thing of fear.

"What is wrong, my dearest?" he asked, brushing his lips against her temple. "What thoughts make a face as lovely as yours frown so?"

She sighed, knowing Chiang would not want her to fret, but she spoke her thoughts out loud just the same. "I was thinking of Pascal."

She wondered if her husband had grown tired of her constant woes, but his expression showed only familiar concern.

"You miss her," he said.

"It's more than that. I feel as if something is not right with her." She pressed her cheek against his shoulder, trying to stop the black doubts that tarnished her blissful marriage. "I fear she needs me. I left her in that lonely house without a friend."

"What you fear is De Dreux. And unnecessarily so. Ling Shi, he is her father. He would not hurt her."

"I do not doubt it, Chiang. She is all that is left of his blood and I know that is important to him. And yet . . ." She couldn't crystallize her worries enough to express them. She pressed her lips together, frustrated with these gnawing doubts.

"Perhaps we should consider visiting her at L'Isle des Rêves," Chiang said after a prolonged silence.

"We?"

"I would never leave you to face that voyage alone. If your worries continue, we'll make the journey."

"Oh, Chiang. I love you so." Ling Shi kissed her husband on the mouth—an act that only a week ago would have filled her with trepidation. Now, the caress came as naturally and as fearlessly as if De Dreux's abuses had been phantoms banished by the morning's light.

Chiang drew her back against him and lifted the counterpane, slipping them both under the covers. "But nothing will be accomplished by your worries tonight." He lifted the hem of her night rail and slipped his hand up her calf with promise. "Rest your fears, my dearest. We will find your answers soon enough. And we'll find them together."

Mercy watched the housekeeper close the French doors behind her, leaving Mercy alone in the bedchamber. She stared at the fire dancing in the grate. The tongues of flame seemed to pulse and leap with the rhythm pounding in her shoulder. She thought of what Mrs. Calder had told her, that Rey waited in the parlor directly outside. "Looking like he's thinking of murder," the housekeeper had said with round, fear-filled eyes and wringing hands. "And started on a second bottle of brandy, madame." Mercy could just imagine the sight of him, his tall, powerful body cramped into one of the delicate Louis XV chairs, brooding over the night's revelations.

She leaned back against the mound of pillows just fluffed by her housekeeper. How many years had Mercy planned, how many chances had she taken to help the women her husband kidnapped? And all along, she'd been giving money to the man who financed these smugglings—the man responsible for the death of Rey's wife.

You are my creation. I made you.

Benoit's words, uttered almost daily those early years, attained a frightening grain of truth. *My creation.* Could the product of an evil man be nothing better than evil?

She'd fought his horrible definition for years. In many ways, Santana was part of her effort to *prove* him wrong. She admitted that she'd enjoyed her role. The disguise had given her power—the perfect antidote for a life spent floundering in a sense of helplessness. As Santana, she'd lived without the fear Benoit had lorded over his fourteen-year-old bride. And yet, her motivation had never been revenge or power. She and Kate had tried to *help people*—those lonely girls who reminded her so painfully of her own fate. She'd always believed her work as Santana showed her capable of good despite the evil man who manipulated her.

Tonight's discoveries had devastated that theory.

For the past hour, she'd faced the possibility that she, not Benoit, had been mistaken. That she *was* his creature—a monster, just as foul as the miscreant produced by Shelley in the book *Frankenstein.*

The prospect left her terrified.

The door creaked open. Mercy's head snapped up. This time, it was not Mrs. Calder's matronly figure silhouetted at the threshold. Rey leaned against the doorjamb, his features shadowed by the lamplight and glowing coals. She couldn't bear to look at him. She knew what she'd find: censure and reproach.

She remembered his expression when she'd told him about the possibility of a child. He'd looked so astonished, and so very betrayed. His disbelief had acted like a torch exposing vermin allowed to thrive and multiply in some forgotten corner. Explanations and rationalizations she'd shared with no one but herself over the years hadn't stood the scrutiny of that light.

When had it all gone wrong in her head, she wondered? When had Santana, crusader for the helpless, turned into a woman who could justify anything—even stealing this man's child? The precious nights Rey had held her, when she'd spun fairy tales of their future together, had been the happiest of her life. And though in her more rational moments she'd known her dreams were unlikely to come true, she'd hadn't thought them dangerous.

The guilt, the misery—she couldn't stand either any longer. Acting on impulse, Mercy opened the drawer of her nightstand, searching beneath the pile of papers she kept there. If there was any fairness in this world, she'd be as barren as she'd once claimed. But that was out of her hands now. Other matters were not. Her fingers closed around cool metal. At least this simple theft could be made right.

Mercy shut the drawer and braced herself against the pillows. She kept her hand fisted on her lap. "I have something I need to give you, Rey."

One dark brow flared upward. He unfolded his frame from the door and paced toward her, each step measured and smooth in a soundless prowl. "And what might that be, Santana?"

The use of her alias was warning enough. Mercy steeled herself against the pillows.

When he reached her bedside, his gaze scanned her face, then settled where the bed sheets hugged her breasts. "What could you offer me now, I wonder?"

She could smell the brandy on his breath. She thought of what Mrs. Calder had said. Two bottles.

"What might sway me to your cause?" With one long finger under her chin, he tipped her face up to meet his. "Money?"

"Don't," she whispered, perfectly miserable.

The pad of his finger trailed down her neck, dipping the bed sheets back to rest at the hollow between her breasts. He leaned closer, so near she could almost taste the brandy on his lips. "Perhaps you have something more precious to offer?"

Mercy closed her eyes. The agonizing brush of his lips against hers made her want to cry. He kissed her with the cunning of a fox. It felt cold, detached: the agent seducing. She turned her face away and clamped her fingers around his wrist, pulling his hand from her breast where he'd stroked with such calculated appeal. She knew his game—he wanted to see the worst in her. He wanted to prove she would do anything, even use her body, to gain his silence.

She pressed the gold chain and medal into the center of his palm. "I wanted to return your necklace," she said, meeting his eyes. She'd thought to tell him about her past, how Benoit had kidnapped her in London, about Laura and Beth, but bit her tongue against useless explanations. He'd turn it all around to prove how immoral she was—a street waif, the daughter of a prostitute, who'd learned to steal at the age of five. Nothing could make Rey understand or forgive what she'd done.

Rey stared down at the medal. He frowned, sorry now that he'd drunk so much and couldn't clear his head. When she'd first spoken, her words had brought to mind Leticia and the more interesting games of intrigue played between men and women. He'd wanted to have everything reduced to that level—no love, no caring, only Mercy, enticing him to let her go and forget tonight's discoveries. Oh, how he'd craved that simple answer: Mercy the bad one, the criminal. She'd never loved him at all; it had all been a game.

He turned the gold medallion in his hand. The St. Christopher surprised him. It was the last thing he'd expected, an act of honesty to meet his deception. For some reason he couldn't fathom, he didn't want the medal back.

He almost pocketed the chain in anger at the thought that he might actually wish to forgive her. But it felt strange to take the medal from her—so final.

Rey tossed the St. Christopher on the coverlet. "Keep the damn medal."

Tears came to her eyes. She scooped up the chain and held it out to him once more. "I don't want it. Not when all I see in your eyes is hate and suspicion—"

"I said, keep it." He stepped out of her reach, leaving her holding the chain. Before she could argue, he reached in his coat pocket and tossed the missive he'd intercepted from the housekeeper onto her lap, his reason for coming in the first place. "This just came for you."

She glanced down at the letter. The seal was broken.

Rey gave her his most wicked smile. The brandy sang in his veins. Good, perhaps now she would shut up about the medal. "It's from your stepdaughter. I think you'll find it quite interesting."

Mercy picked up the note immediately when she heard the letter was from Pascal. She unfolded the delicate paper, forgetting all about the St. Christopher in her hands.

Rey watched her read. The ginger-colored brows furrowed. A wave of amber hair tumbled past her bandaged shoulder to fall across the top of one breast. He tore his gaze from the tempting sight, concentrating on the letter. The note worried him. What was Pascal doing at Bizy? He prayed to God Harlan hadn't done something stupid involving De Dreux's daughter.

Mercy looked up, puzzled. "She says I must vouch for her staying the night here, at the *pied-à-terre,* with me. She wants me to send her a response to Bizy."

Rey appropriated the note, folding it and returning it to his coat pocket. "We'll do better than that, Mercedes. Get dressed. I'll take you to her."

Delicious relief surged through Mercy. After reading the strange note, she needed to make sure Pascal was all right. But then the greater connotation of the journey dawned on her and her relief was replaced by a disturbing premonition.

So. It would begin.

"Are you going to hold me prisoner until you send for Gessler?"

Rey gave her an unreadable look. "What choice do I have?"

Pascal carefully dribbled the potion through Harlan's parted lips, one precious drop at a time until she was sure he'd consumed the entire teaspoonful. She placed the spoon next to the bottle on the nightstand and pushed back a wisp of hair from her forehead.

"Go to bed, lass," MacAfee said from behind her. "It's clear the lad will make it now—thanks to you and yer potion."

Pascal smiled with relief. "Yes. I think so too." She brushed Harlan's cheek with her fingers—warm to the touch, no longer cold or clammy. "He seems to be resting comfortably now." She laid her palm on his chest. "And his breathing is stronger."

Mac frowned at the bottle of brandy he held, then shrugged and poured two fingers into a glass. Moving to the side of the bed where the mosquito netting had been pulled back, he roused Harlan enough to make him drink a good pull, just as the physician had instructed. When Harlan moaned and tried to swat the glass away, Mac coaxed him to take one more swallow. He wiped Harlan's chin where some of the liquor had dribbled and watched the lad fall back into a deep slumber.

Mac sighed. "I'm not sure what good spirits will do him, other than gettin' his back teeth awash and givin' the lad a good case of hot coppers come morning." He placed the brandy glass on the table next to Pascal's curative. "I've the room across the way made up for ye, lass. Rest assured I'll watch Harlan while ye rest."

Pascal shook her head, returning to her seat next to the

bed. "I couldn't sleep a wink. Why don't you go instead? It's useless for both of us to stay up all night." When Mac-Afee said nothing, Pascal turned away from her patient. "Oh, for goodness sake. You still don't trust me?"

MacAfee smiled. "I trust you, miss. You'll not leave the lad, that much I know."

"Thank you."

"Ye'll call me if there's any change?"

"Immediately."

When the door closed behind MacAfee, Pascal studied Harlan lovingly. His color had returned to normal. The swelling on his leg had eased considerably with the poultice she'd made. She sent a silent prayer of thanks. Only when she remembered Lena's request did her sense of dread return.

She stood and sat down on the side of the bed, needing to be as close to him as possible. Taking up his hand, she caressed it between her two. "Oh, Harlan," she whispered, using her own voice to soothe herself. "I don't care what she does to me. It was worth it to see you safe again."

Pascal rested her head against his chest, listening to his strong heartbeat. "Those things I said in the bayou—that you'd hurt me so much that I couldn't love you anymore—it's not true. Yes, it hurt something awful to think you didn't love me. But I guess that kind of pain is just part of growing up." She laced her fingers through his brown curls. "You're the best thing that's ever happened to me. You showed me a side of myself that I was afraid didn't exist. You helped me find the goodness inside, gave me the strength I needed to help Ling Shi and make peace with Mercedes. I love you so much, Harlan. I don't even need your love for mine to exist."

In the murky depths of his dreams, Harlan heard the whispered words of comfort. He wanted to reach up and touch the beautiful creature who uttered those promises of devotion.

"I was so frightened when that snake bit you, Harlan."

He frowned. Frightened? His Pascal worried about him?

"I would promise anything to Lena to see you recover."

An uneasy darkness crept into his sweet visions. Harlan struggled to wake. He didn't want to think of the evil woman he'd seen beyond the windows of the cottage when he'd followed Pascal. He didn't want nightmares about Pascal making promises to that conjo woman!

"I admit I'm frightened of her and her voodoo ceremonies. I'm terrified of what she might do to me—or worse, make me do. But I'd have promised anything to get that potion for you. Anything!"

Anything? *Mon Dieu.* Nightmare, terrible nightmare. Want . . . to . . . wake.

Pascal wound her fingers in Harlan's hair. "She said if I loved you enough, you'd be saved."

She stroked his cheek in a featherlike touch. On the bed, Harlan tossed his head against the pillows. He frowned in his sleep and mumbled something that sounded like, "Just a dream."

A nightmare? Pascal watched his twisted features. Or could he be having some sort of relapse? Instantly, her fears rekindled. She leaned closer, seeking the comfort of his touch. She brushed her lips against his mouth. "I love you, Harlan. I just know my love is strong enough to save you!"

Warm lips cherished his in a kiss so tender it couldn't be a dream, Harlan thought. Was he hallucinating? Living out the desires he'd had for *la petite* in an illusion brought on by the moccasin's poison? Harlan reached out and stroked the waist-long curls falling over him in a curtain of silk. How often had he imagined pursuing his hot kisses with *la petite* to their natural end? How many dreams had he enjoyed with Pascal speaking of her love, and he responding by showing his?

Pascal released a gasp at Harlan's unexpected touch. His eyes remained closed, but his caress was strong and sure against her hair. He murmured something, but this time the sound was too soft for her to understand. His mouth moved again.

"What is it?" Pascal leaned over the bed. "What do you want, Harlan?"

She felt more than heard the whisper. She shifted closer, resting against his body. A band constricted around her chest as she heard the whispered words again.

"Love," he said. Pascal's breath caught in a gasp. "Love . . . you," he repeated.

His eyes blinked open. The indigo color remained a mere fringe, almost wiped out by the dark centers. His hand closed over her breast and a wicked tingling radiated from that spot as his thumb rubbed back and forth. Pascal felt her face flame. No one had ever touched her there.

"Love you," he whispered again.

She pulled out of his embrace and backed away from the bed. She couldn't catch her breath. She told herself he wasn't in his right mind. Between the snake venom, Lena's potion, and the brandy Mac had forced down him, he couldn't possibly know what he was saying. For all she knew, he was dreaming about another woman. She turned toward the door, stopped, bit her knuckle.

"Don't leave," she heard him whisper behind her.

Pascal glanced back at her beloved on the bed. His head was turned toward her.

"Don't leave me, *petite.*"

His voice sounded strong now, his gaze clear. Pascal swallowed a sob. She had him back. He was safe, no longer dying from the snakebite. She raced back to the bed and sat down. She cupped his face in her hands and whispered against his mouth. "I love you, Harlan."

Harlan pressed his lips to hers with unrestrained passion and caressed the curve of her hip, pulling her toward him. He had trouble shifting her on the bed; he felt so weak. But with just a little coaxing on his part, Pascal lay down beside him on the bed, returning his kisses. His hand trailed down the length of her thigh. The prospect of those legs wrapped around him made him hard and hot. She had fine legs, beautiful and long—coltish, like the rest of her. His fingers danced back to her breast. He could feel her heart pounding beneath the material of her gown and he smiled. She felt so good. He wanted to forget everything that had happened tonight, wanted to make up to her about her father.

"Love me, *petite*," he whispered. "Love me."

Heat radiated out from where Harlan's hand caressed her. "I do love you, Harlan," Pascal answered. The tingling inside her confused and enticed. She didn't know what to do. She tried not to move too much, mindful of his leg. "I lied before. I could never stop loving you."

"Pascal," he whispered, kissing her temple. "Feels so good, *petite*. We shouldn't . . . *Mon Dieu*, feels so good." He gave her a gentle tug, trying to shift her on top of him.

Her heart felt as if it would burst from her rib cage. *Lord, she couldn't.* But then she heard his groan as he tried to move her himself. Pascal immediately allowed Harlan to guide her atop him, not wanting him to strain. Harlan pushed the counterpane off them. Using both hands, he worked her skirts to her waist, then stroked his fingers up her legs until they reached the tapes holding her drawers closed. The nightshirt he wore was bunched around his hips. Something warm pulsed against her thigh. Pascal turned and looked down. Harlan's engorged shaft arrowed out from its thick patch of dark curls.

Panic sliced through her. She held herself still and took two deep breaths. She wasn't ready for this. All her romantic notions and Harlan's lovely kisses hadn't prepared her for the reality she faced now. She held herself still as Harlan kissed her neck, lowering her cotton drawers. But when she felt his hands cupping her naked buttocks, she laid her cheek on his chest and burst into tears.

Harlan's hands stopped their stroking. She was crying? *"Mais non, petite."* He dropped her skirts and hugged her, ignoring his own pain. When her cries relaxed into a soft whimper, he held her face in his palms and lifted her head off his chest. He looked at her, really looked at her. This was no vision, no hallucination. Pascal, the woman he loved, lay in bed with him. And she was very frightened.

Harlan kissed her, stroking her lips with his mouth. "I won't hurt you, Pascal. Not again, *mais non.*"

"I wanted to make love to you, Harlan." Her voice broke. Her breath came in halting hiccups. "I wanted to give you everything."

"Shhh, petite. Don't you worry. I'll just hold you. I won't do anything that doesn't feel right." But her body against his, soft and pliant, had felt *very* right to Harlan, too right. His head was swimming. *Zut alors!* What had they given him to drink?

He kissed her again. "I'll stop, *petite,*" he promised. When her breast brushed against his arm, he sucked in his breath and added, "Just tell me to stop."

Pascal returned his kiss, angling for a closer fit with his mouth. She sought entrance with her tongue, quickly granted, initiating an intimacy she'd learned in his arms. Suddenly, she didn't know what frightened her more, the prospect that they would continue their lovemaking—or that they would stop. She only knew she loved Harlan with all her heart and she believed him when he said he would not hurt her again.

She focused on the comfort of his touch, the warmth of his arms. The frantic beat of her pulse calmed, then picked up as his hands again caressed her buttocks, this time through her skirts. A tingling, deep in her stomach, teased, easing away her fears, coaxing her curiosity. Instinctively, she spread her legs wider, bringing her knees to either side of his hips, allowing herself to get closer to him. The effect was startling, a revelation that took her breath away.

"That's it, *mon chou.* Feels good, doesn't it?"

"Yes," she whispered, kissing him, ravishing his mouth. "Oh, Harlan, yes!"

A heat kindled inside Harlan as Pascal rubbed against him. This time, when he lifted her skirt, Pascal helped him. Soon, with some help from Harlan, she'd managed to get most of her clothes off so that she lay in his arms wearing only her chemise. He knew she was young, had barely had time to fill out, but everything was in proportion, soft and sleek. He had one moment of misgiving, but as he lifted the chemise over her head, he reasoned that she was almost seventeen. Where he came from, lots of girls had husbands and babies at her age.

Taking her hips, he guided her until that part of him pressed for entrance. He tried to concentrate on her mouth, tried not to want the sweet union he sensed was so near, but then she nestled against him, rotating, riding him, and he couldn't hold back any longer. Clasping her to him, he plunged inside.

Pascal cried faintly against his mouth, more from surprise than pain. Before she even realized it had gone, the warm pulsing returned, courting her to continue the circling of her hips that had felt like magic. Harlan pulled her thighs higher, tighter against his hips. She caught her breath because of the beauty of his touch. A warm sense of fulfillment teased the edge of her consciousness. The sensation wrapped tightly around her, urging her with the rhythm of Harlan beneath her—until it broke over her in a wave of pleasure.

Chapter 20

Amber rays crested the horizon as Rey opened Bizy's cypress door, allowing Mercedes to precede him. Though his clothes were covered with muck from the bayou, Mercedes had changed into a sapphire promenade gown. The train flowed behind her as she swept past him. She looked cool and elegant despite the sling holding her arm in place. Watching her, Rey experienced a stab of regret. Mac's advice, given so many weeks ago, sounded eerily prophetic: He'd courted disaster when he set out to capture this woman's love.

Mercedes stopped at the bottom of the steps, as if unsure which direction to take. Rey frowned, thinking the choice obvious given the only other direction led to the wine cellar. And then he realized her confusion. She was in fact staring at the cellar door as if already contemplating the cold and lonely hours ahead as Rey's prisoner there. He almost jerked her around to face him, but remembered her injury and forced himself to take her elbow gently instead.

"I do most of my entertaining in the salon," he said, guiding her up the steps. "After you, madame."

It surprised him that he could still feel anger. He'd thought the last six hours had tapped his body clean of that emotion. Yet anger was exactly what warmed his blood as they climbed the stairs. Could she really think him so callous as to hold her prisoner in the cellar? He'd just spent hours nursing her, cleaning her wound, making sure she rested comfortably. Then he remembered he'd never cleared up her misconception about their trip to Bizy—she still believed he planned to hold her prisoner for Gessler.

Isn't that what you wanted, Rey? To torment her with doubts?

Rey's fingers dug into the mahogany banister. At the moment, he didn't know what he wanted. Certainly her fear of him didn't sit well on his conscience as he watched her pale features and injured arm.

At the top of the stairs, he caught sight of Mac carrying a tray of coffee and beignets. The Scotsman almost dropped the lot when he saw Rey with Mercedes.

"Madame De Dreux. And Mr. Parks." Mac regained his composure, giving both of them a welcoming smile as he eyed Mercy and her bandaged arm. "Imagine the two of ye arriving at the same time."

"We came together, Mac."

"Did ye now? Well, it's good to see ye back, sir. And you, madame." He slanted Rey a look. Mac's eyes darted in the direction of Harlan's bedroom.

A cocked-pistol click of warning went off in Rey's head. Something was wrong. "Is Harlan here?"

"That he is, sir," Mac called over his shoulder, leading the group into the salon. "I was just about to bring the lad these." He held up the tray. "Did the evening go well for ye, sir?"

"Not as well as I'd hoped, Mac. And for you?"

"About the same. I expect the Missus is here to ask about Miss Pascal? Ye got the note she sent?"

"Is Pascal all right?" Mercy asked, entering the salon.

She scanned the room, searching for the girl. When she found it empty, she turned her delicate fawn-colored eyes on Mac. Her expression projected such innocence, Rey thought cynically. You would almost believe her incapable of stepping on a flea much less packing a Smith and Wesson.

"Where is she? What's happened to my stepdaughter?"

Mac's glance skimmed over to Rey. He cleared his throat. "The young miss is fine. It's Harlan who's had a wee bit of trouble. He's been bitten by a snake," Mac said. "A water moccasin."

"Oh, my Lord," Mercy whispered.

The fear that rammed through Rey paralyzed, so much so that it took longer than it should for him to piece the proper facts together and wipe out the image of Harlan near death. His gaze dropped to the tray of food Mac carried. A dying man wouldn't need hot coffee and pastries. "Did you send for a doctor?"

"Aye." Mac's considerable brows furrowed. He set the coffee tray on a small table. "For all the good it did the lad. It's the miss who helped him. She brought a special medicine and mixed a salve for the bite. She saved his life, and that's a fact. He's still verra weak. She's not left his side since she brought the potion. I was just going to convince her to get some rest while I watch the lad." Mac spun toward Rey, presenting his back to Mercedes so she could not see his face. "Perhaps Madame De Dreux would like some coffee here in the salon while I show ye the lad, sir?" He wagged his brows, shifting his eyes toward the door.

Rey fixed his gaze on Mercedes. "Stay here."

"But Pascal—"

"Will be out shortly." Rey turned back to Mac. "He's in his room?"

"Aye."

Rey didn't wait for another word. He left the salon with Mac following at his heels. In the central reception hall, Rey took Mac aside. "What the hell's going on?"

Mac looked over his shoulder at the salon door, then leaned closer to Rey. "It's young Miss Pascal," he whispered. "She overheard Harlan and I talking over the mission."

"What!"

Mac nodded. "She came over to bring Harlan flowers last night. She wanted to surprise the lad, and that she did. She hid where we couldna see her. She heard the lot—about Santana, Sotheby, De Dreux. Everything. Harlan chased after the girl to make sure she wouldna warn her father. That's when he got bit by the moccasin. The lass brought him back here. Nursed him through the night, she has. Harlan thinks Miss Pascal will keep quiet. Watching her tonight, Rey, I'd agree."

Cursing under his breath, Rey stepped around Mac, but the Scotsman sped ahead, leading the way to Harlan's bedroom. Swinging the door open, he stepped in—then stopped dead in his tracks. Rey pushed him aside, expecting the worse. But when he managed to sidestep Mac, it wasn't a distressed Pascal and a dying Harlan he found. Through the gauzy curtain of the mosquito netting, he saw they were both in bed. One of Pascal's naked limbs was wrapped intimately over Harlan's legs.

"Jesus, Mary, and Joseph," Mac whispered under his breath.

With a soft sigh, Harlan curled Pascal closer to him. His hand rested on Pascal's bared hip with casual familiarity.

Mac turned to Rey. His red brows shot up, disappearing under the graying curls. "Guess the lad's feeling a might better."

Rey turned for the door without answering. Mac brought up the rear, closing the door quietly behind them. In the hall, they watched each other, both speechless.

"I don't understand it," Mac said, breaking the silence. "When I left the two of them, I thought Harlan couldn't sit up, much less . . ." His wide eyes trailed back to the door.

"Apparently he was inspired." Rey slammed his fist

against the wall. "Damn all! This is exactly what I needed. Harlan bedding down with De Dreux's daughter."

"If I'd thought it even possible, Rey," Mac said, defending himself, "I wouldna have left the two alone."

"The girl's madly in love with him, Mac. You knew that. After seeing him almost die, I'm not sure I'd be surprised by her actions."

"Maybe he didn't . . . perhaps the lad couldn't . . ."

Rey shook his head. "I don't hold out much hope. I just haven't been that lucky of late."

"What are we going to tell the lass's mother?"

"The truth . . . in good time. Get the girl out of that bed and dressed. Rouse Harlan if you can. I'll need to speak to him before I let Pascal see Mercedes."

Rey passed Mac on his way back to the salon. Mac hooked a hand around Rey's arm. "Get her out of bed and dressed?" the Scotsman asked. "And how am I to be doing that without embarrassing the life out of the lass?"

"Knock. Very loudly."

"Do you think I don't know what you're doing, Rey?" Panic flooded Mercy, sweeping away her caution. "You're purposely keeping me from Pascal! Is she a prisoner too? Are you going to use her against me?"

"She's safe and sound, Mercedes. I told you that. She's just . . . very involved with Harlan at the moment. You'll see her soon enough."

Mercy shook her head, not believing a word of it. "Then why won't you let me go to her? I just want to see her."

"That's not possible right now."

Something was wrong. Mercy sensed it. The way Rey looked away each time she mentioned Pascal's name—he was keeping something from her. Suddenly, it wasn't Harlan she imagined near death from a moccasin bite; Pascal lay on the bed, racked with pain from the snake's poison. Rey could have lied to her. Perhaps that was the very reason he kept Pascal hidden away.

Mercy's heart pounded in her chest. Her shoulder burned with each anxious move she made. She had to know her stepdaughter was all right. Pascal could be fighting for her life! Mercy glanced at the tray Mac had left on the table—a good distance from the door.

"All right, Rey," she said, taking a deep breath to calm herself. She walked toward the door, but sat down on the settee closest to it when Rey took a step to follow her. "But truly, I wouldn't have believed you capable of using my stepdaughter against me."

Rey sighed, as if tired of refuting her. "What's between you and me has nothing to do with your stepdaughter, Mercedes."

She took a handkerchief from the Sicilienne pocket of her gown. She made a point of waving it in front of her face as if fatigued. "Is the coffee still hot? Could you pour me a cup? It's been a very long night."

"Of course."

She sat carefully on the edge of the settee and folded the handkerchief back into her pocket as Rey bent over the tray. He picked up a delicate cup with one hand; with the other, he lifted the coffeepot. His gaze stayed on the cup as he poured. "I think what you're forgetting here, Mercedes, is that—"

The instant the first stream of black liquid hit the cup, she dashed for the door.

"Dammit!" Rey spilled the blistering hot coffee across his wrist. He lost precious seconds putting the pot and half-filled cup on the table. In the hall, he was just in time to see Mercy bolt past Mac into Harlan's room.

Rey raced for the door. Reaching Mac, he grabbed the handle—only to have Mac clamp one ham-size fist over the knob.

"Ye canna go in there, Rey," he said, shocked. "The lass might not be dressed yet."

"The lass could be telling her stepmother all about our mission this very second."

Mac frowned, but his grip didn't loosen. "I'll not believe it. She's sweet as candy on Harlan. She'd not betray the lad so quickly."

"I can't rely on a girl's infatuation."

"It's more than that! She loves the lad, took care of him—"

"Save it, Mac. I'm a little skeptical about the power of true love these days."

Rey pushed Mac aside and turned the knob.

Mercy rushed into the room and slammed the door shut. She leaned against the jamb, catching her breath. She ventured inside, her gaze scanning the dark chamber as her vision slowly adjusted to the muted light of one candle. Pascal's gasp immediately centered Mercy's attention on the half-tester bed.

The mosquito netting had been pulled back. On the bed, Harlan lay on his stomach, his naked back partially covered by the counterpane, his mouth slack against a pillow as he snored quietly. Her stepdaughter stood at his bedside, bent at her waist—half-in and half-out of her dress.

"Mercedes!" She dropped the gown and ran to Mercy wearing only her drawers and chemise. "Thank the heavens, you're here!" She hugged her tightly.

At Mercy's groan, Pascal stepped back and stared at the makeshift sling holding her arm. "You've been hurt!" Both her hands covered her mouth. "He hurt you and brought you here." The words tumbled out in a rush. "You're his prisoner. And it's all my fault."

Mercy heard the door open behind her. "Don't say another word, Pascal."

But Pascal wasn't listening, just watching Mercy with guilt-ridden eyes. "I tried to warn you, Mercedes. But Harlan was bitten by a moccasin and I couldn't leave him. I know I should have gone to Kate's, or sent a message—"

Despite the pain the movement cost her, Mercy

clamped her hand over Pascal's mouth. Pascal's eyes grew wide—then wider still as she focused on the door behind Mercy.

Rey waited at the threshold. As he watched De Dreux's daughter by the dim light of the fire, her words echoed in his head. *Tried to warn you: sent a note to Kate's.*

She knew. Pascal De Dreux knew Mercedes was Santana Rose.

A distant memory nudged at him as he studied the two women, their heads bent together like conspirators. For some reason, he remembered Pascal's horse in the stables when he and Mercy arrived this morning. Rey frowned, thinking of that big bay . . . and then the memory jogged into place.

That first time, when Santana had held up the coach, there had been a young boy riding a bay horse. A boy with dark hair.

His eyes met Mercy's. "She's one of your gang." It wasn't a question.

Mercedes stepped in front of her stepdaughter, shielding her from Rey's view. "Is *this* what you didn't want me to see?" She glanced over to the bed where Harlan slept and Pascal's clothes lay in a pile on the floor. "Is this what you call 'very involved with Harlan'?"

Rey smiled coldly at her righteous tone. He wouldn't be so easily diverted. He crossed his arms and leaned against the doorjamb. "It looks like we have a bit more to discuss than I thought."

On the bed, Harlan mumbled in his sleep and turned onto his side.

Mercy licked her lips, a gesture Rey knew meant she was thinking fast. "You said you wouldn't use her against me, Rey. That I could trust you. Don't you think enough harm has been done to Pascal this night? My carriage is waiting outside. Let me help her dress and send her home."

"No, *maman.* I won't leave you here."

He pushed off the door. "It appears your stepdaughter hasn't tired of our hospitality. When Miss De Dreux is ready, she can join us in the salon." He glanced at Harlan snoring softly on the bed. Satisfied with the Pinkerton's condition, Rey swept his hand out in a mocking bow toward the door. "After you, Mercedes."

Mercy squeezed Pascal's fingers with her good hand, trying to calm the wide-eyed look of horror on her stepdaughter's face. Her own emotions pitched up and down like a teeter-totter: relief at seeing Pascal alive, disappointment for the scene of seduction she'd walked into, and now, terror for Pascal's safety. The latter took immediate priority. She had to convince Rey that Pascal had nothing to do with Santana.

She flashed her stepdaughter a reassuring smile. "Get dressed, Pascal. I'll wait for you in the salon. I need to discuss some things with Mr. Parks."

Mercy passed Rey into the loggia. In her mind, she searched for a plan, some bit of reasoning she could use to convince him that his wild accusation was just that—unbelievable and untrue. But the cogs and gears in her head seemed frozen, jammed into place by her fears for Pascal.

When she entered the salon, she rounded the tête-à-tête and looked back. Rey waited at the door, guarding the exit.

She licked her dry lips. "How could you even imagine Pascal—"

"Don't waste your breath, Mercedes. I recognized her. That first time she rode beside you on a big bay horse—the very horse now settled in my stables. She wore a large hat and a red bandanna. I can't imagine why I didn't see it before. Her disguise wasn't nearly as sophisticated as yours." His smile chilled her. "Blinded by love, I guess." He dropped down into the chair next to the door, extended his legs, and crossed one boot over the other. "That takes care of righteous denials. What's the next line of defense?"

Watching Rey, Mercy imagined a cat settling down before the mouse hole. The light reflected off his hair, turning it a startling white in contrast to the shadows around him. She remembered how she'd always believed his remarkable features the very incarnation of good. A man dedicated to justice—it's what had attracted her to him from the first. When had they changed sides?

And then, for the first time in a long and arduous night, she realized the obvious: They hadn't changed sides at all.

Mercy crossed the room and dropped to the carpet beside Rey. She brought her eyes level with his. "Rey, I can help you. I know who you really are, why you're here, and I can help you."

Just a second's pause escaped before he answered. "What the hell are you talking about?"

"The first time I robbed you," she explained, excited now, "I found a letter in Mr. Everard's wallet—from Robert Pinkerton. It outlined your operation with Benoit. A Secret Service agent and a Pinkerton detective here to investigate my husband for illegal gambling. Unfortunately, it failed to mention Sotheby and counterfeiting."

His eyes turned the color of a piece of frozen pond water. The easy recline against the upholstery tightened into coiled anticipation as he leaned forward. He stared at Mercy, his eyes unblinking.

"I could have given you away, Rey." She spoke quickly, trying to show him she could be trusted. "I could have used the information to gain my freedom."

"And now you will." There was absolutely no emotion to the words.

She shook her head. "I'm not bargaining for my silence. Don't you see? We want the same thing; we have from the first—justice. Let Pascal go. She's just a child. She's not some hardened criminal. She rode with Santana as a lark. But she's given it all up now. She knows what she did was wrong. Release her and let me help you. I can catch Harrison Sotheby for you."

He sprang to his feet, giving her his back as he paced to the hearth. "That's not a very tempting offer. I don't need your help, Mercedes."

"You're wrong!" She dogged his steps. She held nothing back, willing to risk everything to secure her stepdaughter's safety and earn back her own lost honor. "There's something else you don't know. Two weeks ago, you were spying around Catalan Kate's. When you tried to pick the lock at the side door, my men knocked you senseless and brought you upstairs. They claimed they'd found a spy. I was meeting with Sotheby when they dragged you in."

He turned to face her. The change in expression was so slight, she might not have seen it if she hadn't been standing so close.

"Sotheby was there?" The flicker of shock sparked again. "He saw me?"

"Not your face." She assured him. "You were on your stomach, your head turned away. Your hat covered your hair almost entirely. But *I* recognized you. I tried to protect you, Rey. I made up some excuse about you being a spurned lover, but Sotheby's a very suspicious man. If he linked you to me, he'd realize your participation in his lottery scheme with Benoit isn't aboveboard. I couldn't take the risk he might recognize you. That's why I kidnapped you when I found out you were riding into town to meet with him. I couldn't let him see you again."

Rey scrubbed his face with his hands. Each new piece of information slammed into his head with the force of a bullet. Mercedes disguised as Santana, the baby, his spying exposed to Sotheby. But he was still alert enough for the last bit of intelligence to slide into its place in the Mercedes/Santana puzzle. The kidnapping hadn't been a game. She'd been trying to protect him.

Confusion boiled and churned inside him. He knew the difference between right and wrong. It was a line that he'd never crossed before New Orleans. Yet the two seemed so mixed up in Mercedes. It seemed his affair with her had catapulted him past the clearly marked boundaries he'd always respected, earning him this turmoil.

Maybe it wasn't a line at all, Parks, more like a cliff you fell off.

Yes, that seemed possible. By falling in love with De Dreux's wife, he hadn't passed a simple mark; he'd fallen off a precipice and plunged into the chaos below.

Rey paced across the hearth, suddenly too anxious to remain still. He ignored Mercy, focusing on how to salvage his plans against Sotheby. *That's it, Parks, think of the mission. The good guys against the bad guys—the basics.*

"Dammit! I needed to get close to Sotheby," he said under his breath. "I *needed* to gain his confidence to find out where he keeps the printing press for the queer— without the plates as evidence, he'll slip right through my fingers. He'll beat any charges I bring, just as he has time and time again!"

Mercy blocked his path, a force not to be dismissed. "I can help you. Sotheby trusts me. We already have a relationship of sorts. I could pretend I found out about the counterfeiting, that I want in on the money. I can get the information you want."

He grabbed her arms, carefully avoiding her hurt shoulder but digging his fingers into her skin. "I don't want you anywhere near that animal! Do you understand me, Mercedes?"

Mercy's breath caught. Rey's expression lodged her arguments in her throat. He seemed more than shocked by her suggestion—he appeared terrified. As if he wanted to protect her.

Instantly, the expression vanished. The planes of his face shifted into those of a gambler calculating odds. He hooked his arm through hers and drew her to the settee, sitting down beside her. "All right, you've got your bargaining chip. When I meet with Sotheby, if he recognizes me, I'll use you as an alibi. I'm the extra security you hired to make sure Benoit takes the bait and sinks more than he can afford into Sotheby's deal. You brought me in, the same way you approached Sotheby. I've lent De Dreux enough money to dig a hole so deep he'll never see light again; that was my job from the first. Anything else I should know?"

She shook her head, a mixture of relief and misery turning her stomach. "You'll let Pascal go?"

"Has she read the letter? Has she known about our mission here all along?" he asked, trying to determine if the girl could be trusted.

"She knows only that you're both government agents. I didn't have the heart to tell her you were investigating her father. Until very recently, she didn't know Benoit was behind the smugglings. And I didn't want her to think Mr. Everard wasn't sincere in his courtship."

Rey's eyes became unfocused, as if he weren't seeing Mercy seated beside him, but an entirely different scenario. He cursed under his breath.

"What is it, Rey?"

He turned more fully to Mercy on the settee. There was a hint of regret in his eyes. "She knows everything now. Pascal overheard Harlan and my valet talking about our plans—against you *and* De Dreux. That's why Mac kept her here. When she ran away, Harlan chased after her to bring her back to Bizy. He was afraid she'd go warn her father."

Mercy stared at the fire, shaking her head. "She was trying to warn me, not Benoit. She loves Harlan so much —she would never have said anything to harm him. How hurt she must have been to realize . . ." Again, she shook her head.

Rey reached out to comfort Mercy, but lowered his hand to the settee before he touched her. He pressed his lips together, brooding over Harlan. The younger man had always reminded Rey of Christopher. In many ways, perhaps because Rey was older and the Pinkerton's superior, he felt responsible for Harlan's many blunders. Thank

God the Pinkerton had survived the moccasin bite—now Rey could wring his neck.

Someone coughed at the door. Rey looked up to see a properly clothed Pascal standing at the threshold with Mac hovering behind. She'd pulled her hair back from her face with a ribbon. Her dress was a simple smock devoid of the sophisticated drapery and lace decorating Mercy's gown. He noticed she'd made an effort to clean the skirt of its smudges of dirt, but the hem was crooked where it appeared she'd torn off pieces of material. Standing at the door, her hands clasped before her and her eyes cast at the tips of her slippers, she looked young. He turned to Mercy. Her face held the same expression that had graced the faces of concerned parents over the centuries.

"Harlan's awake now, sir." Behind Pascal, Mac jerked his head down the hall.

Getting his valet's message loud and clear, Rey stood. "I'll leave you two alone."

Mercy seized his hand. "What about Pascal?" she whispered.

"We'll discuss her after I speak with Harlan." Rey walked two steps, then stopped. Turning back to Mercedes, he couldn't help but add, "Don't worry. I'll make certain she's not hurt more than necessary."

Mercy mulled over the significance of what she hoped he'd intended to be an encouraging statement before turning to Pascal. Her stepdaughter seemed planted at the threshold, her head bowed like a wilted flower.

"Do you think I'm awful?" she whispered when Rey and Mac left the salon.

Mercy ran to the door. She took up both of Pascal's hands, drawing her into the room, then into her arms despite her aching shoulder. "No," she murmured. "But I have a few doubts about myself. Oh, Pascal. I've done a wretched job of mothering you—"

Pascal's fingers covered Mercy's mouth. "You can't blame yourself, Mercedes. I've only lived at L'Isle des

Rêves one year with you there as my stepmother. I've done all my growing up outside your influence. Perhaps if I hadn't . . . You're not responsible for my actions tonight." She twisted away, raised her fist to her mouth. "Oh, *maman*. I'm so very frightened."

Mercy stepped up behind her. She didn't know what to say, or how to reassure Pascal. She settled for resting a comforting hand on the girl's shoulder.

"When I woke up this morning," Pascal said staring into the hearth, "it all hit me—what I'd done. Impulsive Pascal, jumping in with both feet and her eyes closed. Harlan might not even like me any more, much less—" She gasped. She looked over her shoulder; tears sparkled in her eyes. "Can there be a child?" Her voice trembled. "After only this once?"

Knowing what she wanted to hear, Mercy said, "It's doubtful. We'll just have to wait and see."

"I didn't even say good-bye," she cried, stepping back into Mercy's embrace. "I was so scared when Harlan woke up, so embarrassed. I just ran out of the room when he called my name."

"I'm sure he understands." Mercy tilted Pascal's face up to hers. "He cares about you," she said firmly, as if her insistence could make it true. "He must."

Pascal brushed back her tears and walked back to the settee. She sat down. "It *was* beautiful." As she spoke, there was a sweet wistful edge to her voice. "He was so gentle. I only wish . . . well, at least I got the potion." She clasped her hands together on her lap. "I suppose all that's left is for me to accept responsibility for what I've done and go on."

Such mature words she'd uttered, and yet, when she gazed up at Mercy, she looked very young, and very frightened.

"No, Pascal," Mercy said, sitting down beside her. "That's not all that's left. There's one more thing you must accept. You have to understand that no matter what happens, I'll be here to protect you. From Harlan, from your father"—she folded her stepdaughter into her arms—"from the world if need be."

Rey burst into Harlan's room. He would have slammed the door shut if Mac hadn't walked in behind him.

Harlan sat up in the bed, alive and awake but looking as if he desperately wished he were neither. His bloodshot eyes were a virtual collage of red, white, and blue, on the most patriotic order. His furrowed brow and squint bespoke a colossal headache, and his slouch against the pillows indicated a man less than up to snuff. If Rey hadn't known better, he'd say Harlan was fighting off the aftereffects of alcoholic bacchanalia.

He didn't feel the least bit sorry for him.

"I don't suppose he would survive a good thrashing?" he asked Mac, taking out one of the Choctaws and lighting up.

"Not too likely."

"One punch?"

"Ye could give it a try."

"I'll tell you what," Harlan interrupted in a weak voice. "If I had the strength to do it, I'd beat the shit out of myself, *mais* sure."

"Oh, no, Harlan." Rey crushed the lit cigarette in his hand and dropped it to the floor as he advanced on the bed. "You're not getting off so easily. Do you have any idea . . . even the slightest notion . . . just how much damage you've caused?"

"*Mon Dieu*, Rey. Do you think I'd hurt *la petite* if I were in my right mind? I can't even remember half of what happened, just bits and pieces. I thought I was dreaming at first. When I realized I wasn't . . . well, it was jus' too late."

"I did pour the brandy down 'im, Rey," Mac said, empathy slipping into his voice. "Just like that fool doctor ordered. And maybe the potion—"

"Don't make excuses for him, Mac. You have no idea what our companion here has been up to."

Harlan dropped his face in his hands. "You can't say or do anything that makes me feel worse than I do, Rey. You should have seen her this morning. I woke up jus' as she finished dressing, *la pauvre*. When I realized what I'd done, I called out to her . . . I wanted to explain, to let her know I'd make it right. She jus' ran out of the room."

Rey smiled, a cold twist of his lips he spared for criminals under interrogation. "And how do you plan to make it right?"

Harlan's head lolled up. "Why, I'll marry her, that's what."

The Pinkerton watched Rey and Mac with such wide-eyed innocence, it almost hurt to look at him.

"She's the daughter of a wealthy planter." Rey fired out the words as Mac dropped back, letting him take over Harlan's dressing-down. "Why would she marry a poor Cajun boy from the bayous?"

"Pascal loves me! She could be carrying my child."

"Baby or not, her daddy will think he can buy her better."

"Her father's a no-account—"

"Whom you've done your best to alienate. I wonder what he'll say when you get down on bended knee and ask for his only daughter's hand? Do you think 'pretty please' will suffice?"

"Com'on, Rey. You know De Dreux's days are numbered! *Tonnerre!* Pascal will need me more than ever soon enough."

"Sure of that, are you?"

"*Mais oui.* Any day now, Sotheby will be settin' up a meeting and we'll have him and De Dreux like two crabs in a fishing net."

Rey shook his head, stepping away from the bed. "Why didn't I see it, Mac? The sheer innocence, the inexperience—the stupidity! It was there all along, wasn't it? I just refused to see it."

"Sonofabitch," Harlan mumbled under his breath. He looked at Rey as if the simple fact of keeping his head steady took a monumental effort. "For God's sake, man. Make sense."

"Do you know how many criminals I've seen slip through my fingers, Harlan? And none of them had the *incredible* advantage of a letter from Robert Pinkerton outlining my operation!"

Harlan's color blended with the linens behind him.

"When were you going to reveal that little gem? *Hmm?* After De Dreux put a bullet in my back?" Rey let the words sink in, watching Harlan take in the significance of his mistakes. "When I get through with you, Harlan, there won't be a detective agency in the world that will hire you."

"*Dieu,* he got the letter?" Harlan closed his eyes. When he opened them, he looked like he was going to be ill on the bed. "I thought for sure he wouldn't get it, that if Santana's thugs found Robert's letter, they wouldn't bother to read it even if they could, *tu comprends*? It was tucked in the wallet they stole that first day, in a secret compartment—it never even mentioned Sotheby, not him, *mais non.* I really believed they'd take the money and throw away the rest. Rey, I wanted the bastard so badly. . . ."

"That you risked all our lives by withholding valuable information."

Harlan's chin fell to his chest. "I was afraid you'd call it all off—"

"Ye limb of Beelzebub!" Mac raged behind Rey. "How could ye make such a miserable error?" He turned to Rey, his eyes burning with righteous ire. "I knew the lad was trouble!" He wagged his finger at Rey. "I told ye from the first. He's been keeping something from us all along."

"Mac's right," Harlan whispered. "I haven't been honest with you from the beginning."

Rey pushed aside Mac and sat on the edge of the bed. "I'm listening now, Harlan."

The Cajun fell back against the pillows. "It's De Dreux." He examined the canopy of the tester bed as he spoke. "I wanted his hide strung up tighter than a gator's set for market. The convicts who work at the plantation— my brother was one of them. Forced to work because he didn't have the money to pay the fine or prove his innocence." When he looked at Rey, there were tears in his eyes. "They killed him. They worked him to death so that De Dreux could have his L'Isle des Rêves, his damn island of dreams."

Revenge. Rey recognized its draw, the seductive call of blood for blood. He knew just what a man was willing to sacrifice for its taste.

"*Eh bien.* So I've ruined it all," Harlan whispered. "Pascal, the mission, everything's ruined."

Mac's hand rested on Rey's shoulder. Rey looked up. He could see Harlan's story had moved Mac to sympathy. "Och, lad, we all make mistakes. Let 'im rest now, Rey. He was near death not so long ago."

Rey studied Harlan's miserable expression—the shadowed blue eyes. He took out a Choctaw, not looking at Harlan, keeping busy as he lit the cigarette. "You haven't quite ruined everything," Rey heard himself say.

Harlan's head jerked up. "What?"

"The letter . . ." Rey inhaled deeply, thinking on his response, determining how much to reveal, then deciding that it was well beyond the time for complete honesty. "De Dreux never saw it. I found out about Robert's letter from Santana Rose. As it turns out, she wants to help us."

"Santana?" Harlan's hopeful expression vanished.

"Ye'd trust that she-devil?" Mac shouted in disbelief.

"Thanks to Harlan here, I don't seem to have any other option, Mac. And by the way; be careful what you call the lady." Rey took another puff; blew out the smoke in a single breath. He grinned wickedly, knowing that for once someone else besides himself would be knocked over by the night's revelation. "If you speak loud enough, she might hear you. You see, she's just down the hall." He studied the glowing tip of the Choctaw before meeting Mac's puzzled expression. "And I'd hate to have to defend you from her—not when she might be carrying my child."

Rey marched down the loggia, heading for the salon, just as frustrated as he'd been while waiting the endless minutes for Gessler to find his way through the swamp. He'd told Mac and Harlan everything: his affair with Mercedes, the possibility of a child, how he'd discovered her true identity—her relationship with Sotheby and Pascal's involvement. He'd left out nothing. And when he'd waited for much needed advice, neither Mac nor Harlan had been able to spout anything but indignant accusations at Rey—as if he were the criminal under trial.

"You're not going to turn Pascal in to Gessler!" Harlan had shouted.

"The lass saved Harlan's life," Mac added almost in chorus.

"The 'lass' held him up at gunpoint," Rey corrected.

"It's clear to me the ladies are just trying to set some foul wrongs aright."

"They're highway robbers," Rey reminded them viciously.

"They only steal from De Dreux and his cronies, from what ye've said. Seems almost poetic to me."

"There are laws that protect people from De Dreux. That's why we're here, dammit!"

Mac snorted. "Oh, aye. I forgot all about our good Constable Gessler. Och, I'm sure he'd have helped the lass. Fool her not to ask."

"Gessler's wrongs don't change the fact Santana is a criminal."

"*Eh bien,* Rey. *Mais,* if you didn't trust Santana," Harlan interjected, "why did you take her to her men in the swamps? She could have had you killed, *mais* sure."

"The lad's right, Rey. Ye'd never have agreed to helping her if ye really thought her as vile as ye're painting the lass now."

They'd gone round after round—Harlan and Mac defending Pascal and Santana, Rey drowning in the moral dilemma he faced. No matter what the other two said, Rey couldn't forget her lies, her betrayal of his trust and his love. Nor could he dismiss his obligations as a lawman. But in the end, it wasn't moral conviction that had ended the debate.

"I think Santana's right," Harlan had said. "Sotheby might recognize you for sure. It's safer to let her help us. We could use her to get Sotheby, operate through—"

"And get her killed? Brilliant plan, Harlan." He tossed his cigarette to the floor, savagely grinding it out beneath his boot. "Simply brilliant. I'd put it on par with handing over Robert Pinkerton's letter."

He'd spun on his heel to quit the room, stopping only when Mac called out, "What do ye plan to do, Rey?"

He hadn't turned back to face them. Staring at the door, he'd answered, "I've already sacrificed one woman to Sotheby. I'll be damned if he gets his hands on Mercy." Grabbing the knob, he'd added, "I'll get those plates my way. Then I plan to put as much distance between me and Santana as is humanly possible."

Now walking down the dark and empty entrance hall to the salon, Rey considered the one bond that would prevent him from carrying out his plans. The baby. What would he do if Mercedes were carrying his child?

Near the entrance to the parlor, he slowed, hearing a lilting cadence—the subdued music of a woman singing. He stopped at the threshold and peered inside. Before the fire, Mercedes sat on the settee with Pascal cradled on her lap. The flames from the hearth reflected a soft amber glow, surrounding them in a golden halo. Mercy stroked her stepdaughter's hair, smoothing the girl's curls from her face in a languid caress that Rey knew would be soothing. As he watched and listened, Mercy's voice lowered to a gentle humming of the lullaby.

He rested his forehead against the molding at the door. The heat of anger vanished in a chilling sweep of emotions that left only anguish. In the swamps of Louisiana, he'd lost something precious—and he didn't think he possessed the courage to ever reach out and seek it again.

The Medal

It is a comfort that the medal has two sides . . . There is much vice and misery in the world, I know; but more virtue and happiness, I believe . . .

———————

—Thomas Jefferson, *Writings,* 1810

Chapter 21

Mercy lounged back in her chair, one dark-trousered leg propped over the arm. Beyond the slits of her mask, she peered out the second-story window of the saloon to the balcony across Gallatin Street. Despite the noon hour, there was little activity outside. Most everyone had stayed in their beds, recovering from Mardi Gras' last celebration.

As she waited in the quiet room, her thoughts turned to Rey, a phenomenon that occurred with unrelenting regularity of late. Two weeks had passed since he'd released her and Pascal, telling Mercy that he expected nothing from her but continued silence over his mission—and, of course, news about his status as a father. As for Santana Rose, he didn't give a damn if she spent the rest of her days ravaging the countryside. His words had hurt, but not nearly as much as the cold look he'd given her as he'd shut the door to the carriage—a look she'd seen repeatedly ever since.

That night had been agony for Mercy, both emotionally and physically. In the carriage, she'd been obligated to remove her sling before facing Benoit. As it turned out, he was still in town, nestled in the arms of his new mistress—the girl Kate had assigned to curb Benoit's sadistic desires. Benoit hadn't returned for two days. By that time, Mercy had almost full use of her arm. She understood from Kate that her husband had become quite enamored with Teresa, a woman who—though thirty with many years experience in the trade—looked as young and untouched as the sweetest sixteen-year-old. Teresa claimed to have mastered Benoit, telling Kate that he enjoyed receiving her blows and commands to degrade himself. Apparently, Benoit delighted in the role of slave far more than that of master.

Benoit's newfound fulfillment showed in his frequent absences and buoyant mood when home. Under his direction, Mercy had hosted a costume ball at L'Isle des Rêves a week ago. While all of New Orleans prepared for the saturnalian days before Mardi Gras, she had suffered over her upcoming meeting with Rey, hoping for once to breach his wall of indifference. But the night of the ball, Rey had appeared at L'Isle des Rêves dressed as the Sheriff of Nottingham, his message clear: There could be no compromise. They were enemies. Out of some morbid impulse, Mercy had come as Eve, a woman fallen from grace. She'd worn a simple gown trimmed in green velvet fig leaves and had laced a crown of laurel leaves in her hair. She'd carried a basket of apples and had offered the fruit teasingly to her male guests. After one look at her costume, Rey had kept to the opposite side of the ballroom for the evening.

Along with his satisfaction from Teresa, Benoit seemed to thrive on the new tension between Mercy and Rey. Ever cognizant of their relationship, Benoit had soon realized the two had quarreled. With malicious glee, he'd done his best to foist them together over the past week, inviting Rey to the plantation on the slightest whim. Rey's glacial regard on those occasions had left Mercy sorely wounded and Benoit throwing his arm around Rey's shoulders like a comrade. How Benoit had taunted Mercy, saying that her little affair with Parks had proven him right: Despite all her beauty, she had nothing to offer a man between her legs.

She only wished her husband's assessments true, that

her womb were made of ice as Benoit constantly claimed. Ice could not bear fruit. But Mercy's monthly was overdue, her breasts tender, and she'd fought nausea the past five mornings. She'd felt the same symptoms once before in her life and knew well what they signified.

She hadn't found the courage to tell Rey.

It wasn't the kind of thing you could jot down in a note as he seemed to expect. Yet, his hostile attitude made it impossible to approach him in person. How did you tell a man who despised you that you carried his child?

Everything she'd cared about had somehow soured, Mercy thought, turning away from the saloon window. She knew she couldn't face Rey with the news of a child—not until she had something more to offer. To that end, she sat in the upholstered chair, her leg swinging over the arm, waiting patiently for Sotheby to arrive for their meeting.

The Wednesday after Mardi Gras—the first day of Lent —Mercy was doing her own kind of penance.

Mercy heard the door open. She dropped both feet to the floor and watched Sotheby step inside the chamber. His long angular nose and his cigar dominated his profile, leading the rest of him as he met her halfway across the room. His dark brown jacket and pants seemed to hang off his frame. At a guess, she would say the suit was a full size bigger than the lanky man beneath.

"I'm glad you were willing to see me on such short notice, *monsieur,*" she told Sotheby, returning to her chair. "As I said in my note, I am very disappointed that you would take advantage of me as you have."

"Disappointed?" Sotheby laughed, throwing back his head to reveal his enlarged Adam's apple. "Because I used you as my boodle carrier? I'm always looking for a good passer, Santana. I'd of let you in on it if I ever thought you might *want* the money." He puffed on the ever-present cigar, his dark eyes narrowed on her. "Never thought that was what you were after."

Mercy took out the bill Rey had thrown in her face two

weeks before and fanned herself with the money. "But I did not know you were part of such a lucrative business, *monsieur.*"

"So you want in, Santana?"

She straightened the five-dollar note between her gloved hands. *"Oui."*

"And what's in it for me?"

Mercy looked up into Sotheby's greedy face. It was the face of a man who could smell when he had the advantage. She pushed back the revulsion that bubbled inside her as she stood and stepped closer to Sotheby, stopping only when she was within arm's reach. Forcing her hand up the lapel of his coat, she gave a silent thanks for her gloves as her fingertips reached the curve of his face and she stroked his chin. "But why should you want to cut me out? I thought we are friends, *vraiment*?"

He smiled, displaying a set of tobacco-stained teeth. His hungry expression showed he liked the change in her. "I've always wanted to be friends. But you haven't been half accommodating, Santana."

"In the past," she said, leaning closer, smelling his stale breath, "I acted foolishly, *non*?" Drawing on the knowledge she'd learned in Rey's arms, she played her role of seductress. She had to convince Sotheby of her goodwill. "Before, I did not know you had so much to offer."

"Now you're talking." Sotheby ditched his cigar in the hearth. A clammy hand wrapped around the back of her neck while Sotheby's other pinched at her waist, tugging her against him. "I always knew you'd come around. And I'll admit, I'm kinda disappointed it took so damn long. But I'm a forgiving man," he whispered, his breath reeking more foul as his mouth inched toward hers.

Mercy forced herself to endure his kiss, almost gagging when his tongue snaked past her lips and his mouth sucked on hers. She blanked her mind to all sensation. She couldn't allow the man responsible for the death of Rey's wife to walk free. If she had to accept this slobbering and more to trap Sotheby, so be it. For Rey, for redemption, she had to get those plates. But when his fingers pulled at the ties to her mask, Mercy breathed a sigh of relief and slipped out of his arms. "*Non, monsieur.* Not . . . yet. I want a demonstration of your good faith before I reveal all."

He frowned for an instant before a crafty grin slithered across his face. "You think I'm dumb, Santana? That I'd give everything just for a good toss between the sheets?"

Mercy searched her mind for something she could dangle before him—a carrot big enough to coax him into trusting her. And then she thought of what Rey had told her. Sotheby was the man buying Benoit's smuggled women.

"Perhaps I can promise more, *monsieur.*"

"Keep talking."

"I can give you women."

"Women?" Sotheby repeated.

"*Oui.*" The word was an inhaled breath. "De Dreux's business. You have heard perhaps that he's had problems delivering his wares?"

Sotheby watched her slyly. "The only thing Benny's been delivering lately is promises."

"That is because I have been stealing his women from the bayou. I see he did not admit as much to you, that Santana had the best of him. Well, it is true. I take all that De Dreux smuggles into the swamps. Perhaps you might have use for these women?"

"Well I'll be damned!" A genuine smile of pleasure crossed his lips. He slapped his hand on his thigh. "That's been it all along! I knew you were too smart to work up such a steam for revenge. You wanted to bust his business and take over the market. I got to hand it to you, Santana. You're one slick lady. After boodle, girls are my best business. Sure as hell we can deal together. I always gave Benny a fair price. Can't see as how I wouldn't do the same for you."

Something ugly formed inside Mercy, congealing at the pit of her stomach. Though she'd never doubted Rey's information on Sotheby, hearing the man admit his part in the smugglings brought back the sickly unease she'd experienced when she'd first heard of Sotheby's involvement. *Penance,* she reminded herself.

"Yeah," he continued with a pirate's smile. "I like the idea, Santana. You and me working together for real cash has appeal to it. But I want more than a partnership for money." He grabbed her, holding her too tight. "I'll take this as well."

He slammed his lips against hers and pinched her breast. Mercy forced herself to endure it, pulling away only when she thought she couldn't hide her disgust a second longer.

"Yessirree." Sotheby smacked his lips, as if he'd just finished something tasty. "That's more like it." He took out a new cigar, bit off the end and drew on it while he held a match to the tip. "I'll let you know when and where to deliver the girls, but we can definitely do business together."

Mercy watched his wet lips pull on the cigar. An anger seeped through her, reaching deep into her heart. This man had been responsible for the women Benoit smuggled, had killed Rey's wife. The rage seared away her disgust and her doubts, filling her with strength. She thought of her earlier comparison. If Frankenstein's monster could bring about its maker's downfall, Mercy planned to put her powers to good use as well.

In one swift motion, she grabbed the cigar from Sotheby's mouth, leaving him wide-eyed and gaping.

"I want more than Benoit's business, *monsieur,*" she said, throwing the cigar to the floor.

"What the hell—"

She pushed Sotheby up against the hearth, her lips drawn in a curved line of menace. "I want in with the boodle, Sotheby. I want money. More money than the women will get me. *Comprenez!* The counterfeit, Sotheby. You let me into your operation. You let me see those fine plates, *where* you make the queer, *how* you make it, and then we'll be friends, *mon ami.* Friends like you've never dreamed of in your wildest fantasies." Her voice dropped low, with danger and promise. She pressed her hand against the crotch of his pants and squeezed. She could see her aggression excited him. She suspected the sense of danger that surrounded her had always been part of her appeal for Sotheby. "I want to show you those fantasies, *mon chou,* " she whispered close to his mouth, then pulled back just as their lips touched. "But first, the boodle."

"All right," he said, panting. "First the boodle. Just let me contact one more party. I got me a real sweet deal you'll want in on. I'll send you a message soon."

Rey held the folded piece of foolscap Sotheby's man had just delivered. Breaking the seal, he read the splattered lines of ink quickly. With each word, a drone of excitement hummed in his veins.

"What is it?" Harlan asked from the settee. "What's the note say?"

Rey looked up from the creamed-colored paper. "It's from Sotheby. He wants me to meet him. It seems he's ready to set up competition with the U.S. mint on Esplanade, or so he informs me. He needs my help for that."

"He's taken the bait." Harlan leaned forward in his seat. "When do we go?"

Rey shook his head. "*We* don't go anywhere. This meeting happens between myself and Sotheby. Alone."

"*Merde!* You can't possibly take on Sotheby by yourself, Rey."

"The hell I can't."

"He could recognize you. Santana said as much!"

"You're out, Harlan. I told you that weeks ago. Tomorrow morning, I see Sotheby without you."

He watched the dark blue eyes shadow with surprise

and hurt. "*Tonnerre!* If not for me, Sotheby would not be asking for a meeting now. Or have you forgotten that?"

"I'll admit you handled Sotheby well," Rey answered. "But the letter, that was an unpardonable mistake in judgment."

Harlan fell back against the couch, his arms crossed before his chest. "So you no longer trust me. *Bien,* I accept that. But don't be a fool and go alone. Take Mac with you."

Rey shook his head. "It's a simple meeting. I can handle it. Forget about me and concentrate on your own problems. Have you settled with Pascal?"

Harlan sank deeper into the upholstered cushions. "She hasn't answered my letters. Every time I'm at Bizy, she's conveniently away." He shrugged his shoulders and looked away. "Perhaps she'll never speak to me again."

"She risked her stepmother's life for you—and gave you her innocence. She'll see you . . . eventually." And then, thinking Harlan might have forgotten the obvious, Rey added, "Have you told her you love her?"

Harlan looked up. "Are my feelings so obvious?"

Rey shook his head for the man's naïveté. Since his snakebite two weeks before, Harlan had moped around Bizy as if his closest friend had died. Rey knew about the countless letters he'd sent to Pascal—it was almost a daily ritual to see Harlan at his desk hunched over a piece of paper, examining the words he'd written as if he were drafting an amendment to the United States Constitution.

"I don't care how much brandy Mac poured down you that night," Rey said. "You risked our mission and ruined the girl. I believe only the strongest emotions could have motivated you—and judging from the past two weeks, it wasn't revenge. The question is not whether *I* know how you feel. Have you said as much to Pascal?"

"In three languages. And still she won't see me. I'd marry her given half the chance," Harlan said softly.

Rey let out a breath. He'd hoped for at least one simple

solution to their predicament. He'd thought Pascal De Dreux lovestruck. Despite what he'd told Harlan out of anger that first time he'd learned about the stolen letter, Rey had expected that once Harlan proposed, they'd have the girl's complete cooperation. After her father's arrest, Rey had planned to settle back and watch Harlan ankle up the aisle beside Pascal.

Then Mercy wouldn't have to worry about her stepdaughter's happiness.

Rey swept aside his concerns for Mercedes and concentrated on Harlan. But the man's miserable expression reached deep inside Rey to where his own loneliness gnawed at him. Harlan really loved the girl. And like Mac, the Pinkerton had no qualms forgiving her involvement with Santana. Well, why not? Rey thought. Pascal was only a child, misled by the example of a woman she adored and respected.

Yes, everything is Mercy's fault. Always Mercy's fault.

Rey smiled cynically. How simple it was to vent his anger on Mercy. If only he could forget the other emotions she inspired. Then maybe some night soon he'd have a decent night's rest instead of drinking himself into oblivion and waking in the early morning hours with his nightmares still fresh.

Staring out the window behind Harlan, Rey mulled over the past weeks. No matter how many times he ticked off her crimes and lies or how often he reminded himself of his advice to Mac not to get involved with a criminal, each day Rey woke up aching for Mercy to be there beside him. He hadn't heard from her about any pregnancy. He'd taken her silence on the matter to mean there would be no child. His relief had been mixed with a sense of regret he didn't understand. He couldn't seem to resolve his feelings for her. Voices whispered to him from the dark corners of his room that there may be reasons for what she'd done, circumstances other than revenge or greed that motivated her. But with the morning sun came the same unbending resolve he'd lived with since Sophie's death. *Get the plates, then get the hell out of New Orleans.*

Rey turned back to Harlan, again wondering at the man's facile ability to forget Pascal's connection with De Dreux and Santana, a talent Mac seemed to share judging from his frequent trips to Catalan Kate's. Rey might try to differentiate between mother and stepdaughter, but had their situation been reversed—had Harlan fallen in love with Mercedes and Rey with the younger woman—would Rey have been so forgiving? Or Harlan as condemning?

"It doesn't bother you," Rey asked, a devil inside prodding him to pursue the idea, "that Pascal was part of Santana's gang, or the daughter of a man you despise? It doesn't change your feelings for her?"

Harlan seemed to weigh whether he should speak his mind or not. "I love her," he said after a moment. "I have from the first—I was just too big a fool to know it. No matter whose daughter she is or what she's done, she risked everything for me. Everything. That's got to mean something, *mon ami . . .* doesn't it?"

A weighty silence followed. The sensation that Harlan was addressing Rey's own circumstances surged through him.

"Doesn't it?" Harlan insisted.

I asked for this, Rey told himself. *I gave him the opportunity to point the finger and say the flaw lay in me.* But he had no intention of answering Harlan's question.

After a while, the Pinkerton shook his head. "I don't give a coon's ass about revenge against De Dreux anymore. Look what my desire for vengeance did to Pascal. He's an evil man but it will be enough for me if he's behind bars and won't hurt anyone again—including *la petite.* She's led a miserable life because of her father, and still she found the heart to love me. I was a fool to pass up such a gift for revenge. I just hope it's not too late to set things straight between us."

Harlan's blue eyes sparkled with the afternoon sun

streaming through the window. The way he studied Rey, his head tilted, his eyes shining, he reminded him uncomfortably of Christopher, so much so that Rey turned to leave the room. But before he took a step, he heard Harlan say behind him, "Don't put your moral convictions on me, Rey. I jus' don't share them. I choose to forget the past and be happy. I hope some day you'll feel the same. For your own sake."

Rey didn't say a word, didn't turn to face the Pinkerton. Nothing would get past the bitter knot in his throat. Harlan was young, young enough to believe he could wipe the slate clean and start a new life with Pascal. For Rey, that kind of forgiveness wasn't possible. He'd seen too much, lived through too many tragedies. But as he walked out of the salon toward his room, he couldn't help believing that, for all his naïveté, Harlan was perhaps the luckier of the two.

Pascal swung open the door to Doc Chiang's apothecary, blinking as her vision adjusted from the bright sunlight outside. When she saw Ling Shi, she grinned and waved. Her friend returned her smile as she wiped her hands on her apron and walked around the counter.

"Pascal." Ling Shi clasped her hands. "It's so good to see you again, my friend. I have missed you. It's been a full week since your last visit. And I had grown used to your daily visits. What has kept you away?"

Pascal blushed. After her disastrous night at Bizy two weeks ago, she'd sought solace by coming to the apothecary every day. But last week, she'd received her note from Lena. After reading the missive, Pascal had fallen into a depression so deep, she'd been unable to face her friend without revealing the whole sordid tale—something she dared not do. Tonight, she must fulfill her promise to the voodoo priestess. It was her fears about the evening ahead that had brought Pascal into town to say her good-byes.

"I'm sorry, Ling Shi. I've been . . . busy." The lie

sounded weak to her, and she saw Ling Shi frown. Immediately Pascal tightened her grip on Ling Shi's hands and grinned enthusiastically. "You look as marvelous as ever. Shining even. How marriage agrees with you."

"Oh, Pascal, I'm so happy. You were right," she said with a blush. "You were right about love."

A bitter taste filled Pascal's mouth. It was difficult to keep her smile in place.

"Is everything all right? With Mr. Everard, I mean," Ling Shi asked, immediately aware of her friend's change in mood.

"Of course." Pascal released her hands and turned away from Ling Shi's too-knowing gaze. "He wants us to marry. I expect him to come see my father any day now." Oh, how easily the lie came to her lips. Though Harlan had indeed asked to marry her, their courtship could never be a simple matter of asking for her hand. She hadn't even answered his many notes, trying to discourage him. Given what might happen tonight, she thought it best if Harlan forgot about her all together. "But let's talk about you." She twirled around to face Ling Shi, composed once more. "We haven't spoken for a full week. Tell me how things have been."

"Let me get some refreshments for us first."

Grateful for a moment to herself, Pascal sat down at the counter to wait. She marshaled her strength to hide the sorrow and fear that had been too close to the surface. It wouldn't do to let Ling Shi know the things she risked tonight. Her friend would do her best to stop her—and what would Lena do to Harlan if Pascal didn't fulfill her promise? When Ling Shi returned carrying a lacquered tray, Pascal immediately forced a smile. "Really, I have never seen you look so happy, Ling Shi. Is Doc Chiang so wonderful?"

Ling Shi blushed and leaned over to whisper, "In my wildest dreams I could not have imagined such happiness. Chiang and I are expecting a child."

Myriad emotions challenged Pascal as she stared at her friend in amazement. Her monthly had come the week before. There would be no baby from the night she'd spent with Harlan. The thought of the happiness she'd never share with Harlan almost devastated her. But then she took up Ling Shi's hands and hugged her. "I'm glad." Pascal held her tight as tears came to her eyes. "I'm so glad."

"Pascal?" Ling Shi frowned. "Something is wrong, isn't it? What are you not telling me?"

"I'm right as rain." She stood, brushing back her tears. "I'm just happy for you is all." She made a show of glancing down to the watch pinned to her lapel. "Dear me, I hadn't noticed the time. I have to go now, Ling Shi."

"But your tea?"

"Another day, perhaps."

Ling Shi touched her shoulder lightly. "I would not like to keep you if you must leave. But don't wait so long to come back this time."

For a moment, Pascal almost spoke her fears: She might never come back, might never see her friend again. Inside a voice pleaded, "Ling Shi, help me. Please, help me."

"Pascal?"

She shook her head. "Of course, I'll come back. You take care. Take care of yourself and the baby."

Ling Shi watched Pascal close the door behind her. All the fears that had haunted her two weeks ago, during the early days of her marriage, returned with the force and swiftness of demons. She'd been so happy during the week of Pascal's daily visits. Her frequent presence quieted Ling Shi's concerns. It was as if her worries had lain dormant inside her, only to rise up now in fresh flames.

"Was that Pascal?"

Ling Shi hadn't heard her husband step out from the back room. But even now, she didn't turn around, just watched the door helplessly.

Chiang's fingers pressed into her shoulders and turned her to face him. He lifted her chin. "But I thought your concerns for Pascal were forgotten, my love. You still worry about your friend?"

Ling Shi fell into his arms. "Oh, Chiang. Hold me."

Crash! The vase shattered next to Mac's head, showering him with porcelain fragments.

"Katie lass, don't!" He prepared to dive for cover when he saw Kate grab for a ceramic figurine.

"Animal! Bestia!"

Mac managed to duck to the side just before the statue sliced through the air, smashing against the wall at the exact spot where his head had been only seconds before.

"Now Katie, that's quite enough of yer temper. I'm only suggesting this to keep ye out of jail, lass."

Her fine breasts looking to burst past the low neckline of her gown, Kate stopped and stared at Mac. "You want I should marry you to keep out of the jail? *Qué estúpido!*" She searched the room for another projectile. "I will be in jail for killing you, *sinuergüenza!*"

When she reached across the bed for another weapon, Mac made his move. Grabbing her by the waist, he tumbled her to the mattress, pinning her there.

"Katie, I'm here to say I forgive ye lass. Whatever ye've done."

"Forgive me? Bah!"

Through some instinct of self-preservation, Mac released her and rolled to the side, just missing the deadly thrust of her knee between his legs. In less time than he'd thought possible given the elaborate train of her gown, Kate whisked off the bed and marched to the door. Opening it in a dramatic sweep of her hand, she said, "La Kate asks only a priest for forgiveness. *Vete!* Leave here, now! And when you come back, you bring police with you, Juan," she said, shaking a red-enameled nail at him, "because Kate marries no man who thinks she needs his forgiveness."

Not a little angry himself—the lass's knee had nearly

decapitated his Hanging Johnny—Mac jumped off the bed and strode to the door. Slamming it shut with his palm, he cornered Kate's luscious curves against the oak. "Why are ye angry with me, lass? Don't ye want to marry me? An' here I thought I'd won yer heart these past weeks."

Kate's fists slammed into Mac. "*Anormal!* I wanted you should ask me to marry because you love me! Not to keep me from the jail!"

Mac snatched her wrists in his hands, shouting, "Well if that's all that's put the devil into ye, then rest assured, lass, that I do!"

Kate stopped struggling. Her eyes wide, she stared up at him. "You love me?"

"Katie, lass, I know we've not known each other long, but what I feel in my heart for ye tells me it doesna matter."

"*Ay,* Juanito." Her gaze searched his. "Could it be true?" Tears filled her eyes.

"Dinna doubt it, lass, fer I never have."

"This has nothing to do with Santana and my helping her?" she asked, a thread of suspicion still coloring her voice.

"I'll admit the idea of marriage came to me for just that, but I'd swear on that saint of yers that it's my heart that speaks now, Katie. I love ye, lass. Verra much."

Crimson-painted nails laced through Mac's graying curls. "I feel the same. Enough to forget this *estúpido* forgiveness you offered. What can a woman expect from a man but to be an imbecile, eh?" She pressed her lips to his mouth, then his cheek. "*Te amo,* Juanito." A sound between a laugh and a cry escaped her lips as she kissed him. "*Te amo, mi amor.*"

Soon enough, his fingers tugged the sleeve off her shoulder and caressed her bared skin. With a moan that showed her reluctance to stop him, Kate stilled his hand. "But what of Santana?"

Mac doubled his kisses, hoping to distract Kate. "Let's not speak of that now, Katie love."

Kate managed to slip out from under him. Her shrewd blue eyes studied him. "Santana is kindest, most selfless woman I know. She helped many women escape her husband's evil trap. You are right, Juan, when you say I help Mercedes De Dreux. And I am proud that I help! I see her with the girls she brings here. She gives them money. She asks me to watch over them, like a mother. I would not like to see her hurt, Juanito."

"I'm wishing a certain other party shared yer opinion," Mac murmured under his breath. "T'would make all our lives a might easier." Then more loudly, "Dinna worry yerself, lass. Rey's got no plans to turn her in to the police."

Kate brushed aside his hand in a jangle of bracelets. "Bah! You speak only of jail. I speak of her heart. That man has broken her spirit. *Ay*, Juan." Kate shook her head, tears coming to her eyes. "*Qué se puede hacer?* She loves him so, she would give her life for this scoundrel with the white hair."

Mac looked miserably at Katie. "She loves him that much?"

"Why of course! There would be no possibility of a child if she did not!"

"It's not always necessary fer a bairn to come."

"It is for Santana! Because of that animal, her husband, she has trusted no man since she met Reynard Parks. And now he too turns into a demon."

"Now, Kate. Rey's no devil. He's a simple soul who's had his share of heartbreak. Even if I doubted it before, I'd stake my last ten years wages he loves the lass. He'd not be so miserable these past two weeks if he felt otherwise."

Kate's finely-plucked brows arched in surprise. "He loves her? You say she has captured his heart?"

"She's bewitched him, and that's a fact. From the first

day he laid eyes on her as Santana, he's not been the same. But Rey's not a forgiving man—if he were . . ." Mac left the thought unsaid. It was Mercedes De Dreux Katie cared about—not Rey. She wouldn't give a fig about his friend's own battles with guilt and forgiveness. Mac shook his head. "He'll not forget she's on the wrong side of the law."

But Kate didn't respond to his prediction with anger or grief as Mac expected. Instead, she closed her eyes and clasped her hands before her, then quickly crossed herself as if she'd finished a prayer. She took Mac's hand and led him to the bed. "Only a man without a heart would not forgive her actions if he knew the *reasons* that drove Santana. She say to me that I should not speak of this, but I think she is wrong. Juanito." She pulled Mac back to the bed with her. "I have very much to tell you, *mi amor*."

Chapter 22

Pascal seized the doorknob, almost bursting into Harlan's room before she realized what she was doing. Her gloved fingers dropped from the handle and she fell back against the wall, hugging herself. Why had she panicked and rushed past the servant who'd answered the front door? There were plenty of reasons for Harlan to be abed besides his health. Two weeks had passed since Harlan had recovered from the snakebite. Surely he couldn't suffer any sort of relapse now! The maid was probably still standing beside the door with her mouth hanging open, recovering from Pascal's rude entry.

She laced her fingers together and stared at her kid gloves, trying to rein in her imagination. The same brashness responsible for her flight from Ling Shi to Bizy had sent her barging past the entry hall when she'd heard, "Mr. Everard is in bed and not to be disturbed." Mercedes had told her Harlan was perfectly recovered. Why suspect the worst?

She should turn right around and head back to the front door. She started to do just that, but the familiar loneliness she'd experienced at the apothecary made her spin a complete circle and step up to the door instead. Oh, she'd thought to be so brave; to meet her fate at Lena's without so much as a letter to Harlan letting him know what she'd sacrificed for him. But she desperately needed this last good-bye. She raised her hand and knocked lightly. If he were asleep, she would just peek inside and leave.

A strong voice answered, "Come in." She inched the door open, anxious to see him for the first time in two weeks. Sunlight bathed her face, extinguishing the image of Harlan resting in his shirtsleeves on the counterpane, his legs extended in front of him. She heard him whisper, "Pascal. You came."

She closed the door behind her. The first thing she saw clearly was Harlan's welcoming smile.

He tossed the book he'd been reading on the bed and threw his legs over the side, standing up. "Thank *Le Bon Dieu.*" He took two steps toward her, than stopped. He dug his hands in his trouser pockets and watched her from the bed, unsure of his welcome. "*Petite,* why didn't you answer my letters?"

Pascal flushed. "I didn't know what to say. I've never . . . that is . . . under the circumstances . . ." She concentrated on the toes of her slippers before she found the courage to whisper, "I missed you, Harlan. Very much."

It was all he needed to hear. He rushed to her side, taking her into his arms. "Does it help that I feel awful about what I did?" he said, hugging her. "That I regret how I treated you, *chou?*"

Her head jerked up. "You're sorry we . . . we made love?" She couldn't contain her disappointment. "Oh, Harlan. How can you regret it? For me, it was the most wonderful experience of my life."

Harlan smiled. There was such tenderness in his expression, Pascal's concerns for the night faded into the background of her mind. He leaned down slowly, giving her time to avoid his kiss, whispering assurances of his love in French as he brushed his mouth against hers. Pressing her lips to his, Pascal thought how she'd called herself silly and immature for seeking him out. Instinctively, she must have known she'd find her courage here. Harlan reminded her she was a woman, with a woman's strength. No matter what Lena asked of her, she'd be prepared.

"*Petite,* I regret nothing." He couldn't seem to stop touching her with his mouth, his hands. "I meant what I said in my letters. I love you. But I took advantage of you that night. You're so young. Your first time—I should have been more careful, shown more restraint."

"But you're not sorry it happened?" she answered, returning his kisses almost feverishly. "I wouldn't want you to regret making love to me."

He cupped her face in his palms and studied her. His very look made her feel precious. Taking her hand, he guided her to the bed and pulled her down to sit beside him. "I've never hated myself like I did the day you overheard me talking about your *père.* It was like seeing myself for the first time, realizing that what I was doing could really hurt somebody I cared for so much. But later, when we made love here on this bed—" He shook his head, bringing her face so close she could feel his breath against her skin. "Perhaps I should be, but I'm not sorry, *petite.* I'd do it all over again. I'd do it right now, if you'd let me."

Pascal looked into his eyes. She reached out to stroke his face—the face of the man she loved and had nearly lost. She thought of the terrors that awaited her this night when she left Bizy. "I'll let you." She leaned closer, her mouth reaching for his. "Nothing would make me happier."

He pulled her across his lap, wrapping his arms around her. *"Comme je t'aime."*

Pascal's heart spiraled inside her, spinning faster and faster. Harlan brought her true happiness—the kind that left you weak; the kind that made you want more. And though she suspected she would pay a high price for his love, the touch of his mouth and hands made her willing. *Doesn't all love cost dearly?* she thought as she reached for the buttons of his shirt. Her mother had died to give her father a child, even when the doctors had warned her not to conceive. And Mercedes, hadn't her love for Mr. Parks exposed her to imprisonment?

Harlan angled her closer, coaxing her beneath him as he unhooked her gown. "Pascal." His mouth descended to the hollow at the base of her neck. He pulled the sleeves of her gown down her arms. "I've never loved a woman before you. Never leave me." The tension of her corset eased. "Love me, *chou*. Love me."

Thoughts of what was to come wound tightly like a drawn coil below her stomach—not with fear, but with anticipation. For Harlan she'd risk anything. For this moment, when all doubts vanished in an explosion of pleasure and only Harlan's loving touch mattered, she'd pay any price.

"You're like a dream, *chou*," he whispered. "The first time, I thought I *was* dreaming. I couldn't believe anything could be this sweet. *Douce*." His mouth returned to hers while his hands inched up her skirts until they curved over her bottom. *"Très douce."*

"You make me sound like a praline." Her laughter turned into a low moan in her throat as his mouth teased hers. When he pulled away, she opened her eyes to see him poised above her, waiting. He stroked the curls from her face, his expression suddenly serious.

"If I could make you mine as easily as buying a bit of candy, if I could make sure that tomorrow you would still be here with me, still love me as sweetly as you do now, I would be a happy man, *petite*." He held her face in his hands, his thumbs caressing her cheeks. "Say you will marry me, Pascal. You know it's just a matter of time before your father is arrested. You'll need me then."

"I need you now, Harlan."

His expression filled with relief. "Then you'll come away with me? You'll marry me?"

Pascal's throat grew too thick to speak. When Harlan's smile faltered, she wrapped her arms around him and nuzzled his neck so he couldn't see the pain in her eyes. "I'd do anything for you, Harlan," she whispered. *"Anything."*

"Don't sound so serious, *petite.*" He chuckled. "You don't have to make it sound like a death sentence." When he turned to see her face, his boyish smile had returned. "I'll take care of you, Pascal." His hand dropped to her breast. *"Je t'adore, Pascal."* His soft Cajun accent made her name sound like an endearment as he kissed her.

"I love you," she whispered against his mouth, pushing his shirt off his shoulders. "Whatever happens, Harlan. Don't ever forget I love you."

The *Princess* paddled down the river. Enormous clouds of smoke billowed from her stack, stretching like pulled taffy on the wind. The regal figure of a lady, her midnight curls styled fashionably below her feathered bonnet, rested against the filigree woodwork of the railing on the Texas deck. During the two-week voyage, many a passenger had commented on her fabulous peridot-colored eyes, a hue made more striking by her forest-green gown. But only determination of the strongest form could account for the spark in her gaze as she watched the parade of manor homes lining the shores of the Mississippi.

An older woman dressed in widow's weeds attended the small boy between them, explaining in no uncertain terms that the child was *not* to climb the railing to get a better look at the deck below. The small boy—with dark brown curls and eyes bluer than the noon sky above them—settled for watching the shore between the slats.

"I still cannot believe you talked me into this adventure," the older woman complained as she mopped her brow with a lace handkerchief.

"Dearest Auntie Clair, you practically twisted my arm to allow you to come. I feel quite ashamed that I left my poor Michael with only Mother and Nanny to watch over the children."

"Humph! At the time you made it sound as if we were

traveling to Babylon itself. And well, after the phrenologist suggested that I was a woman of adventure, it seemed fate had destined that I accompany you. In any case, Nan, if you could convince that darling husband of yours to allow this wild-goose chase, I shouldn't think your manipulating me shows the least flaw in my character—and you well know that he never would have consented to this trip without me coming along."

"It is exciting leaving Boston, isn't it?" She held her face up to the breeze off the river. "What do you think, Christopher?" She glanced down at the boy beside her. "Isn't this a grand adventure?"

He nodded, then looked up with a smile so radiant, it would have taken the breath from the most hardened soul. "How much longer until we see my father, Nana?"

"Perhaps as soon as tomorrow." She smoothed his brown curls. "But we must be patient; it's a fair distance from Boston to New Orleans."

"Will he be waiting for us? Will he meet our ship?"

The two women's gazes met over the boy's head. Nan brushed back Christopher's hair. "Not at the landing, I'm afraid. But as soon as he is able, he'll come fetch us. Your father will be anxious to see how much his darling boy has grown the past months. And he wouldn't miss your birthday for the world, Christopher."

When Christopher stared ahead, his expression was as satisfied as it had been the scores of times he'd asked the same question and received the same answer. Nan added under her breath, "In his heart, he sent for us, Christopher. It's just a good thing that your Nana can read her brother's heart."

Pascal picked up the skirt of her white lace dress and climbed the steps to Lena's house, trying not to feel as if she were climbing the ladder of a scaffold. She'd brought a crocheted shawl that had once belonged to her mother. She hugged the soft folds around her—more for comfort than warmth against the evening's chill—and looked back at Phoebus grazing in the clearing. She'd braided her hair and twisted it into a knot at the base of her neck, just as Lena had instructed in her note. She shivered as she thought of the dress she wore. Having lacked the courage to wear the requested white until absolutely necessary, she'd packed the gown in her saddlebags. She'd changed in a copse not far from Lena's house. Pascal had read too many stories about virginal sacrifices not to be concerned over Lena's choice in wardrobe for her.

Her fingers clutching her skirt trembled. She told herself that she was only a novelty, a white woman Lena could parade around at her ceremony. Nothing would happen. She would return right after the dinner hour, just as she'd written in the note she'd sent to Mercy from Bizy. She would live to see all her loved ones again.

Fortified by her logic, she took a deep breath and knocked. The door creaked open. As always, Lena's assistant stood at the threshold. Pascal willed herself to move, to take the monumental step toward whatever fate awaited her. But she couldn't. She remained frozen at the door. With a snarl, the woman clasped her fingers like talons around Pascal's wrist and pulled her over the threshold.

Lena waited at the fireplace. The flames blazed behind her and shadowed the priestess as she moved toward Pascal. The legs beneath her checkered dress seemed to float rather than step forward. Lena's lips twisted upward into a smile that looked both cruel and satisfied.

"My magic worked good for dat man of yours, Pas-cal De Dreux?"

"Y-yes." She took a breath, trying to steady his voice. "He recovered."

"So you come pay your debt to me?"

"I'm here, just as you asked in your note."

"Your father. He owe me, Pas-cal De Dreux. Do you know about your father, chil'? What a bad man he is?"

An increased sense of peril snapped inside her. She swallowed. "I . . . know . . . about my father."

Lena nodded her head, then studied Pascal from head to toe. "Dat is a beautiful dress, Pas-cal De Dreux."

"You said to w-wear white." Pascal glanced down at the gown with its single flounce, happy to take her gaze off Lena.

"White is da color of magic. An' dat's what you gonna be tonight, chil'. Magic!"

A shiver crossed her chest and inched down her arms. She felt as if the wind off the bayou had penetrated the brick walls of the cottage and no fire burned in the grate. But when Lena motioned Pascal over to her table, she obeyed, stopping before the scarred wooden table.

The burnt-orange hair peeked out from beneath Lena's tignon. A fire ignited deep in her yellow eyes. For a moment, her dark face looked truly wolflike. Pascal stepped back, almost tripping until Lena grabbed her arm.

"You scared of Lena, Pas-cal De Dreux?"

"N-no . . . maybe."

The taller woman bent down until her striking eyes were on a level with Pascal's. "You *should* be scared, girl."

Something cold nudged her ankle. Paralyzed by Lena's gaze, Pascal ignored the touch until the prodding became a cool grasp, like fingers tightening around her stockinged calf. She looked down. Lena's snake wound up her leg.

"Take it off!" she screamed. Too frightened to reach down and rip the snake from her, she stood perfectly still. Lena's cackle joined her assistant's laughter. "Take it off now or I'll leave!"

"Simone, you put Zombi back in her box. Pas-cal De Dreux don't seem to like our pet."

Pascal felt as if a colony of fire ants had settled on her skin as Simone coaxed the snake from around her leg. When she looked back at Lena, the curve of the priestess's smile looked surprisingly like the snake's. She pulled Pascal to her side and reached behind her for a wooden bowl carved with voodoo symbols. A dark suspicious liquid lapped at the rim as she lifted the bowl to Pascal's lips. A sharp, almost rancid, smell assailed her.

"Drink, Pas-cal De Dreux. Drink from da elixir of life."

Pascal pushed away the bowl. "No. I . . . don't want . . ."

"Drink!"

Lena pressed the bowl to her lips and cupped Pascal's hands beneath it, forcing her to hold the voodoo cup. Her mother's shawl dropped to the floor. Pascal shut her eyes, breathing through her mouth so she couldn't smell the potion. She thought of Harlan's mouth on her lips, concentrated on her memories of their last kiss as she tasted Lena's brew.

"Dat's good, Pas-cal De Dreux." She pulled the cup away. "But don't you drink too much. We gonna make it last a long time."

Ling Shi stepped down from the coach and faced L'Isle des Rêves. Trumpet vines crisscrossed the white wooden slats of the gallery in a lacy pattern that only added to the mansion's beauty. She studied the Ionic columns and Grecian facade. De Dreux's island of dreams—for Ling Shi, it had been a place of nightmares. She'd hoped never to cross its threshold again.

Only her desperate fears for Pascal could bring Ling Shi back down the plantation's oak-lined drive. That afternoon, her friend's good-byes had rung with such finality, that knowing Pascal as she did, Ling Shi dreaded some terrible plot was afoot. Her worries had blossomed until she'd begged Chiang to take her to L'Isle des Rêves. She had to persuade Pascal to confide in her as she'd done so often in the past.

"Come, Ling Shi," Chiang said behind her, pressing his hand to the small of her back. But when she hesitated, the pressure of Chiang's hand vanished.

"You don't have to go in, Ling Shi. I can go fetch her for you. You can wait in the carriage if you wish."

She shook her head, smiling because she'd been blessed with such a considerate husband. "No, Chiang." She took a step forward. "With you at my side, I can face anything. Even my past."

Her heart pounded with the force of the brass knocker against the cypress double doors. Here was the place of her shame. Only with Chiang's support could she have made this journey. Her husband wouldn't allow her to face Monsieur De Dreux alone. She slipped her hand into the warmth of his. He gave her fingers a squeeze as the door inched open.

A young Negress dressed in a servant's uniform stood at the threshold. Ling Shi immediately recognized the girl as one of the downstairs maids. The maid's dark eyes grew large when she saw Ling Shi, and she wondered if perhaps this servant were privy to her scandalous relationship with the master of the house, as many had been. But instead of looking down in shame, Ling Shi pressed her shoulders back. She was here for Pascal's sake.

"Is Miss Pascal at home?" Chiang asked.

"Ling Shi!" The door opened wide and Madame De Dreux stood beside the servant. "I thought that was you. What a pleasant surprise after all this time. I'm afraid I'm the only one in residence at the moment. My husband is in town and I don't expect him until tomorrow. But Pascal should be home soon enough if you care to wait?"

Ling Shi glanced up at her husband. Her fingers tightened around his before she saw him nod. She looked back to Madame De Dreux. "Please, madame. It is urgent that I speak with Pascal."

As she and Chiang followed Madame De Dreux into the parlor, Ling Shi felt a flutter of happiness at the news that she'd not have to face Monsieur De Dreux. Walking into the parlor, it seemed odd to be received in this house as a guest, but then Madame De Dreux had always struck her as a gracious and fair-minded woman, despite Pascal's complaints about her stepmother. Her kindness now did not surprise Ling Shi.

Mercy waited until both Doc Chiang and Ling Shi were seated before ordering refreshments. As she sat on the Belter armchair beside the couple, she couldn't help but notice Ling Shi's glow of happiness. She sent a silent thanks that at least one of Benoit's victims had found shelter. "I'm sorry Pascal isn't here to receive you," she said. "I expect her home any minute."

But one hour followed the next and still there was no sign of Pascal. The tea grew cold and the cakes remained untouched by the three people waiting. Mercy watched Ling Shi glance out the window where the sun sat close to the horizon.

"She's late, of course." Mercy smiled, trying not to let the woman's obvious fears worsen her own. "And as hardheaded as ever. She did say she had a busy day ahead—though I expected her home by now or at least to send a note. I'm sorry I had you wait."

"I do not mind, madame," Ling Shi said, staring down at her lap as she spoke. "I wish only to see her home safely. If it is all right, my husband and I will remain until then."

"Certainly, Ling Shi. I welcome the company."

Mercy glanced at the clock. The fist around her heart squeezed tighter. It would be dark soon. Confound that girl for worrying everyone so! She'd thought Pascal had matured beyond such inconsideration. "It's useless to assign her a chaperone," Mercy said, speaking more to ease the strain in the air than from any need to explain Pascal's thoughtlessness to Ling Shi. "As you well know, Pascal does what she wants most times. I must say, I felt more secure when you were in charge of her activities."

Fresh tea was sent for. It, too, turned cold in the delicate Spode china cups. When at last a servant came in carrying a note, Mercy jumped to her feet to take the folded vellum.

"It's from Pascal," Mercy said, tearing the note open with relief. The last two hours had taken their toll. But as her eyes scanned the penned words, her heart hammered in her throat. The paper fell from her fingers to the tea tray.

"What is it, madame?" Ling Shi called out. "What does she say?"

Mercy dropped her hands to her side. The air froze in her lungs. "The note says she spent the afternoon catching up with you—"

"Yes." Ling Shi leaned forward on the settee. "She came to the apothecary earlier."

"She writes she had such a wonderful time . . . that you've asked her to stay. She's supposed to be having dinner"—her eyes met Ling Shi's and her voice dropped below a whisper—"with you."

Chapter 23

The tingling came again, creeping down Pascal's arms to her fingertips, making her tongue thick, her skin warm despite the cool night. She watched the moonlit dancers sway and dip. Their bodies rippled like the waters of Lake Pontchartrain beyond. Birds floated on the shining surface of the lake, resting like froth before skimming off to disappear on the shore. Birds? Birds vanishing? No, waves. Waves licking the shore.

The white dress tickled her ankles, making her want to dance. She tried to speak, but couldn't form the words of thanks for the heavenly liquid that had opened her eyes to the night's wonders. Above her, the stars shimmered in a silver haze that arched across a sky of black velvet. *My mother had a necklace like that,* she thought. *Ling Shi. Present for Ling Shi. I want . . . I want you to have it, dearest friend. Be happy. Happy. I'm so very happy.*

Someone placed a goblet in her hands. "This is the nectar of life. Zombi's blood," she heard a familiar voice whisper. Pascal clutched the cup. *The nectar of life.* "It will make you immortal," the voice enticed. *Lena,* she thought, but as soon as the word formed, it drifted away like the waves. A firm hand guided the bowl to her mouth. She touched the rim to her lips and the cup was quickly yanked away.

Tam-tams beat. Their short hollow notes struck the rhythm of her heart. *Ra-ta-tat. Ra-ta-tat.* Pascal reached for the skirt of her dress. She wanted to join the dancers as she'd done when she'd first entered the copse of willows on the lake shore. But this time, only in her mind did she swirl around their campfire, lifting her skirt to her knees, sweeping the material right and left to the music of the tam-tams and the song of a high-pitched fiddle. Movement wasn't necessary with the elixir of life singing in her veins —or perhaps, it just wasn't possible.

Men bared to the waist circled the bonfire. Their dark skin gleamed with sweat and firelight. Calico-dressed ladies, white handkerchiefs tied around their foreheads, kept time for the dancers. *Pat-pat, pat-pat,* their hands struck their thighs as a gourd of *tafia* passed from hand to hand. When Pascal asked for a sip of the distilled molasses drink, Lena shook her head. For Pascal, there was only the elixir of life.

A tall youth jumped into the middle of the dancers' circle, shouting, *"Malle oir ca ya di moin!"* Over and over he sang the words "no one can resist me," and Pascal thought of Harlan, the man of her heart. A gentle sweetness filled her. *Harlan, I love you,* she sent her silent message with the singing youth. She watched his sleek ebony skin, the loincloth slung low on his hips, the long muscular legs shaking, stomping, dancing.

Ra-ta-tat. Ra-ta-tat. Malle oir ca ya di moin!

Lena broke into the circle and raised a brightly painted gourd of *tafia* to the youth's mouth. With a blowing sound, he sprayed a fine mist of liquid into her face. Turning, dipping, whirling, he spattered the faces of other women around the circle. Grabbing up a burning brand, he swayed over its tip before bringing it to his mouth. When he blew, a cloud of fire ignited with a loud *whoosh.* A shout of approval flowed from the crowd.

Lena appeared beside Pascal. The painted gourd had vanished. She held only the familiar cup. *Ra-ta-tat. Ra-ta-tat.* The nectar of life. *Ra-ta-tat.* The Zombi's blood.

"Come, Pas-cal De Dreux," Lena whispered. She held

the cup out to her. Pascal tried to take the precious liquid, tried to reach out for the bowl.

Ra-ta-tat. Ra . . . ta-tat.

Another brief taste.

The drum beat deep inside her chest. Slowing, slowing. *Ra . . . ta . . . tat.* Slowing. *Ra . . . ta . . . tat.*

Pascal pushed away the bowl, watched it drop to the ground and spill its magic. Lena's laughter surrounded her, snuffing out the bit of strength left. *I can't move. I can't move!*

Hands tugged at her clothes. They lifted her above their heads, carrying her. The stars became mere wisps of light lacing the night sky through the screen of branches and leaves. Fingers pinched into her skin as she was lowered to the ground. Torch light reflected off white slabs of rock encrusted with lichen and moss. Eerie shadows danced off the sarcophagus-shaped stones.

Ra . . . ta . . . tat.

Pascal glanced down at her feet. In front of her lay an open coffin.

Ra . . . ta . . . Ra . . . ta . . . tat.

"Papa La Bas calls you, Pas-cal De Dreux. You go to da spirit world now. Listen well to his message."

Mercy burst past the servant who opened Bizy's door and raced into the entry hall shouting Rey's name. Doc Chiang and Ling Shi followed close behind. It was dark now and they'd found no trace of Pascal—only a note filled with lies written in her stepdaughter's distinct scroll and a chaperone who'd confessed she'd been bribed to stay home. Added to Ling Shi's worries about Pascal's strange behavior that afternoon was the fact that Phoebus, her horse, had arrived at the stables without Mercy's stepdaughter. The dress she'd worn that morning had been stuffed into the saddlebag.

Reaching the central reception hall, Mercy caught sight of Rey stepping out from the salon. She raced to him, not the least bit concerned that they'd not shared a civil word in two weeks. She didn't give a damn about anger or hate anymore. She'd do anything to find her stepdaughter.

Rey hurried into the hall, a chill rising up the back of his neck. The sound of Mercy's voice had triggered an instinct he'd learned never to ignore. Seeing her only heightened his sense of unease. She was dressed in a lime-green evening gown. Her pelisse was thrown carelessly over her shoulders, not fastened. She wore no hat or gloves, as if she couldn't spare the time to don them. Behind her followed two Celestials—an Oriental man and woman. The woman he recognized as Pascal's maid; Ling Shi's almond-shaped eyes reflected the anxiety Rey had heard in Mercy's voice.

But rather than meet Mercedes halfway, Rey forced himself to wait at the door as she approached him. After weeks of practiced indifference, he found he could disguise his concern. He remembered her costume at the ball: Eve tempting the men in the room as easily as she'd tempted him. Silently, he repeated his conclusions of the morning—he couldn't wipe the slate clean and start a new life with Mercy. For Rey, that kind of forgiveness was not possible.

When Mercy reached out for him, he grabbed her wrists. He lowered her hands to her sides before she could touch him. "What are you doing here, Mercedes? Does your husband know you've come?"

The delicate brows furrowed in pain. He crushed the apology that came too easily to his lips. What had she expected, dammit? A warm welcome? He reminded himself that this woman would take anything he didn't guard carefully.

She stepped away from him, as if needing the distance for composure. "No, of course Benoit doesn't know I'm here. He's in town on business."

"Is that what sent you rushing over?" He crossed his

arms and leaned against the doorjamb. "I suppose I should be flattered."

"I'm here looking for my stepdaughter!"

"Pascal?" Rey tensed, alert once more to the edge in her voice. "To my knowledge, she's not been to Bizy in weeks. Pascal won't even answer Harlan's letters, much less come here to see him."

The door to Harlan's room opened and the Pinkerton stepped in from the loggia to the hall. Mercy rushed to Harlan's side—but not before Rey saw her disillusionment, as if he'd somehow disappointed her.

"Pascal, is she with you?"

"*Mais non,* madame." Harlan focused on Rey over Mercy's shoulder. He seemed to hesitate, then added, "She was here earlier—while you were out riding this afternoon, Rey—but she left. She told me she was returning to the plantation."

Mercy backed away from Harlan, her hand covering her mouth. "I'd so hoped . . ." She turned to face Rey. There was heartache in her eyes. "Her horse arrived at the stables without her. I've had servants searching the grounds." The words sputtered past her lips; Rey could see she was holding back tears. "Nothing. We've found . . . nothing."

"*Mon Dieu!*"

Mercy placed her hand on Harlan's arm, granting him the very touch Rey had rejected. The gesture annoyed Rey, then angered him because he *was* annoyed. He dug his hands in his pockets, and moved back into the shadows. He'd be damned if he'd compete with Harlan for the right to comfort her. But even as the unkind thoughts sounded in his head, he cursed himself. Damn all! The woman brought the worst out in him.

"I received a note from Pascal," Mercy explained to Harlan. "She said she was dining with Ling Shi and her husband, Doc Chiang." She glanced at the couple, obviously too anxious to stop for introductions. "But it was a lie. They came to L'Isle des Rêves looking for Pascal. Ling Shi fears something dreadful has happened."

"Que diable!" Harlan twisted around Mercedes to reach Rey's side, his expression just as pained and demanding as Mercy's. "If her horse returned without her, she could have been thrown. Or abducted! She's worth money, an heiress. Pascal's so trusting. You've no idea the manner of people that girl associates—"

Harlan stopped. He tilted his head to the side in a sharp movement. He looked puzzled, as if he were mulling over what he'd just said.

"What is it," Mercy urged. "What do you know?"

"Nothing, madame. I was remembering another time Pascal disappeared—but no. She has no reason . . ." He stared at the wall with his eyes unfocused.

Mercy spun back to Rey. The soft glow of the lamps reflected in her eyes. Her expression beseeched him, wringing out the anger and suspicion, reaching that part of him he'd made vulnerable to her.

"Please, Rey," she whispered. "Help me."

Those eyes, he thought. He could die for those eyes—and had. Luckily, his had been only a spiritual death.

"Please," she repeated.

He pressed his lips together. As he had when he'd tended her bullet wound, Rey experienced her pain as if it were his own. No matter how much he wished it, he wasn't totally free of Mercedes De Dreux.

With a curse, Rey took Harlan by the elbow and steered the Cajun around to face him. He was letting his anger for Mercy cloud his judgment, he reasoned. "You spoke to her last, Harlan. Think hard about what she said to you." No matter what had passed between him and Mercy, Pascal could be in trouble. She and Harlan deserved Rey's best. "Did she mention anything that could guide us to her?"

Harlan closed his eyes, as if he needed the darkness to concentrate. *"Mais non,* not tonight. But . . ."

"You remember something?"

Harlan's eyes flickered behind his closed lids. His brow furrowed. There was something there; Rey sensed it. Something the Pinkerton knew but couldn't remember. And then Harlan's eyes flared open, their blue color looking like the center of a flame.

"The conjo woman. The voodoo witch. The one who gave her the potion to cure my snakebite . . ." But before he could finish, the light in his eyes dimmed.

Rey grabbed both Harlan's shoulders. "The voodoo priestess? She's part of this? You have reason to believe she's harmed Pascal?"

Harlan shook his head. "*Non*. When I was sick," he spoke as if he were thinking out loud. "*La petite* gave me the potion . . . there's something about the conjo woman." His fingers curled into two tight fists. Rey could almost smell his frustration. "*Zut alors*, it's there, inside my head, but I can't remember!"

"Give yourself a chance."

But Harlan was shaking his head, denying his power to recall. "It was like a dream . . . I only remember bits and pieces." He stumbled back, dug his fingers into his hair, fighting himself despite Rey's command. "My medicine. Something about that potion."

"She got the cure from the voodoo woman," Rey encouraged. "Mac told me as much. Was there something else Pascal might want to get from the woman? Do you think she went there?"

Harlan's head shot up. His mouth dropped open to speak but no sound followed. A full two seconds passed before he whispered, "*Mon Dieu.*" He whipped around, staring at the group of four, watching them with growing alarm. "We must go. Right now!"

Rey grabbed Harlan's arm and swung him back. "Go where, Harlan? What did you remember?"

Misery-filled eyes stared at Rey. "She did it for me." Each word was charged with pain. "Dammit, she did it for me! But I didn't remember—"

"Where can we find her, Harlan." Rey punched the words, trying to make sense of what the man was saying. "You know where she is. Tell us."

"She was afraid of the conjo woman, afraid of a promise she'd made to her—in exchange for my medicine! *My* medicine. She did it to save my life."

"Where, Harlan?" Rey shook the Pinkerton. "Where?"

"She talked about ceremonies. Voodoo sacrifices."

"Lake Pontchartrain," the Oriental man said. "Many ceremonies occur there."

"We have to hurry, *mais oui,*" Harlan said. "Today, when I asked her to marry me—I thought she was just embarrassed. I didn't understand what she meant when she spoke like that . . . as if something terrible was going to happen to her." He grabbed Rey, his fingers digging into his arms. "Rey, she talked as if she never expected to see me again!"

Lightning burst on the horizon, kindling the swamp into a flaming glow. The carriage and two riders blazed a trail to the lake coast, their path ignited by flashes of blue and white across the dark sky and the weak glow of the carriage lamps. But when they reached Lake Pontchartrain, Mercy saw a new source of light. Roaring pine fires spotted the lake shore.

"Dear Lord," she whispered to Ling Shi beside her. "It's as if it were St. John's Eve!"

Rey and Harlan dismounted. As Mercy jumped from the carriage, dark faces bronzed by the eerie flames watched silently. Doc Chiang helped Ling Shi down the landau's steps while Harlan raced to a group of women ladling gumbo to a waiting throng. Mercy watched beside Rey as Harlan asked a calico-dressed Negress for Lena. After receiving a blank stare, Harlan turned to the next woman, then the next. All refused to give him the answers he begged for, watching him with obvious suspicion. In frustration, Harlan grabbed an elderly man by the shoulder and spun him around. He switched to the Creole patois of the swamps.

"My woman," he explained at last. "She has my woman."

A look of sympathy creased the weathered face topped with white hair. *"La petite qui porte la robe blanche?"*

Mercy's heart dipped as she heard the man describe a young girl wearing a white dress. White was the voodoo color for magic. Pascal had stuffed the gown she'd worn this morning in the saddlebags. Had she changed into white for some terrible ceremony?

Mercy stepped in front of Harlan. *"Avec les cheveux rouges,"* she said, mentioning Pascal's distinctive hair color.

"Elle est là." The man pointed down a dirt passage studded with stumps and ruts.

"This way," Harlan shouted to Rey. Both men raced toward the narrow strip of land between the swamp and the lake.

Mercy sped after them, shouting back to Doc Chiang and Ling Shi to wait with the carriage and horses. Dark men and women danced before blazing pine-knot fires, the flames licking high above their heads. What she witnessed here was no less awesome than the sacred voodoo rites on St. John's Eve. The men and women she saw moved with a frenzy fueled by more than the alcohol of the *tafia*. Were Harlan's suspicions correct? Was Pascal part of some deadly voodoo sacrifice?

She picked her way through hanging vines and brush, making sure not to lose sight of the two men ahead of her. Her breath pounded in her throat and drummed in her ears, until she realized it was not her heart she heard, but the faint sound of tam-tams echoing in the copse ahead. She fought back the foliage, reaching Harlan and Rey, helping them carve a path through the swamp toward the orange glow. She opened the purse at her waist and pulled out the pearl-handled gun. She cocked the pistol carefully. One shot. She prayed it would be enough.

The trio burst past a cluster of willows into a clearing. Several torches lit the opening with their yellow flames revealing a wood shanty listing to one side. A shrill wail filtered from beyond the dilapidated building.

Rey grabbed his Colt and checked the chambers. His eyes met Harlan's as he watched the younger man prepare his gun. Sweat glistened on the Cajun's brow.

"They could be in front of the building," he said, jogging his head to the cabin. "I'm going around on the left side. Harlan, you take the right." Rey turned to Mercy. "You stay here."

Mercy grabbed his arm. "She's my daughter, Rey. Don't ask me to stand by and do nothing."

Rey thought of the ceremonies Harlan had related as they'd readied the horses to search for Pascal. The girl was most certainly in great danger. A picture of his own son blazed in his mind, then Mercy's face when she'd spoken of the child she'd lost. No matter what she had done as Santana, Rey had never doubted her deep love for Pascal. To wait helplessly for word of her stepdaughter's welfare would be agony. He glanced down to the pistol in her hand. Ornamental at best, he thought—but then Santana Rose knew how to make her bullets count.

"All right. But stay behind me at all times!"

Pressing his back against the moldering wood, Rey pushed Mercy against the wall of the cabin. Together, they inched around the building, nearing the front until the sound of chanting and drums drowned the chorus of frogs and cicadas. He held up his hand, motioning for Mercy to stop.

"Don't move from this spot until I call for you," he whispered over his shoulder. At her nod, he stepped closer to the cabin's edge. The drums beat stronger, louder, reaching a crescendo. Rey held his gun with both hands, his back flat against the splintered wood. In his head, he counted: One . . . two . . .

He flipped around the building, his gun ready to fire.

Only Harlan stood in front of the swamp cottage, his face bathed in moonlight. In unison, both men looked ahead to a small grove of funeral cypress shrouded by Spanish moss. Dark shapes moved beyond the curtain of leaves, their shadows profiled against the foliage.

Rey called softly for Mercy. When she joined them, he nodded toward the cypress grove. "In there."

Unholy moans and keening floated on the wind. Rey brushed off its eerie spell and led the threesome forward. He shoved aside a tangle of branches. Within lay a small cemetery. A circle of men and women crowded at its center, many holding firebrands. Rey frowned. It was too close to the lake for a graveyard. Any burial plot would soon be reclaimed by the swamp. But even more curiously, the group appeared to have dug a deep pit. In this moist climate, no one was put to rest below ground. The only graves were masonary vaults and tombs.

The circle parted. Rey's heart drove to his throat and ripped the breath from his lips.

Two men lowered Pascal's stiff body into a coffin.

"Mon Dieu! Petite!" Harlan crashed through the low hedges. Shouting a curse, Rey followed.

"Get away from her!" Harlan screamed. He fired his gun into the air. When he repeated his command in Creole patois, a red-haired Negress pushed through the circle.

"Dat girl don't belong to you no more!" she said. "She's drunk Zombi's blood. She belong to Papa La Bas now."

"Shut up!" Harlan lowered his gun on the woman. His hands shook.

Rey stepped beside him and aimed his Colt on the group ahead. Mercy soon joined him, her face as white as Harlan's but her hands steady on her pistol.

"Unless you want a bullet in some vital place of your anatomy," Rey shouted to the dozen men and women surrounding the coffin, "I suggest you turn around and go home." Mercy repeated his command in French. Watching the guns with wide eyes, a few complied, running from the clearing.

"Mercy, watch our backsides," he whispered as a handful more fled. "Harlan, get Pascal out of there."

The moment the Pinkerton stepped forward, the redhaired priestess lunged. She clawed his face and hands, grabbing for his gun. But Harlan pushed her to the ground as if she were nothing more than an annoying insect. He dropped down beside the coffin. With a snarl, the woman jumped on his back, trying to pull him away from Pascal. Angry shouts erupted from the half-dozen men left. A few stepped forward. Rey fired a shot at their feet.

"Last warning!" he shouted.

Mercy's fingers wrapped around Rey's Colt. "Go on; help him. I've held off more men than this by myself," she said, her voice shaking. "Go!"

Mercy's hand trembled as she aimed both Rey's gun and her own. She couldn't breathe, just watched as Rey pulled Lena off Harlan. The voodoo witch twisted and thrust, baring her teeth as she screamed.

Harlan gathered Pascal into his arms. "I think she's alive," he said to Mercy, then shook his head as he glanced at the girl again. "*Mon Dieu.* I'm not sure." He buried his face against Pascal's neck. "I'm not sure!"

"Let's get the hell out of here, Harlan," Rey said, holding Lena. His gaze scanned the waiting men. They seemed to shuffle closer. He could hear one or two chanting something that sounded like "zombi" and Pascal's name.

"No!" Lena pitched her weight left and right, struggling to escape Rey. "Pas-cal De Dreux is mine. Dat girl is mine. Mine to destroy. Just like her father destroy my sister!"

"Her father?" Mercy aimed the Colt at Lena with deadly accuracy. "You stupid woman, how can you hold anything that monster did against this innocent child?"

Lena spit at the ground near Mercy's feet.

Harlan reached Mercy's side carrying Pascal. Mercy glanced down at her stepdaughter before returning her gaze to Lena's men. Pascal's face had gleamed white as moonlight. Mercy's eyes trained ahead, she held her wrist over Pascal's lips. She wasn't sure if she felt a soft puff of breath hitting her skin or a breeze.

Mercy's heart ached with uncertainty. "What have you done to her?"

"She is the living dead," Lena answered with a grin. "No longer part of our world."

"No," Mercy whispered. Then with more strength, "Get her to the coach, Harlan. To Doc Chiang."

As Harlan disappeared down the path, Lena lunged again, screaming for someone to stop Harlan. Out of the corner of her eye, Mercy saw a man creep out from the bushes toward Rey. She fired. The man fell to the ground clutching his shoulder.

"Let's go, Rey," she called out, desperately wanting to check on Pascal. Would Doc Chiang know a cure for this zombi's blood—or was it already too late for her step-daughter as Lena claimed?

"We have to give Harlan time," he answered.

"It don't matter." Lena's eyes gleamed in the torchlights held by her three remaining followers. "My potion is already deep in her veins, poisoning her heart. She's as good as dead, just like my sister. De Dreux killed Anna. Beat her to death when she was with his child. At last I have my revenge!"

A gun shot whizzed past Lena. "Shut up!" Mercy said, tears running down her face. "You may have destroyed the only good thing Benoit De Dreux has ever done in his miserable existence."

"Someone has to pay!"

"Pascal has been paying her entire life! Do you think you and your family are the only ones who have suffered at that man's hands?"

"Hold on, Mercy," Rey whispered in warning.

"Did you see her, Rey?" She choked on her tears, then brushed them aside with her shoulder so they wouldn't blur her vision. "She's stiff. I'm not even sure she's breathing."

Seeing Mercy on the edge of losing control, Rey shoved Lena aside. In two steps, he'd reached Mercy's side. He grabbed his gun and reloaded the Colt, then locked his fingers around Mercy's arm and backed them both toward the shanty. Lena's men watched, their faces twisted in angry snarls. When two reached out to help Lena out of the coffin, Rey shouted, "Leave her there."

Both men looked up in openmouthed dismay. Lena's eyes grew large on her face.

"Stay right where you are lady." To Mercy, he whispered, "Go back to the carriage. Tell them to leave one horse. I'll meet you at Bizy."

"No—"

"Do it, Mercy! Pascal needs you."

Mercy glanced from Rey to the three men and Lena.

"Now, Mercy!"

"I'm afraid to leave you."

"I've faced worse odds," he said, using her own logic. "Don't worry about me. Think of Pascal."

With a final apprehensive glance at Lena and her followers, Mercy backed closer to the screen of branches enclosing the burial site, then turned and disappeared into the thicket. With a cackle, Lena shouted after her, "You're too late! She's dead. Do you hear? She's dead."

A blazing anger ignited inside Rey. The anguish on Mercy's expression remained etched on his conscience. What would he have done if it had been Christopher in that coffin? How would he survive seeing his child in Pascal's condition? The enormity of her pain devastated him as keenly as it drove him to deal with the threat of the voodoo priestess.

Rey took two steps toward Lena propped in her coffin, stopping beside a whitewashed brick tomb only a few feet away. "Why don't you just lay back down and rest," he said to the priestess. "You there," he commanded one of the men. "Get the top on that coffin ready. The lady wanted a burial. Let's not disappoint her."

The man hesitated. Silence reigned, all appalled by what Rey suggested. But one shot fired at the ground served as incentive enough, and while Lena screamed her protests, two men reached for the coffin lid while the third grabbed up a shovel.

Rey leaned against the cool brick, preparing for a good wait. "And when I'm gone, I suggest you forget about following me. It shouldn't take three strong men like you too long to bring her back up—but I'd do it real fast." His smile turned as diabolical as Lena's. "You wouldn't want any bad spirits to get her, now, would you?"

Mercy cradled Pascal in her lap, trying to hold her steady in the pitching carriage. Beside her, Harlan clutched Pascal's hand, as if needing to touch some part of her. Mercy glanced at his face, searching for courage there. But the carriage lamps revealed only a very young man, his face pale and his eyes glassy with fear. Mercy thought of Rey's strength. She and Harlan would have fallen apart at the cemetery without him. She only hoped she'd done the right thing leaving him to face Lena's followers alone. But then Doc Chiang picked up her stepdaughter's limp wrist and examined her pulse. His expression left no room for doubts about past actions.

"Can you help her?" she asked.

Doc Chiang reached into a small leather case he'd brought and retrieved a cone-shaped cylinder. The device had tips, which he fit into each ear while holding the cone against Pascal's chest. "Perhaps, but I fear for her life," he said bluntly, removing the instrument and dropping it back into his bag. "She has barely a pulse. Her heart beats faintly. They have most certainly given her *fugu*."

"What the hell is that?" Harlan asked, his voice breaking.

"Pufferfish. The voodoos mix a potion with the poison of the fish and herbs. It slows the heart. Makes the victim as if dead. Given in small doses over time, the pulse almost stops and the victim is entombed. They become zombis. The voodoo people believe that a zombi can speak with the spirits. At night, zombies are dug out to speak what they have learned."

"Then she won't die?" Harlan asked the question on Mercy's lips.

His eyes filled with compassion, Chiang looked from Harlan to Mercy. "The pufferfish has a very strong poison. She could survive. Many do not."

"Isn't there something you can give her?" Mercy pleaded. "Something to . . . speed up her heart?"

"I can but try."

Pascal's body stiffened against Mercy. Chiang pushed Harlan aside, grabbing the girl's shoulders. Pascal spasmed again.

"Everyone, to the other side of the carriage," Chiang commanded.

Mercy and Ling Shi huddled together on the seat opposite while Harlan remained on the floor cramped near the door. They all watched helplessly as Chiang settled Pascal lengthwise on the bench seat. He placed his ear to her chest, then held his cheek over her lips. He swung back his arm, looking to strike the girl. Harlan lunged and grabbed his wrist.

"Harlan!" Mercy pulled him off Chiang. "He's a doctor. He's trying to save her."

"I must shock her heart into beating again!" Chiang explained, raising his fist once more.

Harlan fell back against the edge of the seat and watched Chiang punch Pascal's chest; her body jolted against the bench on impact.

Hugging Mercy, Ling Shi stared at Pascal, tears running

down her cheeks. Harlan waited, his fist as tight as Chiang's as the doctor struck Pascal again and again. Each time Chiang would stop to listen to her heart, but Pascal's condition didn't improve.

"Give me my bag, Ling Shi."

Ling Shi wiped her tears and reached for the black satchel. She knelt on the floor next to Harlan, holding up the opened bag. Chiang took out a paper filled with white powder, which he fed slowly past Pascal's lips with a tiny silver spoon. After a moment, the girl's body relaxed on the bench seat. Chiang took up her hand, his fingers seeking her pulse. He called to Harlan, giving the Cajun Pascal's hand. "You must hold her small finger, very tight. It will stimulate her heart."

Through the remainder of the wild carriage ride, Mercy witnessed the procedure repeated—too many times without any apparent change in Pascal. Harlan remained on the floor beside Doc Chiang, holding Pascal's finger as instructed. Often, his lips moved and Mercy knew he was praying. Silently, she joined him, adding her own entreaties for Rey's safety.

When they reached Bizy, Harlan carried Pascal to his room. On the bed, her face appeared as white as the gown she wore. The single braid of hair had escaped its coil at the base of her neck and now twisted over her shoulder, down to her waist. Only a few strands curled around her pale cheeks. The simple gown barely reached her ankles, and she looked younger than her sixteen years—barely out of the schoolroom. So innocent, Mercy thought. How could someone so good, die so young?

Mercy focused on Pascal's small chest, watching it rise slightly, then collapse in a breath. She pressed her knuckles to her lips. *Please let her live!* But doubts as she watched her stepdaughter's fragile shape crowded her hope. If only she'd watched over Pascal more closely, guarded her as a mother should. Why had Santana's business always come first? Damn Santana! Damn herself.

Seated on a chair at Pascal's bedside, Harlan hovered over her. To Mercy, he seemed to coax each breath from her stepdaughter. He brushed back a lock of hair from her face. "*Petite?* Can you hear me? I love you, *ma pauvre 'tite,*" he whispered, heedless of the room full of sober-faced observers. "Listen to me, *petite.* You have such a big heart, I can't believe it will fail us now." He took up her hand, and, watching him, Mercy felt tears come to her eyes. "You once said that if your love were strong enough, it would save me. *Petite,* I want the same for you." Then softer yet, "Please let my love be strong enough."

Mercy swallowed past the tightness in her throat. She turned away; Harlan's pain combined with her own, making her heart ache with the weight of it. She searched out Doc Chiang and found him preparing more powders at the washstand.

"Will she survive this?" Mercy asked.

His somber expression offered little hope. "By morning," he said, "we will know."

There was a deep sadness in his eyes—the sadness of regret. *He thinks she's going to die.* Mercy's stomach twisted, the muscles squeezing into a tight knot. *Pascal can't die!*

A wave of cramps seized her. The intensity of her pain took her by surprise. She was thankful Chiang had turned back to the washstand as she struggled to catch her breath. She tried to relax, but her fears for Pascal had become a physical ache she couldn't control. She clutched her stomach as her muscles constricted tighter and tighter.

It was happening again. She was losing a daughter. Almost in sympathy, her body mimicked her miscarriage, flooding Mercy with pain and memories. She straightened, forcing herself to push back the black abyss of her fears. She had to be strong for Pascal. She wouldn't give up hope. Her stepdaughter needed her. She was the girl's guardian, responsible for Pascal's welfare.

Two familiar hands pressed against her shoulders. She

turned to find Rey behind her. Relief at his safe return flowed through her, sweet and consoling. Her pain ebbed, only to clamp down seconds later with renewed force.

"Are you all right?" Rey asked, his gaze slipping from her face to where she held her hands wrapped around her stomach.

Mercy tried to answer. Impossibly, tears choked her voice. She couldn't believe how much she wanted to collapse against Rey, to use his strength to buoy her.

Rey frowned as he watched Mercy step away from him. Her features were pinched, as if she were fighting some great pain. He'd left Lena's men busily digging up the coffin he'd forced them to bury and had hurried back to Bizy. He'd already learned from Mac of Pascal's condition. They could do nothing but wait to see if the girl survived the drugging. It was Mercy who concerned him now. Her shoulders tensed as her hands tightened around her stomach. She looked as if she might collapse. The others in the room had turned to watch them with sympathy as Mercy's body began to tremble.

With a curse, Rey lifted her into his arms. He tucked her close against his chest, ignoring her weak protests, and carried her out of the chamber and into the hall. Entering his room, he didn't bother to shut the door behind him. He took her to his bed and lowered her onto the coverlet. She turned on her side, away from him, and curled up on the counterpane, clutching her stomach.

Rey studied the row of silk-covered buttons curving down the line of her spine. As her body clenched, she brought her knees up to her stomach. The sight of her pain diminished him. This was more than the physical ache; her fears for Pascal consumed her.

Rey laid his hand on her shoulder. "She won't die," he promised, willing to say anything to ease her pain.

He saw her head shake against the pillows. She lifted up on her hands, trying to rise. "I have to help her. Pascal needs me."

Rey eased her around to face him, taking her into his arms. But Mercy pushed him away until he gripped her shoulders, forcing her to look at him. "You can't help her, Mercy. She's not even conscious. She has all the help she needs from Chiang and Harlan. The best thing you can do now is gather your strength."

She clutched her stomach again. If he hadn't been holding her, she would have fallen to the bed.

"Look at you, dammit! You can't even walk out of here. I'm getting Doc Chiang—"

"No!" She grabbed his hand. "No, please. It's only my fears. It will pass. He has to help Pascal." When he would have ignored her, she hung on to him, a desperation to her eyes that he'd not seen before. "I swear I feel better. Please, Rey. Pascal needs Doc Chiang."

He wrapped her into his embrace, unsure how to help her. For the moment, she allowed Rey to hold her. As he rocked her in his arms, Mercy's dry sob escaped against his neck. "God in heaven," she whispered. "Don't let me lose her. Don't let me lose her. My f-fault . . . m-my fault."

The dark confession tore at his soul. He knew the pain of seeing a loved one die. He'd lived through the agony of being the survivor. How many times had he wished he'd died, and not Sophie. "Don't blame yourself, Mercy," he whispered. "There was nothing you could have done to stop Lena. Even Harlan can't take responsibility for that witch's actions—and it was for him Pascal sought the woman. Lena wanted revenge. If anyone is to blame, it's De Dreux."

Another sob burst past her lips. "Benoit . . . I'm just . . . like Benoit."

Rey cupped her face in his hands, forcing her to look at him. "Listen to me. You're making yourself ill acting like this. And what good will that do Pascal? What happened tonight is no one's fault."

"Oh, Rey. You don't know." Mercy placed her fingers against Rey's mouth, stopping his words of comfort. Her hand trembled against his lips; there were tears in her eyes. He'd seen her through the pain of a bullet wound, the fear of capture, and the abuse of her husband—but never had he seen her spirit broken.

"You don't know the truth, Rey; I didn't want to tell you . . ." She bit her lip, in the grip of her emotional torment. "Benoit created me. He's responsible for everything I am, everything I have. He was right all along. I'm just like Benoit—"

Rey crushed her to him, silencing her. Hadn't he said the same of her a dozen times over the past two weeks? He'd wanted to brand her a criminal no better than any other. And yet, hearing her talk like this twisted his insides. He couldn't listen to another word of it. He had to stop her, had to shut her up.

He swept her hands back and quieted her with kisses, knowing he was seeking comfort for himself as much as Mercedes. He brushed his kiss against her lips, then forced his mouth against hers when she tried to evade him. But Mercy would have none of it. She pushed him away, then struck his chest with her fists until he released her.

She backed away on the bed, cornered against the bedpost. "Listen to me!" she shouted. "For once in my life, I'm speaking the truth."

Aren't they the same, Rey? a voice wheedled in his head. *Both criminals. Aren't all lawbreakers the same? The bad guys you fight to put away?*

"What the hell are you talking about," he shouted. "You're nothing like De Dreux."

"I am his creation! Those women you saw in the swamps. I was one of them! Me, Mercedes De Dreux. Benoit's men captured me in a London alley and brought me here. He educated me, bought my clothes, gave me a past. Everything I am . . . everything you see . . . his. Right down to my name! My name was never Mercedes. I was simply Mercy—the street girl who got caught trying to pick pockets! I've been stealing since I was five years old.

It's in my blood. Bad, always bad. I tried to make things right. I tried . . ."

Rey leaned back on his heels, overwhelmed by what he was hearing. She'd been one of the women in the swamps —one of the girls he'd seen herded into the waiting boats? No, it wasn't possible. Yet, there was no denying the truth he saw in her eyes. And in a way, her story made a horrible kind of sense; it explained so much about the strange double life she'd chosen. Mercy, not a criminal seeking money or revenge, but a victim of white slavery.

Her words transported him to the night two weeks ago, when he'd waited on the Barataria shore with Gessler. Had Mercy fallen to her knees and cried for help in the sand just like the girl he'd watched stumble to the ground? What had Mercy sacrificed to be saved from the fate of the brothels awaiting the others? What had she endured at Benoit's side for that escape?

"That's why you did it," he said, understanding now what drove her. "Santana Rose, everything . . . the girls. You were one of them. You wanted to save them."

"It was all wrong, just like you said. I was only giving Sotheby money to create more victims. And now . . . Oh, God, Rey." New tears filled her eyes. "I'm pregnant."

It was his turn to feel a punch to his gut. He should have been prepared, he knew there was a chance. . . . "Mercy, I—"

Her hand clamped around her stomach and she gasped. When she looked up to meet his gaze, a new horror dawned on her face. Instantly, Rey made the same realization.

"The pain," she whispered. "The pain in my stomach."

Another miscarriage.

"Rey." The tears spilled down her cheeks. "I can't bear it, Rey."

He reached across the bed for her, hugging her. He held her as he followed a wild pitch of emotions, the strongest of which was fear that a person couldn't possibly survive so much heartache. Not alone. It did something to you to face that much loss. Hadn't Sophie's death changed him, twisted him until he'd allowed himself only regret and self-reproach?

"Hush, Mercy," he whispered. "I want you to lay back and rest." He pressed her head to his shoulder, stroking her hair as she cried. "Whatever happens is in God's hands now. Hush, my heart."

"I w-wanted your baby so b-badly. Rey, I'm so frightened. P-Pascal, the miscarriage, the g-girls. Everything bad. Everything w-wrong."

"It will work out, Mercy. I'll help you. Together we'll work it out."

She shuddered against him, her breath a series of jolting hiccups. Rey heard a knock at the door. He glanced up, still rocking Mercy. Mac stood at the threshold, waiting.

"The Doc sent this for her." He held up a cup. "It's a tea of some sort. It might help."

At Rey's nod, Mac walked in. Taking the cup from him, Rey helped Mercy drink. She grew lax in his arms as the warm tea did its work. He laid her down on the bed, then stood to watch her as the posset took effect and she eased into what appeared to be a drugged sleep.

Mac cleared his throat. "About what the lass was saying . . . I couldn't help overhearing."

Rey's eyes remained on Mercy. "I'm not accusing you of eavesdropping, Mac."

"Kate told me her story, Rey. It's bad, worse than what she told ye."

It couldn't be worse, Rey thought. She'd suffered so much already—life on the streets, abduction, the miscarriage . . .

"She was only twelve when he took her," Mac said. "He beat her into learning how to be a lady, starved her, Kate said. Whatever it took. The bastard wanted the perfect wife, the kind that wouldna have him because he's got black blood. His first wife werena class. He thought to

make up for her lack in Mercy. Lucky for the lass she's a
fast learner." Mac sighed. "He got her pregnant when she
was all of fourteen." Mac lay his hand on Rey's shoulder,
and Rey braced himself for the words that were coming.
"Kate says he beat the baby out of her."

He remembered the night Mercy had first come to Bizy.
Remembered the bruises. "I can't believe she stayed with
him."

"She has friends in London, two girls De Dreux says
he'll hurt if she leaves him. She was trying to bankrupt him
so he wouldna have the money to harm the lasses. And
then there were the girls in the swamp . . ." Mac shook
his head. "Like I was telling you, Rey. Circumstances
make people do things."

"Yes. I remember."

Mac studied his friend. "You think she'll lose the baby?"

"I don't know, Mac." And then, after a long, thoughtful
silence, "I pray to God she doesn't."

Mac nodded, stepping back for the door. After a slight
hesitation, he turned back to Rey. "Kate said, only a man
without a heart wouldna understand why the lass thought
up Santana Rose. Do you still have a heart in you, Rey?
Or did Sophie take that with her when she died?"

Rey looked down at Mercy's face, still tortured despite
her sleep. "I have a heart, Mac," he answered. "If I didn't,
it wouldn't be breaking now."

Chapter 24

Mercy blinked her eyes open. Her cheek lay against a warm chest. Soothing fingers stroked her hair. She could smell the soft scent of pine. *Rey*.

"You're awake," he said.

She looked up. Sunlight streamed through the window-pane, washing his hair into a flash of brightness against the dark walnut headboard. He was leaning up against a mound of pillows, Mercy cradled against him. His eyes looked very tired, as if he needed to sleep. There was a slight smile on his lips. Mercy almost smiled back when she remembered.

"Pascal." Immediately, she sat up, ready to go find her stepdaughter. Two hands steadied her against Rey.

"She's fine, Mercy. She woke up an hour ago, hale and hearty. She's resting now." Rey turned her to look at him. The same easy smile remained on his lips. "You're fine as well. I mean, the baby. Doc Chiang says your stomach pains were caused by fear, not a miscarriage."

Mercy closed her eyes. The muscles of her throat con-stricted and she took a deep, steadying breath. *Thank God*. She swallowed past the tightness in her throat. Pascal was fine; Mercy had kept the baby. *Thank God*.

She turned to get off the bed. Again, Rey checked her movement, holding her. Mercy looked up at him, startled. "I want to go see her, Rey."

"You will," he said softly. His hand brushed back a few

strands of hair from her face. "I just need to talk to you first." He tipped her face up to his. "About what you said last night."

A dull throbbing pounded in her chest. All her dark confessions rang through her head as she faced Rey. She looked for censure in his eyes, then frowned, seeing nothing in their cool depths but a stoic calm.

He caressed her cheek with his fingertips. "Mercy, I know all about what your husband has done, about the miscarriage, your friends in London—" At her look of surprise, he added, "Kate told Mac."

Mercy dropped her head to her chest. She smoothed her skirt over her ankles as she tucked her feet under her. "I see."

He shook his head. "I don't think so, Mercy. I don't think you see at all," he added more firmly. "You must know what kind of man Benoit is, what drives him. He's selfish, greedy, and very vicious." He steadied her face on his, examining her with his tired gaze. "Don't ever compare yourself to him. What you did as Santana—the robberies, Sotheby—may have been misguided, but not evil. Think of the reasons behind what you did. Were you stealing for money? For power? Do you truly think you're anything like De Dreux?" Again, the gentle smile. "Given choices, we all make mistakes, Mercy. But it's what we feel in our hearts that determines our character."

She blinked back her tears. She thought of Benoit, saw again his distorted features as he beat her, his dark eyes and their hunger to possess. He wanted to hurt people. Their pain brought him solace from his family's rejection. She knew of no other man with more hate and venom in his heart. She remembered her words to Pascal: *You are nothing like Benoit. You could never do the things your father has done. His mind is twisted.*

She looked back at Rey, saw his encouraging smile. The fears she'd kept inside of her the past two weeks—*Frankenstein's monster, evil*—waned, losing their grip. Her heart expanded, filling with hot emotion, with hope. She reached out and placed her palm on his cheek, searching his gaze as she asked, "And what do you feel in your heart, Rey? About me? About the baby?"

His smile faded. His eyes shifted to focus behind her. Inside Mercy, hope slowly died.

"I think I'm in no position to judge you," came the soft response. She felt Rey's chest contract in a sigh. His gaze centered on hers again. "I want you to know, I understand why you've acted as you have. Even why you lied about the baby."

She forced a smile, denying her desire to weep. It had been too much to hope for, Mercy told herself, to be able to banish the past and start over with their love. "So you understand, do you, Rey?"

There was a flash of regret in his eyes before he pulled away, swinging his legs over the bed. "I told you, Mercy. I don't want you to think ill of yourself. Of course, I understand."

She could hear the restraint in his voice. The awkwardness. *But you can't forget,* Mercy thought sadly. Rey, the lawman, could never forget.

"I have to go," he called to her as he buttoned his shirt and reached for his jacket. "Mac will make sure you and Pascal get back to L'Isle des Rêves. We'll talk soon, Mercy. I promise."

He couldn't even face her, she thought. He was leaving her for Mac to take home. "Of course, Rey. Whatever you say."

He shrugged on his coat and turned to her. "I want you to know that no matter what happens, I'll be responsible for this child."

Mercy leaned against the pillows as she watched Rey walk out. She closed her eyes, fighting the tears. Responsible. Such a solid, staunch word. Comforting.

But it wasn't love.

* * *

Rey waited in the chamber above the tavern. The saloon Sotheby had chosen for their meeting could have been any one of the run-down establishments that haunted Gallatin Street. As he surveyed the sparsely furnished room, Rey guessed Sotheby owned the place, or knew the owner intimately enough to think the tavern safe for their rendezvous. Rey studied the dilapidated interior, concluding that, unlike De Dreux, who showed off wealth he could ill afford, Sotheby preferred to play the pauper.

Fighting the urge to nod off, Rey straightened his back against the slats of the wood chair. He'd stayed awake all night watching Mercy sleep under the influence of Doc Chiang's tea. He struggled now to keep alert, but like a haunting refrain his thoughts returned to Mercy and the bitter truths he'd learned.

How could a woman who'd never experienced justice, whose life had been tormented by an animal like De Dreux, ever have faith in a legal system that had abandoned her from birth? Knowing what had created Santana Rose, the forces that had driven Mercy to seek Sotheby's aid, Rey could understand her actions—and yet, he'd been unable to offer total forgiveness or renew his offer of marriage.

He told himself he needed time to digest what he'd learned, that his decision would affect many lives and should be made after honest contemplation. But he knew the reasons for his hesitation weren't that selfless or simple. When he'd left Mercy at Bizy, saying only that they would talk soon, he'd been ashamed at his behavior. He could see in her eyes that she needed more than assurances that he'd be responsible for their child.

He stretched his legs, crossing his arms as he mulled over this new lack he'd found in himself. What prejudices kept him from committing himself completely? It wasn't that he didn't trust Mercy. He didn't fear a life of lies and manipulations any longer. Her deceptions thus far had been the result of few choices in her life and little guidance. After last night, it would take a blind man not to see that the results of Santana's efforts tormented her. Rey couldn't believe her capable of repeating them. Why then this barrier in his heart that stopped him from offering more than the tepid assurance he'd given when he'd left her at Bizy? He remembered his conversation with Harlan just the day before. Perhaps the flaw lay in Rey after all.

No answers came—not for Rey, in any case. Harlan had fared better. Pascal had awakened at dawn to wrap her arms around the nearly unconscious Cajun, who'd sat at the girl's bedside the night through. Rey had wanted to stay and watch Mercy's joy at seeing her stepdaughter alive and well, to take her in his arms and share her happiness, but until he could promise a lifetime of those warm embraces, he wouldn't torment them both with their teasing possibility.

At the sound of the door opening, he glanced up. Almost eagerly, he waited for the loathing that always came at the sight of Sophie's murderer. He wanted to sear his heart with it. But as he watched the lanky man with his oiled hair and protruding nose and cigar instruct the guard at the door not to disturb them, Rey experienced only a spark of the old hatred. He was tired, very tired of the hunt for justice and revenge, the sacrifices he'd forced on himself and his family. Truly, he wanted it to end. He wanted peace.

Sotheby waved out the broad-nosed henchman, who looked as if he'd seen his share of life on Gallatin Street. Stepping into the room, Sotheby turned to greet Rey.

"Good afternoon Mr.—" The dark eyes narrowed almost imperceptibly. The frown that followed was quickly replaced by an expansive smile. "Parks, isn't it?"

A prickle danced up Rey's neck. Stepping into the middle of the room to meet Sotheby, he thought of Mercy's warning. As he returned Sotheby's enthusiastic handshake, he told himself to keep on guard.

"My associate tells me we can do business together, Sotheby."

"Yeah." The cigar moved fluidly to the corner of his mouth as he spoke. "Sit down. Take a rest." He extended his hand to a chair whose springs threatened to burst through the thinning cloth. Rey chose the wooden seat he'd just vacated. With a broad grin, Sotheby dropped into the rejected armchair. "Have we met before, Parks? You look familiar."

"Not that I recall," he said honestly enough. If Sotheby remembered him as the unconscious man at Kate's, Rey would claim Santana had wanted Sotheby ignorant of his involvement. But Sotheby's stare made Rey uneasy despite his ready explanation. The man watched him with eyes that missed little.

"Tell me about these banks of yours," Sotheby said.

"I have connections with many financial institutions around the country." Rey's instincts told him to keep this meeting short. He sensed Sotheby suspected something. Rey would return to Bizy and regroup, seek advice from Mac and Harlan. "As Mr. Everard said, we could be a valuable channel for your goods."

"The boodle, you mean." At Rey's nod, Sotheby continued, "Well, now, I've been thinking it would be mighty handy to have a man in banking join the operation. You ever work with queer before?"

"Certainly."

"Where?" The word was a solitary bark. Sotheby leaned forward in his chair, suddenly more interrogator than coconspirator.

Rey gave him an easy smile. "Havana, Chicago."

"Yeah." Sotheby fell back into the upholstered chair, cigar in hand. "So your man said." Suspicion oozed from every word.

"Perhaps Mr. Everard also mentioned we were referred to your services by Leonard Marcus?" He added the name of the counterfeiter working with the government, hoping to earn Sotheby's confidence.

"Yeah, good ol' Leo. He's a friend of mine."

Another prickle. "Just so."

"Good, good." Sotheby took a leisurely puff of the cigar, deep in thought. "Ever deal in women, Parks?"

The question surprised Rey. He tried to think how De Dreux's smuggling could fit into the counterfeit operation or the lottery scheme, but saw no connection. "I can't say that I have, though I understand it's almost as lucrative as boodle."

Sotheby took the cigar out of his mouth and stared at the tip. "No women, eh?" He shook his head, then glanced up. "That's a real fine head of hair you have. Real distinctive. Believe I've seen it once before."

Rey's smile remained carefully in place. He studied Sotheby, knew in that moment he'd underestimated the man. Sotheby knew exactly where he'd seen Rey before.

"I wasn't sure if you'd recognize me," he said.

"Oh, Santana tried her best to keep me from getting a good look." Sotheby jabbed his cigar between his teeth again, a look of satisfaction curving his mouth. "But I don't miss much, you see?"

"I want it understood my coming to you now has nothing to do with Santana. She doesn't even know about the boodle." Rey sat forward, balancing on the edge of the chair. "That's between you and me. She needed someone to make sure De Dreux put in more than he could afford to lose. And as you know, I've been quite successful. He owes me . . . big. She would have told you, but"—Rey shrugged—"she was afraid you might take offense. She didn't want you to think she didn't trust you to do the job right."

"Smart woman, Santana."

"Not always." Rey leaned back in the chair with studied calm. "She didn't know the money she delivers for you is counterfeit. When I got a look at the bag of goods, I knew immediately where the real money was to be made. I'm familiar with boodle, Sotheby, and it's a game I like. I'd appreciate it if we kept Santana out of this. More for the rest of us, understand? I guarantee that through my connections, I can pass whatever you can print."

Sotheby nodded, a glint of excitement in his eyes. "Your man told me you wanted to see the plates?"

"It's best to buy straight from the source. More profit that way. I'm a careful man, Mr. Sotheby."

"I'll bet you are." The wicked grin broadened. He tossed the cigar to the floor and stood, walking to the back of the room behind Rey.

Rey stared at the smoldering cigar. That one gesture left him more uneasy than anything else thus far. It kept Sotheby's hands free. The business was going wrong, he knew it as well as he'd known the hundred other times his instincts had saved his neck. Mac, Harlan, they'd both been right— Rey should never have come alone. He grinned, almost shaking his head for the foolish risks he'd taken. It seemed, he'd wanted his peace too badly.

Rey stood, spotted Sotheby behind a desk in the room's corner. "Perhaps we can arrange a meeting to see the plates for another time?" Rey said, already heading toward the door.

The sound of a gun's hammer cocking froze his steps. Rey turned to see Sotheby leveling a revolver at him.

"Perhaps, you should sit back down, Rey."

Christopher Parks sat on the pink satin settee across the salon from Mercy. Beside him, his grand aunt, a widow introduced as Clair Falkner, kept her squirming grandnephew in check with an occasional glower. To Mercy's left, the elegant Nan Mattingly held her back straight against the Belter armchair and her gloved hands folded on her lap as she recounted the family's journey by steamboat down the Mississippi. Nan wore her ebony hair in a braid pinned to border a low puff of curls. Her English straw bonnet tipped in a sporty angle over her forehead, its ribbons dyed to match her blue silk gown. Despite the lady's feminine style and china-doll features, there was a striking resemblance between her and her brother. The color of her eyes, the shape of her mouth, the dimple on her chin, were all features Mercy had admired before. Yet, no matter how startling Nan's appearance or the lady's air of command, Mercy's attention strayed with unmannerly regularity to the young boy on the settee.

She tried not to stare. She forced herself to concentrate on Nan's conversation relating the trip from Boston to New Orleans and its many adventures for a woman who had never before traveled beyond her place of birth. But Christopher Parks enchanted Mercy.

Last night, Mercy had fallen into a despair as black as the day she'd lost the baby ten years ago. To Rey, she'd spoken aloud her greatest fear—that she was bad, capable of Benoit's evil. In her misery, she had even believed it. But this morning, with Rey's guidance, she'd made her peace with her doubts.

Rey's strong denial that she could be anything like Benoit had gone a long way to helping Mercy forgive herself for her mistakes. It was as if screaming out her suspicions, sharing them with another—letting Rey judge her—had brought a sobering reality to her comparisons. Rey was right; she had made some bad choices, but certainly she was not capable of the evil that festered in Benoit.

Like the days after her miscarriage, when Santana had risen from the pain of her loss, a new, stronger Mercy faced this day. She'd been given a second chance. Pascal had recovered, though she was still weak and must stay abed for the day. Doc Chiang assured her that Rey's baby still lay nestled in her womb. There was only one taint to her new beginning. Though she'd gained Rey's understanding, she knew she'd lost his love forever. They were too different. Rey the lawman could never forget her past.

"I can't thank you enough for taking us in," Mercy

heard Nan Mattingly say. "I cannot imagine what sort of place Rennie has chosen to live in if it doesn't even have the landing repaired for river passage."

Taking her gaze from Christopher, Mercy answered, "Your brother seems to prefer his carriage."

The woman blushed, then exchanged a look with the older lady on the settee. "Yes. He would." She sighed and picked up her porcelain teacup and saucer from the table. After a thoughtful sip, she asked, "Do you think it will take Rennie long to get my message, Mrs. De Dreux? Christopher is so anxious to see his father again."

"If there's any delay, I'll be happy to accompany you to Bizy in our carriage," Mercy assured her, though she hoped it would not come to that. It would be difficult to face Rey again so soon.

Nan smiled. "We've all missed him dreadfully. My nephew will turn seven next week. It was his wish to spend his birthday with his father." Her proud gaze rested on Rey's son. Nan turned back to Mercy. "Do you have any children?"

Mercy couldn't help her smile. *A second chance.* Before he'd left Bizy, Rey had given her a last comfort: She carried his child with his blessings. God forgive her for ever wishing herself barren. "Just my stepdaughter. I'm afraid she's indisposed with a terrible cold." Pascal was ensconced in her room, where Benoit would not bother her when he returned from his mistress's bed at Catalan Kate's. It was just as well he'd stayed in town, Mercy thought. Pascal's appearance this morning would have been difficult to explain.

"What a shame," Nan answered sympathetically. "I hope she's feeling well soon."

"Ma'am? Do you have any horses?"

At the sound of Christopher's voice, an unexpected anguish pulsed through Mercy. Her child may never know this boy as a brother, or the warm family that gave Christopher his charm and self-confidence.

"No horses that you shall see, young man," Nan Mattingly answered her nephew, as if realizing after the long silence that Mercy would not speak. "Not until your father arrives."

Mercy looked directly at Christopher Parks. He was taller than most boys his age, and slim, but perfectly in proportion. He looked like a miniature of his father in his brown suit jacket and long pants. His dark brown curls covered his ears and his azure blue eyes first sparked with challenge at his aunt's ruling, but catching Mercy's gaze, brightened with knowing appeal. His smile was beyond enchanting—painfully reminiscent of Rey, though Christopher's expression was filled with the abandon only a child sure of the love and devotion of his family could give the gesture. That's the way her child would smile, Mercy vowed. With a freedom that showed his confidence in his mother's love.

Christopher swung his legs on the settee. Having Mercy's full attention, he raised his brows in a rakish imitation of his father and asked, "Any stallions?" At her nod, he added, "Perhaps just a peek at the stables then?"

"Christopher," Nan Mattingly admonished. "You father would be dreadfully disappointed if you weren't here when he arrives."

The boy gave Mercy a look that seemed to say, "It was worth a try," before nodding to his aunt in agreement. He grinned again. "I like horses very much, but my father will want to see me first thing."

Mercy blinked. She swallowed back the tightness in her throat. She'd always known that any child of Rey's would bring her happiness—but until this moment, she'd never suspected just how much.

Water splashed on Rey's face, seeping up his nose, choking him into consciousness. The pain returned, immediately and with an intensity that almost brought the blessed release of darkness before another gush of water

ruined its effect. His jaw burned. With his hands tied behind his back, the joints of his arms throbbed as if someone had rammed hot coals under his armpits. His guts
twisted, crushed in a vice of physical agony.

He blinked his eyes open. A man's face swam before
him until the double image congealed into Sotheby's beak
nose and smug grin. He held an empty glass in his hand.
Behind him, two thugs stood at attention.

"Good to have you back with us, Rey. There's an associate of mine I'd like you to meet. Leo, come and meet the
man."

Rey blinked back the water dripping from his lashes into
his eyes. He could barely keep his head up. But the unexpected information that Leonard Marcus was in town,
when he'd been paid well to be elsewhere, sent a chilling
warning. Marcus had been working with the government
for the last year as an informant, Rey assured himself. The
man had proven trustworthy until now; he knew Rey's mission and had agreed for a price to serve as his cover. But
the minute Rey saw Marcus's face and the rabid fear in the
man's eyes, Rey knew Marcus wouldn't vouch for him. Rey
was as good as dead.

"Never saw him before in my life, Mr. Sotheby."

"Thanks, Leo. That's all I needed to know." Sotheby's
jaw clamped down on the tobacco in a vicious smile. "Why
don't you go back downstairs with Zack here? He'll take
real good care of you, Leo."

The frightened man hesitated, then smiled. "All right,
Mr. Sotheby. Whatever you say."

"There's a good fellow," Sotheby said, thumping Marcus's back encouragingly. When Marcus quit the room,
Sotheby pulled over the remaining bully. "Tell Zack to see
what he can find out. It's a case of easy money that Leo
knows something."

When the henchman disappeared, leaving Rey alone
with Sotheby, the counterfeiter circled Rey. "Well, well.
Leo ain't never seen you. Imagine that." Sotheby crouched

down in front of Rey and blew a puff of cigar smoke into his face. With an air of satisfaction, Sotheby stood, turning away. Rey didn't see the punch coming until Sotheby's fist slammed into his stomach. He doubled over as far as the ropes allowed, groaning in pain.

"I wonder what your game really is, Parks? And how does my friend Santana fit in?" Again, Sotheby crouched down beside him. "She's in on it with you, isn't she, Parks?"

The clouds of pain vanished. Rey's concern for Mercy's welfare wiped out the physical torture screaming through his body. "What the hell are you talking about?" he gasped, trying to get his breath back. No matter what happened to him, Rey had to make certain Sotheby wouldn't hurt Mercy. "I told you, she doesn't know about my coming to you. She didn't even know the money was counterfeit."

Sotheby's man came back inside. Sotheby nodded him over. "Seems like Rey here needs a little more convincing, Al."

A steel fist of flesh belted Rey's head back. Another blow rammed into his gut. He couldn't breathe, but this time, he fought unconsciousness. Mercy's life depended on him.

"All right." He could barely whisper the words, his jaw ached so much. "So I lied about Marcus." Rey managed a weak smile. "But what's the difference? I heard about him from an associate." Rey hoped Marcus was smart enough to keep quiet about Rey, even to save his own yellow hide as an informant working for the government. "I can help you, Sotheby. I can make money for—"

"It don't wash, Parks." Sotheby took a puff of the cigar and squinted through the smoke. "Santana came to me just yesterday. She wanted in on the queer. Said she'd make it worth my while. And"—there was a jeering note to his voice—"she wasn't talking boodle, if you know what I mean. I thought it was kinda strange at the time. She never wanted nothing to do with me before and suddenly she's hot for me. But I tell you what makes me real suspicious. She wanted to see my plates . . . just like you. Not many passers are interested in the plates; they just want the boodle."

The condemning words floated around Rey like obscenities. What the hell was Mercy trying to do? He'd warned her to stay away from Sotheby, dammit. But then he pictured the guilt-ridden woman he'd held in his arms the night before—a woman who'd attempted to set right the world's wrongs in her own Robin Hood fashion.

Every fiber in Rey screamed for him to fight the ropes . . . do something! But he forced himself to remain calm. Sotheby was only guessing Santana was involved. Even if Marcus broke, he knew nothing about Mercy. Rey couldn't afford to implicate her now by defending her.

"Forget about that stupid bitch. I told you why I wanted to see the plates. I like to deal with the source. No middleman. How do I know you're not buying the boodle from someone else and selling to me at a profit?"

Sotheby's face came to within an inch of Rey's. "Nice try, Rey. But I've been in trouble with the law too often not to know a government man when I smell one. They're the ones who'll promise you the moon—endless money and connections—with no catch. And the only thing they want is to see the plates." He took an exaggerated whiff. "Yessiree, Parks. You reek."

Sotheby walked back to his desk, and took out a sheet of paper. "A real shame about Santana, though." With the cigar in his mouth, he smiled wistfully. "I liked her style."

Sotheby scribbled on the paper and folded the note, then took out a second sheet and did the same. Looking up at the burly man waiting by the door, he held out both pieces of folded vellum. "Al. Take these to Catalan Kate's. One's for that whore, Teresa. You know the girl I'm talking about? The one who knows how to give a good wallop when you need it?" His man nodded with a toothy grin.

"The other you give to Kate, and only Kate, understand? Tell her it's for Santana and it's urgent. Oh, and leave the carriage there." He glanced at Rey with an oily smile. "I'm making a pickup of sorts."

His thug took the notes and left the room without a word. Sotheby turned back to Rey. "You and Santana wanted to see my plates?" He threw back his head and gave a full-throated laugh. "Well, it's your lucky day, my friend."

Mercy walked briskly to the servant's entrance, wondering why Kate would come to L'Isle des Rêves to see her—something the Spaniard had never done before. But the woman the maid had described, a purported messenger from the orphanage, could be none other than Kate. Mercy knew only the most dire circumstances would bring her friend to the plantation. Immediately, she'd given her excuses to Nan Mattingly and her aunt, leaving the two ladies and Christopher in the salon with the promise that she would return shortly.

Reaching the door, Mercy saw Kate pacing outside. She was wearing a hooded pelisse that covered her from head to toe. She wore no makeup or jewelry, apparently trying to bring as little attention to herself as possible. When Kate saw Mercy, she immediately raced over and met her halfway up the steps.

"This came for you, *niña*." She handed Mercy a folded note. "It is from that *animal*, Sotheby," she said, lowering her voice.

"But why didn't you just send the note?"

Kate's thin brows furrowed. "This time not feel right to me, *chica. El perro* left his coach at the back entrance of the saloon. He say he want that Santana take this coach somewhere special. I do not like it. He never do such a thing before. I came here to convince you not to do anything foolish."

With a sigh for Kate's worries, Mercy opened the missive. Each word she read whipped her heart into a frantic pace. Sotheby wanted her to see his counterfeiting operation. His coach waited for her at Kate's, ready to drive her to a secret location.

"He wants to show me the plates," she said meeting Kate's blue eyes. "I must go."

"No!" The Spaniard shook her head, dislodging the hood hiding her red curls. "It is no good, this trip."

"Don't you understand? This is my chance. I won't do anything foolish. I just want to find out where he keeps the plates. If I tell Rey their location, he'll be out of danger. He can bring in his men and arrest Sotheby with this evidence."

"And you think these plates bring you back his love, eh, *niña*?" Kate asked sadly.

Mercy sighed. That was exactly what she wanted. It seemed that no matter how hopeless, she couldn't give up her dreams. "I don't know, Kate. Perhaps it's too late for that. But I have to try. For Rey, for myself. I gave Sotheby the money to buy those poor women into slavery. I can stop him now, Kate. With those plates, I can balance the scales."

Kate hugged Mercy. "You too hard on yourself—but I see you need to do this stupid thing to feel right again." She stepped back from Mercy, releasing her with a sigh. "All right, *niña*. But you take Jean Claude with you."

She shook her head. "The letter says I must come alone."

"Ay, no!"

"Please, Kate! I have to do this."

With a sad look of resignation, Kate nodded. She lifted her hood to cover her hair once more, then stroked Mercy's cheek in a motherly fashion. *"Vaya con Dios,"* she said, giving her blessing. "I must go. I nearly kill my horses getting here before your husband. Teresa say he got bad news about business and is on his way home. You take care, *chica*. Maybe he not in so good a mood, eh?"

"I'll be careful, Kate. You tell Sotheby's driver I'll be there as soon as I'm able." She looked back at the house, thinking of Rey's family. She would have her driver take them to Bizy. At least she wouldn't have to face Rey again.

Mercy wrapped her hands around herself in a tight hug, watching Kate hurry to her coach. Just as Kate mounted the carriage, Benoit's phaeton turned down the drive. Mercy steeled herself to greet him, anticipating that he would want to know whose carriage had just left. When the phaeton stopped, Benoit stepped down. His thick lips were pressed together and his dark eyes burned with undisguised fury. He did indeed appear to be in a thunderous mood. When he saw Mercy, he quickly made his way to the servants' entrance.

"Who was that?" he asked, watching Kate's carriage speed away.

"One of the ladies who helps at the orphanage. She delivered a message," Mercy quickly improvised, holding up the missive for proof, then returning it back to the folds of her skirt. "I'm afraid there's been some kind of emergency with the children. Father Ignacio pleads that I come immediately."

"That stupid orphanage again," he snarled, pushing past her. "Those children can all go to—"

"Come now, Benoit," she said, following him inside. "It's part of my mystique. The charitable grande dame. Surely you approve of that." When he kept walking, appearing to care little what she said, Mercy hurried to catch him. "We've had other visitors as well. Rey Parks's family is here. They're in the salon waiting."

Benoit pivoted back so quickly Mercy crashed into him. He grabbed her shoulders. "Rey's family, you say? Is he here as well?"

He barked out the words, an almost rabid expression of excitement on his face. Mercy frowned, unsure why Benoit would react so strongly. "No. He hasn't seen them yet. The landing at Bizy is in need of repairs and the *Princess* was forced to leave them here. His sister and aunt have brought his son down for his birthday. We sent a note to Bizy, but haven't received a response. I thought to let them use the landau."

"Imagine, Rey's family here." He dropped his hands from Mercy as his lips turned into a smile. "What a pleasant surprise."

"I was surprised as well," Mercy said hesitantly, following Benoit. "They've been here all afternoon and are quite anxious to leave and see Rey—"

"And you're pushing them out the door as quickly as possible," he said almost viciously, handing his cloak to a waiting servant. "Your orphanage calls the grande dame after all."

"Well, I did think once they took their leave—"

"I am completely capable of entertaining our guests and seeing them on their way when they wish to leave, Mercedes. In fact, I look forward to it."

Mercy stared at him with honest surprise.

"Oh, don't look at me as if I've grown a second head." He laughed. There was a sparkle in his eyes, something very close to delight. "I feel quite expansive today. Take advantage of my good will."

"All right," she said, thinking that just a moment ago he'd looked anything but pleased. But she'd given up understanding Benoit's strange mood swings years ago. She followed him down the corridor. "I suppose with you here it won't be too rude for me to leave. I shouldn't take long. Perhaps I'll be home in time for dinner. I'll just go to the salon and explain it's an emergency."

"That's right. Mustn't keep your precious orphans waiting. But I want you back tonight, Mercy. Before dark," he commanded as he reached the stairs. "Where's Pascal?"

"Resting in her room. She's very ill, Benoit. She's not to be disturbed. Enough have died from the fever last season for us to have a care," she added, hoping to keep Benoit from bothering his daughter.

"Then I shall freshen up quickly and try to make up for the complete *lack* in the women of my household."

Mercy pressed her lips together as she watched him climb the stairs. But she took comfort in his rudeness; it was so much more like Benoit to make snide remarks. She started back to the salon, preparing to say good-bye to Rey's family and take her last look at Christopher Parks.

Chapter 25

Mercy held on tight to the strap of the carriage as it careened toward the outskirts of the city. Wrapping Santana's cape tightly around her against the chill, she cursed again the need to leave Rey's family with only her husband as host. It wasn't Benoit's genuine pleasure after meeting their guests that puzzled her—he'd always fancied himself a ladies man and Rey's sister was certainly lovely —but she found his cooperative spirit strangely unnerving. She'd eased her suspicions with simple logic: His new-found camaraderie with Rey, based on Mercy's estrangement, was reason enough to be accommodating. In any case, the two women and Christopher would be on their way to Bizy by now in the landau she'd left for that purpose. Benoit had assured her that he would see them safely home as he'd ushered Mercy out to their phaeton carriage.

Gazing through the drizzle at the darkening sky, Mercy imagined Rey's reunion with his family at Bizy. Though he would certainly not be pleased to see his son in New Orleans during so dangerous a mission, Mercy knew how much he'd missed Christopher. And what a beautiful little boy he was. She held her arm around her stomach, wishing desperately that her baby could grow up with Rey in his life. She believed her child deserved a family; she knew how painful it was to grow up without one. Though she prayed Rey could love her again, she questioned whether the plates could really change anything between them. At least, God had given her a chance to stop Harrison Sotheby, she consoled herself. It was an opportunity she dared not miss.

As the dusk gathered, the icy ball of nerves in her stomach grew. Tonight, she would see Sotheby's operation. If all went well, before morning she would tell Rey where he could find the evidence he needed to convict Sotheby. Mercy thought of his wife's death. Perhaps the plates would do more than balance the scales for Mercy. They might buy Rey some peace as well.

The carriage pitched to a halt before a two-story house. The galleried structure was raised high above the ground on brick piers, a precaution against flooding. Dismounting, Mercy held her cape over the feathers of her mask, shielding it from the light rain. She watched the driver take her horse from the back of the carriage where Mercy had tethered him and lead Little John to the stables. When he returned, the driver guided her up the stairs to the main entrance on the second floor. Once inside, Mercy scanned the darkened cottage for Sotheby, her mask firmly in place. He waited in the corner, smiling with his cigar wedged between his teeth.

"Good evening . . . partner."

Mercy pulled back her cape, shaking off the moisture. Her hand instinctively brushed her gun holster. "*Bonsoir* to you, *monsieur.*"

He walked toward her, his gait a cocky swagger. His hand squeezed her arm intimately. Glancing down at her hips where she wore her holster swung low, he reached for her guns. "Why don't I just take these for you."

She braced both hands on the handles, preventing him from lifting the weapons. "*Monsieur,*" she said, putting just the right amount of censure in her voice. "Do you not trust me?"

Sotheby backed away, holding his hands in the air in a conciliatory gesture. "I just thought things might go more friendly without them." He winked. "I'll show a bit of goodwill and let you keep them. After you." He gestured gallantly to the back stairs. "The plates are down in my office."

A troubling disquiet settled in the pit of her stomach. Sotheby had never tried to disarm her before, had never concerned himself in the least with her weapons. Mercy glanced around the room. They were in fact alone, but the edgy feeling would not leave her. Why this sudden distrust? "Would it not be more simple for you to lead the way, *monsieur*?" she asked, taking some precautions of her own.

He grinned, as if he liked her prudence. "Whatever you say, Santana."

Sotheby bounded down the stairs, a spring to his step. Mercy followed, one hand on the rail, the other on her gun.

"You know, Santana. I've been worried about that man of yours, the white-haired one."

The walls of the corridor pressed in on her. Her sense of unease increased. "Old news, *mon ami*." Mercy fingered the Smith and Wesson and looked behind her. No one followed. She continued down the stairs one step at a time.

"Yeah. I know that's what you said. But I got to thinking"—he reached the bottom of the stairs and pushed open the office door, stepping to the side—"I couldn't quite forget about the gent."

Mercy stopped three steps from the door. Sotheby waited by the threshold, leaning against the wall. Clearly, he wanted her to precede him into the room. Mercy peered through the darkened threshold to the chamber ahead, trying to see what danger might await her there.

"Come on down, Santana. You want to see those plates, don't you?"

Mercy took another step. She could just make out a wood burning stove, a desk, a daybed. She eased forward, searching the corners of the office. She scanned the left, then looked right. When she saw the figure of a man seated in the shadows, she caught her breath. A flicker of light from a lamp·flashed white against his hair.

Rey.

She forced herself to stand perfectly still, to show no reaction. As her eyes adjusted to the dark, she concentrated on Rey, trying to get her cue from him. Any misstep now could be fatal. But then she noticed his arms. They were wrapped around the back of the chair, as if tied there.

Mercy jumped down the last two steps, her heart pounding. Slowly, each injury came into focus: an eye almost swollen shut, a trickle of blood from the corner of his mouth, the livid bruises.

Two men stepped out of the shadows behind Rey. One held a gun to his temple; the other aimed directly at Mercy.

"Maybe he wasn't such old news after all, eh, Santana?"

There was a low buzzing in her ears. An unfamiliar weakness coursed through her legs. Dear God, what had they done to him? She kept her eyes on Rey. He looked foggy, as if he were fighting to remain conscious.

Gathering her strength, she turned on Sotheby. "What is the meaning of this, *monsieur*? You dare to meddle with what is mine? This man has nothing to do with our deal. I demand that you release him."

"Shut up . . . Santana," Rey mumbled.

"He's got a point, darling." Sotheby laughed, obviously enjoying himself. "You're just giving yourself away. Rey here kept real quiet, no matter how much we tried to . . . persuade him. Now hand over the guns, or Zack will put a bullet through his brain."

The scene before her became fuzzy, unreal. She tried to focus, to think of some way to help Rey. She followed Sotheby's orders mechanically, lifting both Smith and Wessons from her holster. At the last minute, she emptied the chambers, allowing the bullets to rain onto the floor, then handed the unloaded pistols to Sotheby, butt first.

"Like I told you, Parks," Sotheby said, shaking his head with a smile. "She's got style."

"Let her go, Sotheby." Rey's head lolled to the side, as if it were too heavy to hold steady. "She can't hurt you."

Sotheby dropped the emptied guns to the floor and kicked them aside. He pulled out his own pistol. "That's where you're wrong, Mr. Secret Service Agent." He shoved Mercy into the room. "Ladies first, Santana."

Mercy stumbled inside, trying to digest the information that Sotheby knew Rey worked for the government. But when she saw his injuries up close, she was beyond thought. He was even more hurt than she'd first believed. There were more bruises. More blood. The ugly results of Sotheby's "persuasion."

"Too bad Leo had nothing to say about Santana here. I was real curious," Sotheby said from behind her. He let out a whoop of laughter. "But boy did he sing loud and clear about you, Parks."

"I told you. She held up my coach and I seduced her," Mercy heard Rey explain tiredly, as if he'd said the same time and time again. "Look at her, Sotheby. Can any man pass her up? I just took what she offered. When I found out she worked for you . . . I used her. I wanted in on your operation."

"You know, I really admire you, Parks. Yessirree. You've kept to the same old story for almost two hours now. No agent. Santana not involved. All you wanted was to make some good honest money with boodle." In a lightning quick change, Sotheby grabbed Mercy's shoulders and spun her around. His dark eyes shimmered with the fire from the lamps; his fingers dug into her skin.

"Is that how it was, Santana?" His voice was low, almost sweet sounding. When she said nothing, he shoved her away. He ran to Rey, pushed aside his bully. Sotheby trained his own gun barrel against Rey's temple. "I have it from the word of a good friend that this man's a government agent here to investigate me. Parks claims you have nothing to do with him, that he used you to get to me. You tell me right now it's true, Santana, and I'll pull this trigger and let you walk out of here." Sotheby's thumb pulled back the hammer. "I'm not waiting long, honey."

Rey fixed his gaze on her, urging her to stick with his story, to sacrifice him. It was the last thing in the world she could do.

"We have worked many months together, *monsieur*," she said to Sotheby. "Never have I betrayed you. You can believe Santana. Whoever told you this man is a government agent is mistaken. I know Parks. I can vouch for him."

Sotheby dropped the hand holding the revolver. Mercy held her breath as he walked directly to her. He seized her arm, locking his eyes on hers. "Wrong answer," he whispered. Over his shoulder, he shouted, "Get him on the bed, boys."

The instant the two men loosened his bonds, Rey sprang to his feet. He kicked one of the men in the groin, then slammed his shoulder into the other.

Sotheby pulled Mercy in front of him. He jammed his arm under her neck. Cold steel pressed against her ribs. "I'll shoot her, Parks. I swear it!"

Rey stopped his one-man battle. He turned and looked at Mercy. Sotheby held her arched against him, his revolver jabbing her side.

"No Rey. Please, not for me," Mercy shouted.

Around him, Sotheby's two henchmen slowly recovered. Rey staggered back into his chair.

"NO!" Mercy screamed.

A fist rammed into his jaw. Rey and the chair toppled backward. He curled into a tight ball, anticipating the kick that hammered into his kidney. Another blow drove against his stomach.

"Stop it," Mercy screamed. She lunged forward, but

Sotheby held her. She tried to kick back only to have Sotheby tighten his grip around her neck. The room dimmed; she couldn't breathe. Helplessly, she watched the two men drag Rey to the daybed in the middle of the room and begin tying him there.

"All right, Sotheby. I admit it," Rey whispered through swollen lips. He lay on his back on the bed as Sotheby's men trussed him up with ropes. "I work for the Secret Service. My men know all about you. I've sent all the evidence ahead to Washington. You won't get away with anything now. Why add murder to the charges?"

Sotheby pushed Mercy toward Rey. She stumbled, then ran to his side. Smoothing back his hair with her hand, she wiped the blood from his lip. "Oh, God, Rey. What have they done to you?"

Someone grabbed her from behind and threw her on top of Rey. She tried not to hurt him, breaking her fall with her hands on the scroll end of the daybed.

"I'll take my chances, Rey, ol' boy," Sotheby answered from behind her. "I've been in worse fixes than tonight's."

Following his instructions, Sotheby's men bound Mercy and Rey together in a parody of an embrace. Mercy's arms were forced on either side of Rey until they hung over the bed toward the floor. The two men anchored each wrist to the bed's cabriole legs with rope so she couldn't move her weight and roll off. Rey's arms were strapped around her waist. Their legs were bound together, then secured to the opposite end of the bed with more ropes. When the men were finished, neither Mercy nor Rey could budge from their position on the daybed.

Sotheby hovered over them. In his hand, he held a bar of metal. "It's a shame the plates have to go up with you, but I don't like the idea that you got so close, Parks. Nope, I got me all set up in Honduras. Maybe, in the future, when things aren't so hot, I'll get back to boodle passing. Always been my favorite game." He stroked the plate lovingly, then shook his head and tossed it. Glancing over

Rey's head, Mercy saw it land near the door. "For now," Sotheby added, "it's the sunny South. Burn it, boys."

His men began breaking up chairs. When they finished, they stacked the pieces in the far corner of the office and lit the piled furniture. Chomping on his cigar, Sotheby instructed his two thugs to wait outside as the fire began to kindle. Mercy looked over her shoulder and watched Sotheby take out a knife. He stabbed the sofa near their feet, tearing a gap in the fabric, and laid his cigar in the rift just out of reach of either Mercy or Rey. Smoke immediately lifted from the hole.

Taking a bottle of bourbon, Sotheby doused the couple and the carpet around them. "The two love birds found clutching each other. Such a dreadful accident, falling asleep drunk with a lit cigar." He walked to the head of the bed, then pulled Santana's mask off Mercy and yanked her wig to the floor. His eyes grew wide as he recognized who she was.

Sotheby stood back, watching Mercy with a thoughtful expression. "You know, I don't think I'm going to tell poor ol' Benny about this one," he said. "It would break his heart." He stroked her cheek with the feathers from the mask. "Though we were never properly introduced, I always thought the charming Mrs. De Dreux had the face of an angel." Sotheby gave her a short salute and turned. From the door, he glanced around the room and laughed. "Judging from these timbers, in no time at all, you'll probably be one."

Chapter 26

"Listen to me, Mercy," Rey whispered as Sotheby shut the door behind him. His voice sounded hoarse, as if he'd barely the breath to use it. "There's a chance we can get out of here alive if we work together."

Mercy coughed. The acrid smoke from the cigar smoldering in the couch and the furniture burning had just reached her nostrils. Her face hovered inches from Rey's. "What should I do?"

"Can you slip your hands out of the ropes?"

Mercy yanked viciously. "No! They're tied too tight."

"All right, don't panic. Can you feel where my hands are?" Rey pressed his arms around her waist. She nodded. "I'm going to try to get my bound hands over your head, but you need to move forward and lift your head back. Can you do that?"

She tried to drag her body up. When she saw Rey wince as she pressed against him, she stopped.

"Dammit, Mercy! The minute a spark hits that bourbon, we're going up like a match. It's going to hurt a lot more to roast on this bed than anything you can do to me."

"My ankles are strapped down. I can't move an inch."

"Try!"

She bit her lip. A metallic taste seeped into her mouth. She wriggled her toes in her boots, arched back her heels. One foot slipped a fraction inside her boot. She tugged hard on the other. Another half inch.

"Come on, Mercy. You can do it. For the baby. For us."

She gritted her teeth, straining. Her ankles burned where the ropes squeezed her boots. *Our baby. Think of Rey and our baby.*

"Just . . . a bit . . . more," he ground out. "All right. Now push off me."

Mercy threw her head back. Rey's forearms jammed against her ears, squeezing them forward as he worked his tied hands over her head. His hooked elbows wrenched her arms, causing the joints at her shoulders to scream in pain. Strands of hair caught, ripping from her scalp when he finally managed his hands over her head.

Rey held his tied wrists in front of her mouth. "Can you work the ropes off with your teeth?"

"It's too thick to bite through!"

"Can you unravel the knots?"

Mercy clamped her teeth on the rope. The heat from the fire flailed her back. She could hear the popping of burning wood—a hissing, snarling threat. Her teeth ached. Her jaws throbbed. *The baby. For Rey and the baby.* She bit down harder, twisting the rope, working it loose. The knot gave a fraction.

"That's it," Rey coaxed. "You can do it, love."

His encouragement left her strangely energized. All the old fears, the past battles between them, no longer mattered. They were working together to save the life of their child. Mercy drew on the ropes. *I won't let Rey die! I won't let our baby die!*

With a cry of determination, Mercy yanked—the knot gave. Working with her, Rey jerked the ropes off his wrists. He reached for his belt buckle between them. With a twist and a turn, he pried out a short knife hidden in the leather with the belt buckle as its handle. He sawed through the ropes tying her arms to the legs of the daybed, smiling when he saw Mercy's astonishment.

One rope gave way. He turned his knife to the next.

"We're going to make it, Mercy." Thickening smoke

choked the air. The knife cut through the second line. He reached for the cord anchoring their waists to the couch. "He's not going to get you too," he said almost to himself.

The rope snapped. He hugged Mercy, rolling them off the couch.

The mattress exploded in a bed of flames. In one motion, Rey sliced through the last ropes tying their feet to the daybed and tumbled them out of the reach of the flames. Santana's cloak enfolded them in a cloth cocoon. With the smoke billowing around them, he kissed Mercy hard on her mouth.

"Come on," he said, untangling them from the cloak. The aches and pains of the past two hours vanished. They were going to make it. They were going to live. He jumped to his feet and guided Mercy toward the stairs. Behind them, the timbers creaked ominously. He yanked open the door. Great clouds of smoke snaked down the stairwell. Rey cursed, knowing Sotheby must have set the upstairs on fire as well.

Ducking low, he held his arm over his face and hauled Mercy behind him, climbing. At the top of the stairs, he peered through the dark fog, searching for the fastest exit. An inferno raged up the walls of the cottage; flames licked the wallpaper where curtains once hung. Coughing for air, he wound their way through the darkened chamber toward the front door and safety. But just as he reached the threshold, Mercy gasped. She jerked her hand out of his grasp.

Rey spun around. Before his eyes, a dark cloud of smoke enveloped Mercy. She took a step back, then disappeared into the smoke.

Mercy held her cloak over her mouth, squinting against the burning fumes. She'd forgotten the plate! The one Sotheby had thrown near the door. She crouched down, bending at the waist, and made her way back to the stairs. Breathing the clearer air near the floor, she reached the stairwell. She dropped down to the first step.

The wood snapped. Her foot hit air as the step crumbled beneath her weight. Screaming, she scrambled halfway down before she caught hold of the banister. She almost dropped the last ten feet, but her boot found leverage on a section of sturdy wood. Her eyes watered from the smoke; she couldn't catch her breath. She could see flames tonguing the door and not much more. She caught a flicker—light reflecting off metal. The smoke parted leaving wisps of vapor to curl around the steel edges of Sotheby's plate, giving tempting glimpses of its prize.

Mercy ripped off her cape and dropped down the last steps. She fell to her knees and wrapped the metal bar in the wool folds. Heat sizzled through cloth. She doubled it again.

An eerie whine filled the air, increasing in volume until it echoed like a woman's screams. She looked up. The beams overhead bent, cracked.

Powerful hands seized Mercy. Her heels slapped against the wood as she was hauled up the steps. When she reached the top of the stairs, holding tight to her package, an explosion roared. Plumes of smoke and debris followed as Rey half dragged, half carried her. He scooted them below the thick terraces of smoke filling the front room. On the gallery outside, he dove down the steps to the ground just as another explosion fired and the front room collapsed.

Reaching a safe distance from the house, Rey crumbled to the grass, gulping air. When he stopped coughing long enough to allow speech, he grabbed Mercy by the shoulders and shook her. "What the hell were you trying to do in there, dammit!"

"I got it, Rey. You didn't see where he'd thrown it, but I did." She pushed the smoking wool-covered bundle at him. When he didn't take the package, she peeled away the cloak. Inside, the steel plate glinted from the moon and the light of the fire raging behind them. She looked up, meeting his eyes. "You said you couldn't convict him without the plates."

Rey stared down at the valuable evidence that had eluded him for five years. With sudden clarity, he realized what she'd done. She'd risked everything, even her life, to make good her mistakes. Now she knelt before him, her eyes filled with hope, holding the plate out to him like an offering.

With a curse, Rey threw the plate to the ground and pulled Mercy into his arms, hugging her until his injured ribs ached. When that contact seemed insufficient, he took her face in his hands and kissed her. "I don't give a damn about the plates. I want you, Mercy! You! Alive and at my side for as long as God keeps us on this Earth." He pressed against her mouth, ignoring the searing pain of his split lip. "Even if I have to tie you to me, I'm going to keep you safe from now on!"

"I thought—"

"I know what you thought, dammit. But you're wrong, Mercy. Nothing is worth sacrificing you. When I watched you disappear into the smoke, when I couldn't find you, then heard you scream and saw those beams ready to collapse. My God." He hugged her again. "I thought I'd never reach you in time." He kissed her eyes, her mouth, her cheek. "I couldn't bear to lose you. I couldn't. I love you, Mercy."

She blinked back her tears, putting all the longing she felt in her embrace. "I love you, too, Rey. That's why it was so important that I get the plate. Now you can arrest Sotheby and—"

Rey stiffened in her arms. She pulled back. "What? What's the matter?"

His gaze centered on the road behind her. He sighed tiredly. When he looked back at Mercy, there was defeat in his eyes. "Sotheby's well on his way to Spanish Honduras by now."

Inside her, a new fear ignited. "That's it? He'll go free?"

At Rey's nod, she jumped to her feet. She started running toward the stables, mindless to anything other than preventing Sotheby's escape. She'd lose Rey—everything. Behind her, he shouted for her to stop, but she only picked up speed. An arm hooked around her waist. Mercy twisted out of his grasp, spinning forward. His fingers curled around her arm, wrenching her to his side.

"For God's sake! What's the matter now? Where are you going?"

She almost shrugged off his hand, but stopped when she saw his look of concern. She reached up and stroked her fingers against his face, looking into his eyes. How could she explain her fears? How could she make him understand what Sotheby's capture meant to her? She thought of their child, of Rey and his family, the happiness she craved—and then she remembered. Christopher! She'd forgotten to tell him about Nan and Christopher.

"Rey. Your sister came to L'Isle des Rêves today with your aunt and son."

His dark brows rose; his eyes grew wide. "Nan and Christopher? Here?"

"Yes. The landing at Bizy was broken and their steamboat came to our plantation. But don't worry. When I left, Benoit promised to escort them to Bizy. They'll be there waiting for you." She gave his cheek one final caress. "He's beautiful, Rey. Just like his father. He needs you so. Go to him."

She turned away, making her way toward the stables. After only a few steps, Rey caught up to her. "And where the hell will you be?"

"I'm going after Sotheby," she said. "Little John might still be in the stables. I keep a revolver in the saddlebags—"

Rey planted himself firmly in front of her. "You're not going anywhere except back to Bizy with me."

"I have to stop Sotheby. If I don't . . . without him . . ."

"What, Mercy?" he shouted, angry now. "What happens without Sotheby?"

She turned her face away—but not before Rey saw the tears filling her eyes. He took her chin in his hand, guided her face back to his.

"Don't you see, Rey?" She blinked back her tears. "I have to stop him. For us. For the girls he's bought into slavery. For the people he'll destroy with his false money. You've spent the last five years hunting down Sophie's murderer. You say you love me. But if he goes free, how long will it take for your love to sour? How many years will you stay before you have to hunt him down again. I don't want to see your love turn bitter with the first counterfeit bill Sotheby passes. It's the one thing that will always stand between us."

"Is that what you think?" he asked, searching her eyes. Seeing his answer, Rey dropped his hands to his sides. "I suppose I've given you reason enough to believe that." He shook his head. "You're wrong, Mercy. We both were." Rey pivoted on his heel and jogged toward the stable, holding his side as if each step radiated pain.

"Rey! Wait!"

When she reached the stables, he was backing Little John out of the stall. She searched for another horse. When she saw none, she tried to stop Rey from mounting, but he swung his leg over the saddle with a groan, ignoring her.

Rey pulled back on the reins, controlling the spirited horse. "When I return, you're going directly to Bizy with me. We can't take the chance that Sotheby will get word to Benoit about you."

"No, Rey. You're hurt. At least let me ride with you."

"Dammit, Mercy. How many times are you going to risk yourself and our child?"

Mercy took a step back, her lips parted in surprise. She held her hand against her stomach. To Rey, the gesture seemed so natural, so right.

"I wasn't thinking, Rey. I wanted so badly to . . . all right. We'll go back to Bizy; get help—"

"It will be too late then. We both know that." He steered the horse toward the stable door. Looking down at her, he added, "People can change, Mercy. It's an important lesson to learn. I almost had to watch you die to understand that. And if I have to catch Sotheby to prove it to you, I will."

"You don't have to prove anything!"

"It's not just for me now, Mercy. You're always going to see the faces of those girls in your dreams. I know what it's like to have those kinds of nightmares."

"I didn't mean for you to—"

He kicked the horse's flanks. "Give Christopher a kiss for me."

"Stop, damn you!"

Mercy ran after Rey, cradling her hand to her stomach, stopping only when he rode out of sight. She kicked the dirt in frustration, unbelieving that he would go off to capture Sotheby alone. She blinked, feeling strangely disoriented. Behind her, the burning cottage lit up the sky in flames. Help would come soon to douse the fire before it spread. Mercy had no option but to stay put and pray Rey returned quickly, safe and sound.

She walked back to where her cloak lay on the ground with Sotheby's plate next to it. As she bent down to pick up the precious evidence, she caught sight of a flash of red. Santana's mask lay on the grass a few feet away. Sotheby must have tossed the domino there on his way to the stables. Hugging the wool-wrapped plate, she stepped over and dropped down by the feathered mask—the mask of Santana Rose, a woman who knew few limits. She held it and the plate close to her chest as the drizzle began to fall once again, sensing that before this night was over, she would need all her courage.

*   *   *

Rey slowed his breathing. He'd used up the surge of adrenaline that had gotten him and Mercy through the last fifteen minutes. Now, only his training kept him in the saddle. *Discipline,* he told himself, refusing to give in to his pain. But the air trapped in his lungs with the pounding gallop, testing his control. He could barely see out of his right eye. He tried to ease the agony ripping through his side and jaw by concentrating on the job ahead of him. Sotheby most likely traveled with his entourage of thugs at a leisurely pace, expecting no opposition. Though Rey would be outnumbered, he had the element of surprise. He gritted his teeth against the jarring canter and surveyed the road ahead, the only path back to town. In a matter of minutes, he'd reach the carriage. He had scant moments to think up his strategy.

In his mind, he saw Mercy's face when she'd realized Sotheby was escaping. Terror was the only word to describe her expression. She believed justice and revenge would eventually take Rey from her and their child—as it had drawn him away from Christopher. But Rey had sacrificed enough on the altar of the righteous cause to last a lifetime. When he'd watched Mercy standing with Sotheby's gun jammed against her ribs, he would have broken any law to see her safe. The past hours had opened his eyes to that much. Nor would he allow her to bear the guilt he'd suffered these past five years. If she needed Sotheby behind bars to stop her nightmares, so be it.

Rey clutched his side. Horse and rider turned the bend. Through the thinning mists ahead, Sotheby's coach came into view. Rey spurred Little John off the road and down the embankment.

His mount danced around the oaks and maples, swiveling left and right with the grace of no other horse Rey had ridden. Low-hanging branches and moss slapped at Rey, forcing him close to the horse's neck. When they'd traveled a good distance, he pulled Little John to a stop and dismounted. He groaned in pain as his feet hit the ground, took in a cleansing breath and scanned the moonlit clearing. A fallen sapling lay near the road. It was just what he needed for his plan to work.

Rey dragged the seedling across the road. Pain pierced his side with each step, but he couldn't afford weakness. Not now. He mopped the sweat from his face with the sleeve of his jacket and gathered moss from the trees. He covered the sapling with the long gray-green strands, then kicked dirt over the moss to further camouflage it. His head jerked up; he could hear the rattle of Sotheby's carriage in the distance, quickly approaching. Rey stumbled down the embankment and hid behind a clump of palmettos. Taking deep breaths, he inspected his work. In the moonlight, it would do.

Around the curve of the road, Sotheby's coupe appeared drawn by its two horses. The conveyance still traveled at an unhurried pace, the driver keeping the horses to a slow trot. As the carriage neared the sapling blocking the road, Rey drew out the gun he'd taken from Mercy's saddlebag and cocked back the hammer. He waited, watching the horses. Two hundred feet. He aimed straight up, toward the night sky. One hundred feet . . . fifty feet.

He fired.

The carriage horses reared wildly, then bolted, careening over the sapling. The tree jammed against the carriage wheels. *Crack!* The axle snapped between them. The carriage slammed against an oak, ricocheted into another. The driver shouted as the coach lurched, teetered on the embankment, toppled over.

Rey aimed for the carriage door. The hatch thumped open. Al, the man with the steel fists that had so effectively hammered Rey's jaw and ribs, struggled for the long step. He grabbed the door frame for balance, moaning in pain. Rey fired.

The thug grabbed his knee, stumbled forward. Missing his step, he dropped to the ground and curled up in a ball, howling in pain. Sotheby's other man had only a fraction of a second to aim into the darkness before Rey's bullet hurled him to the dirt next to Al.

The driver jumped down from the boot and unhitched the horses. Without a look back, he threw a leg over one of the mounts and disappeared down the road.

"Harrison Sotheby!" Rey shouted from the side of the road. "In the name of the United States government, you're under arrest. Come out with your hands held high."

Sotheby staggered out, holding his side. "Damn you, Parks!" He sucked in a breath, obviously injured in the crash. "Damn you to hell and back!"

"You did, Sotheby," Rey answered steadily. He ran up the road where Sotheby's men were still writhing in pain. He kicked aside their guns, keeping a close eye on Sotheby, who might be armed. "Five years ago, you sent me and my family to hell."

"What are you talking about, Parks? I've never laid eyes on you before that night at Kate's!"

"You wouldn't remember her, Sotheby, one of the nameless faces of the people you use. Boston, 1874." He stepped toward Sotheby, his hand tight on the gun. "A sting operation gone bad at the Citizen's Bank. Your men took a young woman as a hostage. Under your orders, she was held as ransom to assure the release of the men caught passing boodle by the agents working there that day. Her name was Sophie Parks. My wife."

Sotheby's expression changed from anger to undiluted terror. "That was a mistake, Parks. I never meant for them to blow her up—"

Rey shook his head. "Your man had a different story to tell. You ordered those explosives to go off the minute the police released the passers. No witnesses, you said. Less complicated." Rey took exaggerated aim at Sotheby's chest. "You're all heart, Sotheby."

"Calm down, P-Parks. I'm not even armed. You're talking murder if you fire now."

Rey smiled, a grin that hurt his jaw. But he didn't care.

The weight that had dragged him down for five years had been stripped away. Maybe Mercy was right. Perhaps he'd needed this moment to be whole—but not for the reasons she'd thought. Tonight, Rey was a free man. He wouldn't be Sotheby's executioner, despite his threats; Rey had conquered his need for revenge. He stood here not as Sophie's avenger, but as a government agent putting a stop to a notorious criminal. With the promise of the future, the past had lost its hold on Rey.

"Put both hands against the carriage, Sotheby," Rey shouted, "and shut the hell up."

Rey searched Sotheby for hidden weapons. Finding none, he began tying up one of the men on the ground with the henchman's own belt. From the corner of his eye, he saw Sotheby turning toward him.

"Try something stupid, Sotheby," Rey said. "You have no idea how happy I'd be to shoot you."

Sotheby immediately hugged the carriage wall, laying both palms flat against the lacquered finish.

"You have nothing that will stick, lawman," Sotheby gasped, favoring one side. "No witnesses. No plates."

"Wrong, again, Harry ol' boy," Rey said, mimicking Sotheby's facetious manner. "Thanks to Santana, I have one of your precious plates." Rey put the finishing touches on the second man and turned back to Sotheby. "That evidence will put you behind bars for more years than you have fingers and toes to count."

"It won't be enough!" Rey could see the desperation in Sotheby's eyes as he looked over his shoulder. "You'll need Benny to testify and I warned him about you. By now, he's probably halfway down the river—"

Rey slammed Sotheby up against the coach. Grabbing both the man's hands, he hiked them up his back until Sotheby screamed in pain.

"When!" Rey shouted, recalling Mercy's information that De Dreux was escorting his family to Bizy. "When did you tell De Dreux about me! Answer, dammit."

"This afternoon, when I sent the note to Teresa," Sotheby sputtered. "I always keep track of my people. Benny was in town with his whore. I told him everything in my note. He's hightailed it for sure—"

The pistol crashed against the back of Sotheby's head. The man crumbled to the ground. Quickly, Rey unloosed Sotheby's belt and tied his hands together. He had to get back to L'Isle des Rêves. If what Sotheby said was true, De Dreux knew about Rey before he'd returned to his plantation—before he'd promised Mercy to see Rey's aunt, Nan, and Christopher safely home!

Chapter 27

Pascal pushed the stuffed squab around her plate with her fork. Getting dressed and meeting guests for dinner had drained her energies. Even the silverware seemed too heavy to lift, which was just as well. She had no appetite.

A chill wriggled up the nape of her neck when she glanced at her father to her left. His gaze remained fixed —as it had been all evening—on Christopher Parks. Eating quietly at the end of the table, the little boy peeked from the corner of his eyes at the man watching him, as if he were well aware of his scrutiny. Her father had no love for children; even his sixteen-year-old daughter tried his patience. Hadn't he banished her from the dinner table just scant weeks before? Yet, Benoit De Dreux seemed fascinated by Christopher Parks, had insisted the six-year-old boy join the adults for dinner. Pascal shivered as she watched the way his eyes drifted toward the child, examining him like prey.

"Are you certain you're all right, Miss De Dreux?" Nan Mattingly asked. She turned to Pascal's father. "She looks rather pale."

"Your wife stated very firmly the girl wasn't up for company," added Mrs. Mattingly's aunt from across the table. "She said she had the ague—"

"My daughter insisted on joining us," her father assured the ladies. "She's feeling perfectly fine. Aren't you, Pascal?"

"I'm just dandy," she said, matching Benoit's stiff smile.

"I think she should be in bed," Christopher said from his end of the table, "with the covers tucked under her chin." His eyes narrowed on Pascal's father, as if challenging the older man.

Pascal gave a silent "hurray" for the darling boy with Harlan's blue eyes. Not many stood up to her father. Catching her look of admiration, Christopher flashed an encouraging grin.

"Though I suspect you may be right, Christopher," Nan Mattingly answered, smiling at Benoit to take the sting from her words, "I do believe that is for Miss De Dreux and her father to decide. Eat your dinner, dear."

The table conversation continued to flow in an easy manner, but Pascal remained quiet and ever watchful of her father. When the servants cleared the meal, Benoit stood, showing the guests into the salon.

"Will you be staying long in the city, madame?" her father asked once the ladies had been served a glass of sherry. "It would be a shame to deprive my wife and myself of the honor of your company too soon."

Pascal nearly choked on the sweet liquor she'd managed past her lips. Her father's Creole accent gave his voice a warmth that, combined with his elegant manners, would beguile the most unsuspecting. For the sister of Mr. Parks and his elderly aunt, Benoit De Dreux performed his best. Again, she wished Mercedes home.

Nan Mattingly's laughter floated across the room as she glanced at her aunt. "How gallant you are, sir. I'm afraid we are here for only a short time. A week or two at the most. Just long enough for Christopher to celebrate his birthday and spend some time with his father."

"What a shame your brother has chosen to remain estranged from his family. Were I blessed with such a magnificent son"—his eyes darted back to Christopher seated beside his aunt on the settee—"the boy would never be far from my side."

"Christopher's needs," Nan Mattingly answered, her hand firmly on the boy's shoulder, "are always my brother's first priority." Her lovely smile had changed into the prim look of a schoolteacher about to reprimand a mannerless child. "And though he might have selfishly kept his son at his side during his many travels, Rennie chose—for Christopher's sake—to give him a home in Boston where he could have the stability of a family environment along with my three children. It has been my great privilege to take care of Chris this past year, but Rennie is his parent and has often served both role of father and mother quite well."

"I meant no offense, madame."

"None taken, sir. I perceived a misconception and I saw it my duty to set things aright."

The way she spoke, with her back straight and her vibrant green eyes flashing, Nan Mattingly could have just as likely pronounced Benoit an ignorant ass. To Pascal's surprise, her father merely laughed.

"I always considered Rey an extraordinary man. It's a pleasure to see he commands such familial loyalty."

Nan's smile returned. "I'll admit I have little tolerance for criticism against my brother from others. Rennie and I are just a year apart. I've always been a bit of a mother hen where he's concerned." She glanced down lovingly at Christopher beside her.

But Christopher had not been pacified by his aunt's upbraiding of Benoit. His eyes shone with an intelligence rarely seen in a boy so young. Crossing his arms, he steeled his gaze on Pascal's father. "I think you're very mean to make your daughter sit through dinner when she's not feeling well. *My* father always makes certain I have a tray sent up when I am unwell."

"Christopher! That's quite enough." Nan glanced up at Benoit. "I'm so sorry. It is getting late. He's not his best when he's tired like this." Then, glaring back at her nephew, "Though there's no excuse for such ill manners."

She placed the half-empty glass of sherry on the table in front of her. "Perhaps we should be going. I am getting a bit concerned that we haven't heard from Rennie. Your wife mentioned the use of your carriage?"

"I'm afraid that's impossible." Benoit stood and pulled the servant's bell. "My wife has commandeered the landau. You'll have to wait until she returns, which is just as well. She would hate to miss you. If the boy needs to rest, I'll have someone show you to the guest rooms."

For a moment, Nan looked nonplussed. She appeared about to argue, but instead nodded. "Certainly. Come Christopher."

Pascal watched the two ladies exit. Once the door shut, she struggled to her feet. "What's the matter with the phaeton?"

He turned away from the door slowly, as if he'd just noticed she'd remained behind. He seemed to think a moment, pondering if he should make the effort to answer her question. "They'll be much more comfortable in the landau. Go to your room, Pascal, and wait there. I'll send for you when Mercedes returns."

The disturbing flame of wrongness that had kindled in Pascal through dinner ignited into a blaze. "Are you purposely keeping these people here? They want to go to Bizy. Why are you holding them against their will?"

Benoit grabbed her arms, his fingers biting into her skin. "I'm afraid Mrs. Mattingly was right. You're not at all well to be imagining such things." He released her abruptly. Pascal stumbled back to gain her balance. "Go to your room. Your stepmother should be home shortly."

Pascal backed out of the parlor, reaching for the door handle behind her. She kept her gaze on her father, then slipped into the hall. At the stairs, she tried to find the strength to climb to the next floor. The bit of squab she'd eaten hardened into a lump in her stomach. Her father had lied. He didn't want their guests to leave, had in fact taken steps to make sure they couldn't. Now she knew why he'd allowed Mercedes to leave him to entertain alone. Her absence provided a convenient excuse for keeping Parks's family. She thought of Nan Mattingly's concerns: Why hadn't Mr. Parks sent a carriage or even a note for his family? Perhaps he had—a note that her father had confiscated!

Harlan! she thought desperately. She had to warn him, had to reach him somehow. This morning, she'd insisted on waiting until Mercedes was safely out of her father's clutches before she would elope. Now she wished she'd stayed behind at Bizy as he'd pleaded for her to do. On second thought, perhaps it was for the best she'd waited. Now she could help Parks's family.

With barely a breath left, Pascal wrenched open her door. She found three maids bustling about her room. The armoire stood ajar while one of the maids marched to Pascal's bed with her arms loaded down with folded clothes. Two valises lay open on the counterpane. Pascal's portmanteau waited by the hearth.

Pascal grabbed the clothes from the nearest maid and tossed them to the floor. "What are you doing? Who told you to pack my things?"

The woman's mouth worked up and down like a bellows. She glanced at the other helpers behind her. "Your father, Miss Pascal," she sputtered. "He's who told us to pack. For you and the Missus."

"And so you must," came the deep sound of her father's voice from behind Pascal. "But first I'd like a word with my daughter. Alone."

Pascal grabbed onto the bedpost, suddenly finding her legs too weak to hold her steady. She turned on her heel to see her father guarding the door.

The maids scurried past Benoit De Dreux. Pascal's breath came in panting huffs. She felt as drained as when she'd taken Lena's poison. "Why are you doing this?"

"As soon as your stepmother arrives home, we're taking a trip, Pascal. You, Mercedes, and I. Won't that be nice?"

"What about Christopher? And Mrs. Mattingly and her aunt?"

His smile was just short of vicious. "They'll be coming, as well."

"Don't do this, father," she pleaded. "Whatever you're planning. Please, leave the child and his family out—No!"

Too late, the door slammed shut. She stumbled forward and grabbed the knob. A key turned. The lock snapped into place. She lurched into the connecting room, reaching the door as she heard a second click.

Pascal beat her fists against the cypress, rattling the locked knob. "Don't. Please father. Please . . . don't"—she sank down to the carpeted floor—"don't hurt them."

Mercy studied Rey's profile as he stood near the River Road. The moonlight bathed his face and hair with an iridescent glow. Vivid red marred the underside of one eye. Removing her glove, Mercy reached out and wiped the blood dried on the side of his mouth. Rey jerked back at her touch. He watched her as if he'd forgotten her presence. There seemed no expression to his face until a soft sigh passed his lips and he wrapped an arm around her, pulling her to his side.

"We'll get them out safely, Rey," she whispered, trying to console him.

"I keep thinking about Sophie."

"They'll be free before morning. You'll see." She squeezed his hand, trying to make him believe in her optimism even though inside her own faith teetered.

Rey nodded then looked back to Harlan and Mac near the River Road. The group of four was just a mile outside L'Isle des Rêves, waiting for the appointed hour when Rey would travel to the plantation to meet with De Dreux.

When Rey and Mercy had delivered Sotheby and his men to Bizy, both he and Mercy had prayed to find his family there. But in the salon, only Mac waited with De Dreux's letter stating Rey must come to the plantation—

unarmed and alone, if he ever wanted to see his loved ones alive. Harlan had been trussed up like a downed steer in his room. Mac explained, "T'was the only way to keep the fool lad from going after Miss Pascal."

Rey flipped open his watch and glanced at the face. "Almost midnight." He seemed to memorize Mercy's features, then sighed. "I'd better go."

Mercy seized his arm. "Not alone, Rey. Please! I know Benoit. You've ruined his dreams. He'll want revenge. If you go in there, he'll kill you. How will that help your son?"

"Five years ago, I let Christopher's mother die. Mercy, I have no choice."

"But you do! Let me go instead. Benoit is expecting me; I should have returned from the orphanage hours ago. He won't hurt me. Once I'm inside, I can smuggle out your family and Pascal!"

Rey's gaze flicked over the clothes she wore, Santana's black garbs.

"I'll sneak in and change first," she said. "He won't think I'm involved! When he's not looking—"

"Rey!" Mac jogged toward them, then huffed to a stop. "It's time. Harlan and I will ride out first, get into position—"

"He can't go!" Mercy jumped in front of Rey, as if protecting him from Mac. "Don't you see? Benoit isn't sane! He'll kill Rey—even if he must destroy himself in the process."

Mac glanced nervously at Rey, then looked back at Mercy. "Don't ye worry, lass. Rey knows how to take care of himself."

With a frustrated groan, Mercy spun back to face Rey. "Listen to me! Now more than ever it makes sense to give my plan a try."

Rey grabbed her hand and dragged her aside, away from Mac. "Don't you understand," he whispered almost harshly. "I love you. I can't sacrifice you as well."

"It wouldn't be that. Benoit won't hurt me—"

"The note said for me to come before midnight. Alone." He glanced over her shoulder. Following his stare, Mercy saw Harlan wave for Rey to hurry. "Mercy, I told you who to contact if something goes wrong. Mac knows all about the baby. If anything happens to me, he'll make sure you're both taken care of."

She shook her head, refusing to accept his terrible verdict.

"I have to do this." He kissed her gently. When she would continue their embrace, he set her firmly from him. "I don't want to see you anywhere near L'Isle des Rêves, is that understood?"

"Don't go," she whispered, reaching for him. "Don't—"

"Do I have to tie you up as Mac did Harlan or will you stay here?" Then, more gently, "If not for me, Mercy, think of the baby you're carrying."

Mercy closed her eyes. A lone tear slipped down her cheek and she dropped her arms. "All right."

Rey squeezed her hand. Not wanting their last words together to be said in anger, he whispered, "I love you," and kissed her again. He walked back to Mac. "Let's go."

Rey mounted his horse and galloped down the road toward L'Isle des Rêves. Though Mac had done his best taping his ribs, every jolt pierced Rey's side with pain. Ignoring the steady ache, he concentrated on the road ahead, reviewing his hastily made plan. There hadn't been time to round up reinforcements, though they'd been able to cut a deal with Gessler, neutralizing his threat. An earlier reconnaissance showed De Dreux waited in the salon. He held a gun on Rey's family and Pascal as he paced before them, speaking at length as if holding court in his gilded throne room. Harlan and Mac would climb the trees outside the salon. It was Rey's job to make sure they'd have a clear shot of De Dreux through the window.

A paralyzing fear gripped Rey as he thought of the lives of his loved ones depending on the whimsy of a man who was half mad. The similarity between tonight's confrontation and Sophie's death plagued him. But tonight there would be a different ending to his nightmare, even if he had to throw himself in front of De Dreux's gun to free his family.

At the next turn, Harlan and Mac veered off the road. Rey slowed his mount to a trot, giving his companions enough time to get into place. Not until they determined that De Dreux still waited in the salon would Rey venture up the steps of the devil's white palace.

A series of images flashed through his head as he traveled down the oak-lined drive: Sophie on the deck of Sotheby's ship, Christopher as he'd seen him last, playing ball with him in the Commons. He banished his visions, refusing to dwell on the chances of his plan not working. In front of L'Isle des Rêves, he dismounted and waited until he saw Mac wave from the side of the house. Rey took a deep breath and climbed up the steps, thinking of Mercy. She needed him, needed his love and acceptance to recover from the years of torment she'd suffered from De Dreux. He prayed he'd get the chance to return to her.

At the front door, Rey swung the knocker against the cypress. The door creaked open and a servant, her eyes wide with fear, gestured him inside. He followed the young woman into the salon. From the threshold of the double parlor, Rey spotted De Dreux, then immediately saw Nan, Aunt Clair, and Christopher huddled near the window behind him. The sight of their fear raged through Rey, pushing him to the point that he had to look away or lose control. He scanned the chamber for others. He found only Pascal seated in an armchair, her face pale, her fingers clutching the upholstered arms.

"Christopher!"

Nan's voice echoed across the room as Rey's son dashed past De Dreux and launched himself into his father's arms. De Dreux pivoted around. He held the revolver aimed at Chris.

Rey twisted Christopher to his side, placing himself between his son and danger. "For God's sake, De Dreux! He's only a child. Put that gun away!"

"Then get that bastard back across the room. I don't want to kill him if I don't have to, Parks!"

Christopher clung to his father, ignoring De Dreux. "Daddy! Nana is so very frightened—though she doesn't show it. Please make that awful man leave us alone."

"I mean it, Parks!"

Rey pressed his cheek to his son's warm skin. "Everything will be all right Chris, but you must go back to your aunt now." He cupped his son's face in his hand, studying every treasured feature. "I think it might help her feel better to have you by her side, don't you?"

He watched his father bravely. "Yes, Daddy." He leaned forward and whispered, "But I'm a bit scared too."

"Of course you are, Chris. But trust me; this will all be over soon."

Rey turned his son back toward Nan, urging him forward. When the boy reached her side, Nan took Christopher's hand in hers, giving Rey a quick nod. Rey stepped purposely away from his family, forcing De Dreux's attention back to him. De Dreux looked calm and strangely satisfied.

"All right, De Dreux. I'm here. Why don't you let the others go and we can get down to business."

"Not quite, Parks. I find their presence comforting." He circled Rey, swinging the gun from him to his family, then back again. "A bit of insurance."

"Insurance?" Rey measured his steps toward the window, hoping to lure De Dreux within shooting range of the men waiting outside. "I'm alone; just as you asked. I would have thought escape might be more tempting."

"I thought of escape. Then Gessler wouldn't answer my summons—something about circumstances out of his control? I stand alone now, thanks to you. Powerless. There is no escape."

"Perhaps we should discuss that very thing, then? I think I might have some options you might want to consider." He held his hands out and smiled. "Mind if I smoke?" When De Dreux looked about to refuse, he added, "A last request, so to speak. Before you get on with your . . . business."

Apparently finding Rey's comment humorous, De Dreux grinned. "As you wish." He trained his gun on Christopher. "But bring the cigarettes out very slowly."

Rey reached in his coat and drew out his package of Choctaws. He lit a cigarette and turned to the window, signaling Mac and Harlan outside that the situation was dire. They should shoot to kill at the first chance. All he needed to do now was coax De Dreux to his side, closer to the window. There was plenty of light in the room to give his men a good target. "You're right about Gessler. His allegiance has shifted with the tides after receiving instructions from my men. I suggest you do the same, De Dreux. You and I could come to some kind of arrangement, like I did with Gessler. But I won't talk with my family here. Let them go. They've served their purpose. I came; just as you asked. They're of no use to you now."

"I disagree." De Dreux moved away from the window—toward Christopher.

Rey felt the skin at the back of his neck crawl. Christopher watched him with his chin up, not even allowing a moment's fear to creep into his gaze.

"I've enjoyed getting to know your family. Your son is a fine boy," De Dreux said brushing Christopher's hair with the muzzle of his gun.

"Come on, De Dreux. Women and children? I'm the one who can make the deal you're after. You're in trouble with the law. I can help you escape. I can give you the money—"

"I'm not stupid enough to believe you! The minute I let your family go, there won't be a corner in this world where I can hide. I know that!"

"Then come here and get me, you bastard," Rey said. He held his arms out, making himself a target. He'd seen the reckless glint in De Dreux's eyes. He had to draw De Dreux away from Christopher, back to the window. "If you want your revenge, I'm here."

De Dreux's fine nostrils flared. He stepped closer to Rey. "You destroyed my life, Parks." De Dreux took another pace toward the window and the men outside. "Everything I've ever had was here on this plantation; respect, money, my pride." Again, a step. "Did you know my father started L'Isle des Rêves? But it wasn't so magnificent in his days. Oh, no. It was modest at best. And what little he had, he threw away on Henri. Henri, his precious, perfect boy, ran this plantation into the ground until it wasn't worth the dirt that filled its arpents! That's when I bought it, Parks. It took his bastard son to make L'Isle des Rêves into the palace it is today. Everything you see"—he glanced around the gold-patterned walls—"is mine. Paid for by me. Built by me! I bought my respect! And now, it will all go away. The most I can do now is flee—but to what?"

De Dreux stopped, still out of shooting range.

"I have no money." De Dreux looked at Pascal in the armchair; his expression left no doubt that he found her lacking. "I have no son." He focused on Rey with new venom. "No future. They'll all ridicule me now. I'll be Benoit the Bastard again. Worthless. Society, my family . . . they'll be able to turn their backs on me as they did before. Do you know what that feels like? Do you?"

Rey waited silently, praying De Dreux would keep coming closer. But instead, De Dreux cocked his head, as if thinking. He glanced over his shoulder, back at Christopher. When his gaze returned to Rey, De Dreux's wide lips were turned into a smile. "I want to hear you beg for their lives. I want to see you on your knees, Parks, begging."

There was a wildness in De Dreux's eyes that frightened Rey. De Dreux was a man who'd lost everything—and therefore had nothing more to lose. Rey flung away his cigarette and dropped to one knee. "Let them go, De Dreux."

"I don't hear you groveling, Parks." He took a step backward, closer to Christopher. "I want to hear you grovel."

"He'll never beg for the likes of you!" Christopher shouted, delivering a swift kick to the back of De Dreux's knee.

De Dreux stumbled, his leg folding beneath him. Rey lunged. But De Dreux was ready, twisting around to meet him with his gun.

"Benoit!"

De Dreux's startled gaze turned to the doorway. Mercy stood at the threshold dressed in black pants, shirt, and cape. She held her hands behind her.

"Mercedes?" De Dreux looked at her with confusion, keeping his attention between her and Rey. "I've been waiting for hours—what are you doing dressed like that?"

Mercy stepped into the room, her hands hidden in the folds of her cape. "Don't you recognize me, Benoit?"

"Get out of here, Mercy," Rey warned.

De Dreux glanced at Rey, then back to his wife. *"Mercy?"*

"No, *maman*!" Pascal shouted from her chair.

But Mercy ignored all their warnings. She drew her hand forward. "Perhaps this might refresh your memory." From her fingers dangled Santana's singed mask.

Rey's heart pounded in his chest. "For God's sake! Leave here now!"

"Don't you understand, Benoit?" Mercy asked, diverting her husband's attention from Rey and his family. "Can't you guess." She held the mask just before her face. "Does this make it easier to remember?"

A cry of despair fell from Pascal's lips. The girl scooted to the edge of the armchair, watching her stepmother with fear.

"You bitch!"

"That's right, Benoit," Mercy answered. "It was me. I was the one who stole from you. I was the one who released those helpless women. I even set it all up with Sotheby. He couldn't really fix the lottery. It was very naïve of you to believe he could. Rey's not to blame. Sotheby and I had you ruined. Do you have any idea how much we laughed at your gullibility, Harry and I, while you poured more money into his scheme? I bet he didn't mention that in his note to you."

De Dreux's face grew purple. He rose to his feet, stalking her. When Rey moved to intercept, De Dreux spun back on him.

Mercy pulled her second hand from behind her back. "I've always been the one."

She held a gun aimed at De Dreux. Catching sight of the pistol, he stared at her, speechless.

"And now, I'll be the one to end it, Benoit."

"You're going to kill me?" Suddenly, the fear left his eyes. He laughed, ignoring Rey, concentrating on Mercy. "Like you tried to do ten years ago?" He shook his head, smiling now. "I don't think so, Mercedes."

Mercy dropped Santana's mask. She used both hands to steady the revolver. "Don't underestimate me, Benoit. I've changed from the fourteen-year-old girl you tormented."

"Have you really?" There was an edge of disbelief in his voice. His eyes shone with a strange light as he stepped toward Mercy. "Do you remember that first year, Mercy? After we married, when you lost the baby? How you screamed at me that I was to blame, that I beat that baby out of you with my little games. But it wasn't my fault, Mercy. We both knew that. You were too frail to take the love of a real man. A better woman wouldn't have lost my child. Wouldn't have become barren."

Mercy took another step back as Benoit moved closer. Her hands dropped slightly.

"De Dreux," Rey shouted. "I'm here waiting for you! It's me you want. I stole your money."

But De Dreux had found his target. He kept his focus on Mercy. "You pulled a gun on me then, remember? But you couldn't pull the trigger."

Mercy appeared mesmerized by the fiend's taunts—just as De Dreux was captivated by Mercy.

"You won't hurt me, Mercedes," De Dreux whispered, his voice almost sweet-sounding. "I made you. I found you and molded you. Without me, you wouldn't exist. You can't kill your maker."

She shook her head. She lifted the gun level again.

"I'm the one who created you, Mercedes. I am your God."

With a curse, Rey glanced out the window, then looked at Nan. She grabbed Christopher and dropped to the ground, pulling Aunt Clair down beside her. Nan hid Chris's face in her skirts.

"I have the place surrounded, De Dreux," Rey shouted. "My men are waiting outside, right by the window. The minute you fire, you're a dead man."

De Dreux rocked halfway around, swinging his gun between Mercy and Rey. He laughed, holding the pistol in both hands. He took exaggerated aim on Mercy, switched to Christopher, then Rey. "You can't destroy God."

Behind him, Pascal lunged with a strangled cry. Her fingers curled like claws, scratching her father's face. De Dreux flung Pascal off, his momentum taking them both toward the window. His eyes were wide and wild as he stared at his daughter.

"So you'll betray me too?" he screamed. He raised his gun and aimed at his daughter.

Mercy fired.

The room exploded in gunfire. Glass shattered, fragments spilling across the carpet. Nan and her aunt flung themselves across Christopher. Benoit's body jerked with the force of each bullet that entered his body. De Dreux fired wildly at the window, then pivoted and shot at Mercy. More bullets pierced through him. He fell to his knees; the gun slipped from his fingers. "You bitch," he whispered. A smile spread across his face. "You . . ." He dropped to the floor.

Rey lowered his head. Immediately, Christopher and Nan ran to his side. He wrapped his arms around them, keeping Chris from seeing De Dreux. Through their hugs, he glanced up at Mercy. She was staring at Benoit's body on the floor.

"It's over, Benoit," Rey heard her whisper. She swayed on her feet. She held one hand pressed against her chest. Blood stained her fingers.

"No!" Rey sprang across the room as she crumbled to the floor.

Chapter 28

"Ay, niña." Kate wrung the cloth over the washbasin and leaned over the bed. She laid the linen moistened with Doc Chiang's medicaments on Mercy's shoulder where the bullet had grazed the skin. "You listen to Kate. No more fighting. You settle down and give this baby a family."

Propped against a mountain of pillows, Mercy stared out her bedroom window at the dawn's light. She placed her hand on her belly. "That would be my fondest wish, Kate."

In a jangle of bracelets, Kate turned Mercy's face back to hers. "Why so sad, then? This Parks man, he no offer marriage?"

Mercy thought back to the night Rey had proposed at the *pied-à-terre.* She smiled wanly at Kate. "Not recently."

Kate frowned. "Bah!" She stood up, jerking her skirts aside. "My Juanito talk some sense—"

"No, Kate." Mercy grabbed onto Kate's hand, pulling her back down to her chair. "Rey can't be bullied into accepting me, we both know that."

"But this *estúpido.* You love him." Kate held one palm up. "He love you." She held up the other, then looked from her hands to Mercy. "He does love you, eh, *niña?*"

Mercy sighed, twining Kate's fingers with hers for comfort. "Yes. I think he does."

But Mercy wondered if a lawman—a man who had dedicated his life to justice—could accept her past as he'd hinted when he'd saved her from the burning cottage. Or would Rey, in the clear light of day, again retreat to his world of rules, a world that would never accept Mercy.

She squeezed Kate's hand between her palms, anxious to have her answers. Meeting Kate's worried gaze, she whispered, "I just hope love is enough."

Rey watched Christopher stuff yet another sweet biscuit into his mouth. Smiling at his son, he leaned back against the slats of the kitchen chair. The lamplight bronzed Christopher's curls with red highlights; the smell of freshly baked bread filled the air. All the aches of Rey's body disappeared in the joy he felt at watching Chris eat across the table from him in L'Isle des Rêves' kitchen. After the night's events, Rey had been happy to wait here and let Mac see to the details of disposing of De Dreux's body, as well as contacting the federal authorities about Sotheby and Gessler.

Christopher grinned up at his father. Around a mouthful of cookie, he said, "He was a terrible man, Mr. De Dreux. He made Miss Pascal come down, even though we all knew she was very sick." He spoke as if that were De Dreux's greatest crime. "And he made it sound like *you* were a bad father," Christopher added for good measure.

An uncomfortable warmth flushed Rey's face. He drew closer to his son. "And what do you think about your father?"

Christopher frowned, as if he'd expected Rey to see the absurdity of De Dreux's accusation rather than ask for his son's opinion on the matter. When Rey waited patiently for an answer, Chris dropped his cookie on the plate. He pushed back his chair and ran around the table. Unconditional love beamed on his face as he threw his arms around his father.

"You're the best." His arms squeezed tighter. "You let me practice my letters on your desk while you work. You take me riding, and fishing, and let me visit Nana whenever I want. And when you're away, you always write me very long letters and come see me, even though Nana says it is very difficult for you to come to Boston sometimes." He wiggled out of Rey's embrace. He watched his father closely with his striking blue eyes. "And you always answer all my questions about my mother, and let me talk about her a whole lot, even when I know it makes you terribly sad."

Rey saw the devotion in Chris's face, recalled how his son had stood fearlessly by his aunt's side and kicked De Dreux in the shins. Christopher was a fine boy, a son to be proud of, and he loved Rey. He might not have been the best of fathers—but perhaps he'd been good enough.

"I love you," Chris said, an octave higher. "That's why I missed you so much." His normally vibrant eyes turned solemn. "You're not going away again, are you? Because, if you are"—he leaned closer, about to convey a confidence—"Nana said we would follow you again."

"*Are* you leaving again, Rennie?"

Rey turned to the door where Nan stood with their aunt. Both ladies waited at the threshold.

Rey smiled at his sister. He looked down to meet Chris's expectant eyes. "I'm not going anywhere without you." Over his boy's shoulder, Rey saw Nan's wide grin of approval. She pressed her fingers to her lips and blew him a kiss from the door. For the first time, Rey realized what his family's love meant to him—acceptance. No matter what his failings, they always saw beyond his faults to the good.

Rey wrapped his arm around Chris's shoulder, enjoying another warm hug. This is what he'd sacrificed when he'd turned his back on his family to seek justice. He'd thought himself undeserving of love then—or more likely, he'd been afraid of it. Yes, perhaps fear lay at the heart of his quest for justice these past five years. As long as he remained focused on balancing the scales against Sotheby, he could avoid love and the possibility of losing someone he cared for, as he'd lost Sophie.

Rey almost laughed at the irony. He'd thought he'd taken so many risks as a government agent; now he realized that for him, work had been the safer occupation—much easier than risking his heart.

Nan cleared her throat from the door. "Now that that particular matter is settled," she said, glancing lovingly at her nephew and Rey, "I believe you're needed in the bedroom. Doc Chiang said she's asking for you."

The door opened and Rey walked in. To Mercy, he looked a bit pale and very tired, but never better. He was safe at last. Neither Benoit nor Sotheby could hurt him now. As she watched, he sat down in the cane chair Kate had just vacated. Immediately, he took up her hand. Mercy grew hopeful at the comforting touch. She knew Rey cared about her, even loved her. She prayed that despite the doubts she'd voiced to Kate, it would be enough.

"Doc Chiang tells me you're fine," he said. "That you only fainted because of the baby." He touched the bared shoulder where Benoit's bullet had grazed the muscle. "Looks like you'll have a wound to match the one I gave you." He studied her pensively, then sighed. "I'm here to offer you a job, Mercy."

His words startled her, but seeing his smile, she knew there was more to his offer.

"Mac believes you'd make a fine addition to the Secret Service," Rey said. "He thinks I should talk to the Chief about you."

Mercy's heart sank. She swallowed back the knot in her throat. Perhaps love wasn't enough after all.

"But before you consider the benefits of government work, I'd like to make you another offer. It's not as glamorous or exciting, I'll admit."

"Rey, I don't—"

"It's quite a staid life"—his eyes met hers—"to be a banker's wife."

Mercy caught her breath. "You want to marry me?" she asked in a very low voice. "Oh, Rey. Do you really think you can forgive—"

He pressed his finger across her lips. "You don't need my forgiveness, Mercy. What you need—and what you've always needed—is my understanding and acceptance. I'm asking the same of you." He stroked her cheek with the tip of one finger. "I want to tell you about the man I was before Sophie died. Young, a bit too brash, perhaps—certainly too daring—but *never* quick to judge. It wasn't until after Sophie died that I turned rigid, becoming someone who clung to the letter of the law and forgot its spirit." He brushed the back of his fingers against her temple. "For years now, I've thought only in terms of right and wrong— black and white. In my world, I was to blame for Sophie's death, because my job put her in danger. I had to tip the scales back for justice before I deserved the love of my son." He cupped her chin in his hands. "You taught me there can be a lot of gray in the world. It's an important lesson, one I needed to understand before I could forgive myself for Sophie's death." He stared at her with an intensity that left her weak. "Do you think you can do the same?"

She frowned, puzzled. "Forgive you? I never—"

"Forgive yourself, Mercy. And believe that I'll love you forever, and that I'll never judge you or find you lacking again."

He could see she still doubted him. He didn't want her to spend her life trying to prove herself, to make up for every mistake, as she'd done by retrieving Sotheby's plate. He thought of how to convince her that limits and mistakes didn't take away from her own self-worth—then he remembered his recent lesson from Christopher. Unconditional love.

He lifted her face to look at him. "You know why Pascal attacked her father, don't you?"

Tears filled Mercy's eyes. "Because the poor thing loves me and risked herself for me!"

Rey shook his head. "No. She did it because Pascal knew her own father would shoot her—but that her stepmother, who loves her greatly, would never allow him to hurt her. She told me, she remembered that Santana never shot to kill; it was a steadfast rule of the gang."

Mercy nodded, feeling the tears running down her cheeks.

"She was afraid her father was right, that you wouldn't fire on him, that he would kill you instead. But she knew you would shoot to save her life."

"Oh, Rey." She buried her face in his shirt.

"Pascal sees the good in you, Mercy. I would be a fool not to see it too—and so would you. You've sacrificed for the people you love. You've fought for them, and protected them. You've given completely of yourself. You'll be a wonderful wife to me, Mercy. And an even better parent." He kissed her lightly on the mouth. "The only one I want for my children."

She blinked up at him. "Children?"

"If it's all right with you." He grinned. "I think I'd like half a dozen."

She smiled, her first heartfelt smile, and Rey knew she understood the hidden message. He was ready now. Ready to leave the doubts of his past and believe in himself and their love.

"Here." He pulled the St. Christopher medal from his trouser pocket. "I found this in your saddlebag." He fastened the chain around her neck. "We slew the dragon together, Mercy."

She held the medallion in her hand. The breadth of her smile made her radiant. "Just like in the stories," she said softly, staring at the St. Christopher.

Rey lay down in bed beside Mercy. She cuddled against

him as he wrapped his arms around her. "And when our children gather around us," he said, "we'll tell them all those stories, Mercy. In particular, the one that goes like this." He cleared his throat theatrically. "Attend and listen, ye gentlemen, that be of freeborn blood—"

Mercy stared at Rey with an expression of surprise and love on her face. He smiled, feeling the same.

"—I shall you tell of a good yeoman." He kissed her and whispered against her lips, "And her name was Santana Rose."

Epilogue

Mercy cradled her daughter in her arms, waiting for the feeding bottle. Christopher dribbled a bit of the watered milk with sugar on his hand and tasted it. He screwed up his face. "Does she really like this, Mother?"

"Give her the bottle and see," she answered with a smile.

When Sabrina latched on quickly, Christopher whooped with laughter. "Wow! Look at her! She must be starving."

Mercy tousled her seven-year-old son's hair, threading her fingers through the dark curls. Sabrina was a voracious eater, so much so that Rey's sister Pamela had suggested supplemental feedings with the bottle as well as breastfeeding. Mercy sighed, thinking of all the details left for Sabrina's christening. At least Mercy would see all her friends again, she consoled herself.

She'd received Kate's letter just yesterday. She and Mac were coming from New Orleans, despite Kate's many complaints that since Mac had made her close up the brothel upstairs she could barely afford the clothes on her back. Just thinking of the outrageous Spaniard made Mercy laugh to herself. Ling Shi and Doc Chiang had also written that they would be coming—with their new infant son. They planned to travel with Pascal and Harlan. Though in the early months of her own pregnancy, Pascal had sworn nothing would keep her from being Sabrina's godmother.

Still, there was so much left to do that Mercy sometimes worried half would go unfinished. She reminded herself that now she had Nan and Rey's other sisters to help her. Never again did she need to see to important matters alone.

The door to the parlor opened and Rey stepped in, closing the door behind him. He had the look of a man well content, and a secretive smile that told Mercy he had a surprise for her.

"What's in your hand?" she asked, seeing that he held his arm behind his back. Christopher had told her about a very pretty ruby necklace Rey had bought for Mercy in honor of Sabrina's birth. Her heart skipped a beat as Rey brought his hand forward. In it, he held not a jeweler's box, but a letter.

"It's for you," he said.

Mercy put down the bottle. She took the note and gave Sabrina to Rey. He gurgled down at his daughter, before jogging his head to the letter and saying, "Go ahead. Open it."

Mercy studied the vellum. On the outside, in long fluid strokes, was written her name. She broke the seal with a puzzled frown. There was no postage on the letter. It must have been hand delivered. She glanced at the bottom. When she read the name penned there, she gasped.

Beth. Beth had written to her.

My Dearest Mercy:

I thought never to hear from you, my friend. How it makes my heart glad to know that you are alive and well. When you didn't return that day, Laura and I feared the worst. We both knew nothing short of death could keep you from us. We always did rely on you so. Your husband's man informed me that you have been searching for us all these years. Well, I suppose street waifs like Laura and myself would be difficult to find. I must commend Mr. Parks on his effort!

When you did not return, Laura and I took refuge in a church. The nuns at St. Catherine's were very kind to us, and it was through them that we found a wonderful patron, Madam Lavinia Freedman. By her good graces, I had a home and an education. I am sorry to write Laura died giving birth to her daughter, Katarina, named after the patron Saint of the nuns who sheltered us. I always brought flowers to her grave, and ironically, it was there that I met the wonderful man I married. Daniel kept the gardens at the church. We adopted Katarina. The money Mr. Parks delivered will be kept for her, so she will always have a better life than her mother.

I hope the years have been as gentle to you as they have been for me, my friend. In his missive, Mr. Parks said you have a little girl! I have two daughters of my own, as well as Laura's girl, whom I think of as my own flesh and blood. And when I rock them to sleep at night, or hold them when they wake from nightmares, I always think of you, dear Mercy, and how you comforted me those many years ago.

"Oh, Rey." Mercy held the letter against her heart. "Thank you!" She pulled him down for a kiss. "Thank you so much for this!"

Sabrina wailed between them and Rey pulled back and rocked her in his arms as Mercy wiped the tears from her eyes.

"What's the letter say, Mother?" Christopher looked over her shoulder, anxious to share in the news Rey had delivered.

"It's from a very close friend, Christopher. Someone I love dearly, but I couldn't find."

"Daddy found your friend for you"—he looked proudly up at his father—"didn't he?"

Mercy drew her arm around Chris. "Yes, he did, darling."

"The man I hired told me a great deal about Beth," Rey said, still rocking Sabrina. He watched Mercy almost sadly. "It seems that after all your worries and sacrifices, she's led a better life than you have."

Mercy stood. She took Christopher's hand and together they walked to Rey and hugged him. She looked down at Sabrina. Her tiny fists flailed and her eyes scrunched as she whimpered in her father's arms.

"No one could have a better life than mine, Rey." She smiled up at her husband—the man who'd given her yet another happy ending—and wondered of the day when she'd questioned whether love would be enough. She had her answers now. Kissing Rey, she whispered, "Mine is the most wonderful life of all."

Author's Note and Acknowledgments

The United States Secret Service was established in 1865. Its purpose was to protect the new federal currency from counterfeiters.

On March 27, 1879, Governor Nicholls signed Act No. 44, a bill designed to abolish the Louisiana lottery. The lottery company sought relief in the federal courts. Within a few months the courts declared Act No. 44 of 1879 unconstitutional and the lottery continued. In 1890 Congress passed a law prohibiting the use of the mail for transfering lottery materials, striking the death knell for the Louisiana lottery.

I take this opportunity to thank the people who helped bring New Orleans to life for me. Thelma Parker, who opened the back door to the Madewood one fateful January night. The staff at the San Francisco Plantation and the Gallier House, two institutions that are a historical author's dream come true. Lorri Baldwin, who gave me a home in the French Quarter (I wrote some of my best scenes in your parlor, Lorri). Cindy Falk, who kept me from flooding the swamp and other disasters; Gail Snyder, who stopped me from jumping into a swamp when it seemed appropriate to do so. Mary Lou Widmer, who went beyond the call of duty in directing my research.

Meagan McKinney, who never tired of my visits and always had one more treasure to show me.

Most of all, I thank Jessica Travis of the Historic New Orleans Collection, who never refused my phone calls. Jessica, I could never have done it without you.

Experience the Passion and the Ecstasy

Heather Graham

☐ 20235-3 Sweet Savage Eden $4.99

☐ 11740-2 Devil's Mistress $4.99

Meagan McKinney

☐ 16412-5 No Choice But Surrender $4.99

☐ 20301-5 My Wicked Enchantress $4.99

☐ 20521-2 When Angels Fall $4.99